PRAISE FOR JUDITH E. FRENCH AND *THE CONQUEROR!*

"Historical fiction fans will have a feast!"

—*Romantic Times*

"Judith French has skillfully crafted not only a top-notch romance but an excellent work of historical fiction."

—ARomanceReview.com

"Don't miss *The Conqueror.*"

—*Romance Reviews Today*

"Extremely compelling . . . [this book is] a difficult one to put down."

—LikesBooks.com

"*The Conqueror* is a strong historical tale . . . action packed."

—*Midwest Book Review*

BREATHTAKING...

For a heart's beat, her gaze locked with Prince Kayan's. Mayet's throat constricted. She felt as though she'd been knocked off the edge of a precipice into empty space.

His appearance was so foreign, so savage, yet wildly magnificent, that the Greek officers and Egyptian noblemen in their spotless white linen appeared as soft and helpless as doves flushed by a hunting falcon.

Mayet sat immobilized, unable to breathe, unable to tear her eyes away from him. A great rushing storm filled her head, stunning her, as thoughts, images, and memories whirled too fast to grasp or comprehend.

Trapped like an insect in a drop of amber, she could only stare.

The barbarian's hips were narrow, his muscled legs encased in skintight trousers cut in the Persian fashion. The doeskin garment fit without a wrinkle and revealed far more of his considerable male attributes than it concealed, before disappearing into thigh-high, soft leather boots with scarlet tassels.

He must be an imposter, she thought. This is no prince, but a warrior, a man whose powerful hands appear more accustomed to wielding a sword than a royal seal. . . .

Other books by Judith E. French:
THE CONQUEROR

The Barbarian

Judith E. French

LEISURE BOOKS NEW YORK CITY

For Evan Marshall, my agent and friend.
Thank you.

A LEISURE BOOK®

August 2004

Published by

Dorchester Publishing Co., Inc.
200 Madison Avenue
New York, NY 10016

ISBN 0-8439-5379-9

The name "Leisure Books" and the stylized "L" with design are trademarks of Dorchester Publishing Co., Inc.

Printed in the United States of America.

Visit us on the web at www.dorchesterpub.com.

Prologue

". . . Now must I depart . . .
and as I long for your love,
my heart stands still inside me . . ."
        —*Love Songs of the New Kingdom*

High in the mountains, nestled between a craggy outcrop and a sheer wall of rock, two boys huddled under a sheepskin as the first flakes of a late spring snowstorm drifted down to melt on their hair and faces. Beyond the circle of flickering firelight, feral eyes gleamed in the dark as shadows crept close.

"Tell us about the Amazon princess held prisoner by the evil witch for a hundred years," Val begged.

Yuri shook his mop of tangled curls. "No, Kayan. Not that story. Tell about how Alexander leaped over the city wall and fought off five thousand enemy swordsmen and—"

"Why do you need me to tell it?" The man squatted to place another log on the fire. Cords of muscle tightened along a powerful, battle-scarred forearm as he poked the glowing coals with the tip of his sword. "Sounds as though you know those tales by heart. It's late, and we've far to ride tomorrow. Best you both sleep while I keep watch."

"Can't." A lock of sandy hair fell across Val's forehead, and the eight-year-old brushed it away. "You need me to help guard the horses."

Yuri yawned and rubbed his gray eyes with the back of a grimy fist. "Me too! I'm not scared of wolves."

"Think you can kill a steppe wolf with your slingshot?" Val taunted as he elbowed his younger brother.

"I could. Couldn't I, Kayan?"

"A wolf would gobble you in one bite," Val said.

Yuri shook his head. "Would not. I'd pick a good stone and fling it right—"

"You need a bow like mine to kill a wolf. Doesn't he? He's too small to pull—"

"Am not!"

Val nudged Yuri again. "Hush. You want a story, or not? Tell us about Princess Roxanne, Kayan. Please."

For long seconds, the warrior stared into the flames before rising and gazing off into the night with eyes as fierce as those of the wolves. "There is a legend of a princess held captive by an evil spell," he began softly. "So beautiful was she that evil men went blind when they looked upon her shining face . . . so brave that she could turn a charge of Indian war elephants with the golden arrows from her magic bow—"

"And tigers." Yuri leaned forward in excitement. "She fought tigers with her sword. Two tigers . . ." He broke off as the haunting refrain of a ram's horn echoed down the canyon.

None of them spoke as Kayan tied scraps of woolen cloth around the heads of three arrows and then loosed the shafts from his bow. The flames arched high overhead before falling to earth. Within seconds, the horn sounded again.

In the time it took to saddle their horses, all three could hear the muffled clatter of hooves on rock. Kayan drew his sword and motioned the boys to take positions behind him. Yuri set a stone in the leather pad of his sling while Val notched an arrow in his bowstring.

Four fur-clad riders materialized out of the falling snow. "General!" one cried. "A message from Prince Oxyartes!"

"Cyrus? Is that you?" Kayan demanded.

"Aye." A whip-thin veteran reined in his snow-covered mount and tossed a leather-bound scroll. "Cursed weather. We've been a week hunting you down."

Kayan unrolled the parchment and held it close to the fire to make out the message. A quick glance at the familiar signature told him that the letter came from his prince.

> *Kayan,*
>   *Today, word came from our friend in Egypt. It is over. Our prayers have come to nothing. Ptolemy sends his regrets and the bitter words that Cassander has done what we feared most. He has taken both her life and that of the boy. My only comfort in this, the most bitter hour of my life, is that Lord Ptolemy's informants assure him that her end was swift and merciful.*
>   *She is lost to us who loved her most, and to the one who never knew her. In the Macedonian's son we must place our hopes and the future of the twin kingdoms.*
>   *Oxyartes*

Kayan read it through twice before tossing the scroll into the fire. It seemed as if the cold of the frozen earth seeped up to chill his blood as he watched the parchment blacken, flare, and crumple to ashes. When he raised his gaze to meet Cyrus's unspoken question, the soldier blanched and took a step backward.

"What is it, General?" another of the riders asked. "Bad news? Not our prince?"

Val and Yuri crowded close. "Kayan?" Val began.

Kayan shook his head, caught the nearest horse, and vaulted into the saddle. "Wait here. Keep them safe!" he commanded, before lashing the animal into the teeth of the rising storm.

"Where are you going?" Val called after him. "The wolves!"

Wide-eyed, Yuri caught hold of his brother's hand, but uttered no sound.

Kayan rode until he was far enough that his voice would not carry to those he'd left by the fire. Then he reined in the horse, flung himself off, and dropped to his knees in the snow. "Roxanne," he whispered hoarsely. "Roxanne."

For seconds . . . minutes . . . he rocked back and forth in excruciating pain, unable to draw enough air into his lungs or to fathom the reality of the message branded across his mind in flaming letters.

How could she be dead? The sun had risen in the east this morning. The sky still stretched over mountains and endless steppes. Hawks soared. Fish swam. Children laughed. And his flesh had not shriveled and fallen from his bones.

How could she be dead and the world still be whole and shining?

A cry of anguish writhed in the pit of Kayan's gut. Knotting his hands into fists, he thrust them toward the black, swirling heavens. "I will have my vengeance," he screamed into the wind. "On your immortal soul, I swear it!"

Abruptly his horse whinnied. Snorting in alarm, the animal lashed out with flying hooves as red eyes glowed in the night. Kayan leaped to his feet, drew his sword from his scabbard, and turned to face the wolves with a fierce and terrible joy.

Chapter 1

The Mediterranean Sea
Spring, 315 B.C.

The flame-haired woman hung suspended between life and death, each breath coming when all hope of another had failed. So faint was her heartbeat that the Phoenician physician despaired of ever seeing the face of his young son again. His mysterious patient would die before the ship ever reached Alexandria, and the sole of the pharaoh's sandal would grind him into the Egyptian sand as mercilessly as if he were the smallest cockroach.

The poison had been too strong.

He had feared the dose was too powerful when he mixed it, but the stakes were high. The Macedonian general, Cassander, had ordered the prisoner's death, and Ptolemy, pharaoh of Egypt in all but name, ruler of Cyprus, master of the greatest navy the world had ever known, had demanded that he bring her to him in Alexandria alive and unspoiled. Only one ancient poison was reputed to plunge a man so deeply into sleep as to make its victim appear a corpse . . . and he had never tried it on beast or human, let alone a woman.

He dipped a sponge into a basin of vinegar and fresh water, squeezed it, and wiped the beads of sweat from the lady's brow. So fair she was that it seemed the rays of the sun had never touched her alabaster face, but whether the hue of her complexion was that of death's approach or her natural color, he was at a loss to tell. He leaned close, so close that his lips brushed her earlobe. "Live, lady," he whispered. "Live so that you might taste the wine of Egypt on your tongue . . . that the sound of a baby's laughter might bring joy to your ears. Live . . ."

She was no untouched virgin, nor was she in the first flush of womanhood. Yet she was not old, certainly no more than twenty-five . . . and she had given birth to a child. Her face was unlined by age or weather, her mass of glorious hair the vivid copper-gold of sunset on the rim of the western sea.

The woman's boldly etched cheekbones were high; dark brows arched gracefully over long, thick lashes that fluttered at rare intervals to reveal wide, almond-shaped eyes of cinnamon scattered with flakes of raw gold. His mouth went dry as his gaze rested on her sensual lips . . . lips so perfectly shaped that they would tempt a man to risk his soul to taste them.

Her body . . .

Sweat trickled down his face, and he swallowed, attempting to dissolve the thickening in his throat . . . clamping back the primal need that fired his blood and turned him hard. He flushed with shame. Was he not trained to put aside his human urges in order to heal the sick and afflicted? The woman was dying. What physician would sink so low as to allow base urges to cloud his reason?

But the lush curves of her sweetly formed breasts and hips, the silken texture of her skin, and the feminine glory of that thick mane of shimmering auburn hair were all too real. Her legs were long and shapely . . . her calves . . .

The physician rose to his feet, closed his eyes, and inhaled deeply, drawing in the pungent odors of sea and ship, letting the familiar sounds of creaking timbers, groaning oarsmen, and snapping canvas remind him of where he was and why. Making the sign of the blessed lady Asherah for protection, he moved away from the woman, wondering if she was a sorceress who had bewitched his senses. With a foul curse, he scrambled up a ladder to the splintery deck and let the salt spray and wind blow the shadows from his mind.

She tossed restlessly on the mat, caught in a tangle of nightmares and memories. Images swirled; the face of a golden-haired man flashed before her and faded in shadow, his familiar voice drowned out by the snarl of a hunting leopard and the granite-etched features of another man, dark, with eyes as fierce and haunting as those of the great cat. Wind and snow whipped through rugged mountain passes that gave way first to trackless green jungle and then to desert wasteland as lines of grim-faced soldiers struggled through knee-deep sand beneath the burning disk of a pitiless sun. She tried to cry out, but her lips were cracked and her parched throat was as dry as the empty riverbeds. She could not summon the strength to run or even to raise her head. Her fingers, once strong enough to control the reins of a rearing stallion, lay limp and motionless.

Only her eyelids fluttered, clenching tight against the onslaught of thundering hooves and blood-streaked swords . . . opening to see towering city walls rise and crumble to windblown dust. And always the golden man returned, his powerful arms lifting her, his whispers sweet in her ear. She groaned, struggling for each breath, feeling her will to fight seeping away, sensing the cool night of eternal oblivion that waited to swallow her.

"Come," he whispered. "Take my hand and come away with me. Away from pain and darkness."

Pain surged in her head, plunging her world into chaos, dragging her down into a morass of choking mud and tangled roots. She struggled to breathe, gasping for air and screaming soundlessly. In her torment a pinpoint of light flared and blossomed into a world of radiant blue sky and green Sogdian meadow. She could smell the sweetness of wildflowers, see the vivid red and yellow petals, and hear the clear, bright song of birds. And across the valley pranced a magnificent black horse carrying a golden rider. Nearer and nearer they came, the man's gilded hair and the horse's ebony mane and tail rippling in the gentle wind.

The golden man beckoned. "It is time."

Strength flowed through her as she reached out, easily extending the hand that had been so weak only an instant before.

"Trust me," he called.

"No!" Kayan sat bolt upright and shoved away the wolf-skin blanket. So real. She had been so real. Her scent still lingered in his nostrils. With a curse, he rose naked from the bed and threw open the massive wooden shutters, letting the cold, white moonlight pour into the room.

Footfalls pounded in the stone passageway. The door banged open, and a servant stood clutching a torch in one hand, a sword in the other. "Prince? I heard—"

"You heard nothing!"

"But I—"

Kayan drew back a clenched fist. "Leave me!"

Mumbling excuses, the intruder fled. The torchlight dimmed and vanished, leaving the chamber in darkness. Kayan turned again to the open window, heedless of the frigid wind that chilled his sweat-sheened skin and hair.

His eyes ached for lack of sleep. His gut churned. Would the pain never recede? Would he live on in torment, eking out the hours and days listening for her footfall . . . looking for her face around every corner? Would she haunt his dreams? And if he could banish her from his heart and mind, would it leave him as empty as a drained wine bladder?

If only he could remember his dreams. That they were of her . . . only her, he knew. He could still feel her skin against his, taste` her mouth, hear her laughter. Did she come to tell him that she was safe in the heaven of Ormazd's peace? Or did the evil god Abriman hold her captive in his dark kingdom?

He slammed his fist against the stone sill until his flesh split and blood ran, but he gained nothing more than the realization that he had acted the fool—again. "By Zoroaster's promise, am I such a coward?"

Dry-eyed, he turned and snatched up the first piece of clothing that came to hand. He thrust his legs into the doeskin trousers and pulled on a pair of high, soft leather boots. Strapping on his sword belt, Kayan stalked out of the bedchamber and down the ancient stone corridor. He followed a wide, curving staircase to a lower floor, passing several sentries, and strode down a long gallery to the private section of the palace. Once there, Kayan paused to speak to two more guards before continuing on to the end of a passageway.

He stopped, pushed aside the heavy silk drapes embroidered with scarlet Chinese dragons, and paused in the archway of the elegant paneled chamber. The man he sought sat in a high-backed chair before a fire. His eyes were closed. Two hunting leopards slept at his feet.

Oxyartes, High Prince of Bactria and Sogdiana, was dressed in an unadorned Persian tunic and trousers of Phoenician blue. His gnarled feet were bare, the discarded slippers half buried under a leopard's front paws, but his thin gold diadem gleamed in the firelight, and a naked sword lay across the old warrior's lap.

The leopards opened their eyes and the female, Naheed, uttered a deep warning rumble. The male, Veer, younger and sleeker, rose to his feet and bared ivory fangs. Kayan spoke to them, and they sank down again. Naheed's tail flipped back and forth, and she watched him approach through yellow slitted eyes. The man did not stir, and Kayan called softly, "Uncle?"

The proud head rose, once-auburn hair streaked with gray, shrewd eyes narrowed in thought. "Come in, son." He gestured toward a table spread with an embroidered wool cloth and set with a matching Egyptian alabaster pitcher and cups so thin that the light shone through them, a platter of flat bread and cheese, and a bowl of dates. "There is food and honey wine."

Kayan shook his head. "I'm not hungry."

"You're never hungry. You need to eat and to sleep."

"You sound like my mother."

Oxyartes uttered a snort of amusement.

"It's late," Kayan said. "You should be abed."

"Me? I'm an old man. I'll have plenty of time for rest soon enough."

Kayan crossed to the fire, dropped to one knee, and added another log. The male leopard rolled onto his back, exposing his lighter-colored belly, and stretched lazily, claws extending and retracting. Kayan scratched the animal's chest and was rewarded with a lick from a rough tongue. "It's been long since I've slept," he said.

"Since we received Ptolemy's message." Naheed laid her chin on Oxyartes's bare foot and continued to watch Kayan. Both cats were tawny saffron with black rosettes, but the female's beautiful face and coat were marred by an old scar from a Greek javelin.

Kayan made no reply. He doubted his adopted father expected one. He rubbed Veer's head and scratched behind his ears. The big cat yawned and wriggled contently.

"You cannot go on like this," Oxyartes said. "You are a prince of the realm. You have a duty to Bactria, to Sogdiana . . . to your sons. The cord of your life remains strong."

"And you, Uncle?"

Oxyartes's mouth tightened. "She was my only child."

"We have the boy."

"Yes, there is that. And he is as dear to me as my Soraya."

"But he cannot take her place in your heart." Veer batted playfully at Kayan with a big paw, claws sheathed.

"He has his own place. As you do. And the other lad."

Kayan nodded. "I've been a poor father to them lately and a poor prince. You were wrong to name me your successor."

Determination flared in the older man's eyes. "Do not presume to tell me what I should and should not do. I am yet high prince of the twin kingdoms, and I know better than any what burden I laid on your shoulders when I made you my son." He rose from his chair, and Naheed got to her feet and shadowed him. Veer rolled over and crouched, muscles coiled, eyes wide and alert.

Oxyartes rested a callused hand on Kayan's shoulder. "Without you, there is no hope for our people. And without the power that the title gives you, you are no more than any ambitious soldier seeking his own throne."

"That title should be his alone."

"In time, it will be his. But not yet. Since before he was born, evil men and women have sought his death. If it were known now who he is, the Greeks would send a dozen armies to destroy him." Oxyartes scoffed. "I could name you a quiver full of our own warriors who would kill him for who his father was, let alone for their own schemes."

"He has you."

"I'm old, Kayan. No." He raised a palm to silence protest. "We've always been honest with each other. My years are numbered. I'm not ready to go into the grave tomorrow or the next day. This gray wolf has a few tricks left. But it's better that men know you as my successor. You're no child to be smothered in his bed or drowned crossing a river. You are the shield that protects him while he grows to manhood."

Kayan brushed a lock of black hair away from his eyes.

"But it tears at me that you have given me what should be hers. She was crown prince of the Twin Kingdoms, female or not. She was always your successor."

"She is dead, Kayan. And if she could breach the chasm between this world and the next, she would tell you to take my throne and hold it for him."

"All you say is true, Uncle, but why do I feel like a thief in the night?"

"You never sought a crown."

"No, I didn't. All I've ever wanted was to be a soldier. I'm a warrior, not a statesman."

"All the more reason you should be high prince. When the time comes, if he becomes what we believe he will—you'll willingly hand him the throne."

"You put too much trust in me."

Oxyartes chuckled. "I've known you since the day you were born. I know your strengths and your weaknesses. Your father might have been my second cousin, but we were blood brothers. He was a nobleman who lived as he died, a man whose name stood for honor and courage. He would be proud of you."

"So be it." Kayan bowed his head and crossed both arms over his chest in salute. "But I won't hide here in this fortress. Not when Greeks, Egyptians, and Scythians raid our borders and warlords spark rebellion in every valley."

Oxyartes nodded. "I did not think you would."

"I intend to raise an army unlike any the Twin Kingdoms have ever seen. I mean to ally Bactria and Sogdiana with the mountain and steppe tribes to create a force that will defeat both the Greeks and the Egyptians. Ptolemy deserted her when she most needed him, and he will pay for it with his life. Cassander will die as well."

"And Olympias."

"By my own hand."

"A woman?"

"No woman, but a she-demon. She condemned her own grandchild to death. She deserves no mercy."

"Dreams," Oxyartes said. "Idle talk. How could you match the numbers in Pharaoh's army? In those that Cassander and the Greek generals can assemble?"

"They have infantry. Some cavalry units, but nothing compared to Alexander's great army. Cassander's might rests on hired mercenaries."

"But still," Oxyartes said. "Tens of thousands, professional soldiers who will lay waste to our country."

"Not if I hit them first. With cavalry. In India, I have seen warriors mounted on saddles of cloth padded with grass." He took a burning branch from the fire and ground out the flames, and then used the blackened tip to sketch a crude horse on the surface of a marble table. "The saddles have leather or rope straps here and here, with a wooden or bronze loop to hold the rider's foot. They are called stirrups."

"And it works, this invention?" Oxyartes asked. "A man's legs don't tangle in the straps?"

"I've had these saddles made for twenty of my best riders. You can witness a demonstration the day after tomorrow. I'll pit them against any twenty warriors you choose." Kayan grinned. "It takes some getting used to, but with my feet in the stirrups, I'm as solid as standing on rock."

"If Alexander's generals saw this marvel in India, why hasn't anyone else—"

Kayan shrugged. "Why are our swords different from the Greeks'? Our bows shorter? Each culture has its own strengths, developed over thousands of years, and soldiers do not like change. We will take this idea from the far side of the Indus River and make it our own. My craftsmen stretched a Scythian leather saddle over a wooden frame and increased the height of the pommel—the front. The back is higher too, so that the rider sits not on top of the saddle, but in it. With the leather straps and the stirrups, the rider is near impossible to dislodge."

"I'll come and witness this marvel. If it is as you say, it will give the Twin Kingdoms a new weapon." He gazed thoughtfully down at Kayan's drawing. "But you still will have to convince the Scythians to stop killing their neighbors and join us. Can you do that?"

"I will do it."

Oxyartes settled heavily onto his cushioned throne. "You seek more than to defend Bactria and Sogdiana. You want revenge."

"I will have it."

"It will not bring her back."

Kayan's voice grew thick with emotion. "No, it will not. But her enemies will pay one hundred fold for every drop of her blood."

"You would become another conqueror?"

A bitter smile played across his lips. "The Macedonian, of all men, would understand."

Chapter 2

"Open your eyes."

She heard a voice coming from far away.

"You must wake."

She sensed that the man speaking was accustomed to being obeyed. Yet what he asked was impossible. She was so weary, and she felt no pain while the gray mist enfolded her. The meadow had faded from sight. She could no longer see the golden man on the black horse . . . couldn't hear birdsong. She distinctly remembered the rhythmic splash of waves against the hull of a boat.

"Your fever has broken. You must open your eyes."

She struggled to do as he asked, but the blackness closed over her, carrying her down to the place of swirling memories. For an instant she saw a silver goblet . . . tasted bitter wine . . . and then . . . nothing.

Time passed. She knew that it had, but had no idea how she knew. She smelled incense and felt the blessed coolness of water on her parched lips. Strong arms lifted her. She swallowed, choked, and swallowed again.

"You can hear me. I know you can. You're safe now."

Safe? A cooling breeze caressed her hot skin, and the sweet notes of a five-string harp wafted on the air. She wondered if she was dead.

"It is hopeless, Your Majesty. If she has not the will to live, nothing can—"

Not the will to live? Anger surged through her. She opened her eyes and looked up into the face of a man. "Do I . . . do I . . . know you?" Her lips formed the words, but she could not speak. The thought that he was Greek and therefore her enemy chilled her, but she had used up the last of her strength and could only lie there struggling to draw breath.

"Thank the gods." He raised her hand to his lips and kissed it. "I am Ptolemy. You must . . ."

Her eyelids drifted shut and she tried to link the name to the strong, aristocratic face. The Greek was tall, neither old nor young, and clean-shaven with a straight nose and chin-length, light brown hair that curled around his face. Lines creased the corners of his sensual mouth and eyes, and his skin was tanned by sun and weather, giving him the look of a soldier.

He seemed familiar . . . and yet . . . Was he her enemy? Trying to think brought back the pain, and she winced.

"Stay with me," he commanded with both authority and affection.

"Where . . . where am I?" This time, she managed a hoarse whisper. She did not recognize the chamber, but she lay in the center of a spacious, columned room. The linens were crisp and fresh with the scent of sunshine, and the mattress was soft beneath her. Filmy drapes hung from the ceiling around the wide, raised bed, affording the illusion of privacy.

This was no prison. She could hear the sound of water trickling from a fountain, catch a glimpse of a lush garden through the open windows. The air smelled of cedarwood and cinnamon.

"Alexandria. In the Palace of the Blue Lotus." Ptolemy smiled down at her. "You're safe here."

She tried to remember what frightened her, but the fog was too thick, and she wanted more of the cool water. "Please," she said; "water."

He brought the cup to her lips. The water was sweet, the rim of the blue glass smooth. The fingers that held the cup were lean and strong, heavy with rings. She blinked, and Ptolemy's face came sharply into focus. For the first time, she noticed that he wore a coronet of laurel leaves exquisitely crafted of beaten gold.

"Don't you know me?" he asked.

She exhaled softly and shook her head.

"Rest—I'll come again when you are stronger." Ptolemy gestured to a young woman kneeling on the far side of the draped bed. "Hesper."

"Yes, Your Majesty."

"Attend her. Do not leave her side."

"Yes, my lord."

"Send word immediately if her fever returns."

"Yes, sire."

He gripped her hand again and brought his face close to hers. "Affairs of state demand my attention, but I'll be back when I can. Sleep now."

The olive-skinned beauty was the first thing she saw when she woke. "Hesper?" she murmured. Again she smelled the incense and heard soft music. This time she could make out the bright notes of a flute and zither.

The woman nodded. "Yes, lady. I'm here to serve you. Are you in pain?"

"No." She tried to smile. The compassionate dark eyes stared down at her. She'd never seen Hesper before; she was certain of that. The woman wore a peplos and chiton of snow-white linen, so finely woven that they were almost transparent, clearly not the garments of a servant. Her thick black hair was braided into an elaborate knot and held by a linen scarf embroidered with silver thread in a design of lotus blossoms. Silver and faience earrings dangled from her delicate lobes.

Hesper smiled. "Are you hungry?"

She nodded. "Yes, and thirsty enough to drink the Tigris."

"Good." Hesper clapped her hands, and two naked girls came with laden trays. "There is wine and chicken broth, grapes, roast goose, and bread with honey." She chuckled. "I do not expect you to eat all of it, just a bite or two. I didn't know what you'd like, so I ordered—"

"Broth . . . please." It tasted wonderful, as did the honey. She could not bring herself to drink the wine. But she finished nearly half a cup of the rich soup. After each spoonful, Hesper gently wiped her mouth, caring for her as tenderly as if she were a baby. When she'd had enough, she shook her head.

Hesper sent the girls away. "You look much better, lady," she said. "We were so worried. The priests said you would die." She smoothed the sheet. "You've grown so thin. We'll have to fatten you up." Hesper poured scented oil from a jar into her palm and began to massage it into her patient's hands.

Moistening her lips, the woman in the bed looked around the airy, high-ceilinged room with its brightly colored columns and cool, white-plastered walls decorated with murals of fruit trees, waterfowl in flight, and graceful reeds. "I'm in Egypt," she said. "In the city of Alexandria?"

Hesper smiled and nodded.

"In the Palace of the Blue Lotus. And the man . . . who was here . . . His name is Ptolemy."

"King Ptolemy, lord of Egypt, Phoenicia, Cyprus, Palestine, and Syria." Hesper smiled encouragingly, as if to a shy child.

"You're not a servant. Are you the king's . . ."

Hesper laughed. "No, my lady. My husband, Argo, is one of His Majesty's generals and his friend."

She hesitated. "And who am I?"

Ptolemy stared at the Egyptian physician in disbelief. "Is it possible, Djedhor? She doesn't seem to be witless. How can she not know me or her own name?"

"It is possible, mighty one. I have not seen such a case with my own eyes, but years ago, one of my teachers spoke of a man who saw his pregnant wife devoured by a crocodile. By all accounts, he retained his skill at making pots, but he could not remember his own name, his young son, or the faces of his parents and brothers and sisters. He lived another fifteen years and raised his boy. But he claimed never to recall a single day before the tragedy."

"I've seen soldiers lose their wits after receiving head wounds, but they either recovered fully or remained helpless."

"The lady has suffered a high fever. It may have left her damaged."

The thought was repugnant. He'd not be cheated again. "No! I refuse to accept that. There must be another answer. Is she deceiving us with this tale of memory loss?" She was clever, this woman. And that made her all the more desirable to him.

Djedhor paled. "No, Your Majesty, I do not think she is attempting to trick you. I have carefully examined her, and I believe she is telling the truth as she knows it. I summoned the Phoenician physician to question him further on her condition, but he has vanished."

"Without waiting for payment." Ptolemy averted his eyes. "A pity."

Visibly trembling, the physician bowed his head and crossed his hands over his chest. "It may be that another, one skilled in the care of women or in trepanning the skull, might better cure her. I have anointed her with healing oils, called for the priests to offer prayers, and hung a holy amulet over her bed to protect her. It could be that an evil spirit has—"

"Don't give me that superstitious nonsense. Will she recover her memory or not?"

The Egyptian began to babble. "None but the gods can say, my lord. It is in the hands of the gods. Do you wish me to summon other physicians to—"

"No. You're sure she's out of danger?"

Djedhor bowed lower. "Her urine and blood are as they should be. Her fever is gone. She eats and talks. What mortal can say if he will draw breath at the next sunrise?"

"Truthfully, what is your best guess?"

"That the lady will live, great lord, and that she will recover her full health and strength. But whether she will ever regain her past, that I could not say—not if my life depended on it."

It may, Djedhor. It may indeed, Ptolemy thought.

She was sitting up and sipping a goblet of fruit juice when the king returned to her bedside. He motioned to Hesper, and she quickly dismissed the musicians, made an obeisance, and backed from the room. He approached, and she smiled at him.

"How are you?"

"Better, thank you."

"I understand that you have questions."

"Many."

"I'll try to answer them for you." He sat on the edge of the bed and took her hand in his. "You had us worried. Can you remember anything of your illness?"

She shook her head. "Nothing before I awoke and saw you standing over me. I asked Hesper, but she—"

He nodded. "It's my fault. You've been through so much that I was afraid . . ." He squeezed her hand. "Your name is Mayet. You were the wife of my friend Philip."

"Was?"

"You are a widow. He was washed overboard in a storm on his way home to Alexandria from Athens. A little more than two years ago."

She shook her head. "You say that he was my husband? I'm sorry, I don't remember . . ."

"Philip and I have been friends since we were boys in Macedonia. I've known you since you and he were wed, nearly five years ago."

"But I don't understand. How can I have forgotten a husband—a life?"

"Your fever was very high. The physicians say that they have seen few live after such a fever." He lifted her hand and kissed it again. "There is more, my dear Mayet. Are you certain you feel strong enough to hear—"

"Please." She leaned forward. "I must know."

"The fever took your only child, a boy, Linus."

"I had a son?" She swallowed, wondering how such a thing could be possible. Could she have lost a child and not know it? What kind of person was she, that—even now—she felt no loss for her own flesh and blood?

"I'm so sorry, Mayet. As soon as I heard, I had you brought here from Philip's estates. It was too late for little Linus, but at least we were able to save you."

"How old was he?"

"Three." Ptolemy's eyes held hers. "He was a fine boy, worthy of Philip."

She murmured something and sank back against the cushions. "Thank you," she said. "For telling me. And for . . ." She should feel something, but when she tried to reach inside herself there was only the familiar gray mist. "And thank you for all this . . . for taking the trouble. As soon as I'm able, I'll repay you for—"

"Mayet. Mayet. There can be no talk of repayment between us. Your husband was my dearest friend. We were more like brothers than friends. There is nothing I wouldn't do for you . . . won't do for you." He squeezed her hand again and leaned over to kiss her forehead. "Regain your strength, that's all I ask. Let me come and talk to you so that we can build our friendship again."

"I will be honored, Majesty."

He chuckled. "No, my little Mayet. When we are alone, there will be no formality between us. We will be simply Ptolemy and Mayet, old friends who enjoy each other's company."

"Yes," she answered. "If it pleases you, but I cannot remain here imposing on you indefinitely. You say that I . . . that Philip left estates. Surely I can return to—"

"You must consider this palace your home as long as you like. What use is it to be king if I cannot indulge myself a little? Promise me that you will stay—at least until you have completely recovered?"

She tried to think of a reason why she could not do as he asked. "Surely I must have other family," she began. "Parents . . . brothers or sisters—"

"None that I know of," Ptolemy said. "Philip told me that you were born far away in Nubia, and that you were the only child of a wealthy Egyptian nobleman and his foreign wife. He said your mother died when you were born. I believe that your father arranged your marriage only months before he too, died. You and Philip did not meet until your wedding day, here in Alexandria."

"Were we happy?"

"Yes, I think you were, although Philip had a wild streak in him. I know he was more than content with you. You were the love of his life."

"If only I could remember . . ."

"Perhaps it is better this way." He smiled reassuringly. "Your sorrows are all behind you, and only contentment lies ahead."

"You say that as if you were sure of my future."

"Ah, my dear Mayet, but I am. Very sure."

* * *

Berenice was waiting for Ptolemy when he returned from a ceremony honoring Alexandria's greatest poets. It was late, and he was weary of listening to praise of his wisdom and courage. He'd eaten more than he should and was more than half intoxicated. He wanted nothing more than to crawl into his bed and sleep, but his Greek wife Berenice had been drinking and showed all the signs of staging a royal tantrum.

She'd trailed him here to his bedchamber, whining and haranguing him each step of the way. His four bodyguards had had the good sense to ignore her presence and keep up the pretense of not hearing her demands and accusations. How he'd often wished he could do the same.

"Can't it wait until tomorrow?" Ptolemy asked, dismissing his guards. Here in his private apartments, he was safe from assassination, if not from the attack of a vindictive woman. He glanced at her, wondering how he could ever have believed her attractive. Berenice was tall and sharp-featured with a pale complexion, long patrician nose, and small blue eyes. He supposed her waist-length white-blond hair was her best feature. Her figure was adequate, slim rather than lush, and her breasts were small and cone-shaped with protruding, rose-colored nipples. At least they had been the last time he'd seen them.

Berenice was the epitome of the proper Greek noble-woman, proud, uneducated, and frigid. A man with blood in his veins could take more pleasure with his own right hand than in her bed. If Berenice were a bird, she would have been an Ibis, slender, cool, and reserved, with a long, sharp beak to pry into places where it didn't belong.

"Isn't it enough that you set Artakama over me as first wife?" Berenice shrieked. "That you must wallow with Zeus-knows-how-many concubines? Is there no end to your whoring?" She planted herself directly in front of him, waving her arms dramatically.

"Leave me, woman. I've no patience for this tonight. How many times do we have to discuss this?" He turned his back on her. "Artakama is the only living daughter of the last pharaoh. The crown of Egypt comes through her royal blood. Without Artakama as first wife, I'm only a Greek usurper."

"And me? What am I?" She began to sob. He didn't have to see the tears; he could imagine them. Berenice cried as easily as tavern sluts passed wind.

She tried once more to command his attention, and again he turned away. "Don't press your luck, woman," he warned. Her footsteps receded, and he heard the clink of a stopper and the faint trickle of liquid. Berenice was into his favorite wine.

Ptolemy's male body servants came to undress him and see to his bath. The oldest removed the heavy crown from his brow while another took his linen himation. A third undid the gold clasps at the shoulders of his short chiton while the first returned to loosen his sandal ties.

"Ptolemy, I won't be ignored," Berenice said.

"Are you still here? I thought you'd taken the wine bottle and gone."

"Macedonian bastard!" Berenice hurled a wine cup shaped like a griffin's head at him. It missed and shattered on the marble floor. The servants didn't look up from their tasks.

"A little late for that, isn't it?" Ptolemy said. "You should have taken my breeding into consideration when you accepted my offer of marriage."

Eyes bulging, she rushed at him. "You needed my father's support and his troops!"

"True enough." Ptolemy avoided her and stepped into the bathing pool. Two naked slave girls followed with sponges, scented soap, and bath oil. He couldn't remember seeing them before. They had dark almond eyes, small breasts as sweet as ripe plums, and skin the color of old ivory. One was as identical to the other as a reflected image in a mirror. He supposed they must be twins.

Berenice squawked and fluttered around the pool, wings flapping. "The Palace of the Blue Lotus is mine. How dare you put one of your half-breed *hetaerae* in my home?"

Ptolemy ducked his head under the water and wondered how he could ever have been foolish enough to make this shrewish creature his wife. She was still berating him when he stood up and shook the water from his hair. He felt the buzzing that always signaled the onset of one of his headaches, and knew that his longed-for sleep was now impossible.

"Leave me, before I have you bound, gagged, and carried out like a goose to market," he threatened.

She drew herself up to her full height and wrapped herself in wifely plumage. "I will not go a step until you give me your word that you'll rid yourself of that orange-haired creature."

"Mayet's hair is red-gold, not orange. Who told you about her?" One of the girls scraped the soap from his back with a wooden blade while the second massaged the old arrow wound in his shoulder.

"You think you and that Egyptian bitch are the only ones who have spies?" Berenice shook an accusing finger. "I am your queen, Ptolemy. Your queen, if you've forgotten it!"

He rubbed his temples. Yes, he did have a headache coming on, and Berenice could take full credit. For a few seconds, he toyed with the idea of drowning her in this pool, but as he always did, he decided that being rid of his Greek wife wasn't worth the political price that it would cost him. "I forget nothing," he replied. "Least of all the yellow-haired musician who sings you to sleep. Get out of here. I don't want to see your face or hear your mouth until I summon you."

Her eyes widened in surprise. Pale claws fluttered in the air.

Did she forget whom she was speaking to? Whom she'd shamed in front of his soldiers and servants more times than he cared to remember? "I'll not ask you again," he said. "Unless you'd like to find your pretty lyre player's head in your wine bowl."

"You wouldn't!" Her thin face turned fish-belly gray.

"Wouldn't I? Continue to try my patience and you'll see." He smiled. "If you prefer, I could leave him his pretty head and have his phallus removed, pickled, and served to you in a jar of Egyptian beer. I hear you have a taste for both."

With a wail, the plucked ibis fled his apartments.

Ptolemy climbed the steps out of the pool and allowed the slaves to dry his body and wrap a clean tunic around him. Since he couldn't sleep, he thought he'd pay Mayet a late-night visit. Maybe she couldn't sleep either.

Chapter 3

From a hiding place in a small stand of wind-stunted trees, Kayan's stallion Sidhartha snorted and laid back his ears as he caught the scent of the Scythian raiders. As Kayan scanned the valley, painted tribesmen sprang up from their hiding places in the tall grass and lashed their shaggy ponies toward the herd of Bactrian mares and foals.

Each spring and summer wild nomads came howling off the steppes to attack isolated farms and settlements in Bactria and Sogdiana. The Scythians came in search of slaves, plunder, and livestock—especially women and horses. The mares and stallions of the Twin Kingdoms were larger than steppe ponies, with longer legs and broader chests. Their speed, endurance, and intelligence proved the wisdom of years of improving the bloodlines by interbreeding the hardy Bactrian mountain horses with the finest Macedonian and Arabian mounts. The beautiful and strong women of Bactria and Sogdiana were equally prized by bandits.

Thus, Kayan had known that this herd of exceptionally fine mares, which appeared to be guarded only by young girls, was too good for any Scythian marauder to resist. Grinning, he brought a curled ram's horn to his lips and blew long and hard.

Twenty Bactrian soldiers, clad in Greek cuirasses and carrying bronze shields and swords, charged out of the mountain pass. Uttering a war cry as fierce as any steppe bandit, Kayan urged Sidhartha into the fray. Guided only by the prince's knee pressure and vocal commands, the powerful black warhorse thundered toward the raiding party with mane streaming and teeth bared.

As he neared the first of the screaming Scythian warriors, Kayan caught a glimpse of his son Yuri flinging off his horsetail wig and whipping his dun pony into the frightened herd of mares. Riding bareback, the boy flattened himself over the gelding's withers and clung like a burr.

Kayan couldn't see Val in the confusion. *The Good God keep them safe*, he thought in the last seconds before an arrow whizzed past his head and battle lust possessed him.

Bactrians and Scythians clashed. Naked blades gleamed and rang in the bright sun. Javelins and arrows darkened the sky. The scent of blood drove the mares wild and set the herd into a frenzied gallop. Horses and men screamed, bled, and died. A gray Scythian pony sank a foreleg into a hole and somersaulted. The agonized cry of the pony mingled with the screech of a golden eagle swooping low over the battlefield. The rider flew through the air and landed directly in front of the stampeding herd.

Kayan cut down a bearded tribesman with a single stroke, parting the man's head from his shoulders and driving his shaggy pony to his knees. Another nomad took aim at Kayan and let fly an arrow. Kayan blocked the missile with his round shield and kneed his stallion toward the archer. The Scythian snatched another shaft from his quiver and notched the arrow to the bowstring.

Kayan's black horse slammed into the smaller animal before the Scythian could draw his bow to full release. The force of the collision knocked the smaller horse off his feet. Leaping free, the enemy warrior slashed at Kayan's bare thigh with a curved saber. Kayan blocked the blow with his sword, parried, and skewered his opponent with a powerful thrust.

The Bactrians were outnumbered two to one, but the Scythians—as fearless and skilled horsemen as any in the world—were outmatched, both in weapons and by the effectiveness of trained cavalrymen equipped with the radically designed saddles. The clash of the men became a skirmish and then a rout. Of the forty-three looters who rode over the mountains into Bactria, no more than six would live to see their homeland again.

Kayan's force had lost one man. Another had an arrow through his thigh and was bleeding badly. Three others had suffered minor injuries, but should recover fully. He had yet to find out how the four boys who had disguised themselves as girls had fared amid the carnage.

Kayan reined in Sidhartha, sheathed his sword, and shaded his eyes with a bloodstained hand to search the valley floor for the children. He saw two small figures on foot leading mounts on the far side of the scattered herd. The ponies and riders were too far away to identify, and there were two other boys to account for.

Earlier, Kayan had given the order to take no prisoners. With a nod to his trusted man Tiz, a one-eyed veteran old enough to be his father, Kayan rode to find the youngsters. Tiz would see the enemy wounded swiftly dispatched.

The boys Kayan had seen turned out to be the sons of a local farmer and horse trader, who had been recruited for the mission. Both had divested themselves of their sisters' clothing and were nearly overcome with excitement at their exploits. Kayan complimented them on their courage and offered each his choice of a mare and foal from the herd. "Do you know where Yuri and Val are?"

The older boy shook his head, but his brother pointed to the trees where Kayan had kept watch. "They're not hurt. Yuri said he was going to throw up."

"He's the littlest," the first said in Yuri's defense. "He got scared. A Scythian almost yanked him off his pony."

"It's all right," Kayan said. "I'm proud of all of you. You did a man's work here today. Ask your father to take you to Prince Oxyartes's court. He'll reward your family well."

Kayan tightened his heels against Sidhartha's sides and turned the stallion's head toward the grove. The warhorse was streaked with sweat, head tossing, muscles coiled to bolt at the slightest windblown leaf. He wanted to run, Kayan could feel it, but he soothed the spirited animal with endearments and held him to a trot.

Kayan signaled Sidhartha to halt at the edge of the trees. Dismounting, he caught sight of the boys almost immediately and felt a surge of relief that they were safe. Allowing his two sons to take part in the operation had been a difficult decision. The Scythian raiders were not only fierce opponents, they were cannibals. But in good conscience, he could hardly risk the lives of other men's children without having the courage to put Yuri and Val in harm's way. As much as he wanted to protect them, they were soldiers born. If they were to survive, they would need to learn the warrior's path.

For a few seconds, he let his gaze linger on the Macedonian's son. The lad favored his mother enough to make a lump rise in Kayan's throat, but the boy had his father's blond hair and light Greek eyes. Whether he would have his strength and genius, only time would tell.

Kayan had taken the child to raise at birth. His other son, also fatherless, he'd adopted several years later. Both were half Greek, and in truth, the two looked enough alike to be siblings. More than one high-born lady had hinted that Val and Yuri were sorely in need of a mother, but Kayan had no wish to marry again. When he needed the ease that only a woman could provide, he could find it easily enough. Only one lady had ever captured his heart, and she was lost to him forever.

Kayan commanded Sidhartha to stand and strode with him toward the two boys, getting within a knife's throw before Yuri saw him.

"Kayan!"

"I killed a man," Val proclaimed, running to meet him. "He almost got Yuri, but I shot him with my bow and the horses ran over him. It still counts, doesn't it?"

Yuri came slowly toward Kayan. His face and hands were streaked with dirt, and his gray eyes were sunken in dark circles. His complexion had a pasty hue, and he looked older than his years.

"It counts as my kill, doesn't it?" Val persisted.

The man ruffled the taller youth's yellow hair and hugged him hard against his chest. "Yes. It counts." Kayan's voice was rough with emotion. He held the boy a few more seconds before reluctantly releasing him to turn to Yuri.

Kayan crouched to take hold of the younger child's shoulders. "Are you hurt?"

Yuri bit his lower lip and shook his head.

"Good."

"He got sick," Val said.

Kayan took Yuri's chin and raised it so that he could look into the child's eyes. "How old are you?" he asked.

"Eight." Yuri swallowed. His eyes glistened with tears.

"He's only seven," Val said.

"Almost eight."

"He threw up."

Kayan hugged Yuri. "Were you afraid?"

He nodded. "A little. It wasn't what I thought it would be. I was scared you'd get killed. I saw—"

"I told him that you're the best. Like Alexander," Val said. "No Scythian could beat you."

Kayan let go of Yuri and stood up. He glanced down at his bloodstained hands and clothing. "I was scared too," he said quietly. "Any man who tells you that he's not afraid when he goes into battle is either a madman or a liar."

"Really?" Val asked. "Even Tiz?"

Kayan shrugged. "I said *sane men* were afraid."

Val giggled.

Yuri hung his head and kicked at the grass. "The men . . . they're . . . they're killing the wounded Scythians."

"Yes," Kayan answered. "I ordered it done."

Yuri kicked harder at the small hole he'd dug with the toe of his soft leather boot. Kayan could smell the damp soil and the crushed grass. The shadow of the golden eagle flashed across the tiny clearing and a ground jay dove for cover in the branches of a silver birch.

Yuri's voice dropped to a strained whisper. "But it's not fair."

"Is too!" Val insisted. "They're Scythians!"

"Ah." Kayan nodded. "So it wasn't the warrior who frightened you—the one Val shot with his arrow?" Yuri shook his head emphatically. "What's bothering you is the slaughter of the wounded. You don't understand why we had to kill helpless men?"

" 'Cause they're monsters," Val said. "They eat people."

Kayan nodded. "It's true. Some steppe tribes do eat their captives, but not for food. They do it because they think that by eating the hearts of their enemies, they gain the fallen warrior's power."

"That's silly," Val said.

"We think so, but we are followers of the light. The gods of the Scythians are dark. They demand blood sacrifice."

"But . . ." Yuri frowned. "If we do bad stuff, does it make us bad?"

"Scythians are a harsh people." He glanced at Val to make certain he was paying attention. "They admire strength and hate weakness. If we allowed the wounded warriors to go free, they would never live to get back to their tribe. If they couldn't keep up, their comrades would abandon them on the steppes. Either they'd die of hunger and thirst, or wolves would eat them."

"I thought we killed them because we could," Val said.

Kayan put his arm around him and pulled him close. "You know that I mean to raise a mighty army of horsemen . . ."

"To kill the Greeks," Yuri said.

"And Egyptians," Val said.

Kayan nodded solemnly. "There are not enough Bactrians and Sogdians. We need the wild men of the mountains and of the steppes. But they won't come to the council fire if they don't respect us. We must show that we're strong. Warriors worthy to claim as allies."

Color was beginning to seep back into Yuri's cheeks. "How will they like us and want to be our friends if we kill them?"

Kayan chuckled. "We don't want them to like us. We want them to respect us. And if I'd spared the wounded, they would have had contempt for us. Alexander did that once. He showed mercy to the tribe that had attacked him. He left men alive, and they called him soft. He had to fight them again and again."

"So Alexander wasn't always smart?" Val asked.

"Most of the time, but not always." Kayan rose to his feet. "Even Alexander had his weaknesses."

"But not you," Yuri said.

"Mount up," Kayan ordered. "It's time we joined the troop and you boys got these mares and foals settled."

He crossed the small grove to where Sidhartha waited, pawing the ground and nickering with impatience. Yuri's childish words lingered in Kayan's head, and he unsuccessfully tried to push them away. He supposed that if he was honest about it, those two rascals were his weaknesses, but none would ever be so vast as the weakness he'd had for *her*. He wondered for the hundredth time if she would still be alive if he'd not done as she asked—if he had been stronger.

It was a question that haunted his dreams, and one for which there was no answer.

"I tell you that we cannot permit this to go on," Berenice whispered to Ptolemy's first wife, Artakama. "Something must be done before we find ourselves exiled to some mud hut in Memphis."

Artakama nibbled another grape from the bunch in her hand. The two royal wives lounged on the open deck of a royal barge beneath a striped and fringed canopy. Around them clustered groups of gossiping noblewomen, servants, musicians, a group of dancers, two poets, three philosophers, a dozen members of the household guard, four parrots, a pet monkey, and five dogs.

Court cruises on Lake Mareotis were popular diversions, especially with those who had something to conceal. The palaces were full of spies, and the freshwater lake provided a place where delicate subjects, especially those concerning King Ptolemy, could be discussed. Between the poet delivering his latest work, the zither, the double flute, the cymbals, the chattering monkey, squawking parrots, and the rhythmic chant of the oarsmen, Berenice and Artakama could talk freely without any danger of being overheard.

"It is an insult," Berenice said.

Artakama tossed a grape to the monkey. The animal caught it and popped it into its mouth. The Egyptian queen laughed. "Don't scowl at him, Berenice. He's cleaner than those filthy parrots."

"I didn't ask you here to have you insult my birds. This is serious. When has he last invited you to his apartments? Or gone to yours?"

Artakama yawned and extended one leg so that the masseuse could continue rubbing her foot with scented oil. The Egyptian refused to wear proper Greek dress, preferring a linen gauze shift and tunic so transparent that, when she shifted her limbs, not even the most intimate parts of her body were hidden from view.

Berenice felt her throat and face grow warm as she averted her eyes. One naturally became accustomed to seeing naked servants, but when a queen did not preserve her dignity, it was an affront to all decent women. Pharaoh's daughter or not, Artakama was nothing more than a painted Egyptian slut.

A young Nubian girl offered wine in a blue glass vessel decorated with lotus leaves. Berenice accepted the brimming goblet and waved her away. Artakama nibbled at a slice of melon. The Greek woman could barely hide her disgust. Her rival hadn't the decency to acknowledge their shared problem. To all appearances, the Egyptian hadn't heard a word she'd said. Swallowing her anger, Berenice tried again. "You don't seem to realize what this means."

"Our lord may take his pleasures where he pleases," Artakama purred. "I don't understand why you feel threatened by—"

"She came by ship from Greece. And he had the physician who accompanied her disposed of. Why? What is so important about her that her existence must be kept secret?"

The dancers had finished their performance. Artakama smiled and motioned to one of her attendants. The woman tossed a gold ring to the lead dancer. Twittering like birds, the troupe bowed and retreated. "See that they are fed," Artakama said to her servant. "They please me. Tell them that I will mention their skill to His Majesty."

The ugly Thracian poet trailed away, following the dancers. Artakama offered her other foot to be massaged. The monkey scampered across the table and made off with a fig. Berenice drained her cup and called for more wine. "So you will do nothing? You will give your approval to this barbarian whore?"

The Egyptian queen's kohl-black eyes widened in amusement. "It is hot, my dear sister. The music is pleasant, and the melons are the sweetest I have tasted this year. Will you ruin such a pleasant afternoon by wailing over so small a matter?" A smile played over her full lips. "We are his wives, Berenice. She is nothing, a plaything, a few evenings' diversion. How can you deny him his hobbies when his burdens are so heavy?"

"Our positions are in danger," Berenice said. "He will—"

"Wait," Artakama chided. "You have done all the talking. Now have the courtesy to listen to me. War, famine, plague—those matters are serious. Under our lord's hand, Egypt lies secure and the city of Alexandria glistens like a beacon on a dark night. Our husband has built libraries, universities, and a magnificent tomb to the memory of Alexander the Conqueror. Learned men flock here from all the civilized world. Ptolemy's army is mighty and invincible; his ships command the seas. Kings tremble when his ambassadors approach." She rested two slender fingertips against her delicate chin and chuckled. "All these things our lord has accomplished. And you would dare risk his wrath over a bedmate?"

"I'm not afraid of him," Berenice retorted.

"No?" Artakama lay back against the cushions and closed her eyes. "You should be, my dear sister. For all men are unpredictable creatures, and kings most of all."

A mile away, in the Palace of the Blue Lotus, Ptolemy and Mayet lay facing each other on couches beside a reflecting pool in the garden. They had spent the afternoon talking and playing at senet. She was still weak, but each day she found her appetite both for food and for life returning. She looked forward eagerly to Ptolemy's visits, and today had been nearly perfect. So long as he was here with her, charming and cosseting her, she could almost forget that her life had begun only weeks ago and everything before that was a gray swirling void.

Almost . . . except for the repeated dreams that both troubled and excited her. Dreams of two men . . . one golden . . . a second, dark and wild . . . and the sound of an infant wailing—an infant she could not see. Each time, she thought that what she searched for was within reach, but whenever she opened her eyes nothing remained of her shadow world. Nothing but emptiness . . .

"Mayet? Are you tired? Should I have the servants—"

"No. No," she answered, willing herself to remain here in this magnificent garden amid the sounds of birds calling, flowing fountains, and the faint rustle of the breeze through the date palms. "I'm all right. I would finish our game. Please."

Each had won once, and Ptolemy was only two squares away from declaring himself the victor in the playoff. "Your turn," he said, offering Mayet the throw sticks. "But you're well beaten, woman. You may as well admit it." He waved away the two slave girls with their ostrich-feather fans.

"I admit nothing," she said. Bringing the sticks to her lips, she kissed them for luck and cast them onto the table. "See," she cried triumphantly. "A three! I win."

"You cheat," he teased.

"I do not cheat. It is impossible to cheat at senet."

He laughed, and she thought again how attractive he was—not classically handsome, but strong and appealing with his fair hair, strong chin, and light eyes that sparkled with intelligence in his tanned face. His well-formed shoulders and lean, muscled arms showed to their best advantage in the elegant Greek chiton and mantle bordered with a band of silver embroidery. Few men could wear the himation, the draped over-garment, without appearing stout and pompous, but it fit Ptolemy's slim figure with grace and style.

"Nothing is impossible," he said. "I am ruler here. I say you cheat, and you deserve to be punished." Playfully he lobbed two grapes at her.

She ducked, and the grapes sailed over her head to plop into the pool. "For shame to attack a helpless woman. And you a mighty king." She threw a grape back at him and cried out in triumph. Her aim was true, and struck squarely in the center of his forehead.

Ptolemy clutched at the point of impact and groaned dramatically. "Struck down in the prime of my life."

"Serves you right," she said with a giggle. "And I never cheat."

"All women cheat." He flashed a boyish grin, and a warm feeling of security embraced her. "So long as they believe they can get away with it."

"Liar."

Smiling, he rose and crossed to sit on the edge of her couch. "It's good to see you getting better, Mayet. A few more weeks should put the pink back in your cheeks." He took a small silk bag from the folds of his mantle and poured the contents into his hand, revealing golden earrings crafted in the form of the cross of life. "For you," he said. "It would please me to see you wear them."

"You spoil me," she said, removing the silver cowry-shell earrings she wore and replacing them with the beautiful ankhs. "Thank you." He had already given her so many lovely things that she was reluctant to accept these earrings. But how could she refuse? He was her only friend. She didn't want to think what would have happened if he hadn't brought her here . . . if she'd been alone . . . without past or future.

"Why shouldn't I spoil you?" He touched her face. "We've been friends for a long time. Now I'd like us to be more. And I think you would too." He leaned forward and his lips brushed hers.

Her eyes widened in surprise. Before she could decide what to do, he pulled away and stood. "Admit it, I'm irresistible."

She felt herself flush with pleasure. The kiss had been tender and pleasant, so pleasant that she wasn't certain she could have resisted. "A little," she said. "But you don't play fair."

"I play to win, sweet. Always." He chuckled. "Duty calls, but I'd like to come back . . . later."

She hesitated, her thoughts in turmoil. "It's too soon," she began. "I—"

"Why too soon? You've been a widow for years. You're free, Mayet, free to live your life. Why shouldn't it be with a man who has loved you and desired you for so long?"

She covered her face with her hands. "But I can't remember. How can I go on when I don't know where I've come from? When I'm unable to mourn the loss of my own child?"

"You must trust me, dear one. I would never do anything to hurt you."

Trust me. His words struck a chord, and for an instant she felt that she stood on the brink of . . . Of what, she couldn't say, but instinctively she felt that it was important. "I do trust you," she answered. "It's myself I don't trust . . . don't know. I need time, Ptolemy. I must have time."

"And if you never recover the memory of what is past? How long will you wait? Life is short. As your physician told me, 'What mortal can say if he will draw breath at the next sunrise?' Perhaps you remain in this state of confusion because you cling to all that's lost to you. And once you decide to go on living, you will be restored to health."

"You may be right," she conceded. "But if you truly care for me, you will be patient a while longer."

An expression that might have been displeasure flashed

across his face, instantly replaced by the good-natured tenderness that had characterized his behavior. "I will try," he said, "but patience has never been my strongest asset."

"I think I might recover sooner if I had a change of scenery," she said. "Could I venture beyond this palace? Visit the city? The place where my son is buried? Make the acquaintance of other noblewomen?"

He frowned. "There is something here that displeases you? Hesper fails to show you the proper respect? The servants do not—"

"The servants are wonderful. Hesper has been as kind to me as any sister." She gestured. "My quarters are fit for a queen, but I grow restless, Ptolemy. I fear I'm not suited to endless days of having my body rubbed with precious oils and my hair dressed and—"

"You would overtax your strength. I cannot allow it. Not yet. Your physicians have been quite adamant. You must have rest and quiet. Sightseeing must wait, but if you desire anything . . . anything I can provide . . . jewels . . . new gowns . . . a pet . . . Would you like a parrot? A kitten? You have only to ask."

"A boat ride?" she suggested. "A chariot—"

"No chariots!" He smiled indulgently. "You must learn patience, Mayet. And you must trust me to do what is in your best interests." He patted her hand. "As you say, you are still recovering from a near-fatal illness and the shock of losing your only child."

"One? Was there only one child?" She shook her head. "It seems as though there were two."

"No. You had one son. Linus is dead, Mayet. You must accept it."

"I suppose you're right."

"I am. You are fragile, still too close to your own death. You are in no condition to make decisions. And until you are, as much as it pains me to deny you anything, I must insist that you follow physicians' orders."

"In other words, I'm to be treated like a child." *Or a prisoner,* she thought, unwilling to hurt him by saying those words aloud.

"Not a child," he said, "but a beloved lady." He spread his palms. "Promise you'll allow me to come this evening?"

"And if I say no?"

"I would be stricken."

She laughed. "Come, then. For if you don't, I may die of boredom."

Chapter 4

As soon as Ptolemy left the garden, Mayet retreated to her bedchamber. She was weary and troubled by her confusion. She wondered if she'd made a mistake in agreeing to let him return in the evening. Would he take that as a license to advance his seduction? It was clear to her now that he meant to come to her bed. What was unclear was whether or not she wanted him to.

Hesper supervised as the maids bathed the Lady Mayet and dressed her in a sky-blue linen tunic in the Greek style that left her arms and throat bare. Hesper offered a tray of golden bracelets and necklaces, but she refused them with a wave of her hand. Likewise, Mayet rejected jeweled pins and a diamond-studded diadem for her hair.

"Send away the musicians," she commanded. "Send them all away, Hesper. My head aches."

"Go, go," Hesper said. "I will attend the lady." Giggling and chattering among themselves, the slave girls, maids, ladies-in-waiting, and flute and zither players departed.

"It's kind of you to stay, but there's no need," Mayet

said. "I'm capable of braiding my own hair. Your husband and baby have more—"

"My son is in the capable hands of my mother-in-law and her staff," Hesper replied "And my husband is away on the king's business."

Mayet glanced curiously at the olive-skinned woman with the gentle brown eyes. In the weeks since she had recovered from her fever, Hesper had been vigilant in her care. She seemed sensible, and Mayet liked her, but there had never been personal conversation between them.

Hesper lowered her eyes. "Please, lady. I must know if I can trust you."

"Are you in trouble?"

"No." The dark eyes were shrewd. "But *you* may be."

"What trouble could I . . ." Mayet exhaled slowly. "Ah . . . I see. The king."

"He is a good man, a great ruler."

"But . . ." Mayet felt a shiver of unease. She grasped Hesper's hand. "Something is not right. Tell me what I should know. I swear to you that I will do nothing to harm you or yours."

Hesper glanced around the shadowy chamber. The sound of wind chimes and trickling water drifted in from the garden, and the air was rich with the scent of flowers, cloves, and myrrh. "I am no traitor to the House of Ptolemy," she murmured. "Or to my husband."

Mayet sank onto the bed and turned her back. "Comb my hair," she said. "If anyone sees us talking, they'll think nothing amiss."

Hesper applied the brush, divided a section of Mayet's thick red-gold tresses, and began to style intricate plaits. "King Ptolemy gave you a gift this afternoon."

"These gold earrings." Mayet resisted the urge to touch the ankhs and folded her hands in her lap.

"They are beautiful, but they are ankhs." The woman's

capable fingers continued weaving the heavy braid. "In the land of Egypt, none but royalty—kings and queens—may wear the ancient symbol of everlasting life."

Mayet made a small sound in her throat. "He is already married."

"Twice. He has two royal wives, lady. Queen Artakama, daughter to our last pharaoh, and Queen Berenice of Greece."

"I see."

"Of course, a king . . . a ruler of Egypt may have as many wives as he chooses. Queen Artakama's father had fourteen. But Queen Berenice is a jealous woman. My friend heard from her most trusted eunuch that Her Majesty, Queen Berenice, has been asking questions about you." Hesper pulled sections of Mayet's hair taut. "My friend's servant told her that he believes the queen wishes you ill. Lady"—Hesper's voice dropped to a whisper— "King Ptolemy is powerful, but so are his wives. If Queen Berenice thought you a threat to her position . . ."

"I've done nothing to be ashamed of," Mayet said. "At least, nothing that I'm aware of."

"You have not, I'm sure of that. You are a most honorable person."

Mayet toyed with the fabric of her tunic. "Then you have more faith in my past than I have. But what am I to do? I'm not free to leave this place." She wasn't sure she wanted to, but she didn't need to share her indecision with Hesper.

"You must have guessed that a king would have a queen."

"Yes, I did suspect." She'd deliberately not asked. Did that make her deceitful, or simply a coward? Knowing, she would have to take his marital state into consideration. So long as she remained innocent . . .

Hesper coiled the braid and secured it on the crown of Mayet's head with ivory pins. She leaned close and whispered in her ear. "Eat only what King Ptolemy eats or what I bring you. No one would dare to poison the king, and my cook has been with my husband's family since he was a child. I will bring fruit and food from my own kitchen."

"You think that necessary?"

Hesper shrugged, took another section of hair, and ran a silver comb through it. "Two of the king's concubines died last year," she said, keeping her voice low. "Both were with child and in good health when they were stricken by a sudden and fatal affliction of the belly."

"Poison?"

"The king was furious. Some say he cursed Queen Berenice. Others that he struck her in the face. But I didn't witness it. I do know that he invited her to dine with him and the main dish was one of her tame parrots, baked and served on a bed of grape leaves."

"You're certain it wasn't the king himself who wanted to be rid of these concubines?"

"No, lady." Hesper began braiding. "He is reputed to have a great appetite for women, but he is never unkind. When he tires of a favorite, he finds her a wealthy husband and gifts her with jewels and estates. Of course, not all are unwed. Many a noblewoman has increased her husband's fortunes by spending a night in the king's bed." She answered the unspoken question. "No, not me. I am shamefully fond of my good husband, and he of me. And King Ptolemy is not one to force a lady, neither noble nor commoner. He has no need to."

"So I am not the first to reside in the Palace of the Blue Lotus?"

Hesper uttered a sound of amusement. "You are the second. King Ptolemy built it for Queen Berenice. She thought it too Egyptian and too close to the banks of Lake Mareotis for her delicate constitution. The queen abandoned it after only a week's residence and insisted he build her a new palace in the Greek style. His Majesty has brought no one else here until you."

"And where did he bring me from?"

"I can't say." Hesper stood and clasped her hands. "There. I'm finished. You have beautiful hair, my lady. I'm sorry if I've frightened you, but I felt that it was my duty to warn you. If you seek King Ptolemy's favor, the stakes are high."

"So far I haven't sought it. But I'm not fool enough to believe his interest is nothing more than friendship." She sighed. "Thank you for telling me, but . . . Why would you risk so much for a stranger?"

Hesper averted her eyes. "I have my reasons. Besides, I think you would do as much for me."

"I hope I would." She hesitated and then asked. "You don't know where my home was, or are you afraid to tell me?"

Hesper shook her head. "I have said too much already. Forgive me, but I must go."

"One more thing, please. Can you get me a dagger?"

Beyond Persia, in far-off Bactria, the day was as fair as that in Alexandria, if not as warm. Spring rains and snow-fed mountain streams had turned the meadows to lush carpets of wildflowers. Prince Oxyartes, riding down from his mountain stronghold, halted his mount to take in the beauty of the green meadows framed by ancient forests and snow-capped peaks.

"Another year, old friend." Oxyartes patted his sorrel's neck and chuckled. "Much to our enemies' dismay, we've survived another year." Nudging the animal's sides with his heels, he guided the spirited gelding across an open training field and through the teaming military encampment at a quick trot. Everywhere men paused at their tasks to salute their monarch and exchange greetings.

How alike all armies were, Oxyartes thought as he surveyed the lines of archers practicing their marksmanship at straw targets. Greek, Indian, Egyptian, or Bactrian, it made little difference. Armies and wars tended to blur in his memory until they became one. No matter the language or the color of their skin, soldiers were much the same. They gambled, cursed, boasted, and complained of their betters.

To his left, green broke horses pranced and shied as trainers patiently coaxed the animals to accept the weight of a man on their backs. Dogs barked; boys watched wide-eyed. Tame hawks flapped and stared from their perches. Anvils rang as smiths hammered out arrowheads, spear points, and shields. Warriors, stripped to loincloths and boots, wrestled and crossed swords under the critical eyes of their officers, while others mended bridles and polished weapons. Craftsmen and merchants haggled and gossiped, shouting their wares. Vendors, both male and female, wandered up and down the lines of tents with baskets and trays of hot food for sale.

Veterans, men that Oxyartes had served with since he was a boy, hailed him, offering ale and gossip. He stopped to speak to each one, but didn't linger among his old comrades. He was anxious to meet the returning troop of cavalrymen, to hear the details of the battle with the Scythians, and to tell his adopted son what he had received in Kayan's absence.

Yuri spied Oxyartes first and shouted, "Grandfather!" The boy urged his pony out of formation and galloped toward him. Val trailed him, kicking his pony into a canter. By the time Kayan dismissed his men and reached Oxyartes, Val was already relating the story of his first kill.

"A Scythian nearly got Yuri!" he exclaimed. "I shot him with my arrow."

"The herd ran him down," Yuri said. "And he didn't get me. I kicked him. Hard!"

"Greetings, my prince," Kayan called, saluting the regal figure on the bay horse. "You've heard?"

Oxyartes nodded. "News of your victory against the raiding party preceded you. One of my commanders received word from an outrider last night."

Kayan noticed that Oxyartes's saddle was fitted with leather stirrups. The older man sat erect on the horse, shoulders back, heels down. His years told on his face, but he remained one of the best riders and the shrewdest generals Kayan had ever known.

"You sent up signal arrows?" Oxyartes asked.

Kayan nodded. Arrows tipped with flame carried messages swiftly across the rugged terrain. A man on foot might take days to cross a mountain range, but lookouts posted at intervals throughout the Twin Kingdoms linked the far-flung population in hours rather than weeks. Oxyartes's ability to send and receive information was vital. That and the loyalty of his followers had kept him in power through three rebellions and four all-out Greek invasions in the turbulent years since Alexander's death.

"Fortunately, most of my hair is already gray," Oxyartes said. "I didn't know you meant to take these boys hunting Scythians."

Kayan smiled grimly. "Without them, the plan might not have worked."

"Yes." Oxyartes nodded. "It's not their bravery I worried about. It was what my life would be worth with their grandmother if you'd come back without either of them." He grinned at the boys, and for an instant, years fell away from his face. "Ride up to the palace. Soraya will not be satisfied until she has hugged and kissed you and stuffed you both with sweetmeats."

Yuri and Val did not need to be told twice. They glanced at Kayan, and he waved them off. "Go, go. Like as not, Soraya will scold me for not seeing the two of you decently bathed and dressed—"

"As a prince's sons," Oxyartes finished. "Go, lads. But do not forget to see to your ponies first. They look hard used." He laughed as the boys rode off toward the fortress. "They remind me of two other troublemakers I knew a long time ago."

"I worry about them," Kayan answered. "Yuri, especially. He has a soft heart."

"And the world is hard?"

Kayan picked a burr from Sidhartha's tangled mane. "Too hard for some."

"And Val?"

"Better suited to a soldier's life, I think. He has the makings of a general." He gazed at Oxyartes thoughtfully. "There is something you would tell me?"

"I received a message two days ago. I would have you read it. I don't know if it's genuine or a cruel jest."

Kayan stiffened. "Came from where?"

"Macedonia. By post."

The mail system, which Alexander had borrowed from the Persian kings and refined, still functioned after a fashion. Relay riders on fast horses carried letters to towns, cities, and armies from Macedonia to Syria, Egypt, Persia, and the borders of India. So terrible was the punishment for attacking one of these agents—who carried no valuables other than the mount beneath them—that even the savage hill bandits dared not interfere with their mission.

Now that Alexander's empire had shattered, the mail routes did not officially extend to the rebellious Twin Kingdoms. But Greeks and Bactrians had intermarried and possessed mutual friends and interests. What custom could not accomplish, gold coin would. Oxyartes received regular mail deliveries from the centers of the Western world.

The high prince tossed Kayan a scroll of stained calfskin. "Read it and tell me what you think."

Kayan unrolled the thin leather and studied the crude and misspelled Greek.

For the sake of Apollo's lady who gave my wife water in the desert, I Tito, son of Thanos, Macedonian citizen and infantryman what followed him beyond the Hindu Kush to the towers of Babylon, bear witness to what I saw three nights past.

Cassander's soldiers brag in the ale houses of murdering a queen. All the city watched her coffin carried through the streets to the grave. They lie. With my own eyes I saw a woman with the mark of a leaping tiger branded on her thigh . . .

Kayan swore and gripped the scroll so tightly that his finger pierced the leather. The next words were smeared and illegible. His heart hammered against his ribs as he scanned the rest of the message.

. . . carried aboard a Phoenician merchant ship flying the banners of King Ptolemy . . . bound for Alexandria.

By the foreskin of Mighty Ares, I do swear. Apollo's lady did not die. She lives.

Kayan crushed the scroll in his fist. "He lied. That bastard Ptolemy lied."

"You believe this Tito?" Oxyartes asked.

"He's telling the truth. There can be only one woman with such a mark. Besides, if he was caught sending this, Cassander would boil him alive."

Oxyartes nodded. "I thought as much. But why? Why would Ptolemy rescue my daughter and tell me she was dead?"

Banked fires ignited behind Kayan's eyes. His voice thickened with barely controlled fury. "He wants her. He has always wanted what was his brother's."

"Ptolemy was her friend. Our friend."

"No more." Kayan struggled to control his rage. "He

sees himself as Pharaoh," he muttered. "All-powerful."

Oxyartes's weathered face softened. "I was afraid to let myself hope that she was alive. Afraid it was an old man's unwillingness to accept the truth."

"I should have gone for her long ago. I was wrong to leave her in the power of her enemies."

"No." Oxyartes shook his head. "You were right to remain here. You are the heir to the Twin Kingdoms. Attempting to rescue her from Cassander's prison would have been suicide, a useless sacrifice."

"The boy is heir, not me!"

"Not yet. Not for many years. And never if you do not remain to protect and guide him."

"He has you."

"I won't live long enough to put him on the throne. Once, I was as you are. I thought there was nothing I could not do. But I have seen too many battles, endured too many winters. I have the will, Kayan, but not the strength. She was wise. She put the child in your care. And you swore to make him king in his own land."

Veins stood out on Kayan's forehead. "I will see him crowned. And she will be at my side to witness it."

"You're a fool! If you had no chance of rescuing her from the Macedonians, how from the might of Pharaoh?"

"You think so little of me?"

"Where is your reason? Egypt is far away."

"It would not matter to me if she were in the farthest province of China. I will go for her."

"Ptolemy is the most powerful man on earth. He commands more ships than Greek and Macedonian cities put together. His soldiers number as many as the sands of the Nile. And your army is two years away from being ready to invade Greece, let alone Egypt."

"You expect me to leave her to Ptolemy?"

"Would you rather she was in her grave? If Ptolemy

bought her or stole her from under Cassander's nose, he will—"

"He will take her to his bed!" Kayan gripped the hilt of his sword. "No more!" he said. "No more will I stand aside for a lesser man. Roxanne is mine. She was always mine. And I will bring her home or die in the attempt."

"And what of the boys? Would you take them to their deaths?"

"I can't leave them here. I'll be gone a year, maybe two. It's too long for me to be parted from my sons. But I will return with her. You can hold the Greeks and your rivals at bay for that long. You may be more cautious than you once were, but you have lost none of your wits."

"Madness," Oxyartes said. "Do you expect to attack Ptolemy's palace and demand that he give her to you? You'll be dead before you cross the Nile. You'll never lay eyes on her."

Kayan shook his head. "Ptolemy will welcome me as an old friend and an ambassador of the Twin Kingdoms. He's taken North Africa and Palestine. He's ambitious. He lusts for the riches of Bactria and Sogdiana. If he controls them, he can control the trade routes and use them as a stepping stone to invade Persia."

"You'll dangle a treaty in front of his eyes," Oxyartes surmised. "Yes, that might work." His face grew grim. "And you have the one possession that he might trade anything to have."

"No. The boy is mine. I won't give him up."

"Not even for her?"

"I'll have them both."

Oxyartes paused, and when he spoke again, his eyes were old. "You risk too much. This is not a game of courage, Kayan."

"I can only answer with her words, my prince, the words her waiting woman told me in those last desperate hours.

'The game nears its end. We must risk all on a final throw.' "

"I fear for you, Kayan. For all of us."

"It's Ptolemy you should fear for. I'll carve his heart from his chest and lay it at the Macedonian's tomb."

Chapter 5

An hour after leaving Roxanne in the garden, Ptolemy reached the harbor, accompanied by couriers, members of his military council, and an assortment of noblemen, scribes, officials, priests, and servants. He waved away the entourage to walk along the wharf with Hector of Pella, admiral of his southern fleet.

Ptolemy wanted to appear to be inspecting the warships, but he had little interest in the ranks of seamen or the day-to-day operation of his navy. That was Hector's job. All Ptolemy was concerned with was results. Whoever commanded the sea lanes held power in the Mediterranean, and he meant to be that power.

What an odd pair they must appear, Ptolemy thought with amusement: a king, richly clad in linen and gold, and the barefoot naval commander, wearing nothing but a stained and patched, thigh-length tunic. Ragged attire or not, Hector of Pella possessed courage, a keen mind, and unshakable loyalty. Ptolemy had known him more than twenty years. They had fought side by side, shared dock-side trollops, and possessed the same ability to command men. Ptolemy trusted Hector as he trusted few others, certainly more than either of his wives.

Now Ptolemy listened only halfheartedly as Hector delivered his detailed assessment of Cassander's sea force and a skirmish near Cyrene. He could not stop thinking about Roxanne, about the feel of her mouth against his, and the sound of her laughter. Thinking about her made him grow hard and walking uncomfortable. For once, he was glad for the cumbersome peplos, the formal draped cloak of Phoenician purple that custom decreed he wear over his tunic. The folds of the material, of linen rather than wool, discreetly hid his physical condition from the public. Evening and his return to Roxanne's bedchamber could not come soon enough.

". . . sent them to the bottom," Hector said.

Pretending interest in Hector's report, Ptolemy paused, shifted his stance to ease his burgeoning desire, and gazed around him at the merchant vessels streaming through the heavily fortified harbor entrance. Ship followed ship, each heavily laden with the riches of Africa and the Aegean: ivory, spices, cattle, gold, slaves, olives, oil, wine, bronze, and wheat.

Yes, that was better, Ptolemy decided. He must concentrate. Thinking about commerce, about possible hostilities with Carthage rather than Roxanne's perfume or the texture of her skin, would help the hours pass.

Endless lines of near-naked men moved from the docks to ox-drawn carts and columns of mules and camels. Their backs sweating under the hot sun, bearers staggered under the weight of sacks of grain, baskets of fish, and bundles of animal skins. Gulls and sea birds shrieked and dove and squabbled for scraps. Stewards and scribes and city officials shouted and shoved through the throngs of sailors, soldiers, priests, priestesses, urchins, harlots, and beer sellers. Oxen bawled, mules brayed, hounds barked, caged birds squawked, and parrots cursed.

"By Zeus's ass, this city smells like a whore's purse,"

Ptolemy said, forcing himself from his reverie and hiding the fact that he had heard barely a word Hector had said. "A man cannot get a breath of fresh air. Sometimes I wonder if I would have been wiser to retire to Macedonia and turn farmer."

The admiral grinned. He was a small man of middle age, whip-thin, his skin bronzed and seamed by wind and salt water to the consistency of ship's dried beef. "I cannot see you behind a plow, Highness."

Hector's eyes were blue, but as faded as the rest of him. Faded or not, they sparked with intelligence. Ptolemy knew he had a prize in this admiral, and it was in his own interest to give the little man the respect he deserved.

"It's been too long since I've wielded a sword," Ptolemy said with affected comradeship. "Let no one tell you that dealing with these fawning bureaucrats and preening ambassadors is easy."

"True enough," Hector agreed. "Although a good port town has its compensations after weeks on sour beer and hard bread."

"But the stench," Ptolemy exclaimed. "How can you stand the stink after the clean sea air?"

The admiral laughed. "There are far worse cities. And we've fought our way in and out, haven't we? At least the sewers function here." Hector's gold and ivory teeth glittered in the sun. What remained of his salt-and-pepper hair was cropped close to his head, and he was clean-shaven, revealing deep pox scars and a sagging left cheek where an arrowhead had broken teeth and severed muscles. "Alexandria smells of money," Hector said. "And of power. What city can match her? What land, Egypt? Because of you, my king."

Ptolemy grunted, but he was secretly pleased. Hector's news of Carthage and the southern campaign was good, and the new fleet was well on its way to completion. Soon he'd have no need to be wary of Cassander. In two years,

Macedonia would be sending tribute to Egypt, to him. He slipped a heavy gold ring off his thumb and handed it to Hector. "Sell it and buy yourself a pair of sandals," he said. "Poseidon take me if you don't look more like a pirate than my admiral. If I met you in a dark alley, I'd look to my sword."

Hector took the ring and bit it to test the quality of the gold.

Ptolemy roared with laughter and slapped him on the shoulder. "Win me Carthage and I'll make you governor. You can spend your old age in comfort."

"I'd have to leave my wife in Greece."

"Which one? Old Circe? The Phoenician beauty or the Nubian princess I hear you have stashed in a villa on—"

Hector cut him off with a sailor's oath. "You know too much," he protested, laughing heartily. "You know what they say about you, Majesty. They say a man cannot pinch a louse between Athens or Persepolis without your spies reporting the size and weight, and you thinking of a way to turn a profit on the murder."

"Do they, now?" Ptolemy chuckled. "I—"

A rotund eunuch with a shaven head and eyebrows darted forward to prostrate himself on the dock. Hector yanked the curved blade from his waist and moved to protect his King. Ptolemy motioned Hector aside. "What is it?" he demanded.

"Great and glorious king," the messenger piped. "Most high and esteemed—"

"Skip the formalities. What do you want? Speak, man, or I'll have Hector slice open your pate and use whatever's inside for fish bait," Ptolemy said.

The messenger pressed his face closer to the wooden boards. "Her Royal Highness, Queen Artakama, favored daughter of Isis, High Priestess of Bastet, Tawert, and Nekhbet, begs you to come to her at your earliest convenience." One stubby-fingered hand fluttered to indicate a flower-bedecked vessel anchored beyond the naval fleet. The barge, gaily painted with the Eye of Horus and golden lotus blossoms and bedecked with flowers, flew the banner of Ptolemy's Egyptian queen.

"What does she want?" Ptolemy asked and then laughed. "You wouldn't tell me if you knew, would you, you perfumed bastard?" He glanced at Hector and shrugged. "You see, royal wives are as troublesome as any man's. Can you provide a craft and oarsmen to row me out to her yacht? If I don't go, she'll retaliate by building herself another tomb, and the last one cost me a year's income."

Hector saluted. "At once, my king." He beckoned to an aide, and within minutes, Ptolemy was climbing the rope ladder to the deck of Queen Artakama's luxurious barge.

The royal lady's guard, armed with bows, spears, and thick wooden staffs, stood rigidly at attention while a host of slave girls chanted a welcome. Wearing only garlands of flowers around their hips and cones of perfumed wax on their heads, the girls knelt and tossed lotus blossoms in his path. Ptolemy stopped amid the shower of flowers and looked around for his wife. He saw priestesses, dancers, musicians, oarsmen, eunuchs, and cats, but nothing of Artakama.

An older lady-in-waiting, a woman he recognized as one of his wife's favorites, came forward and prostrated herself. "Your Highness, Queen Artakama begs that you—"

"Yes, yes," Ptolemy said, becoming more annoyed by the moment. "Where is she and what does she want?"

The Egyptian noblewoman smiled and gracefully indicated a curtained pavilion near the stern of the barge. Two enormous eunuchs garbed in Persian trousers and turbans stood guard. Each man held a double-headed axe.

Ignoring them, Ptolemy pushed aside the curtain and stepped inside the area, then stopped short and stared. He nearly gasped, but caught himself at the last moment and merely spoke his wife's name. "Artakama."

She didn't reply, but remained motionless, on her knees, clothed only in her long black hair. He swallowed, his mouth suddenly dry. He knew that she shaved her head and this was just a wig, but the effect was stunning.

Artakama had oiled her body and sprinkled it with gold dust. As she slowly raised her head, he saw that her eyes were outlined in kohl, her lashes long and thick, her mouth painted scarlet.

He sucked in the moist sea air.

He'd been mistaken. She did adorn her womanly charms with more than her hair. Around her neck, she wore a slave collar of beaten gold, set with blood-red rubies. From the collar to the bracelets adorning her delicate wrists ran thin chains of gold, each minute link engraved with tiny hiero-glyphs, while the wide bands of collar and bracelets bore figures of Indian men and women happily engaged in prodigious sexual feats.

"I beg your pardon, mighty bull," she said in her lisping Greek. "I have offended you in some way. Forgive me, husband."

"You haven't . . ." He trailed off as she moistened her red lips with the tip of her tongue. She smelled of musk and something elusive, something heady and alluring. Her dark lashes fluttered. "You have not come to my bed," she whispered. "So I know that I must have committed some—"

"No, no." He stepped nearer. Fierce need knifed through him.

"I have been very bad," she said. "I need to be pun-ished." From the heaped cushions, she produced a leather whip with a silver handle and offered it to him. "Please," she murmured. "Teach me a lesson in obedience."

His fingers closed on the delicate whip. It seemed al-most a toy, yet the thin strips would sting well enough. Sweat beaded on his forehead.

Incense curled from a brazier beside the bed. Slowly, teasingly, Artakama turned away from him and lowered her face to the pillows, presenting him with luscious bare cheeks and the hennaed soles of her bare feet. Her bottom was oiled and firm and glistening, her thatch a dark curtain of fleece.

Ptolemy groaned, shook off his cloak, and fumbled for his stiffening rod. Outside, the musicians increased the tempo of their performance, but he was barely aware of it. Louder and more incessant was the pulsing of his blood, the whisper of the leather strips against Artakama's flesh, and her moans of ecstasy.

Hesper's infant son was sleeping when she returned to her husband's estate later that night on the outer edge of Alexandria. She did not stop to bathe and change into a fresh tunic, but went straight to the child's bedchamber. Suddenly, the most important thing in the world was to make certain her son was safe.

A cool breeze off the lake wafted through the spacious room. Sixteen-month-old Jason lay with a thumb in his rosebud mouth, sprawled on his back in the silk-lined cradle woven of reeds and hung securely from sweet-smelling cedar beams. Hesper's mother-in-law, Lady Alyssa, sat beside him on an ivory stool. Across the room, ever vigilant, hovered Jason's Macedonian wet nurse.

"He's not feverish, is he?" Hesper demanded.

Lady Alyssa smiled at her. "No, daughter. He is fine. Perfect." She sighed, and her round face beamed with joy. "You cannot know how happy he makes me, how happy you make me. To have a healthy grandchild after so many disappointments."

"Isis bless him," murmured a kneeling slave girl. "May the gracious goddess watch over him and grant him a hundred years."

"Has that tooth come in yet?" Hesper asked the nurse. Resisting the urge to pick the infant up, she stroked the crown of his head, reveling in the feel of Jason's silky, dark hair against her fingertips.

The wet nurse shook her head. "No, lady. His gums are swollen, but he has yet to produce the pearl of a tooth."

"You look tired," Lady Alyssa said. "Is the foreign woman difficult?"

"No, to the contrary," Hesper replied. "She is most pleasant. You would like her."

"Come, we will let him sleep." Lady Alyssa brought two fingers to her lips, kissed the tips, and pressed the caress to Jason's head. "Keep him safe," she commanded. The nursemaid murmured assent.

Hesper gave a final instruction to the nurse and followed her mother-in-law to a private sitting area. Lady Alyssa sent a slave for roast chicken, fruit, olives, and cheese, and bade Hesper to make herself comfortable. "What troubles you, daughter of my heart?" the lady asked. "There is no need to worry about your husband. He is likely to come to no harm entertaining the Etruscan scholars."

Hesper shook her head. Argo's mother had welcomed her with open arms, despite her lack of breeding or family. She'd been more than kind; she'd treated her with respect and affection. But Hesper wasn't certain how much it was safe to reveal.

"Out with it," Lady Alyssa said. "You know there are few secrets in this household. And a burden is lessened if there are two to carry it." Her eyes suddenly grew concerned. "You haven't had bleeding, have you? The child you carry—"

"No, lady," Hesper assured her. "I felt him kick only hours ago. This babe will be as strong as Jason. No, this is something more dangerous . . . to me and to this house."

The lady motioned for silence, rose, and led her out to the enclosed garden. She didn't speak again until they reached the far corner, beyond the reflecting pool. She took Hesper's hand. "Tell me."

Hesper drew in a slow breath. "Long ago, the woman whom King Ptolemy calls Lady Mayet saved my brother's life. Mine also, I think. At least, her compassion rescued me from a life of poverty and provided my substantial dowry."

"Your brother Jason—but I thought he was dead."

"He is," Hesper answered, "but his death came long after in war. I was fostered by the general Julian and his wife, who were childless. They treated me as their own. Before, Jason and I lived . . ." She shook her head. "I don't remember much about that time, and I don't want to. What I do recall is that we were often hungry. And once, I had a puppy, but wolves took it."

"Then you should be happy to serve the Lady Mayet."

"I should," Hesper said. "But there are things about her past that I know." She hesitated and went on in a rush. "Things that she doesn't."

"Why is this knowledge dangerous?"

"King Ptolemy."

"Ah." The lady folded her arms over her full breasts. "You are torn between your loyalty to our monarch and this mysterious stranger?"

"Yes. I am."

"But the debt is real."

"Yes, it is." She clasped her mother-in-law's arm. "What do I do? I would not bring harm to you or my husband—to my baby son or the child that is to come. But my conscience will not let me forget what I owe to her."

"Then you must do as your heart bids, Hesper. If there is anything of worth in this world, it is honor. Honor to one's self, to one's house. Ours has always been a loyal family. Do what you must, but only what you must. And do not risk more than you can bear to lose."

"When I first laid eyes on her, I wanted to run away."

"But you didn't."

"No. Am I weak? Was she wrong to do so much for Jason and me and thus make this debt between us? Do I dare to help her?"

"Go to the temple of Hera tomorrow morning and make sacrifice. Promise the goddess . . . promise her two white bulls and three slaves. I will give you the price. Pray to her and listen with your heart. Hera watches over women and children, and she is all compassionate. She will tell you what to do."

Senbi passed through the west gates of Queen Berenice's summer palace, crossed the street, and walked quickly to the alley that led to the rear of the newly constructed temple to Demeter. Several yards from the entrance, a Greek wearing the uniform of the king's guard waited.

"Senbi?"

"No names, fool!" the eunuch said.

"Have you got it?"

Senbi opened the drawstring bag and poured a cascade of silver four-drachma coins, bearing the image of the head of Alexander the Great, into the guard's cupped palms. "Do it tonight, and do not fail in your task. If you do—"

The soldier grunted assent. "You've told me twice. I should be able to dispose of a sickly woman."

"No mistakes. In. Out. Her Highness was adamant. No fuss. No unpleasant details to deal with."

"I said, I can do it."

"Knife, noose, or pillow. It makes no difference so long as you aren't caught. If you are, and if you mention my name or—"

"Don't get your bowels in a twist. I've done this before."

"Good. If there are any miscalculations on your part, your end will be unpleasant. If you complete your mission satisfactorily, there will be an equal reward waiting, and doubtless, more opportunities to play the butcher."

The soldier snatched the bag from Senbi's hand and stuffed the coin back inside the folds. "She dies tonight.

And tomorrow night, you'd best be here with the rest, or the crocs will dine on your guts by midnight, you greasy lump of—"

"We are agreed," Senbi said. He turned back toward the palace, smiling. Let the Greek dog say what he liked. Senbi would be at the appointed meeting place, at the appointed time. But he wouldn't come alone. Her Majesty had asked that all loose ends be tied up. He, Senbi, would increase his income by a substantial number of silver drachmas, and the lady's assassin would be in no position to mention any names, ever.

Chapter 6

Mayet cried out as the dark form bent over her. Eyes wide and unseeing, she sat bolt upright and lashed out with her hands to defend herself. But against what? She began to tremble. Her heart raced, thudding so hard against her ribs that she thought it would break.

Gasping for breath, she slid off the wide bed, stood unsteadily, and listened. All was silent. She could hear nothing but the pulse of her own blood and the warning scream in her head. She reached for the goblet of water beside the bed. Her mouth was dry, her silk tunic damp with sweat.

A nightmare? Had she been dreaming? The memory of what she'd seen was jumbled—as unreal as the invisible assailant she'd struck at. What had frightened her so?

She strained to hear, but there was nothing, not a sound. She lifted the glass to her lips and then remembered Hesper's warning. "Eat only what I bring you." Did that mean that her water might be poisoned? But what if Hesper wished her ill? Could she trust her?

Mayet returned the glass to the table and sat on the bed, clasping her hands to keep them from shaking. The dream began to surface in her mind. A baby. An infant boy. Could it be her little Linus that she was remembering so clearly? She'd heard his first cry. There was blood . . . His birth . . . Was she recalling his birth? It was so real. She could feel the weight of him, feel her overwhelming happiness. But there was something more . . . sadness. No, not sadness— grief and acute apprehension. But of what? Surely the birth of her child would have been a time of joy. The baby was healthy, strong. She could see the chubby face, the little hands, the blue eyes.

But Linus was dead. Her child was dead. Ptolemy had said so. Words rose in her mind, words that she seemed to have heard before. *Not until I touch his cold flesh and close his eyes with my own hands will I believe.* Where had that come from? She didn't remember Linus as a toddler, only his birth. Was that natural? But . . . she'd remembered nothing . . . until now.

No, there was something more. Her dead husband? She remembered giving the child to a dark-haired man. . . . *You who are dearest to me in all the world, you must take him and* . . . And what? She was certain she had said that . . . but to whom and why? She strained to hold the image of the dark-haired man's face in her mind's eye. Black hair, thick and long. Features carved of granite . . . no courtier's face, but that of a warrior. A scar . . . a thin scar through his lip. Strong hands that she knew almost as well as she knew her own flesh, and eyes so deep and intense she could lose her soul in them. His eyes had been a dark brown, almost liquid, darker than black, black as pools of—

A twig snapped outside in the garden. Hair rose on the back of her neck. Were those footsteps? Icy fear gripped her as she reached under the cushions for the copper dagger Hesper had brought her. On bare feet, she inched away from the bed, into the darkest shadows of the room.

It occurred to her only then that there was no oil lamp

burning before the shrine of Isis. The light had never been extinguished before. And where were her maids? Where were the slave girls who slept on pallets at the foot of her bed? She'd not heard the guards speak since she'd opened her eyes. How long? Was she still dreaming? Or was she caught in the tangled web of her own twisted mind? Had she lost the ability to tell reality from illusion?

No, she was definitely awake. She could feel the cool tiles beneath her feet, feel the chill night air on her skin. She wondered what hour this was. How long had she slept? She had waited later than usual for Ptolemy, but finally she'd decided he wasn't coming. The two girls had been there when she'd gotten into bed. The blonde, Dirce, with the tattoo of a bird on her right ankle, and Vema, the Indian girl. Where were they?

Mayet pressed her back against the wall and clutched the knife in her hand. What if it was a gardener, or worse— Ptolemy, come to woo her in the middle of the night? Would he believe that she'd lost her mind? Or would his soldiers strike her dead for daring to raise a weapon in the presence of the king? Was she truly in danger? Or was she possessed by madness?

She stared at the colonnaded passageway that led to the garden. Moonlight spilled through a roof vent and washed across the floor between the entrance columns. All else was inky darkness.

Gooseflesh prickled her spine. Her mouth tasted of tin.

A sandal scraped on tile, and for an instant, the pool of light was marred by the shadow of a man. Her breath caught in her throat.

The shadow wore a Greek cuirass and carried a naked sword.

The king of Egypt crawled drunkenly on hands and knees to the rail of the queen's barge and quietly vomited over the side. Guards stared straight ahead, watching over him but pretending not to see his shame. Everywhere women and eunuchs slept, some curled on the bare wooden deck, others on pallets.

Ptolemy's head felt as if it were going to explode, and his mouth tasted like camel dung. Worse than camel dung, he thought as he wiped his lips with the back of his hand and stood up. Dizziness assailed him. He felt as though he was going to vomit again, but he forced himself to maintain his balance. What in the name of Dionysus had he been drinking?

He was mother naked. His hands felt sticky. He hoped it wasn't blood, but it was too dark to see. Shocked by his own loss of control, he returned to the queen's pavilion and parted the curtains. The draped area was lit by oil lamps, casting a yellow glow over the royal enclosure.

Artakama, Ptolemy's first wife and queen, lay on her back amid the heaped cushions, her breasts bared, her wig askew, one leg thrown over another human's naked thigh. A streak of kohl ran from the corner of Artakama's left eye to her open mouth. Bald, without garment or jewels, her body slick with oil, she was still beautiful in the way that a wild lioness was beautiful.

No, not a lioness, Ptolemy corrected himself, a tigress. Beautiful, sensual, and possessing lethal claws and teeth. He looked down at his scratched and bitten torso. What had they done tonight? What had he done? He wondered if the androgynous dancer sprawled under his wife had been part of the performance. Was the lovely creature male or female? Did he care?

You've become as decadent as a Persian satrap.

The familiar voice caught him unaware, lancing through his gut with the shock of a Scythian spear point.

He could not have been more astonished if a bolt of lightning had struck him out of a clear and sunlit sky.

"Alexander—" The word was out of Ptolemy's mouth before he realized what he was saying. He turned, half expecting to see his brother standing on the deck. But there was no one.

Alexander's laughter echoed in Ptolemy's head. *Yes, it's me. Do you doubt your own senses?*

Ptolemy blinked. He stared, looking for what? A ghost? His brother, dead nearly eight years, risen from his tomb?

The laughter came again.

Gooseflesh rose on Ptolemy's bare arms. He sprinted to the side of the barge and dove into the sea. A guard shouted. Men and women rushed to the edge of the barge. Ptolemy swam for shore with powerful strokes. The current was swift, but he didn't care. Better to drown or be eaten by sharks or saltwater crocodiles than stay there another instant.

He wasn't that drunk. He'd heard a dead man speak to him. It was impossible. His blood ran cold. Had Artakama poisoned him? Was he already dead and too foolish or cowardly to know it?

If he believed his own senses, he'd heard the voice of Alexander. Reason failed him. He wouldn't try to think. He'd simply swim, because if he didn't, he'd end up in some croc's belly.

A quarter of an hour later, Ptolemy waded from the Mediterranean onto a sand beach. His muscles ached and his head was still splitting, but his mind was no longer clouded with unwatered wine. Several reed fishing boats were pulled up on the shore. He crawled into the nearest one, rested his head on a coil of rope, and stared up at the stars. No more voices troubled him. He heard nothing but the lap of water and the shouts of searchers.

When the sun came up, he would hike to the nearest military outpost. Morning would be time enough to consider what had really happened.

What was it Alexander's specter had said to him? *You're as decadent as a Persian satrap*? Maybe the voice was right. Maybe he'd become too fond of being king to remember that the crown of Egypt was his only as long as he could hold it.

Old stories claimed that the gods warned their chosen of plots against their lives. Had that happened to him tonight? Or were the gods chastising him for heedlessly taking his pleasure at Artakama's wish?

He'd never been a religious man. He'd paid lip service to the gods, more as insurance than as an act of faith. He'd sacrificed in the temples and murmured prayers before battle. But if truth were told, he'd often doubted whether the gods existed, or if they did, whether they cared an ass's turd about the troubles of mortals.

Maybe he'd been wrong.

The thought was unnerving, but also reassuring. If the gods were real, they favored him. And as Alexander always said, it was better to be lucky than smart. Maybe he was both.

One thing he knew for certain. Neither of his queens had his best interests at heart. Theirs were marriages of state, political unions. He had no one that he could trust as his brother had trusted Roxanne.

Until now.

The Greek soldier crossed the chamber to the dais where Mayet's curtained bed stood. She heard the sound of the sword striking the cushions. He cursed and brought the heavy weapon down again and again.

Run! Every instinct bade her to flee. But where? She could run into the garden, but it was walled. If the gate was locked, she'd be trapped. He was between her and the hallway that connected her apartments to the rest of the palace. Could she outrun him?

"My lady! My lady Mayet!"

A torch flared.

The assassin sprang up from the bed, saw her, and lunged toward her. Two eunuchs burst into the room. One carried a torch, the other an axe.

Hesper followed. "Help! Help!" she screamed. "An assassin! Guards, come quickly!"

The eunuch swung his axe at the soldier. The intruder dodged the blow and drove his blade through the Egyptian's chest. The dying man staggered backwards, blood spilling between his lips and down his bare chest.

Mayet tried to reach Hesper in the doorway, but the killer wrenched his sword free and charged at her. Mayet whirled and fled through the columns to the garden.

Behind her, Mayet heard Hesper's frantic screams. The soldier dashed into the garden. Mayet ducked behind a date palm.

"You can't escape!" the killer said in Greek.

She didn't move a muscle.

The moonlight was bright, but the trees cast long shadows, throwing areas into darkness. The man moved toward her hiding place. She stepped backwards and stumbled over something on the ground.

With a curse, the soldier closed the distance between them. "You're a dead woman."

Frantically Mayet clutched the dagger and tried to get to her feet. What was it she had fallen over? It was too black to see anything, but the shape felt oddly familiar.

The curve of a bow! If there was a bow, there had to be arrows. He was only yards from her. He swung his sword high to deliver an overhand blow.

Mayet's fingers brushed a quiver. Without thinking, she raised the bow and set the feathered shaft in place. The bow was tall and heavy. She strained to draw the string.

Her would-be murderer swung the sword.

At the same instant, she released the arrow. She flung herself aside as the bronze blade sliced through the air. Twisting, she brought the bow crashing down on the back of the man's neck.

Abruptly, torches lit the garden. Shouting men poured onto the grass. Mayet sat down hard. For an instant, she felt nothing. Not fear, not regret. And then a chill seized her and she began to tremble.

"My lady!" Hesper cried. "There! There she is!"

Mayet glanced at the body lying on the grass beside her. In the circle of torchlight, she could see the bronze arrowhead protruding from the nape of his neck.

"He's been shot!" a eunuch shouted.

Someone rolled the Greek soldier onto his back.

"He's dead."

"Who killed him? There's no one here but . . ." The guard's words were lost in the clamor.

Hesper knelt and took hold of Mayet's hands. "Are you hurt, my lady?"

"No." She shook her head. "Why are you here? Why did you come back?"

"I couldn't sleep. I was afraid you wouldn't heed my warning about . . ." She squeezed Mayet's hands. "My warning. It's a good thing I did. When I arrived, the guards were missing. Vema and Dirce were gone as well. When I found the corridor deserted, I shouted the alarm."

"Is he really dead?"

Hesper questioned the nearest eunuch in Egyptian and turned back to Mayet. "He's dead. Do you know who shot him?"

"I did." Her eyes widened as she stared at Hesper. "He must have left his weapons here when he crept into my room. But how? How did I—"

Hesper put her finger to Mayet's lips. "Shhh, lady. Not now. Later." In a louder voice, she said, "I must get the lady back to bed. Someone must inform the king. At once. Iuty? Is that you?" She addressed a tall guard. "Yes, Iuty, see that the guard is doubled around my lady's chambers. Send word to King Ptolemy that someone attempted to murder Lady Mayet tonight. And find those who were supposed to be on duty. Be swift, unless you want to share in their punishment."

* * *

The sun was high the following morning when Hesper came to the garden to tell Mayet that the king was on his way. Mayet motioned to the seat beside her. "You look exhausted," she said. "You're with child, aren't you?"

"Yes, my lady." Hesper glanced around.

Slaves had carried the assassin's body away, and gardeners had replaced the blood-soaked grass. All appeared as serene as it had been the afternoon before, but Mayet felt that everything had changed.

"You were right," she said quietly to Hesper. "You saved my life."

"No, you saved your own life," the young noblewoman replied. "You killed him with the arrow. I couldn't have done it. I don't know of another woman who could have."

"How did I? That was a man's bow. How could I—"

Hesper shook her head. "There's no time."

"What of Dirce and Vema? Are they all right?" Different slaves had served the morning meal and helped Mayet to bathe and dress. When she'd asked about the missing girls, no one would admit to knowing their whereabouts. She hoped the two were safe.

"Yes," Hesper said. "They are unhurt. A washwoman discovered Dirce and Vema in a storage room just after daybreak. The guards who should have been on duty bound them hand and foot, blindfolded and gagged them. They're frightened but unharmed."

"And the guards? What of them?"

"We don't have much time. The king will be here any moment. I won't be able to return for a few days. My husband will be home for the first time in weeks. But you'll be safe. Now that the king knows that Queen Berenice—"

"You're sure she's the one who wanted me dead?"

Hesper looked around nervously. Mayet noticed that her eyes were red and sunken in her face. Hesper wore Egyptian dress this morning, and she was nearly as pale as the white linen. "Both of the guards who were not at their posts last night are dead. Their throats were cut to prevent their talking."

"What is happening?" Mayet cried in frustration. "Why?"

"You must be patient," Hesper said. "Your memory will return, if you give it time. Then all your questions will be answered."

"I want to know what you know." Mayet grasped her hand. "Please. If you hadn't warned me, I would have been in bed. He would have killed me. I'm in debt to you."

"Never." Hesper bit her lower lip. "You must not let anyone know that I told you, but the Greek who tried to kill you was one of the king's own guard."

"Ptolemy's?"

Hesper put her finger to her lips. "Be careful. Nothing is as it appears. The king wants you alive. If he hadn't, he'd never have brought you here. You would have died without any of us seeing you. Queen Berenice is your enemy. She failed this time, but don't expect her to stop trying. You must be on guard. The murderer and the guards weren't the only ones to die last night. One of Queen Berenice's servants, a eunuch by the name of Senbi, was found on the street near the temple of Demeter this morning with his throat slit."

"That he was murdered makes him and his mistress the queen suspect?"

Hesper grimaced. "Senbi was a pig. He had a name in the city for procuring young girls for sacrifices to the Egyptian crocodile-headed god. He did many other things, things that would only foul your mind. Trust me, lady. If someone chose last night to dispose of Senbi, he had dealings with the assassin."

"You're out here," Ptolemy called from the doorway.

Mayet rose to her feet.

"Your Highness." Hesper made to prostrate herself, but

the king shook his head. "No, no. I won't have it. You do your husband great honor, Lady Hesper. Please, accept my thanks. If not for your bravery, I might have lost her."

"Thank Hera, great king. I prayed to her, and it seemed to me that the goddess wanted me to check on Lady Mayet. When I found her guards missing, I summoned help as anyone would have done."

"Not anyone. And I won't forget. Your sons shall be educated with mine."

"Thank you, lord."

"Go, go now. You should be at home.

"I could not come sooner," Ptolemy said after Hesper had made her farewells and hurried away. "I blame myself for this. I should have protected you better." He embraced her and kissed the crown of her head.

"Who would hate me enough to try to kill me?" Mayet asked, once he had released her. Now that she'd had time to think about what had happened, she was afraid. Afraid and confused, and grateful for the king's strong arms around her.

Ptolemy shook his head. "I don't know. I have my suspicions. But it won't happen again, I promise you."

"Did they tell you what happened? Who killed him?"

"No. Hesper was hysterical, as you can imagine. One of the eunuchs. I'll find out the man's name if you—"

"No, no, it's not important," Mayet covered, realizing that Hesper had lied to the king. But why?

Ptolemy took her hand and raised it, pressing his lips to the underside of her wrist. "You must know how much I care for you, dear Mayet. How devastated I'd be if anything happened to you."

Shivers of pleasure coursed through her veins, and she raised her gaze to meet his.

"Am I so wrong?" he asked. "Or do you return that affection?"

When she didn't answer, he pulled her into his arms

again and kissed her tenderly. Mayet savored the caress, slipping her arms around his neck and raising herself on tiptoe to return the kiss. What could be so wrong with this? she wondered. If her life were in danger, who better to protect her than Ptolemy, the high king?

He kissed her again. She clung to him, returning his ardor with equal desire, and when he slid his hand to cup her breast, she made no protest.

Chapter 7

Mayet rolled over in bed, felt the empty place beside her, and opened her eyes. "Ptolemy?" Five months had passed since the attempt on her life, and she and the king had fallen into a comfortable domestic relationship. He came to her bed several times a week, and they dined together most nights. Ptolemy was a generous and accomplished lover. He was also intelligent, complex, and witty. Mayet supposed she should consider herself the most fortunate of women, but his possessiveness and her failure to remember her previous life kept her from allowing herself to trust him completely.

She sat up and looked around the dimly lit room. It was very early in the morning and still cool. "Oh, there you are," she said sleepily. Ptolemy stood near a window inspecting a map of Alexandria. Strewn across the surface of the marble table beside him were scrolls of figures and engineer's drawings. "What is it that has you enthralled this morning, my lord? An expansion of your library? A new temple?"

He turned his head. "A lighthouse, for the harbor. One such as the world has never seen." He smiled at her. "I meant to let you sleep."

For a man nearing forty, Ptolemy retained the physique and vigor of one much younger. Naturally lean, he kept his waistline by eating sparingly and exercising with sword and spear every afternoon. Gray flecked his fair hair, but his comely face was untouched by pox or disease, and he possessed an endearing charm. Ptolemy's belly was flat, his buttocks firm, and his chest and arms sleekly muscled. The king's male parts were all they should be, as was clearly revealed this morning.

"I see that you certainly find the plans exciting," she teased. She had discovered her own nature to be highly sensual, and at times, bordering on bawdy. She enjoyed food, and fine wine, and sex. And to her surprise, she felt not the slightest fear of King Ptolemy. Was it courage or stupidity? She had yet to learn that. What she did know was that she had a sharp tongue, and didn't hesitate to use it on him.

He chuckled, dropped the map on the table, and returned to her bed. She went into his arms, laid her head against his shoulder, and trailed her fingertips through the sprinkling of fair hair on his chest. "Surely Egypt's mighty bull has more to do today than linger with his concubine," she said.

He slid her silk sleeping shift off her shoulder and kissed her throat and breast. "Mmmm," he murmured. "You smell good."

His touch never failed to stir her physically, but she was not in the mood to make love. The dreams had troubled her sleep again last night. She kissed his forehead, wiggled away, and pulled the linen sheet to cover herself. "You will be late," she reminded him.

He tucked an arm under his head, lay back, and closed

his eyes. "You're not my concubine," he said. "You have only to agree, and we will be married."

"I'm not sure I want to be one of many wives, my lord. I don't like the idea of sharing my husband."

His eyes snapped open and narrowed with suspicion. "You share me now."

"It's not the same. You are here in my bed because I invited you in. If I become your wife, I am subject to your will."

He sat up. "And you aren't now?"

"Not in the same way. If I closed my door to you, you would not order your guards to break it down so that you could ravish me."

Ptolemy frowned. "Don't be too sure. You're mine, Mayet. Body and soul. I'm your king." He threw a leg over hers and rolled on top of her, pinning her beneath him. "I may be your slave, but I am still master here."

She didn't struggle. But when he kissed her mouth and nibbled at her lower lip, she didn't respond.

He pushed himself away. "You're insufferable. What more do you want, Mayet? Jewelry? Perfume? Land? I'll have one of my greedy governors executed and give you his lands and income."

"Spare your faithful supporters." She sat up and wrapped her arms around her knees. "Why should I marry you? You could find a dozen women who would please you more than I do."

"No, there is no woman like you. We are destined to be together. I mean to found a dynasty. I will be pharaoh in name as well as might. And I want you to give me sons to sit on the throne of Egypt after me."

Mayet's eyes glistened with moisture. "Would that I could give you a child." The vague ache in her belly told her that her menses would start within hours. Another cycle of the moon had passed without her quickening with his seed. Her friend and companion, Hesper, was growing larger every day. The girl was barely twenty and this would be her second child. "I've had one baby," Mayet said. "Why should it be so hard to have another? You must have what? A dozen?"

He waved a hand. "I'm potent enough. But they are girls. And how would you know?"

"Slaves' gossip. Nothing happens in Alexandria that isn't common knowledge within hours."

"You shouldn't listen to such prattle. I'm sure there aren't a dozen, and at least two may not even be mine. None are by my official wives, so they hardly count. I did have one boy, a long time ago. His name was Paris."

"In Greece?"

"No, Persia. His mother was a noblewoman. But it was wartime. She died, and he was lost to me."

"As my own child was lost."

He traced her bottom lip with his finger. "I must have a royal son, Mayet. Many sons. It's expected of me."

"What if I did marry you and I never could give you an heir?"

"Impossible."

"Not impossible. I'm old."

He laughed. "You are not yet thirty. My mother was your age when she had me. My father was King Philip of Macedonia. Did you know that? The great Alexander and I shared the same sire."

"You served with him?"

"As brother and Companion." His mouth thinned. "For years I walked in his shadow. This is my time."

"Yet, you brought his body here and built him a magnificent tomb."

Ptolemy's features softened. "Yes. I did. And a damned hard job it was to get it here. He died in Babylon. Did you know that? In summer, yet his corpse did not decay. Even now, he looks as though he is asleep in his glass and crystal coffin."

"I would see this wonder."

"No. I'll not have you wandering the city where harm might come to you. My soldiers could protect you from knives or arrows, but there is always fever and pestilence. They are silent killers. You are too beautiful to have your face pitted by pox."

"I am a woman of flesh and blood. Not a babe to be swaddled in goose down and sheltered from every peril." She rose from the bed and struck a small gong. "You must eat and bathe, my lord. No one will blame you for being late. They will blame me."

He groaned. "Now you sound like a wife."

She stepped out of her gown, pulled the ivory pins from her hair, and let it tumble down her back. Crossing to the pool that took up a full quarter of her chamber, she descended the steps into her bath. The water, always the perfect temperature—neither too warm nor too cool—rose to lap against the underside of her breasts.

"Don't ever shave your head," Ptolemy said. "Your hair is your greatest treasure."

"Perhaps I should cut off my hair and give it to you to keep in a copper-bound box. Then the rest of me could go free."

He came to the edge of the pool and glared at her with hard eyes. "You think you're a captive here?"

Stiffening, Mayet lifted her chin. "Go, do whatever it is that kings do. Conquer Carthage. Build a pyramid. And leave me to the idle chatter of women and the claustrophobia of these walls."

He returned to the bed and grabbed his tunic from the stool where he'd tossed it the night before. "How many rooms does this palace have? Fifty? A hundred? Haven't I sent you books, musicians, scholars, entertainers? I seem to recall bills from sandal makers, rug merchants, and jewelers. The price of a vial of your perfume would buy the services of a platoon of archers for two years. What do you want of me, Mayet? Is it too much to ask that you appreciate my generosity?"

She ducked her head under water to try to cool her temper. When she lifted it, Ptolemy was halfway to the door. "I want the rights that every freeborn Egyptian woman has," she called after him. "The right to walk the city streets, to see your library and your temples—the right to administer my own property, and to choose whether or not I wish to marry."

He paused long enough to make a rude gesture before striding away. Mayet covered her face with her hands, held her breath, and sank down until she rested on the tiles at the bottom of the pool. Seconds later, her slaves were grabbing her and pulling her up.

"My lady! What are you doing?" Dirce cried.

Vema clucked over her like a hen. "Lady, you will harm yourself."

"Don't," she protested. "Don't tug at me. Ouch! You're pulling my hair. I wasn't trying to drown myself. By the light, I . . ." She gritted her teeth and tried to ignore them.

Her headache was coming back. How tired she was of being oiled and perfumed like some ivory statue. No matter what Ptolemy said, she was a prisoner here, surrounded by women and eunuchs who refused to let her lift a finger to care for her own needs, let alone do anything useful. The king claimed he was protecting her from assassins, but if she didn't get away from this palace, she would lose her reason.

If she hadn't already.

She hoped that Hesper would come today. Now that her pregnancy was advancing, the noblewoman did not serve her regularly. When she did come, Hesper brought news of the city, gossip, and laughter. She told her about the great library of Alexandria, the new observatory for studying the stars, and the magnificent gold and crystal tomb of Alexander the Great. Once, Hesper had brought her son Jason with her. The two of them had played games with him in the garden, fed him honey cakes, and watched as he sailed his toy reed boat in the reflecting pool.

It was hard to see Hesper's little boy and to know that the young woman was about to have another baby. The loss of her own son, Linus, had made her desperate to have another child. If she had a babe, perhaps she would stop yearning for Linus. Strangely, she never envisioned him as a child. All she ever saw was the moment after his birth— that, and passing him to the dark-haired man, who she felt must be her dead husband.

Maybe she was foolish not to have accepted the king's offer of marriage. Surely he would not keep his queen so close. There would be court banquets, state affairs, processions. She'd even wished longingly that she could go to a temple and worship. The trouble was, she couldn't remember to what god or goddess she owed allegiance.

As queen, she could command her own guard, influence trade, deal with ambassadors, and confront her enemies from a position of power. Here, in the Palace of the Blue Lotus, she remained a plaything, as much a toy as Jason's reed boat.

"Enough," she said to her women. "I'll go to the garden and practice my archery. Have Iuty set up my targets."

The bow had been a gift from Hesper. A week after the failed attempt on her life, Hesper had appeared with a short, curved bow fashioned of horn, and a beautiful leather sheath of arrows. The bow was much lighter than the one she'd used to kill the Greek, and it was easier to draw.

Archery had become her favorite pastime, other than the bed sport she shared with Ptolemy. Surprisingly, she found that she rarely missed a target. Keeping the weapon near her eased her mind. She still had the dagger Hesper had given her, hidden under a loose tile behind the shrine of Isis, here in her bedchamber. It was a secret she shared with no one, not even Ptolemy.

For more than an hour she launched arrow after arrow while Iuty and the girls cheered and applauded and Egyptian musicians played softly from a secluded spot under the trees. But today, the physical exercise did not ease her unrest. Again and again, she scanned the high walls, wondering what lay beyond and what she would have to do to get there.

Ptolemy's driver and escort took him by chariot from the royal reception room of the grand palace to the library. There he met two renowned magi and listened to an interminably long and boring dissertation from a visiting Chinese philosopher, whose every word had to be translated first into Parsi and then Greek and finally into Egyptian. Ptolemy had yet to settle the dispute between Berenice and Artakama over an estate near Memphis, to receive Lord Yakdast and his wife from Syria, and to meet with the ambassadors from Hermes-knew-where.

His breakfast had been a mug of strong Egyptian beer. He was still out of sorts with Mayet, and he wearied of the crowds of courtiers, army officers, and noblemen who followed his every step, fawning and agreeing with everything he said, regardless of how bizarre. It had become a game with him to make vague comments about the possibility of rain in a country where it never rained, or to offer an absurd opinion on the height of the Nile's next crest. Then he would wait to see how long it would take for some shaven-head priest to come running with a bloody calf's liver and recite his exact prediction.

Did you think it would be easy to be king?

Ptolemy stiffened. He glanced behind him to make certain there was no opening in the stone wall where a speaking tube could carry a voice.

Not here, he wanted to shout. In dreams, or when he was drunk, but not here. It was impossible that he should hear Alexander's voice while he was awake and sober.

The hollow sensation in his gut became nausea.

The voice was in his head. Nothing more. He was not hearing Alexander's—

A chuckle. Faint. So faint that had he been listening more closely to his vizier, he wouldn't have heard it.

Mark me, Brother. She is no tame partridge. Beware her claws.

Ptolemy stood up. "Enough." He gestured to the captain of his guard. "Offer my excuses," he said to the white-faced official on his knees in front of him. "Tell the illustrious gentleman that I am called away by a matter of vital importance to the realm."

Outside, his charioteer Eli waited, idly chatting with an attractive young woman. When he saw Ptolemy, he snapped to attention. "I'm going to his tomb," the king said.

Instantly, one of the soldiers galloped ahead to clear the monument of visitors and prepare the honor guard for a royal inspection. Ptolemy leaped into the chariot, took the reins in his own hands as his cavalrymen vaulted onto their mounts, and slapped the leather over the team's backs. Eli barely had time to gain a foothold on the back as they sped away through the streets to the magnificent domed tomb of the Conqueror.

Ptolemy yanked hard on the reins, and when the horses came to a halt, he threw the lines to Eli. Soldiers on either side of the entrance stood like statues as Ptolemy stalked past them into the outer chamber. Here, armor and likenesses of Alexander lined the walls. A life-sized marble statue of Alexander's warhorse Bucephalus, complete with gold and onyx saddlecloth and crystal eyes, kept vigil, with his long mane and tail eternally blowing in an invisible wind.

The duty captain stammered and bowed. Ptolemy hurried through clouds of incense, past the raised wall map of the world showing the route of Alexander's conquest through silver mountains, golden cities, and across rivers crafted in blue turquoise.

The inner room blazed with sunlight, filtered through mirrored and barred ceiling vents. The ceiling was painted to resemble the blue of the Macedonian sky set with diamonds and crystal that reflected and intensified the light. Fountains bubbled out of the marble floor tiles, and songs of praise drifted from the adjoining chapels where priests and priestesses recited constant prayers for Alexander's soul.

Ptolemy ignored it all, walking past the statues of the gods and goddesses, going straight to the jeweled and canopied bier. "Are you there, you bastard?" he demanded.

Alexander lay as he had since the day his body had been entombed in a bath of pure honey in the gold, crystal, and glass coffin. His eyes were closed, arms folded over his chest, sword in hand, his shield on one shoulder. A simple golden coronet rested on his yellow curls. Golden elephants and life-sized lions stood at the corners of the tomb, while columns of silver antelope, griffins, horses, and camels filed around the base.

"You're dead," Ptolemy grated. "Dead. Not a god, just a man. And dead as Perdiccas."

He waited, half dreading an answer, but Alexander made no reply. Ptolemy dropped to his knees beside the coffin. "I've immortalized you, Brother. In this tomb and in the history I shall write of our exploits. Now leave me alone!" Tears welled in his eyes. "In the name of Zeus, please leave me alone."

Again, the faint echo of laughter.

"No, damn you. She's mine. She'll give me a son, and I'll not lose him as you lost yours."

When no reply came, Ptolemy got to his feet. He swallowed and wiped the sweat from his brow. "You failed to protect her," he said. "I won't. I'll crown her my queen. And if you don't like it, I'll tear this monument down stone by stone and throw your stinking carcass to the hyenas."

Mayet followed the chamberlain to the wide, curving marble staircase that led to the king's audience hall. Lady Hesper followed a few paces behind, and when Mayet glanced back at her friend, the noblewoman winked at her.

Ptolemy's invitation to join him at the palace for the ceremony welcoming the foreign dignitaries had shocked her. He'd been so angry when he'd left her this morning, she hadn't expected to hear from him for days. Instead, his runner had come bearing a golden chiton cut in the Ionian style and shot with silver threads. Woven sandals of gold and emerald earrings accompanied the gift, along with a glittering crystal and silver diadem.

She'd left off the circlet for a modest hairstyle, and she'd not worn the king's peace offerings. Instead, she'd chosen a simple chiton of the finest ivory linen, white leather sandals, and exquisite gold filigree earrings.

Hesper had smiled at her choice. "The king may not be pleased," she warned.

"My lord is both wise and generous," Mayet had replied. "But I'll not be displayed like an expensive harlot."

Now, facing the royal gathering, she almost wished she had been more obedient. A hundred pairs of eyes turned toward her as she descended the steps.

"The Lady Mayet of Thebes," the Egyptian high chamberlain lisped.

Ptolemy rose and came to take her hand. "Welcome to

our court, lady," he said. His gaze traveled from her eyes down over her breasts and thighs to her toes and back again. Then he chuckled. "Very nice," he said so low that only she could hear. "Again I am bested by a woman's intuition."

Murmurs washed against her like waves on a beach.

"That's her."

"She's a beauty."

"She won't last a month. Berenice will . . ."

"Haven't you heard? She's the king's new favorite."

"A widow, you say, Hippogriff? I'd have . . ."

Mayet held her head high and tried not to make eye contact with anyone. Ptolemy led her up onto the dais and indicated a stool beside him. She sat, glad that her legs were no longer forced to hold her upright. The vast columned chamber swam before her as she struggled to maintain her composure. Greeks, Egyptians, Phoenicians, Persians, Nubians—men and women of every hue and origin crowded the room. Priests and serving men, merchants, noblemen and women, guards, soldiers, eunuchs, and entertainers edged and jockeyed for position. Of the two queens, Berenice and Artakama, there was no sign.

Ptolemy laid a hand on her shoulder. "This won't take long," he said. "Afterwards, we'll retire with a hundred or so of our most important guests and eat. I don't know about you, but I'm starved." He nodded to a eunuch, who whispered to another official. He motioned to a third. A dour man in Egyptian clothing struck a brass gong. The room grew silent.

The same stout and self-important chamberlain who had announced her stepped forward. "Great lord of the two lands, king of Egypt, lord of . . ."

Mayet searched for Hesper in the crowd and saw her standing beside a distinguished older Greek.

"Pay attention," Ptolemy whispered. "He's about to introduce the foreign ambassadors. Zeus only knows what

they'll bring as tribute. The last brought a spotted bear
from China."

Ptolemy's fingers tightened on her shoulder as the chamberlain bellowed, "Prince Kayan of Bactria and Sogdiana."

Chapter 8

Mayet winced as Ptolemy's grip bruised her flesh. Perplexed, she glanced at the king and then back down at the man who had obviously caused Ptolemy's alarm—the barbarian who had dared to come so close to the royal dais without prostrating himself.

For a heartbeat, her gaze locked with Prince Kayan's. Mayet's throat constricted. She felt as though she'd been knocked off the edge of a precipice into empty space.

Fierce almond eyes glared at her from a rugged face. Two thin braids interwoven with strands of red silk hung on either side of his proud face. Behind the braids, barely contained, a thick mane of gleaming dark hair framed a high forehead, a strong jaw, and a square, stubborn chin, to tumble loosely below the line of massive shoulders. Gold disks dangled from shapely ears, and a thick, golden torque clasped his strong neck. His sleeveless doeskin vest, lined with red silk and embroidered with a border of red stags, revealed a broad, hairless chest and heavily muscled arms with biceps encircled by thick armlets of Scythian gold.

His appearance was so foreign, so savage, yet wildly magnificent, that the Greek officers and Egyptian noblemen in their spotless white linen appeared as soft and helpless as doves flushed by a hunting falcon.

Mayet sat immobilized, unable to breathe, unable to tear her eyes away from him. A great rushing storm filled her head, stunning her as thoughts, images, and memories whirled too fast to grasp or comprehend.

Trapped like an insect in a drop of amber, she could only stare.

The barbarian's hips were narrow, his muscled legs encased in skin-tight trousers cut in the Persian fashion. The doeskin garment fit without a wrinkle and revealed far more of his considerable male attributes than it concealed, before disappearing into thigh-high, soft leather boots with scarlet tassels.

He must be an impostor, she thought. This is no prince, but a warrior, a man whose powerful hands appear more accustomed to welding a sword than a royal seal. She leaned forward, fingers clenched, her chest tight.

"I bring greetings, King Ptolemy," Prince Kayan said in the courtly Persian tongue. "From Prince Oxyartes." He placed a knotted fist over his heart and inclined his head slightly in a stiff salute.

"It's been a long time, General," Ptolemy replied rigidly. "Are we to understand that you are now heir to Oxyartes?"

"I have that honor." Something that might have passed for a smile if not for the murderous gleam in his eye tugged at the corner of the prince's mouth. "It seems both our fortunes have improved since last we met."

The obsidian eyes flicked back to Mayet with so much animosity that she felt a rush of blood to her throat and cheeks. He terrified her, but her fear arose from more than his obvious disapproval. The kingdom of Bactria was far away. They could never have met, so why did he insult her? Why was she so unnerved by a savage ambassador? And how did he dare to come before Ptolemy, king of kings, without offering the proper respect?

She blinked. Her whirling thoughts slowed. She seized on one and then another. Did Prince Kayan hold her in contempt because she was the king's concubine? Could all females be treated so poorly in his backward country? Or . . . she suddenly noticed the handsome boy at his shoulder. Could he be a lover of boys, one who despised all women?

She attempted to pry her tongue from the roof of her mouth and regain her shattered composure. How dare this stranger judge her? She drew herself up to her full height and regarded him with disdain. She wasn't ashamed of who she was, and she'd not cower before some mountain savage—even if he did call himself royalty. Prince of goats and moth-eaten camels, more likely.

"Welcome to Alexandria and to Egypt," Ptolemy said. His tone was stronger than before, more regal, yet still hollow, as though the Bactrian had struck him a mortal blow. "It is our wish to extend the hand of friendship to former allies."

"My prince bids me offer you a treaty of peace," Kayan answered.

Where was the respect due a monarch? The barbarian's courteous speech was a mockery. The man might have been addressing a gatherer of dung from the market square.

The air between the two men seemed charged with energy. Mayet shivered. It appeared to her as if Ptolemy and this stranger might suddenly leap barehanded at each other's throats at the slightest provocation.

To her right, a bejeweled and ringed Egyptian noblewoman boldly ogled the Bactrian. She wore a gown of draped linen so sheer that the rouge on her nipples and the shadow of her shaved pubic hair showed plainly. Fluttering her lashes, she nudged her companion and whispered. The other woman covered her mouth and twittered. Prince Kayan flashed them a look of admiration.

No, Mayet decided. He didn't hate all females. From what Hesper had told her, a barbarian stud would have no problem acquiring the favors of Alexandria's ladies, married or single. Morals were no better here at Ptolemy's court than in Athens.

For the first time, Mayet noticed the three men in Kayan's party. The prince's followers were as fierce and bronzed as he, all dark-haired and grim-faced, except for the boy. The sturdy child, whom she guessed to be about ten, had a Greek look about him.

Gray-eyed and fair-haired, the boy was clad too richly for a squire, with golden armbands, fine garments, and high embroidered boots much like those of his prince. His blond curls had been shaped into a loose cap that bounced when he moved, making him almost too comely for a lad. Yet no one would take him for a girl. There was a steely confidence about him, so much so that she wasn't surprised when the prince introduced him as his son Val.

"Prince Val," Ptolemy said. "It is a pleasure to have you with us as well." He rose abruptly, ending the audience. "Unfortunately, our time is exhausted. Perhaps you will do us the honor of dining with me some evening, Prince Kayan."

A court official whispered to his superior, who murmured to the vizier, who looked at the king, held up his index finger and mouthed the word *gifts*.

"Yes, yes," Ptolemy said with great indifference. "I believe you have brought tribute."

"Not tribute but a token of Prince Oxyartes's friendship," Prince Kayan said. "Horses. Stallions such as you have never seen. And these—" He lifted a hand and another foreign warrior trotted into the room from a side entrance, holding the chains of a brace of snow leopards. "They will give you good sport, King Ptolemy. They are trained to hunt lion, deer, and antelope."

"But not men?" the king asked.

"They are intact males," Kayan replied. "You may get them to track women, but they have no interest in their own sex."

There was gaping silence, and then Lord Yakdast guffawed loudly. Other men began to laugh, and then the women joined in. The two highborn ladies who had flaunted themselves laughed shrilly, drawing further attention to themselves.

Mayet did not laugh. She regarded the Bactrian prince as she might a stray dog that had found his way into her chamber and soiled the floor.

Ptolemy caught her arm as he stepped down from his throne. He walked so fast that she had to hurry to keep from being dragged. He led her through a private corridor into a small room not far from the great reception hall and shoved her through the doorway. "There was no need to make a spectacle of yourself," he said.

"Me? What did I do?"

"Do you fancy him? I doubt he's had a bath since he left his mountains. Maybe I've been too gentle with you, Mayet. Do you prefer a rougher touch?" He seized her by the shoulders and ground his mouth against hers.

She gasped as he groped her breast.

"Your Majesty—" A rotund court official appeared in the entranceway.

"Get out!" Ptolemy roared. He tore the clasp from one shoulder of Mayet's tunic and pushed the material down to bare one breast. "If you want—"

She jerked back and slapped him as hard as she could.

For an instant, he didn't react. He stood there, all blood drained from his face as the imprint of her palm and fingers appeared on his skin. "How dare you?"

He grabbed for her, but she darted around a table, snatching a twelve-inch wooden statue of Horus from its ebony pedestal. "How dare I?" she cried. "How dare *you*? Come near me and—"

"And what? What will you do?" His voice dropped to a low tone of quiet fury. "You forget your place. I own you."

The profanity that she flung back was so foul and so original that it shocked herself as much as Ptolemy. He lunged across the table at her, but she hurled the little Horus, striking the king full in the chest. He cursed and charged her, but she tipped over the table and dashed through a narrow door at the rear of the room. Breathless, she slammed the carved wooden door and dropped the bronze bar into place.

"Mayet!" Ptolemy pounded on the door with both fists, but she didn't hesitate. Holding her torn chiton in place, she sped through a vestibule, ducked into a passageway that smelled of incense, turned right at the first opportunity, and then right again. She cut through a small chapel, pausing long enough to pin her torn chiton with a hair ornament, and strolled calmly down the steps into the large audience hall from a side entrance.

A palace guard spied her and hurried toward her.

Mayet caught her breath and smiled. "His Majesty is occupied," she said. "Find transportation for me to the Palace of the Blue Lotus."

"Yes, lady," the soldier replied. He called to another guard, and the two found four men not presently on duty in the king's palace, and escorted her to a courtyard where bearers waited with enclosed carrying chairs. The first guard assisted her into the cushioned conveyance. When the men lifted the chair, Mayet drew the heavy curtains to shield herself from passersby.

As guards and litter bearers filed through the crowded streets of Alexandria, Mayet's fear grew. Why had she had such a reaction to seeing the barbarian prince, Kayan? And why had Ptolemy, who'd never been cruel, treated her like a common harlot? Now that she had escaped his attentions, what would the king do to her? Why was he so angry with her? Or had it been the arrogance of the Bactrian that had set the king into a rage?

If she weren't so furious, she would weep. She'd been so excited to receive Ptolemy's invitation to the palace reception. She'd looked forward to meeting members of the court and talking with his friends and advisors.

Prince Kayan had ruined everything.

But perhaps he was not the one at fault. Had she been foolish to believe that she would be welcomed at Ptolemy's court? What was she but a trollop? She wasn't a wife. She was a plaything that the king could enjoy and toss away when she no longer amused him.

But she had enjoyed his attentions as well. She'd welcomed his company and their lazy afternoons and long, hot nights together. He had treated her as though she were a princess, gifting her with luxuries and satisfying her sexually and intellectually. What woman without friends or family wouldn't do the best she could for herself? Why hadn't she accepted Ptolemy's offer of marriage?

. . . Because she hadn't trusted him.

Ridiculous. It was herself she hadn't trusted. So long as she was of unsound mind, what right did she have to become a wife? Whatever else she was, she was honest. She hadn't lied to Ptolemy, hadn't sworn eternal love or used her wiles to gain a crown.

He'd offered it freely. What king who wasn't being honest with her would do that?

Suddenly the thought of returning to the Palace of the Blue Lotus was intolerable. She parted the curtains and peered out, expecting to see the broad avenue she and Hesper had been carried along on the way to the reception. But instead of elegant homes and temples, she saw beer houses and small shops. She was unfamiliar with the city, but caught the distinct cry of seagulls above the clamor of the men and women along the street.

"Stop," she called.

The bearers slowed, and one stumbled, but a harsh voice said something and they picked up the pace again.

"I commanded you to stop," she said, jerking back the curtain and leaning out. The men turned into an alley and trotted faster. The chair swayed. Here, the houses pressed together so closely that only a thin line of sunlight filtered through to the lane ahead. The air was thick with the smell of garlic and rotting animal hides.

Apprehension prickled the hairs on the nape of her neck. She tensed her muscles, wondering what to do, when suddenly the chair stopped moving. A male voice swore. She looked out again but could only see the soldiers' backs.

". . . blocked," one said.

A soldier behind the chair moved to the front. "I know another way, past the sail maker."

". . . get it over with."

The litter tipped. More cursing. The grumbling bearers began carrying the chair back the way they had come through the alley.

The bearer on the left rear pole screamed. The chair tilted and dropped onto the street. The jolt knocked Mayet sideways, and she gasped as a bronze arrowhead pierced the curtain only inches from her face.

Kayan stalked from the audience hall with his men and Val close behind. He didn't trust himself to speak, and even the boy had sense enough not to ask questions.

No weapons were permitted inside the palace other than those carried by the king's personal guard. That order had saved Ptolemy's ass, and probably his own, the two boys', and his followers'. When he'd seen Roxanne sitting there beside the king, he'd wanted Ptolemy's blood.

That she could look at him and say nothing seared his soul. He'd crossed desert and mountains, fought storms and bandits, and lost the lives of nine faithful warriors to reach her. And the woman he'd loved all his life—the mother of his son—had stared at him as though he were a stranger.

Had she ever given a thought in all these years to the son she'd given away at birth? To the father and country she'd left behind? Had she been dazzled by the riches of Egypt and the naked power of the man who claimed the throne of the pharaohs? Had she traded one conqueror for another?

"Prince Kayan. Sir. If you please, sir." A servant ran after them, calling out in Greek. "Sir, I have a message. An invitation from my mistress, the Lady Nofritari. She begs you to join her at her home this evening. A private reception. A few friends." He thrust a tablet into one of Kayan's men's hands. "The hour, and the street where my mistress's home is located."

"I have not made the lady's acquaintance," Kayan said brusquely.

"She thought you might say that, sir," the servant said. "She wished me to remind you that you favored her and her friend with a smile." He bowed. "She says to tell you that the food will be the finest to be had in the city, and that her entertainment shall be second to none."

"All right, you've told me."

"Please, sir. My mistress bids me to tell her if she may expect you. And these gentlemen as well."

The prince's eyes narrowed. "Give your lady our thanks," he said. "Tell her we are honored to accept her gracious invitation."

The man bowed again and hurried back inside the palace. Kayan, Val, and the other three crossed the large courtyard to the section of the palace where important visitors were housed.

Kayan stormed into the guest rooms he and his men had been assigned to. Snatching up his weapons, he strapped on his sword and knife without speaking to Tiz and Bahman, who'd remained to guard Yuri while Kayan had his audience with Ptolemy.

Only his sons and this small band of trusted warriors had accompanied him to Alexandria. The remainder of the force, another two score of crack cavalrymen he'd brought with him from Bactria, hid on the far side of the Nile.

"What's wrong with him?" Tiz asked Jandel. He and Bahman, a young, good-natured Bactrian, had been teaching Yuri the finer points of dice.

Jandel shook his head and gestured for silence. "Later."

"Did you see the king?" Yuri asked Val. "I won four silver pieces from Bahman." He held up the coins, stamped with horse's heads. "Tiz promised to take me to the market tomorrow morning so that I can spend them."

Val eyed the silver pieces longingly. "We saw him. I didn't like him. He was rude."

Kayan motioned Tiz aside. "You and the boys aren't staying here. Don't let the others eat or drink anything from the palace kitchens. I don't trust Ptolemy."

Tiz nodded.

"Zar speaks Egyptian," Kayan continued. "I'm sending him to rent us a house near the waterfront. There are many foreigners there. If we dress as Greeks, we'll be less conspicuous."

Tiz looked down at his worn leather trousers and boots. "You want me to trade a man's clothes for a dress?"

"You're lucky I didn't ask you to shave your head and wear Egyptian garb," Kayan said. "You, Val, and Yuri leave right now. Take the boys to the temple of Artemis. Zar can come for you as soon as he finds a house. Ram and Izad can leave separately, buy what we need in the market, and wait for you outside the temple."

"Homji and Jandel?" Tiz glanced at the two Bactrian noblemen.

"They're staying here with me. We have an invitation for this evening. From an Egyptian lady. She may have information about the princess's whereabouts. We'll join you in a day or two, as soon as I find out where Roxanne is."

"You're certain she's alive?" Tiz asked. "We've not come all this way for nothing?"

"Oh, she's alive," Kayan said. "Alive and well. I've seen her."

"She knows you're here?"

Kayan nodded.

"You're certain she's willing to come with us?"

"She'll come," Kayan said. "One way or another."

Chapter 9

Mayet rolled out of the litter, hit the ground, and crawled back through the tangle of chair poles, soldiers' legs, and fallen bodies. Dust filled the air as sandaled feet churned the earth. The men who'd brought her away from the palace were injured, dead, or dying. Arrows hissed overhead, snapped against dried mud walls, or buried themselves in living flesh. Shouts of triumph echoed from the alley's entranceway; groans and sobbing rose from the chaos surrounding the abandoned chair.

A bloody fist closed on Mayet's ankle. She kicked it away and continued moving on hands and knees, keeping her head down. Two of the surviving soldiers fled toward the obstructed end of the alley. One guard raced ahead of his comrade. The second hobbled, clutching a wound in his side. The first gained the barrier, an overturned two-wheeled cart. He clawed up, getting one hand over the top rim of the wheel before a six-foot spear—launched from the far side—struck him through the chest. Screaming, he tumbled backward. The injured man, only a few paces behind, sank to the ground and slumped forward, his face a mask of utter terror.

More shouting came from beyond the cart, followed by three feathered shafts. One bronze-tipped arrow plunged into the packed dirt between Mayet's index finger and thumb. She shuddered, too frightened to cry out. Behind her from the other side of the carrying chair came male voices, louder and closer than before.

She had to find a way out of the alley in the next few breaths or she wouldn't live to draw more. When the first bolt had struck the bearers, she'd thought that a rescue party had arrived to save her from her abductors. It hadn't taken long for her to realize just how foolhardy that assumption was. Whoever had attacked these men wanted them all dead, herself included.

Frantic, she looked around and saw a narrow doorway that she hadn't noticed before. She leaped to her feet and pushed hard on the door. The wood creaked and gave slightly, and then stopped. Mayet threw her shoulder against it, using all her weight, and the inner bar cracked. She flung herself into the shadowy interior of the room, kicked the door shut, and ran through an opening into a chamber stacked to the ceiling with coils of rope, lengths of folded sailcloth, and tall amphorae of oil.

She dashed down one aisle, nearly tripped on a sleeping cat, and ducked through a curtain into living quarters at the back of a merchant's stall. The smoky area was small, holding little more than a sleeping pallet, a stool, and a carved wooden chest. A gutted and featherless duck hung from the ceiling beams along with dusty strings of onions and garlic. In the center of the clay floor a wizened old crone squatted, turning fish and leeks over a charcoal brazier.

Before the startled ancient could cry out, Mayet tore the silver clasp off her tunic and held it out to her. "Help me," she pleaded. "They'll kill me."

The woman took the clasp and pointed to the bed heaped with baskets. Mayet hesitated, and then noticed a crude ladder beside the cot. She ran to it and glanced back at her savior. The woman nodded, and Mayet climbed the deep footholds carved into the single cedar beam to a storage ledge about eight feet above the floor. She expected to find an opening to a second story, but there was none. Desperate, Mayet flattened herself against the wall and stood motionless as Egyptian soldiers exploded into the space below.

The old woman cursed and waved her arms, gesturing to the front of the shop. The intruders shouted questions, overturned baskets, kicked over a tall amphora of wheat, and thrust swords through the bed. Mayet was afraid to breathe. If they looked up, she was lost.

They didn't. One man, obviously in command, gave an order, and they all hurried out the front way to the street. The last straggler snagged the duck as he went.

"Thief!" the old woman shrieked. "Spawn of Seth!"

Mayet waited a long time before she ventured down from her hiding place. Her ally sat on the bed, eating the fish and spitting the bones into a basket. "Amon curse them," she muttered, eyeing Mayet through filmy eyes. "Who are you that the queen herself would send her guard to murder you?"

"Berenice hates me." Mayet glanced nervously over her shoulder, half expecting the soldiers to come back.

"Berenice?" The old woman cackled. "The foreign queen despises you too? You must be important to have so many enemies."

Mayet knotted the torn shoulder of her tunic. "Those weren't Berenice's guard?"

Her hostess sucked a carp bone clean and discarded it, then began to chew a leek. "I'm half blind," she said after a few moments of silence. "You're young. Are you too stupid to recognize the royal axe on their tunics? They are Queen Artakama's soldiers."

"Artakama?"

"Don't think you can take back your silver now that they're gone. Try, and I'll scream loud enough to bring half of Alexandria down on your pretty head."

"No, no, I wouldn't," Mayet said. "I'm new to this city myself." She plucked an earring from her ear. "These are worth far more than the brooch. You may have the pair if you find someone to show me the way to the Palace of the Blue Lotus."

"Let me see the earrings."

Mayet shook her head. "One now, one when I reach the palace safely."

Laughter. "So untrusting." Her head bobbed up and down vigorously in assent. "They say in the marketplace that the king keeps a foreign concubine there. The most beautiful woman in the world, they say. Look at you. Your hair and face are dirty. Your tunic is ripped and stained with blood. Why would she want such as you in her palace?" She howled with glee at her own joke.

"A good question," Mayet said. "But one I don't have to answer. Do you want the earrings? Or—"

"Yes, yes. My grandson Userhat will take you. He knows the city like a dog knows his own ass. Userhat will guide you, and whatever befalls you there will be on your own head."

Userhat motioned for silence and pressed back into the shadows of the wall of a great house. A group of men passed, and Mayet thought she recognized one as a man who had accompanied Prince Kayan to the king's audience hall. The barbarians had obviously been drinking. One sang loudly, a bawdy tune about the fat wife of a tavern keeper, a heifer, and a thick-headed infantryman.

The revelers halted at the nobleman's gate and pounded

for admittance. The gatekeeper welcomed them in, closed and locked the door. The street fell silent.

Userhat tugged at Mayet's elbow. Keeping well away from the torchlit entrance, they hurried past the well-guarded private homes of the wealthy. Mayet could smell the lake and knew they must be nearing the area of the Palace of the Blue Lotus.

A quarter hour later, the boy stopped and pointed to a columned entrance on the far side of the street. Mayet looked in that direction, and when she glanced back, her guide had vanished.

Two guards stood at attention in front of the high-walled enclosure. She didn't recognize the structure, but she assumed that a palace would have many gates. Waiting until morning wasn't an option. Hesper had told her that the city was plagued at night with packs of feral dogs, some inter-bred with wild dogs or jackals. Not long ago, she'd brought word of a sailor who'd been torn to pieces sleeping off a drunk. Human predators also prowled the streets of Alexandria, cutthroats and criminals who used darkness to hide their crimes.

"May the Creator protect me," she whispered without thinking. But what god? Which god did she pray to? Would he listen if she didn't even remember His name? Summoning all her courage, she crossed the avenue and approached the guards.

"I am the Lady Mayet," she said with as much dignity as she could muster. "Open the gate in the name of the king."

Kayan finished the goblet of unwatered wine and held out his cup for another. The hall was over-warm and smelled of sex and sweat and perfume. Three Egyptian slave girls, bodies oiled and wearing little more than ribbons around their hips, were performing a physically challenging dance that involved a large snake, a pot of honey, and several os-trich feathers.

The skirl of pipes and the heated throb of drums grew louder and faster. Now Lady Nofritari joined the dancers, her lithe body swaying and twisting to the primeval strain. Once, twice, she undulated around the open area before dropping to her knees, throwing back her head, and pleasuring herself in full view of her guests.

Jandel groaned.

Kayan glanced at the couch where Jandel lay. A woman with enormous breasts leaned over his face, while two more gave attention to other parts of his body. Jandel was renowned for his skill at archery, wrestling, and mastery of the short sword, yet he seemed to be putting up little struggle.

Homji was equally engaged, although he no longer occupied his couch but rather lay half under it with his boots in a bowl of sliced melon that a naked dwarf had been feeding him. Pairs of Indian acrobats, male and female, had joined the dancers and immediately engaged in diverse sexual acts, paying no heed to gender or common sense.

Kayan yawned. There had been a time when such a gathering would have fired his blood, but he feared that at thirty-three he was growing too old and sensible to fully enjoy such a lascivious evening.

Lady Nofritari, now attempting to devour what looked like a rhinoceros horn, was as good as her word. She and her friends, Hippogriff and another Egyptian noblewoman whose name he couldn't recall, did indeed provide unique entertainment.

Kayan wasn't drunk, at least not drunk enough. He'd wanted to become very drunk, drunk enough to forget the pain that cut through him and filled his soul with a black emptiness. But Greek wine served at a lady's table, even the finest that Alexandria had to offer, had little effect on a man who'd imbibed the potent spirits of the steppe tribes.

Now that his rage had cooled and he'd sampled the delights of Nofritari and Hippogriff in and out of the bathing pool, reason was beginning to creep back into his stubborn mind.

Something wasn't right.

Roxanne had not given the slightest indication that she recognized him. He had looked straight at her, made eye contact, and even glared at her. She might have been a total stranger for all the response she'd given him. He knew she was a skilled actress; on more than one occasion, he'd seen her give performances that would rival any in an Athenian amphitheatre. But she wasn't skillful enough to pretend she didn't know the man she'd been promised to since she was a child.

Had Ptolemy drugged her? Or was she under some spell? Was she a victim of foul Egyptian magic?

Whatever was wrong, he meant to find out. To do that, he'd have to learn where Ptolemy kept her. And Kayan was certain he knew who had that knowledge.

With a shout, he leaped onto the dance floor, seized Lady Nofritari, and threw her over his shoulder. She squealed and kicked, feigning protest, an act that would have been more convincing if she hadn't been laughing so hard and trying to caress his ass.

Mayet barely had time to bathe and change into a clean chiton before a tearful Hesper rushed in and embraced her. "We thought you were lost," the noblewoman said. "Word is all over the city that you and the king argued and that your broken chair was found in an alley beside the bodies of five of the king's guard."

"And the bearers," Mayet said. "I know at least two of them were dead. But . . . are you certain it was five guardsmen? There were six soldiers and the four men to carry the chair, ten in all."

"I'm sure they said five. No one mentioned the bearers."

Hesper squeezed Mayet's hands. "One soldier must have escaped."

"Yes, that must be what happened. Unless he was in league with those who attacked us." She was sure there was no other way out of the alley than the way she'd found. And she doubted that a wounded man would be allowed to live to tell what he'd seen. Mayet dropped her voice to a whisper. "I wonder now if it is the king who wanted me dead."

Hesper shook her head. "He was frantic. Troops are searching the city for you. How did you get away? And how did you find your way back here?"

"Luck and a few gold trinkets."

"It must be the Greek queen who is to blame." Again Hesper dismissed the maids and dressed Mayet's hair. "My husband is here, in the outer courtyard. He has sent word to the king that you're safe."

"I don't believe the murderers were sent by Queen Berenice. I saw an axe on their tunics. Isn't that the Egyptian queen's insignia?"

"Yes, but it wouldn't be beyond Queen Berenice to use men disguised as Queen Artakama's guard to commit a crime."

"I asked one of the king's guard to escort me home, but I think he betrayed me as well. We were in a poor section of the city when the attack occurred. I don't know the way from Ptolemy's palace, but I know how long it took us to get there. I believe they meant to kidnap me, but"—Mayet shrugged—"they didn't live long enough for me to discover their intentions."

Hesper secured Mayet's crown of braids with silver pins and let a cascade of curls fall down her back. "Put on your finest jewelry and rouge your lips and cheeks. You must mend your falling-out with King Ptolemy, and quickly. He is all you have."

Mayet looked at her. Hesper's advice was reasonable, but Mayet could not help feeling that the young woman wasn't telling her all she knew. "You saw Prince Kayan and the barbarians who accompanied him. What did you think of them?"

Hesper flushed. "I . . . I . . ." she stammered. "As you say, my lady, they were savages. Amusing, but—"

"Have you seen the prince before?"

"No, lady. I haven't. How could I?" She stood up. "I must go now. My husband will remain with his men until the king arrives." She rushed forward and hugged Mayet tightly. "I may not be able to come again before the birth of my child."

Mayet nodded. "I understand. You have your safety and that of your baby to worry about. I'll be all right."

"Mend your quarrel with the king," Hesper said. "Only he is strong enough to protect you." She glanced nervously over her shoulder. "Alexandria is a nest of vipers. Only the strong survive here, lady."

"Thank you. I'll remember that."

An hour later, accompanied by archers, charioteers, and forty of his crack guards, a repentant and joyous Ptolemy appeared. "I was half out of my mind," he declared, pulling her into his arms.

She stood stiffly, not resisting, but not returning his affection.

"Mayet? Do you blame me for—"

"How do I know?" She pushed him away from her. "This is the second time someone has tried to kill me."

"And you think it was me?" He swore. "Damn you, woman, you're dearer to me than . . ." He broke off. "I'm sorry—I overreacted. I never should have treated you the way I did."

"No, you shouldn't have. I'm not ashamed of what I've done, but I'm not a whore."

He frowned. "I thought you made a fool of me, staring at . . . Never mind, what's important is that you're safe."

"Am I?" He reached for her hand and she moved back out of his reach. "Berenice or Artakama, maybe both of them, want me dead."

His frown became a scowl. "Berenice, certainly. I wouldn't put anything—"

"The men who attacked us wore the sign of Artakama's axe."

Ptolemy swore. "I wouldn't have thought . . ." He shook his head. "I'll find out who's responsible. Whoever it is, she'll pay for this. I promise you that."

"I can't stay here. I want to return to my own home."

"Impossible. We will be married, and the sooner the better."

"I'm not going to marry you, Ptolemy. It wouldn't be fair to either of us."

His features hardened. "Why not?"

"I don't love you."

He shook his head in disbelief. "Love? When does love have anything to do with marriage? Are you a fool that you must believe in poets' babbling or songs of eternal devotion?" He advanced until he could mold his palms to her face. "You will be my queen, Mayet. I will crown you with my own hands, and I'll breed a line of sons on you."

"Why? Why me? You have a queen! Two of them. What are you hiding from me, Ptolemy? And why did that Bactrian prince—"

"Enough. I can see you are distraught tonight. I'll come again tomorrow, when you're in a more reasonable mood."

"And if I feel the same way by daylight?"

"Then you will learn who is king here." He pressed a cool kiss on her forehead. "Good night, Mayet. Sleep well, and consider what you gain by continuing to oppose my will."

She bit back the curse that rose on her tongue and turned her back to him.

"Until tomorrow, sweet wife."

"Why? Why can't I remember?" Mayet whispered into the night. No answer came but the chirping of insects and the rustle of a desert breeze through the palms.

Unable to bear the curious eyes of the servants, she had banished them all from her presence and paced the garden paths alone. There was a logic to all this, a game, but no one had told her the rules. The feelings she'd had for Ptolemy seemed hollow, her future dark and uncertain.

Who was the mysterious Mayet? How had she captivated a king? And why was she unable to settle for a life that most women would kill to have? She was certain that the truth lay in the twisted corridors of her dreams, but her dreams were as muddy and trackless as the Nile marshes.

In desperation, she dropped to her knees in prayer. "Help me," she begged. "Help me find the way." She waited for a long time, hoping to receive some sign, but there remained nothing but emptiness. Weary, dry-eyed, she rose and made her way to bed.

Sleep wouldn't come. She tossed and turned, dozing and then snapping awake, certain that she'd heard an approaching footstep or felt the presence of someone in the dimly lit room. But whenever she opened her eyes and looked around, whenever she strained to listen, there was no one there.

At last she fell into a fitful state, half dozing, half awake. In this altered state of consciousness, she was certain she saw a man standing beside her . . . a man holding an infant in his arms. She reached for the baby. "Give him to me," she murmured. "Give me—"

Her fingers touched not the tender flesh of a baby, but

the hard muscle of a man's arm. Mayet opened her eyes, saw the figure looming over her, and drew in a breath to scream.

A callused hand clamped over her mouth.

"Shhh," the deep male voice whispered in her ear. "What kind of greeting is that after eight years?"

Chapter 10

Roxanne's fist connected with his jaw. So fierce was her resistance that she nearly caused his hand to slip off her mouth. He used his weight to pin her legs and body against the bed, but she continued struggling, kicking and bucking against the bed. He caught one wrist, but her left hand was free. The palm of her hand smacked into his right cheekbone and her nails scratched his face.

"Beloved," he said in their native tongue. "It's Kayan. I'm not going to hurt you." Thrashing wildly, she attempted to bite his finger. "Stop it, I say! Must I bind you like a goose for market?"

She tensed, breathing heavily. He could feel her muscles coiled to react. If he relaxed his hold for even a fraction of a second, she'd start the battle all over again.

"I'd cut off my right arm before I'd harm you," he whispered. "You must believe me."

He could feel her heart pounding through her thin sleeping garment. Her breath was warm on his face.

It wasn't supposed to be like this. He'd expected her to welcome him with open arms and tears of joy.

"Nod if you understand. It's Kayan. I've come to take you home."

She nodded.

He started to remove his hand. She uttered what would have been a shriek loud enough to raise the dead pharaohs from their tombs, but he clamped his palm over her mouth again. "Do you want to get me killed?"

She made a sound that he took to mean agreement.

Bewildered, he asked, "Do you know who I am?"

She nodded.

"Either you've lost your mind or I have. I didn't come all this way to have you turn against me." His throat constricted, and he leaned close to murmur in her ear. "Hear me out, Roxanne, for the sake of your son, if not for me."

She groaned and mumbled, "I can't breathe."

His own breathing was nothing to brag about. He could feel himself growing hard. The sensation of her nearly naked body, warm and moving beneath his, was torture, causing him greater discomfort than his lacerated cheek or swelling eye.

"Let me go," she mumbled against his hand.

He knew she felt his increasing arousal and her anger was fast becoming fear. "I didn't come here to rape you," he said. "If I take my hand away, will you give me your word that you won't scream?"

She nodded.

Cautiously he took his hand away from her mouth. "Say something."

She called him a name so foul that he would have laughed if the situation hadn't been so lacking in humor.

"That, at least, is the Roxanne I knew."

"I am Mayet," she said. "I am the king's—"

"No! You're not. You are Roxanne, Crown Princess of Bactria and Sogdiana."

"Liar. Get off of me."

He let go of her wrist and shifted his weight. "I've known you all your life. I'm your—"

"You are Prince Kayan. The Bactrian barbarian." She sat up, rubbing her wrist and scooting to the far corner of the bed.

He scoffed. "No more barbarian than you. And Sogdian, not Bactrian. You carry the blood of both royal houses. Your grandmother, the warrior queen, was Bactrian."

She folded her arms over her chest. "You were right when you said you'd lost your mind. You have the wrong woman. I'm Egyptian. By coming here you've signed your own death sentence." Her eyes narrowed. "How did you get past the guards?"

He shrugged. "It wasn't easy. But I had to get to you. You've been bewitched."

"King Ptolemy will have you garroted."

"He'll have to catch me first." He rubbed his smarting cheek and grinned at her. "And you'll have to scream and summon the guard."

"You believe I won't?"

"You stopped fighting me when I mentioned your son. If they come and kill me, you won't learn—"

"My son is dead."

"He's very much alive. Who told you he was dead? Ptolemy?"

"He's been my friend and protector."

She was trembling now, and he wanted to pull her into his arms. "He was your friend a long time ago. Was it Ptolemy who told you that your name is Mayet—that you're Egyptian?"

She nodded.

"Did he tell you that you are a widow, and that your husband was his friend?"

"Yes." She buried her face in her hands. "Yes, yes. Stop. I don't know what to think. I don't know whom to trust."

"You still think you don't know me? We were sworn to

each other when you were still a child. You were to be my wife."

"Why should I believe you and not him?" she demanded. "I don't know you."

"If I'm wrong, and you are this Mayet, who is your father? Can you remember his face?"

"No. I can't." Tears came now, spilling down her cheeks.

He pressed her. "Your first pony? What color was she? What was her name? Who taught you to ride?"

"Stop. Please stop," she begged him.

"I taught you, Roxanne. As I taught your son."

"No." She scrambled off the bed. "No more. Go away."

"You know it's true. Call the guards. Call them and have me put to death."

"Leave, please," she begged.

"I'll go, but I'll be back. I won't leave Alexandria without you." He met her gaze. "I love you, Roxanne. I've always loved you."

"Go!"

He choked back the sorrow that knotted his stomach and left by the garden passage. It would be simple enough to climb the wall and untie the kitchen slave he'd bribed to show him where Roxanne slept. Whether the cook or Roxanne would cry the alarm and bring Ptolemy's soldiers down on him before he could escape, he didn't know. Any sensible man would cut the cook's throat to be certain of his silence, but Kayan knew he wouldn't. He could kill when he had to, but he was no mindless murderer. And there was no point in killing the slave when Roxanne might run to Ptolemy with the news that he'd broken into her palace.

He cursed himself for a fool as he went up the thick flowering vine, hand over hand. He should have waited, taken her unawares, and carried her off. She hadn't believed him. Whatever hold Ptolemy had on her was strong. The Egyptians were known for the spells of their priests and magi. It was said that they could turn water to blood and raise flying serpents from the ashes of a fire.

On the top of the mud-brick wall, Kayan waited, listening, waiting to hear Roxanne scream. But he heard nothing but the wind over the lake and the cry of a night bird. The clouds which had provided cover only a short time before had drifted away, and the moon shone bright and cold. He tensed to jump, then remained where he was. A man's laughter came from the compound. Kayan slid a knife from his boot.

Footsteps. Not one guard, but two, approached the garden wall. ". . . I swear it's true, every word. Amoy can tell you. He was there. She had breasts like . . ."

Kayan heard two streams of urine hitting the base of the wall. Then the men moved off in different directions. He counted to three hundred slowly before leaping to the ground. Once in the outer compound, he used the smaller structures for cover as he returned to the spot where he'd left the bound slave.

The man lay where Kayan had left him. Kayan knelt beside him. "Listen well," he said. "No harm has come to the lady, and you are the richer for aiding me. But if you report this, you will suffer the king's wrath." He pressed another coin into the slave's hand. "I'll let you go, but if you make a sound, I'll return and silence you once and for all. Do you understand?"

The cook mumbled that he did. Kayan cut the bonds with his knife, climbed the outer wall not thirty paces from a sleeping sentry, and vanished into the trees beside the lake.

Mayet wanted to call out for the guards, knew she was making a terrible mistake not to. But doubt held her paralyzed. What if Kayan had spoken the truth? What if Ptolemy had lied to her?

Why would he? Yet why would Prince Kayan take such a chance to come here if he wasn't telling the truth?

Something was terribly wrong. She felt it. But which man was deceiving her? Hesper knew more than she was willing to say, but whether she had recognized Prince Kayan, Mayet couldn't guess.

What had the barbarian said? "Your son is alive."

If he was, then maybe she wasn't crazy. Perhaps her dreams revealed more than a tortured mind. There had been a dark-haired man in her visions, but was he Prince Kayan? A scar . . . she remembered a scar on his lip. But she hadn't seen his face clearly enough tonight to see whether he had a scar.

Kayan had confirmed that she was a widow, and that her late husband had been a friend to Ptolemy. If both told the same story, why did their accounts differ as to her name and origin? And why would Ptolemy tell her that her child was dead if it wasn't so? How could he be so cruel as to deny a mother's heart?

Pulse still racing, she went to the garden entrance. All was quiet and still. Was Kayan still lurking there? She didn't believe so. He would have made his escape while she hesitated. But he'd said he would come back. She shivered in the cool night air. Whoever he was, Prince Kayan seemed to be a man who wouldn't make idle threats.

She looked up at the moon, hanging like a huge white melon in a diamond-studded black sky. Was her son somewhere staring at that same moon? Did he wonder where she was and why she had abandoned him? Tears sprang to her eyes, and she dashed them away. Such thoughts would tear her heart to shreds. Her child was dead, his body committed to the sands, his spirit . . .

Mayet dropped to her knees, hugged herself, and rocked back and forth, sobbing. "Where are you?" she cried. "My arms ache for you."

The only answer to her plea came from her own empty soul. Without memory, she had no faith, no god, no home or country. Without a past, she could sit on the throne of Egypt and hold nothing in her hands but sorrow.

* * *

Ptolemy threw open the double doors to his wife's sleeping chamber. Slave girls screamed and scattered. A tame gazelle dashed back and forth in panic, and a monkey scrambled to the head of a towering black basalt statue of the goddess Sekmet and shrieked at him.

"Artakama!" Ptolemy roared. He wished he had ordered her to come to him. He didn't like her palace, hated these apartments. They were so . . . Egyptian. Brightly colored murals of the afterlife covered the whitewashed walls. Incense burned before countless shrines to her grotesque animal-headed gods. Shaven-headed priests and dozens of cats roamed the shadowy maze of passageways, making him uneasy . . . causing him to feel himself a stranger in his own kingdom.

"Artakama!" he called again.

She rose from her narrow bed, rubbed her eyes, and yawned. "What do you want, mighty bull of the black land?"

He wasn't a man who enjoyed abusing women, and he'd rarely done so. But if she wasn't careful, tonight he might make an exception to his rule.

Behind the drapes where her slaves huddled, someone giggled. Artakama glared, and the laughter ceased. She clapped her hands, and an older woman emerged from the alcove.

Artakama stood, arms extended, while the servant retrieved a wig and pleated kilt. The queen allowed her attendant to settle the wig on her shaven head and fasten the white linen around her hips. She nodded, and the woman hurried back to her companions.

His wife strolled toward him as calmly as if he made a practice of invading her palace unannounced in the middle of the night. The kohl beneath one of Artakama's eyes was smeared. Her beautiful breasts were bare, her protruding nipples tinted with rouge, and she smelled of musk.

Sinking gracefully on her knees in front of him, she asked, "What would you have of me, great king?" Her eyes were heavy-lidded, her mouth red and inviting. She grasped his leg and leaned forward, her fingers inching up beneath his tunic. "Ask anything in my power to give you."

Ptolemy shut his eyes, savoring her sensual touch, the feel of her warm tongue laving the skin of his thigh. Her hand closed on his staff, and he groaned. From the shadows came the rippling chords of a harp and the strong scent of incense.

She stroked the length of him, and cupped his sacs in her capable fingers. His breath came in short gasps. Need burgeoned as her wet tongue caressed him. "Do it," he commanded.

Her lips closed on his swollen flesh. He swallowed, tangling his fingers in her hair. In seconds, he had her down on her back, driving into her wet folds. Artakama laughed and wrapped her long legs around him, thrusting her hips and clasping his rod eagerly as she screamed with pleasure.

It was over in the time it took a man to put on his sandals. His breath came in deep gulps, and sweat ran down his chest. He rolled over, pulling her on top of him. "You are a bitch," he said.

"I know, but you love it."

She arched her back like a cat and beckoned to one of her waiting women. The girl came with a brimming goblet of wine. Artakama took a sip, leaned down, and dribbled the wine between his lips. It was too sweet for his taste. He shook his head and pushed her off. She clapped, and the same girl returned with another wine cup.

Ptolemy tried it and nodded. "Better." He reclined on a couch, and his wife settled at his feet.

"What have you done?" he asked her.

She smiled. "I would have thought that was obvious. Pleasured you."

"And yourself. You're insatiable."

She laughed throatily. "But I never put horns on you. Unlike another I could mention."

"You call what you do with your slaves moral?"

Her eyes widened. "Surely you don't trouble yourself with what I do or don't do with slaves?"

"Snakes."

"Husband, you wrong me." She twittered and began to stroke his leg again. A cat, thin and black, appeared from beneath the couch and rubbed against him.

He hated cats.

Ptolemy grasped her chin and lifted her head so that he could look directly into her eyes. "You tried to murder Mayet today. You didn't succeed, but you did kill five of my household guards."

"Me? I'm innocent." The expression in her eyes told him otherwise. "Did you ask your Greek wife—" she began.

"Enough. You know better than to interfere in my affairs, Artakama. Our arrangement works well for both of us, but I will not be crossed by a woman."

"It was not me," she protested. "It is Berenice. She told me that you were infatuated with a new concubine, and that we could not allow—"

"Take your household to Thebes," he said. "You will be gone from Alexandria by midday. You will send no messages and have no contact with anyone here until I give you leave. Do you understand?"

"Thebes? You can't send me to Thebes!"

"I can send you to Hades if I like. I am your husband. You have not yet provided me with an heir. If you die, I still rule here."

"You would not." Her eyes clouded with tears. "Have I not been a good wife to you? Do I not—"

"I have ordered Berenice to Memphis. She leaves at dawn, under guard. If you would not suffer the same indignity, make yourself scarce."

"Am I under arrest?"

"Not unless you force me to it."

She nodded and sighed. "Then I am resigned to my fate. Thebes it is, although it is very dull at this time of year."

"You admit your guilt?"

"No, I do not. I maintain my innocence in this matter. I confess, I cannot understand why you would suspect me of troubling myself with such a trivial matter as a concubine." She smiled at him and sipped her wine. "But if we are to be separated, perhaps we should not part as enemies." She moistened her lips with a pink tongue and offered a suggestion so novel that he could not resist.

Chapter 11

Ptolemy stood at the archway that led to Mayet's bedchamber in the Palace of the Blue Lotus and watched as two slave girls rinsed the suds out of her hair. The three naked women, one fair-haired, one dark, and one with hair a glorious golden-red, made a charming picture standing waist deep in the tiled bath. He hesitated to disturb them, but finally one of the servants caught sight of him and emitted a yelp of distress. Immediately both slaves made a great show of attempting to prostrate themselves. The blonde swallowed a mouthful of bathwater and dissolved into choking spasms.

Mayet glanced at him for an instant before shooing the girls out of the water and slapping the blond girl on the back until her breathing returned to normal. Dismissing the slaves, Mayet wrapped her wet body in a fresh linen towel and smiled at him. "A good day to you, my lord. I hope you've not come back to continue our disagreement."

"No, I haven't." Ptolemy approached her and leaned forward to kiss her. She smelled of flowers, and he wanted to pull away the towel and feast his eyes on her. His night of abandon with Artakama should have quenched his thirst, but it hadn't. He yearned for Mayet in a way he hadn't desired any woman in many years.

She avoided his caress and took a seat in a chair with three running gazelles carved into the low back. She began to run her fingers through her wet hair. Her skin was pink, and her face had lost the awful paleness of her illness. "I'm grateful for all you've done for me," she said softly, "but I want to return home. I presume I do have a home somewhere."

Stubborn. She was always stubborn about having her own way. And she'd not talked this way until Kayan's appearance. Ptolemy would not permit her to continue in this manner, but neither would he allow this morning's meeting to dissolve into another senseless argument. He forced a smile and waved to a slave boy waiting in the corridor. "I haven't come to bring you grief," he said. "I've brought you a gift."

"No more gifts. I'm already too greatly in your debt."

He shook his head. "You must. It is as close to an apology as you will get from me. I've come to take you on a tour of my city. Isn't that what you've been insisting that you wanted? I want to take you by boat out to Pharaoh's Island, at the harbor entrance. You have a magnificent view of the library from there. It's where I mean to build my lighthouse." He motioned to the boy. "Here, Gyes, bring it to me."

The child hastened to obey. Ptolemy nodded approval. The youth was but recently come from the Land of Punt and his cost had been exorbitant. Gyes's Greek was only rudimentary and his Egyptian worse, but he showed promise of great intelligence. His skin was a light, creamy brown and his features delicate. Gyes had been gelded as an infant by his family and raised to obedience to bring the highest price on the market. Ptolemy thought that with the proper training, he would make an excellent servant, a proper addition to the royal court. It was important to make the right impression on foreign ambassadors and nobility if Alexandria and Egypt were to topple Athens as the cultural capital of the Western world. The more pomp, Ptolemy reasoned, the greater his own splendor.

He took a box wrapped in red silk from Gyes and offered it to Mayet. "At least open it," he said. "Then you can decide if you want to insult me by refusing."

The exquisitely carved and inlaid wooden box had come from India, but Egyptian artisans had crafted the kohl containers and the tiny alabaster pots holding cosmetics and precious oils. There were tweezers, tiny brushes, and flasks of ointment and cream as well as rare perfumes. Each object was a work of art, yet designed to be used for many generations. A silk-lined compartment contained golden combs and hairpins set with amethyst and turquoise stones.

Mayet gasped. "It is beautiful," she said. "But I can't take it."

"You have no choice." He pointed out the raised hieroglyphs around the sides of the box. "My own ancient Egyptian script is rusty, but my bailiff assures me that it says, 'This belongs to the Lady Mayet. May she live for a thousand floods of the Nile.' If you don't accept it, I'll be forced to hunt for another Mayet, and she could have the face of a hippo."

She chuckled. "Must you always have your own way?"

"That is one of the advantages of being king."

"Thank you," she said with a sigh. "But I still want to go home."

He brushed a lock of hair away from her forehead and kissed the crown of her head. "I'm bringing you to my palace," he said, "where you'll be safer than here. You were right. I've been keeping you locked away. But I've dealt sternly with Berenice and Artakama. I've sent them away. I want you in my bed and by my side."

Her face lost its light. "And if I don't want the same thing? Do I have a choice about that?"

"No," he said. "You don't. You've shown that you have affection, even love, for me. You're vexed with me now, but that will pass. Make ready. My soldiers will escort you to the palace within the hour. Later, when you're stronger, you'll thank me. You'll realize that this is right for both of us. For us and for Egypt."

She rose abruptly, and the cosmetic box clattered to the tile. The lid flew open and the precious contents rolled out. "Don't mistake me for one of your slaves, Ptolemy. You'll find I'm not so easy to manage."

"You always did need a stronger rein than your husband was willing to use on you." He grabbed her and kissed her, forcing her head back and grinding his mouth roughly against hers. "You're mine," he said when he released her. "And you'll learn to come at my whistle or you'll find the bars of your cage not golden but iron."

She threw him such a look of raw fury that his stomach clenched. But it wasn't the defiant woman staring him down that caused the chill to flash under his skin. It was the peal of sardonic laughter that echoed from the deepest chamber in his head—laughter that only he seemed to hear.

Didn't I warn you? the haunting voice of his dead brother taunted.

A shaft of pain skewered through both eye sockets. Ptolemy put a hand to his brow and planted his feet, waiting for the next blow. He'd suffered arrow and sword wounds in battle that had not caused him such blinding agony.

Nothing. Mayet gave no indication that she'd heard anything in the room other than his own words. Ptolemy turned away, choking back the bile that rose in his throat. "You will join me today," he commanded, wanting nothing more than to have her cradle his head in her lap and rub his aching temples. "I'll send my own chariot and a company to escort you. Ride in it like the royal consort you are or walk behind it in chains. I don't care which." He strode away.

"Bastard!" she flung after him.

She has you there, the mocking voice whispered as Ptolemy retreated down the passageway with little Gyes half-running to keep up. *Nothing you accomplish can ever change that.*

"I've exchanged one prison for another," Mayet thought as she walked through the garden in the king's palace two days later amid a green landscape of flowering trees, fountains, and Greek sculpture. When Ptolemy's soldiers had come for her that morning, she had not resisted. She wondered now if she was a coward, and if she had always been one. Was she a woman who bent to the wishes of men? Or had she simply not fought a battle she had no chance of winning?

She told herself that she'd ridden in Ptolemy's chariot because she could see no advantage to being dragged behind it. The test of her will would come in the days ahead. Each night since she'd arrived, the king had sent a servant bearing gifts to bring her to his chambers, and each night she had refused, pleading her woman's courses. What would she do when six days had passed? Would Ptolemy allow her to put him off with another lie, or would she weaken and submit?

She could not fool herself that the king had taken advantage of her. She had eagerly accepted his sexual favors and given hers without hesitation. Why was everything different now? Was she awakening from a dream . . . or sinking deeper into madness? How could Ptolemy's touch, which had been so welcome, now fill her with disgust?

A splash caught her attention. She parted the leaves of a flowering shrub and saw two boys skipping stones across the surface of a reflecting pool. They wore the linen kilts of highborn Egyptian youth, but they were not natives of Kemet. They had to be foreigners. Their heads were not shaved except for a single braid, as was the custom for highborn Egyptian boys. Instead, both of those children had thick, blond mops of hair tied back in a queue.

Fascinated, she watched them play for a quarter-hour until the younger turned and spied her. He nudged his companion and pointed to her. "Good day, lady," the lad called in courtly Greek.

Mayet came around the hedge and returned the greeting. The older boy frowned and whispered to the first. His guileless smile vanished, to be replaced with an expression of suspicion.

"We did no harm here," the taller one said. Mayet guessed him to be about ten, but foreigners were often taller than Egyptian children. The smaller boy appeared to be no more than six or seven. Both were attractive, with high foreheads, fair skin, and intelligent eyes. They looked so much alike that she decided they must be brothers.

On closer examination, the older held himself with an almost regal bearing. The little one appeared a scamp. Freckles spattered his nose, and his knees and elbows bore the scars of a dozen scrapes. His kilt was grass-stained, and the toe of one reed sandal was caked with dirt.

"Didn't I see you at the king's audience?" Mayet asked the elder lad. She'd been fooled by the clothing, but the taller boy had been with Prince Kayan when he was presented at court. "You're Prince . . . Prince Hal?"

"Val," the younger one corrected. His voice was sweet and childish. "He's my brother. I'm Yuri." He grinned as if sharing a joke. "Prince Yuri."

"We're just leaving," Val said. He tugged at Yuri's arm, but the child broke free and did a handstand on the lush grass. "Come on," his brother urged. "Let's go." The little show-off continued into a cartwheel, which didn't quite materialize. He landed on his bottom, giggling merrily.

This time, she realized, Prince Val hadn't spoken in Greek. But what was the language? Could it be their own barbaric tongue? "Is that Bactrian? The words you—"

"Parsi," Yuri proclaimed. "I can say it in Persian and Scythian too. Want to hear me?"

A lean figure stepped from the trees and called to the children. Both boys ran toward him.

"Wait," Mayet called. "Don't go. I won't tell anyone you were here."

Prince Val turned and flashed a grin at her. She had the strangest feeling that he reminded her of someone, but the thought was gone as quickly as the boys. The man said something to them that she was too far away to hear, but she sensed he was scolding them. Then all three vanished behind a shrine to Artemis.

Mayet sank to her knees beside the pool. A small pile of stones remained, and she tossed them one by one into the water. The garden seemed empty without the children, and she thought again with longing of her own lost son. She needed to fill her arms with her own babe so that she wouldn't yearn so strongly after others.

"You are here."

Shocked, she twisted to see Prince Kayan standing only a few feet behind her. "You . . ." She drew in a strangled breath. "What are you doing here?"

"I might ask the same of you."

How fierce he is, she thought. Not made for this soft expanse of man-made oasis, but someplace wilder. She shivered at the expression in his eyes. "You are a madman to risk your life so heedlessly," she said.

His thin lips tightened. He had spoken to her tenderly in her bedchamber, but there was no tenderness here, despite the armlets of gold and the rich garments he wore. Her heart hammered against her chest. She knew she should leap to her feet and run from him as she might from a ravenous steppe wolf, but she couldn't.

"You didn't call the guards."

His tone was brusque, almost mocking. Here in the bright sunlight he seemed larger, more ferocious. He wore no weapons other than a small eating knife, yet he radiated an aura of danger.

"I should have summoned them," she said. "I will do so now, if you don't leave at once."

He regarded her with an air of amusement. "You have the manners of a fishwife." He spread his legs and rested scarred fists on his hips with unconscious arrogance. "I am here as Ptolemy's guest. He wishes to sign a treaty of peace with the Twin Kingdoms. My sons tired of the vizier's long-winded speeches, and your king suggested the boys might enjoy his garden."

"You dare to show your face here after invading my—"

"You haven't heard a word I've said, have you?" His mood darkened, and the hawk face became as unyielding as granite. "You are the crown princess of my country. You have people who need you. And instead of fulfilling your responsibilities to your family and your nation, you linger here like some tame gazelle, licking sweets from the hand of your betrayer."

Anger brought her to her feet. "Prove it," she said. "Prove one thing you've said. You can't. And I can't trust you any more than I can trust—"

"Ptolemy?"

She shook her head. "Myself . . . my own judgment. I can't remember. Can you understand that? I don't know who I am."

"I know," he said. "If you doubt my word, look at your

own flesh. You bear the mark of a leaping tiger on your thigh."

Her eyes widened, and she clapped a hand over her mouth to keep from screaming with rage. "That proves nothing," she protested. "You were in my bed. You laid hands on me."

"I'm not the first, am I? I can think of at least two other men who have shared that pleasure. Doubtless, Ptolemy has—"

She flew at him in a fury, hand drawn back to strike. But before she could, he seized her wrist in a powerful grip.

"No," he said. "I'm no Greek eunuch. Raise your hand to me and prepare to pay a price."

She did cry out, but only for an instant. Kayan crushed her against his hard chest and covered her mouth with his own. Her first instinct was to fight him with every ounce of strength and will, but the intensity of her own emotions betrayed her. Her bones turned to water, and her knees went weak. Sweet, unfamiliar sensations rippled through her body, making her heart flutter like a moth's wings.

She slipped her arms around his neck and let the demanding kiss go on and on until she was breathless and shaken. When he released her, she swayed, unsteady on her feet. "I . . . don't . . . I didn't know I . . ."

He didn't wait to hear what she had to say. Turning away abruptly, he left her without another word . . . left her dazed and bewildered. And wishing he had not abandoned her to her own despair.

"Who was she, Val? The beautiful lady in the garden?" Yuri asked as he, his brother, Tiz, and Jandel walked away from the palace.

"I saw her sitting beside King Ptolemy," Val answered. "She is his wife or a concubine."

"Or his sister," Yuri suggested. "She might be his sister."

"Ptolemy has no sisters," Tiz put in. "Or if he has, he's married them."

They ducked to avoid the lines of drying linen that hung over the street. The paving bricks were wet where the laundresses had spilled out the dirty water. In an open doorway, an old woman pressed yards of linen into a mold to pleat an elaborate tunic.

Melon and sweets sellers cried their wares. On the far side of the street, a potter sat cross-legged at his wheel, pressing coils of wet clay into the shape of a tall ewer. A farmer strode by with a string of ducks over his shoulder. A cheerful countrywoman followed, a babe in her arms and a naked girl child scampering behind.

A boy in his mid teens stood juggling three brightly colored clay balls in front of a narrow shop. "Toys and games," he called. "Sir, buy a game for your sons! Senet boards! Whistles. Cunning toys from India. Balls!"

Val and Jandel paused to inspect a round game board propped against the doorway. "What's this?"

"Snake," the vender answered. "A fine game. Don't go home without it."

"Come on," Tiz urged. "You don't need that."

"How do you play?" Yuri asked.

"Yuri, I said come. We've no time for—"

"I want to see it," the boy insisted.

"I saw it first," Val said. "How much? Is it hard to learn?"

"Easy to learn, hard to master," the merchant said. "You move this way. It's a game for two or more. The first to reach the snake's eye wins."

"Buy it, Val," Yuri said. He eyed the balls the young man had dropped into a basket as he displayed the snake game. "You get that one. I think I want these."

A fat priest wearing nothing but a kilt of leopard skin and sandals shuffled past. His kohl-painted eyes lingered on Yuri, and for a moment Tiz glimpsed something unclean in the man's eyes. The Bactrian dropped his hand to his sword and stepped between the priest and the boys.

"Tiz!"

Tiz looked up as Kayan dodged a laden camel and hurried toward them with a frown on his face. "Didn't I tell you to take them back to the house?"

"I'm trying," Tiz grumbled. "Go on, get out of here," he snapped at the priest. "You'll get nothing here but the taste of my blade."

"Kayan!" Val said. "Look at this game I just bought. It's called *snake*. Will you play with me?"

Yuri quickly parted with his coins for the three balls.

"The quicker we get what we came for and get out of this accursed city, the better," Tiz said. "Too many corrupt people."

"I agree," Jandel put in. "Another month and these two young ones will be as soft as Egyptians."

"You're right," Kayan agreed, motioning to his sons to come with him. "I don't trust Ptolemy, and the longer we stay, the more we risk."

"I saw her," Tiz said, so low that only Kayan could hear him. "And so did they."

"I was afraid of that. Do they have any idea who she is?"

"I don't think so."

Kayan's frown became a scowl. "I shouldn't have brought them with me to the palace. I wouldn't have if the invitation hadn't mentioned Val by name."

"Did he sign the treaty?"

"Ptolemy?" Kayan shook his head. "He's stalling. I'm not sure why. But we'll not wait to find out."

"He always was smart. He won't let her go without. . . ." Tiz fell silent as a platoon of Egyptian marines, bristling with weapons, shouldered their way down the avenue.

Kayan stepped into an alley. His sons and Jandel followed. Tiz waited to let the boys get ahead of him, so that he could guard the rear. The good food and beer of Alexandria didn't make up for his uneasiness in this foreign den of iniquity. Tiz hated cities. Princess or no princess, he longed for a horse under him and an open plain in front. Kayan had never led him wrong yet. He hoped this wouldn't be the first time.

Chapter 12

"My library is the envy of every scholar in the Western world," Ptolemy said as he slowed the chariot team to a walk. "This is the center of science and mathematics, not to mention art and philosophy. There." He pointed to a building under construction, rising stone by stone from a wide marble terrace. "That will be an academy for the study of medicine. The first class has already assembled with students from as far away as India and Syria."

"You have much to be proud of," Mayet said. She stood beside him in the open chariot, clinging to his waist.

"You have no idea how difficult it is to find workmen skilled enough to complete the task," he said. "I've brought artisans from Macedonia and Athens. Egypt can provide master stoneworkers, but they don't understand the form and line of Greek building. I've employed an army of scribes and common laborers, but these natives simply don't want to put in a full day's work. How the ancients created the pyramids, I can't understand."

She nodded.

"It takes years to become a competent scribe, and my need is greater than you can imagine. It isn't enough to store the wisdom of the past in my library. We need to copy the texts, so that if anything should happen to the originals, the knowledge won't be lost. I've had agents in Palestine collecting Hebrew lore. Their records go back . . ."

She let him talk without interrupting. There was so much to see, and she'd been too long confined. Alexandria was truly a marvel, a feast of sights, sounds, and smells. Not content to build in the Egyptian manner of dried brick, Ptolemy wanted his capital erected of stone, marble, and granite. Streets and avenues must be wider than normal and laid out precisely to the plan. No expense was spared; even the public market was graced with tall columns, mosaic wall panels, and tiled roofs.

Mayet wondered if she'd ever seen so many temples and shrines gathered in one place. Greek gods and goddesses were honored as well as the Egyptian ones. On this street alone, she had counted four sanctuaries, to Ares, Isis, Artemis, and Demeter. Worshipers thronged to make offerings and ask for special favors or safe passage. She wondered if she had ever prayed in one of these holy places. Her gods must be Egyptian, but she took no comfort from their images.

Unless Kayan was telling the truth.

What gods did the barbarian worship? And why did he haunt her waking hours?

"Wait until you see the plans for my stadium," Ptolemy said. "That's the theater over there. It seats ten thousand. I'll take you to a performance if you'd like."

She nodded. He turned onto the street that ran along the waterfront. Greek cavalrymen flanked the chariot on both sides. Ptolemy leaned close. "Prince Kayan upset you at the reception hall, didn't he?"

She steeled herself to keep from reacting. Had she murmured his name, or was Ptolemy an oracle that could read her thoughts? "No," she lied. "Why would you say that?" Again she was protecting the barbarian. But why? And what if the Sogdian was telling the truth? What if she wasn't Egyptian and all Ptolemy had told her was false? If her son was alive? Could the king be hiding him from her?

"You haven't been the same since he arrived in Alexandria."

"That's not true."

"Have you ever defied me before? Have we ever had cross words?"

She sighed. He'd promised that this was to be a special day for her, that he wouldn't press her on setting a wedding date. "You grew angry with me because I wouldn't agree to marry you," she reminded him. "I'm not ready to make that decision."

"I am," he said. "And I have. We will be married in ten days, here in Alexandria and again in Thebes. I have already sent out the invitations."

"No. I won't go through with it. You can't make—"

Ptolemy reined in the team of matched bays. A line of bullock carts carrying cargo from a ship blocked the royal procession. The ship's captain came forward and dropped to his knees in respect. Ptolemy glanced at Mayet. "Stay here. I wish to speak to him." He threw the reins to a cavalryman and jumped lightly down from the chariot.

The officer commanding the soldiers and six of his men surrounded Ptolemy. The eyes of the remaining horsemen followed their king as he approached the sea captain. No one paid any heed to Mayet in the chariot—except for a street urchin.

A barefoot boy wearing only a loincloth darted forward. He held out his hand as if begging.

"I'm sorry," she said. "I don't have anything to give you."

"But I have something for you," the beggar said in a mixture of street Greek and Egyptian. "A friend asks that you meet him at the Temple of Isis at the hour of the ninth watch. For the sake of your son, he bids you to come."

"What friend?" she demanded, but the messenger had already ducked into the crowd and disappeared.

Ptolemy returned to the chariot and took up the reins again. "A full cargo of spices," he said. "Ten percent of the profit is mine. You're not only marrying a king but one who possesses riches beyond anything you can imagine. Down here are twenty of my newest warships. I want you to see—"

"Please," she said, swaying against him. "The sun. I don't feel so well. I'm not used to—"

"Very well. Another day." He called to his commander. "We'll be returning to the palace."

Once back in her apartments, Mayet bathed and retired to her bed. There she proceeded to devour dates, pomegranates, and honey cakes until her stomach revolted. She summoned a palace physician, and he arrived in time to hear her vomiting into her water closet. An hour later, after the physician had administered medication to Mayet and hung an amulet with the image of the god Asclepius around her neck, servants tucked her back into bed and extinguished all but one oil lamp.

Ptolemy came to her room twice that evening to inquire after her health. He spoke with the physician and the oldest of her serving women and then offered his condolences.

"You didn't believe that I was really sick?" Mayet asked wanly.

Ptolemy shook his head. "You wrong me. I only want to see that you have the best of care. Our wedding is approaching, and you must be well for that." With a final admonishment for her not to do anything to endanger her health, he went away.

Mayet listened as the watch passed. Time seemed to crawl by. Eunuchs lingered in the hallway talking and laughing longer than usual, and she was afraid she wouldn't arrive at the temple at the appointed time. Finally, when she felt it was safe, she climbed from the bed, stepped over the slave girls sleeping on a pallet beside it, and crept through the passageway to the garden.

The king's palace enclosed the garden, but there were several gates leading to different sections. Although Mayet didn't know the layout of the sprawling complex, she knew where the kitchen wing was located. She followed her nose through the hallways to the food preparation area. Slaves and dogs lay sprawled in the passageway between the bakehouse and the kitchen.

Mayet picked her way carefully through the sleepers and waited, uncertain how to get out of the palace without being seen. After what seemed like half an hour, someone stirred, rose, and walked groggily through the service area and down a twisting staircase. Mayet followed at a safe distance through a damp cellar and up more stairs to a grove of trees outside the palace walls. The slave she'd seen leave the kitchen went to a low area, but Mayet didn't need to go farther. The stench of human waste told her that this was where the staff and probably the soldiers relieved themselves.

After a few minutes the servant returned to the palace. Mayet skirted the foul area, cut through the trees, and discovered an alley. That byway led to a stables area and a street containing smiths and armorers. Again, she could tell what the area was used for because of the strong scent of horses, manure, and forges. She hurried along, aided by the full moon. She still didn't recognize the streets, but her sense of direction was good. In a short time, she passed into a neighborhood of artisans' homes. The next intersection was a wider street that she remembered crossing with Ptolemy earlier that day.

The steps outside the Temple of Isis were empty. They glistened white and cold in the moonlight. Nervously Mayet ran up the marble stairs, through the columned portico, and into the sanctuary. Immediately, clouds of swirling incense enveloped her. There were people here, worshipers and priestesses, praying, kneeling in front of the smaller shrines, and placing offerings of flowers and fruit. Lamps glowed in the alcoves, and a skylight over the huge statue of Isis flooded the interior of the holy place with the moon's light.

Mayet breathed a sigh of relief. Although she felt no allegiance to Isis, she felt safer here than she had on the darkened streets. She could make out no faces, hear only low murmurs, yet peace permeated the air. She stood in the shadows, letting her eyes adjust to the interior of the temple. Figures entered and left, but she saw no one tall and broad enough to be Prince Kayan. And if he hadn't summoned her, who had?

A priestess, clad in a long tunic and wearing a linen cloak and headdress, made her way to where Mayet waited. "You're late."

Mayet flinched. It wasn't a woman's voice, but a boy's, one she recognized as Prince Val's. "Why did you—"

"Follow me." He immediately turned and walked toward the back of the sanctuary, past the great statue and into a smaller chapel where Kayan waited in the shadows.

"I thought you weren't coming," he said.

"I'm sorry. I couldn't get away earlier. Why am I here? What has this to do with my son?"

"The king has announced your wedding. We're leaving Alexandria. This is your last chance to escape him. Come with us to your homeland—to your father and your son."

"What you ask is madness," she whispered. "You don't know Ptolemy. He'd come after me. All your lives would be in jeopardy." She heard breathing and sensed that others waited in the shadows. Val, but who else?

"You think we aren't in danger now? Ptolemy knows me," Kayan said. "He's afraid that seeing me will break whatever spell he's cast over you."

"Give me proof," she begged. "If you are who you say you are, wouldn't I recognize you? Wouldn't I know the truth of it?"

"For the last time," Kayan said. "Will you come with us willingly?"

"I can't," she said. "I can give you no better answer than I gave Ptolemy. If I can't trust myself, how can I trust you?" She grasped his arm. "I came here to learn of my son. Tell me what you know, unless that's another lie."

"You give me no choice." Kayan grabbed for her.

At the last second, she leaped away. A small figure charged into Kayan, tackling him at the knees. "No! No!" Yuri cried.

Val seized her arm, but she twisted out of his grasp.

"What's happening here?" a woman's authoritative voice cried in Egyptian.

Mayet pushed past two priestesses. At almost the same time, shouts and the clatter of running feet came from the portico. Someone screamed. Torches flared. A spear caught a worshiper through the belly as he rose from the area in front of the statue of Isis. He staggered back, falling onto a lamp. His linen tunic caught fire. Men and women ran screaming as soldiers stormed the sanctuary.

"You betrayed us!" Kayan shouted as he ran by her, sword drawn to engage the first wave of guards.

"No!" Mayet protested.

A woman fell face down, an arrow protruding from her back. A small figure burst from the chapel, and Mayet saw the gleam of a knife in the child's hand. She snatched Yuri by the hair and dragged him back, fleeing toward the rear of the temple.

"This way," a priestess said. She placed both palms against

what looked like a solid wall of granite, and the blocks of stone slid soundlessly aside. She gestured, and Mayet—still clinging to Yuri—ran into the secret passageway.

Two more priestesses and a woman with blood streaming down her face followed. One of the priestesses activated the lever from inside and the portal swung closed, muffling the sound of fighting. Mayet's guide led the little party through a corridor so narrow that they had to turn sideways to get through into what appeared to be living quarters for the holy women.

Trembling, the injured Egyptian girl sank down on the floor and began to weep. "Why would the king attack the temple?" she wailed. "What wrong have we done?"

"They did not seek you or us," a grim-faced priestess said. "One of the soldiers warned me to run as he entered the sanctuary. They came seeking someone."

"They killed my brother Nesamun," the girl sobbed. "He could not hear or speak. What harm had he done anyone?"

Mayet released Yuri. The boy glared at her with such hatred that she flinched. "I had no part in this evil," she said to him. "I swear it."

"If my father or my brother are hurt, I will cut out your heart and feed it to the jackals."

"Be at peace, little one," a priestess soothed him. "Trust in Isis."

"I can't stay here," Mayet said. "I must get back to . . . I must get home." She glanced back at Yuri. "But"—she turned to the oldest priestess—"can you keep him safe for a day or two? I will make an offering to—"

"Do not insult us," the woman answered. "We will treat the child as our own."

"No," he said. "I won't stay here."

"He would want you to," Mayet reasoned. "Stay with these good folk. I will come for you as soon as it is safe. I promise."

"What good is your word, Egyptian witch?" He turned the knife on her. "I could kill you now," he said.

She took a step closer to him. "Trust me," she said softly. "I will not betray you, and I will not betray your father. I swear on my dead son's soul."

Tears ran down the boy's cheeks. "You'd better not," he threatened. "Because if you do . . . if you do, I'll find you. I'll find you and I'll make you pay."

"Don't despair," Mayet said. "I don't think this is the first battle your father has fought, and I don't think he's that easy to kill."

One of the novices at the Temple of Isis led Mayet back to the king's palace and showed her a secret entrance used by Greek priests and priestesses. A few whispers and Mayet was passed from the care of Isis to that of Hera. Another young woman guided Mayet through a chapel devoted to the wife of Zeus to the wing where Mayet's apartments lay.

A guard station stood between Mayet and a hall that opened to her quarters. Hera's servant created a small incident to distract the two soldiers so that a grateful Mayet could return to her bed before anyone learned that she had been absent.

By the time the sun was high, the palace servants were abuzz with news of the riot at the Temple of Isis the night before. Mayet listened to the snatches of gossip as she allowed her slaves to bathe her and dress her hair.

"Barbarians robbed the Temple . . ."

". . . shot through the heart in the holy . . ."

". . . blood on the feet of Isis."

"The king called out the army to bring order to . . ."

Once she was garbed in her finest tunic and bedecked in a pectoral and armlets of gold, Mayet sent word to Ptolemy asking if she might wait upon him.

A messenger returned almost at once, begging the lady's indulgence, but saying that the king was pressed by urgent demands and could not see her now.

"Where is he?" she demanded of the slave.

"In council with the vizier and a general," the eunuch replied.

"Take me to him."

The youth paled. "I dare not, lady. It would mean my head."

"My lady!" Hesper called from the archway.

Mayet went to her and embraced her. "I've missed you," she said. "Are you well? The baby—"

The dark-haired noblewoman nodded. "I'm fine. My child is strong and healthy. He kicks like a donkey." She patted her swelling belly and drew Mayet aside. "May we walk in the garden?" she asked. "It is such a lovely day that fresh air might—"

"Of course." Mayet was as eager as her friend to be away from the eyes and ears of ever-present slaves. The two strolled arm in arm to the trees beside the reflecting pool.

"What's happened?" Mayet demanded. "I've heard there was fighting at the Temple of Isis last night. What do you know?"

"Little else, lady," Hesper said. "My husband was called up before dawn to lead troops into the city in search of the Bactrians. I heard him tell his lieutenant that three of the king's guardsmen had been slain. I think worshipers were killed in the sanctuary, and at least one priestess was injured."

Mayet took her hand and gripped it tightly. "What does this have to do with me?" she asked. "Who is this Prince Kayan? Why is Ptolemy threatened by him?"

"The barbar . . . Prince Kayan's men attacked the temple," Hesper said.

"Kayan escaped?"

"Yes, he and his men. One was killed, but—"

"Why? Why do people say he did this?"

"No one knows. Perhaps robbery. The shrine is rich and—"

"Don't lie to me," Mayet pleaded. "It wasn't Prince Kayan who attacked the sanctuary. It was the king's men."

"No," Hesper said. "My husband is a pious man. He would never do violence in a holy place. He says that his orders are to arrest Prince Kayan for murder."

"Kayan is innocent. Ptolemy's soldiers committed the atrocity. He wanted the Bactrians dead. And there's more—I've talked to Prince Kayan. He says that I'm from his country. That I'm their queen, and that I'm not even Mayet."

"Don't." Hesper pulled away from her. Her eyes widened in fear. "I can't . . . Forgive me, lady, but I cannot risk the lives of my husband and children." She burst into tears.

"It's true, isn't it? I'm not Mayet, but . . . Roxanne of Bactria?"

"Please," Hesper sobbed. "I cannot . . ."

"No, I won't ask you to put your family in danger. No matter what I say or do, remember that I am eternally grateful for your friendship."

Hesper raised a tear-stained face to stare in bewilderment.

"Thank you," Mayet murmured. She pulled off the heavy golden armlets and pressed them into Hesper's hands. "For your unborn child," she said. "A birth gift."

Hesper shook her head. "I don't understand."

"I do this for the sake of our friendship and your loyalty," Mayet said. She screamed an obscenity. "Get out of my sight!" she shrieked. "Go! You fat cow! I never want to lay eyes on you again!"

Leaving Hesper beside the lake, Mayet stormed into her bedchamber. She dashed a pitcher of wine onto the floor and scattered the slaves with harsh words and threats of beating. "Take me to the king!" she commanded the chief eunuch. "Take me at once, or I'll tell him that you offered me insult and laid hands on me in a foul manner."

Chapter 13

Ptolemy scowled and rose as Mayet entered his council chamber. "This is not the time to come here. I'm discussing important matters with General Telephus."

"Pardon, my lord." She bestowed her most adoring smile on him. "I'll just wait." She nodded to the stern-faced general and to Ptolemy's vizier, a pompous man whose name she didn't recall. "I'll be as quiet as a moth," she promised.

The king spoke tersely to the general. "Continue the search. I want to know the action is complete."

Mayet sighed and toyed with two bracelets, clicking them together.

"All, Your Majesty?" Telephus asked.

"All."

The general and vizier saluted. Mayet felt their disapproval toward her as they left the room. Ptolemy's brow was furrowed with suspicion. "Why did you disobey my orders and come here when I distinctly told you not to?"

"What's happening in the city?" she asked. Ptolemy was sharp. She sensed that her charade of innocent foolishness wasn't working. "I've heard gossip that—"

"Prince Kayan and his followers attempted to rob a temple. Someone alerted the city guard. They clashed. Three of my soldiers were killed, along with four or five innocents who were worshiping at the shrine. I've sent forces into the streets to find Prince Kayan and arrest him for murder."

"Why would he do such a thing?"

"He's a Bactrian. A hill bandit blinded by the riches of Alexandria. I suppose he thought he could get away with it."

"I'm sorry."

"Why should you be sorry? It has nothing to do with you. It's a small matter. Alexandria attracts criminals as well as wealth. The brigands will be found, tried, and put to death."

"Even the children?"

Ptolemy offered an outstretched hand. "Come here."

She forced herself to offer a half-smile, to go into his embrace, and rest her head against his chest. How strange, she thought, that someone she'd trusted so completely could turn out to be despicable. "Prince Val is so young," she said. "His brother can't be seven. Surely the king's justice—"

"If we pardon Kayan's sons, we make blood enemies of them. And robbers would find it profitable to use boys in their thieving. Crime would run rampant, until no citizen was safe on our streets or in his home. Attacking a temple is an offense against the gods. Civilized laws, Greek and Egyptian, are clear on such issues. Thieves lose their right hand on the first offense. Murderers receive the death penalty. If it will ease your heart, I'll show mercy to the youngest, if he's captured alive. He will merely have his right hand amputated."

A chill ran through her.

"The older boy was arrested during the struggle in the sanctuary."

"How can a ten-year-old be accountable for murder? You can't blame—"

"Eyewitnesses proclaim his guilt. He was taken with a bloodstained knife in his hand. I judged him just after daybreak. Don't think you can obstruct my sentence. He'll be garroted at sundown in the public square in front of the great library."

"What?" She opened her eyes and gazed up at his face. Had she heard him right?

"The square. The space between the library and Alexander's tomb."

"It is harsh," she murmured. "I understand the need for justice, but . . . is there nothing—"

He tilted her face and kissed her mouth. "Shhh," he said. "Trouble yourself about this no longer. You don't have to watch. No one will think less of you for remaining in the palace. After your illness last night, it would be natural for you to avoid disturbing events. You'll understand that I must be there to see my orders carried out."

He traced the outline of her lower lip with his thumb. "I see now that it was the onset of your sickness that made you so contrary yesterday."

She stroked his hand and twisted so that her back was nestled against him. He hugged her and kissed the top of her head. "I'm sorry if I gave offense," she said. "I have had time to think, and I see now the wisdom of your decision that we should marry."

"Good." He squeezed her again. "Now go back to your apartments and let me tend to my affairs. I'll come to you this afternoon. You have my word on it."

She clasped his hand and looked down, not trusting herself to meet Ptolemy's gaze. His middle finger bore a heavy gold ring with a lion's head motif. Mayet saw it and inhaled sharply. The ring . . .

It was Alexander's ring.

Alexander had ordered it made in remembrance of his friend Hephaestion's tragic death at Hamadan. She'd seen it last on Alexander's hand. He'd sworn never to take it off in this life or the next.

Alexander.

She gave a choked cry and her knees buckled as a rush of memories swept over her. Alexander's death in Babylon . . . Perdiccas's treachery . . . Faces swirled in her mind's eye. Voices. The wail of a newborn as she passed him into Kayan's arms. Her own words echoing through the years.

"*. . . My son you must take home to our mountains. You, who are dearest to me in all the world, you must take him and make of him a prince.*

"*. . . Go and seek out another infant, one with a Persian mother and Greek father, fair of skin as my babe shall be. I'll switch them and claim the foundling as my own.*"

"Impossible," Kayan had claimed.

The memory of her reply rose as clear as a drop of water from a Sogdian mountain stream. "*. . . A lone man on a Bactrian racing camel? Who would notice a single rider carrying so small a bundle? No creature on earth runs as swiftly as a Bactrian racer. The distance is far; the Greeks will never hold the Twin Kingdoms. They will scramble for Persia and Greece like beggars for crusts in a gutter!*"

As Ptolemy had scrambled to seize Egypt.

Roxanne. She was Roxanne . . . daughter of High Prince Oxyartes and Queen Pari, rulers of Bactria and Sogdiana. She was the widow of Alexander of Macedon. She was Roxanne, who'd followed Alexander the Conqueror to India and been captured and branded by a sadistic Indian ruler. . . . The desperate woman who'd switched her royal newborn for a foundling to keep his enemies from destroying him, and spent the next seven years a prisoner in Macedonia.

Colored lights pinwheeled in her head. The voices of the past were drowned by a buzzing that grew louder and louder. She felt no pain, only the pulsing glare of a star that shone brighter than the desert sun.

"Mayet?"

She looked into Ptolemy's eyes and truly recognized

him, not as Pharaoh of Egypt but as Alexander's Macedonian Companion, half-brother, and trusted friend. "Why?" she asked. "Why?" And then the earth parted under her feet, the light dimmed, and she sank into oblivion.

Roxanne became aware of Ptolemy's voice. It sounded hollow, as though he were a long way off. She opened her eyes just enough to see that she was lying in her own bedchamber before she let them drift shut.

She remembered everything.

So why wasn't she dead? Seven years she'd been held a prisoner in a Macedonian cave, first by Alexander's mother, Queen Olympias, and later by her greatest enemy, the Greek general Cassander, Olympias's murderer. For seven years Roxanne had dreamed of sky and mountains and green valleys. And when the end had come, when she'd realized the game was over and Cassander's assassins were coming to kill her, she'd drunk the poisoned wine her friends had provided. Poison seemed a cleaner death than torture and rape. She'd no wish to provide sport for Greek assassins, especially since she'd known they meant to kill her when they were finished with her.

She'd tasted the bite of poison on her tongue . . . felt its cold fingers creeping through her, felt herself dying. She'd even seen Alexander and Bucephalus come for her across a Sogdian meadow strewn with flowers.

"You said it was nothing serious! And now you tell me that she has a fever?" Ptolemy shouted.

"A relapse." She recognized Djedhor the Egyptian physician by his voice. "She should never have been allowed to overtax herself."

"If she dies—"

"She won't die, Your Majesty. Not if she follows my instructions and takes this medication."

A spoon banged against her teeth. She knocked it away. "No," she said. Ptolemy lifted her head and brought a cup to her lips. She remembered the smell of the tainted wine. "Poison," she murmured.

Djedhor leaned over her. His breath was foul. "Lady, you must drink this."

"It's poison," she repeated, but didn't know if she was awake or still reliving the past.

"Poison?" Ptolemy asked.

She moaned and tossed her head. "I feel sick." That was true, but it was her heart that felt strange, not her stomach.

She turned her face to the cushions. So many memories . . . She could almost see 'Zander's dear little face, so delicate and pale that the blue veins were visible beneath his skin.

'Zander, the fosterling she'd passed off as Alexander's son . . . the unwanted child she'd come to love . . . her adopted son who'd lived his too few years as a prince and died in her arms. How could she have forgotten her precious little 'Zander?

Tears welled up and spilled down her cheeks.

Why wasn't she dead? "Poison in the wine," she whispered, remembering. "I won't drink it."

"What is this of poison?" Ptolemy demanded.

The weight of heartache pressed against her eyelids. Not remembering was contentment compared to the pain of knowing. She forced her eyes to open. "I'm not ready to die," she whispered, caught in a storm of emotion between what had been and this moment. "I was, but not now."

With a cry of rage, Ptolemy seized the Egyptian and forced the man to his knees. "You drink it!"

Djedhor's face twisted into a mask of fear. He tried to break away from the king, but Ptolemy bent his head back and forced open his mouth in the same way she'd seen him force a bit between the teeth of a half-broken horse. Djedhor moaned and begged, but Ptolemy was merciless. He poured the wine into the man's mouth, holding his nose to make him swallow.

NAME: _____

ADDRESS: _____

_____

_____

TELEPHONE: _____

E-MAIL: _____

_____ I want to pay by credit card.

__ Visa   __ MasterCard   __ Discover

Account Number: _____

Expiration date: _____

SIGNATURE: _____

Send this form, along with $2.00 shipping and handling for your FREE books, to:

Historical Romance Book Club
20 Academy Street
Norwalk, CT 06850-4032

Or fax (must include credit card information!) to: 610.995.9274.
You can also sign up on the Web at <u>www.dorchesterpub.com</u>.

Offer open to residents of the U.S. and Canada only. Canadian residents, please call 1.800.481.9191 for pricing information.

If under 18, a parent or guardian must sign. Terms, prices and conditions subject to change. Subscription subject to acceptance. Dorchester Publishing reserves the right to reject any order or cancel any subscription.

The poison was fast-acting. In the time it would take for a trained archer to shoot all the bows in his quiver, the Egyptian no longer tried to escape. He lay on his back on the floor and gripped his belly in agony.

In the time it would take to boil a pot of water over hot coals, foam bubbled from Djedhor's mouth, his eyes rolled back in his head, and he drew his last breath.

Ptolemy sat on the side of the bed and rocked her in his arms. "I'm sorry," he said. "I'm so sorry. I shouldn't have trusted him. I should have known."

"What?" she whispered. "What should you have known?" She was vaguely surprised. The poison had been a memory, something that happened before . . . not now. But the Egyptian physician was dead. Slaves were dragging his body away.

"Throw him on the midden heap," Ptolemy commanded. "Let the stray dogs eat him." He covered her face with kisses. "You didn't take any of the wine, did you?"

She shook her head. She was weary, confused. And if she closed her eyes, she could see them, the ones she'd loved, the ones who'd gone before her—her mother; Wolf, her faithful bodyguard; her son, 'Zander; and Alexander, the golden god of her dreams with his intense blue-gray eyes and boyish grin.

"Dead," she said. "He's dead, isn't he?"

"Yes," Ptolemy said. "He's dead, but he died too easily. I should have had him staked out on the desert over a nest of scorpions." He kissed her lips. "I should have known. He was Berenice's physician before he was mine. This is her doing. She tried to poison you, and I almost helped her."

Alexander? What was he talking about? Alexander wasn't Berenice's physician. He was Ptolemy's half-brother. Ptolemy loved Alexander. Why would he want to stake his brother out in the desert?

She closed her eyes and drifted for a while in a twilight state, only half asleep and half aware of what was happening around her. This time, when her head cleared, the water clock showed her that it was past the hour of noon. She was alone except for musicians playing in the garden. Her servants had drawn painted screens in front of the windows to keep the sunlight from disturbing her rest and had left her to sleep.

She remembered Kayan.

She sat up abruptly. Val. Ptolemy was going to put Kayan's son to death at sundown. If she lay here and did nothing, Val would die. Yuri would believe that she had abandoned him.

She would have abandoned him.

She got out of bed. She felt hungry, no longer confused. Her life had fallen into place like the pieces of 'Zander's alphabet puzzle. Val needed her. Kayan needed her.

She had been Ptolemy's helpless pawn too long.

Knowing the truth, she realized why Ptolemy wanted her to be his queen so badly. Alexander had promised to crown her if she gave him a son to inherit the world he meant to conquer. But he hadn't lived to see the birth of his son, and she—who'd never wanted to sit on a Macedonian throne— had never received that honor.

Ptolemy had always stood in his brother's shadow. If he took his brother's wife and made her his queen . . . if she gave him sons . . . he would get the better of Alexander.

Poor little 'Zander, whom the Greeks knew as Alexander IV, had died more than a year ago in that Macedonian cave. Ptolemy believed Alexander's heir was dead and saw himself as successor to the conqueror. But Kayan had outsmarted them and taken Alexander's true son to Bactria.

Her child was waiting for her there now. Kayan had promised her that, and he had never betrayed her, never lied to her. Kayan had been telling her the truth all along, and she'd refused to accept it.

Unless . . . A thought rose in her mind, a thought so

wonderful and yet so terrifying that she nearly fell back into the daze that had gripped her since the moment she'd recognized Alexander's ring on Ptolemy's finger.

What if Val was her child? Or precious little Yuri? No, she told herself. That was impossible. Kayan wouldn't risk her son's life by bringing him to Egypt. He was too precious to Sogdiana and Bactria, and the danger to the boy was too great. Surely her son, the real Alexander IV, was safe in Bactria in his grandfather's arms.

She had to act, but what should she do? This was a time for reason, not emotion. If she agreed to marry Ptolemy in exchange for Val's life, she would be Queen of Egypt. She would hold power in her own right.

Egypt was the most powerful nation in the civilized world. Couldn't she do more for her Kayan and his sons . . . for her own son and her country as Ptolemy's queen?

She dumped out her jewelry chest, removed the dagger that Hesper had given her from the hidden space beneath the false bottom, and used a silken scarf to tie the weapon to her thigh. Then she bundled together the sturdiest clothing she could find—tunics, Egyptian kilts, and two wigs in the Theban style. Into this bundle she tucked golden earrings, bracelets, amulets, and a cascade of jewelry. If she was to rescue the boys and flee Alexandria, she would need all the wealth she could carry.

She could not remain here as Ptolemy's queen. He might welcome her by his side, but she knew she could never bear his touch again.

Ptolemy was not the man his brother had been. Ptolemy had lied to her, stolen her past, and given her a false identity. Worst of all, he had tried to keep her from her son. The fact that he didn't know she had a living son didn't matter. She still blamed him. They had once been friends, but no more. She would sleep alone all her days rather than sit a throne beside a man she couldn't respect.

She dressed in her finest Egyptian tunic and topped it with a headband of gold and precious gems. Then she did the only sensible thing that came to mind.

She set fire to Ptolemy's palace.

The fire was a small one, but it would grow, fed by the oil from two lamps and an armful of scrolls. Strange, that she who loved learning so much would destroy knowledge. But Val's life hung in the balance, and the Crown Princess of Bactria and Sogdiana could not afford to hesitate. A princess must do whatever was necessary.

Carrying her unwieldy bundle, she thrust it into a woven basket and then into the arms of the first slave she found. "Summon a guard for me. At once," she commanded.

"But, lady," the eunuch said. "You are ill. The king has left orders—"

"You dolt!" She smacked him soundly alongside the ear. "Offspring of a flea-bitten goat! Were you sleeping that you did not see His Majesty's messenger? I am to go to the barbarian's execution. He wants me at his side as an example to the people of Alexandria. Unless you wish to dispute the king's word?"

"No, lady. No," the man squeaked.

"These trifles go with me to the Temple of Isis, gifts of charity for the injured worshipers. Bring them." She swept past him down the passageway. "And my chariot and driver had best be waiting. If I'm late, heads will roll."

Three-quarters of an hour later, Roxanne arrived at the temple. A dozen armed guards trotted beside her chariot as escort. She directed them to wait while she consulted with the priestesses of Isis. Roxanne declined the offer of a man to bear the bundle. It would show greater humility, she informed them, if she brought the cast-off clothing for the unfortunates with her own hands.

Persuading Yuri to dress in female garb and to cover his hair with the black wig was more difficult than getting out of Ptolemy's palace. She was even less successful in parting him from his knife.

"I may need it," he insisted. "If you betray me—"

"Yes, yes," she said impatiently. "You'll chop me in little pieces and feed me to the crocodiles."

"Hyenas."

"Be still," the priestess said as she painted the boy's eyes with kohl. "Don't touch it until it dries or you'll look like a whore instead of a holy initiate."

Roxanne rewarded the temple with three armlets of gold, more than enough, the priestesses assured her, to win the favor of Isis and assure her help in whatever scheme the lady intended. Roxanne didn't explain, and they didn't ask. When she returned to the chariot, Yuri minced beside her in an exaggerated feminine walk. He carried the basket containing the clothing and jewelry.

"I will deliver the clothing to the injured myself," Roxanne said to her driver. "To the waterfront. The street of the rope makers." She glanced at Yuri, a very young, very short novice wearing a large amulet with the image of Isis embossed on it. The small faux priestess wore a formal tunic with a pleated skirt that hung almost to the toes of his reed sandals. "Are you coming?" Roxanne asked him.

Yuri mumbled something, yanked up the hem of the skirt, and hopped into the chariot. He wedged himself between Roxanne and the side and clutched the basket against his chest with a death grip.

The driver cracked the whip over his team.

"Where are you going?" Roxanne demanded shrilly. "I told you the street of the rope makers."

"Yes, lady. That's where I'm taking you."

"No," she said. "Not that way. Go by way of the library. One of the injured women sells fruit on the corner near the main portico to the Conqueror's tomb."

The driver, a middle-aged Egyptian with a lean body

and bowed legs, shrugged and turned his horses in the other direction. A soldier galloped by on horseback. Then a second rider followed. As Roxanne's party rounded a corner, they were forced to pull up short as a platoon of Greek infantrymen ran past.

"What's up, Endre?" one of Roxanne's guards called.

"Fire," a soldier shouted back. "Fire in the palace."

"Look," the chariot driver said, pointing to the sky. Black smoke curled above the rooftops.

"Go!" Roxanne shouted. "What are you waiting for? King Ptolemy will need every pair of hands to fight the fire. My lord may be in danger! Go!"

The sergeant shook his head. "Can't do that, Lady Mayet. You need protection."

"Fool. Who would harm me? Leave two men if you must, but go before it's too late."

The soldier looked from her to the driver and back to his men.

"My driver can take us to the library. Surely we'll be safe there. I order you to attend your king."

"You heard the lady. Take her to the library!" the sergeant said. He pointed out two older guards. "You and you, stay with her. Guard her with your lives."

"Well, what are you waiting for?" Roxanne said to Yuri, once the group of guards had trotted away around the corner. "Give it to me."

Yuri's eyes widened.

"The knife," she whispered. He shook his head. "Now." She pinched him.

The boy swore and passed her the weapon under the basket.

She smiled. "Good. Now be ready to grab the reins."

"What?"

"Faster!" Roxanne shouted to the driver. "Faster!" The two guards, trotting now, were falling behind the chariot. Both men were past their prime, and the midday sun was hot. Sweat poured off them as they struggled to keep up. "Faster!" she urged.

"Lady," the driver protested. "I can't—"

"Then you'll have to lighten the load." She whipped the point of Yuri's curved dagger to rest against the man's throat. "Get out!"

The driver squeaked in protest, and she pressed harder. With a yelp of pain, he leaped off the back of the chariot. Yuri grabbed for the reins and caught one. Roxanne caught the other.

Snatching the leather from the boy, she slapped the lines over the horses' backs. "Haa!" she cried.

"You can drive a chariot?"

"By the Great God, I hope so!"

Yuri gave a yell of pure delight as team and chariot sped down the center of the broad avenue, sending pedestrians scattering for their lives.

Chapter 14

Roxanne raced through the streets, leaving her pursuers on foot far behind. People turned to stare at the noblewoman and the young priestess driving so recklessly through the center of Alexandria in a chariot bearing the king's seal, but no one attempted to stop them. Most attention seemed to be drawn to the black smoke rising over the section of the city containing the palace. Groups of men and boys hurried in that direction. Women pointed at the sky and commented anxiously to those around them.

Again, Roxanne could catch only fragments of conversation.

". . . Fire! It looks bad."

". . . My Ion says . . ."

"The wind is blowing south away from . . ."

Yuri kept his head down and remained silent as Roxanne guided the matched team of black horses around a train of donkeys carrying jars of oil, past the angry patrons of an outdoor tavern, and through the center of a rug market.

She continued on, keeping the team at a fast pace as they left the merchants' stalls behind and entered an area of public buildings, wealthy private homes, and temples. She was afraid she might be going in the wrong direction until she recognized an exquisite marble temple dedicated to Aphrodite rising on the left side of the wide thoroughfare. She distinctly remembered Ptolemy pointing the structure out to her the day he'd shown her his city.

At the next corner, Roxanne reined in the team just enough to make the hard right turn. The Egyptian-style chariot was heavier than any she had driven before, larger and not so agile, designed more for stately processions than speed.

The vehicle careened around the corner, tilting precariously onto one wheel and nearly overturning. Yuri could no longer contain himself and cried out with excitement. Roxanne threw her weight to one side and the rogue wheel touched down on the paving stones, and bounced hard. The axle held, and the chariot sped down the center of the street.

This boulevard was wider still, with more stately structures on either side, and had much less foot traffic. The street ran only a short distance before opening into the square that stretched between Alexander's tomb and the enormous complex of buildings that housed Ptolemy's library.

Kayan had gotten there ahead of her.

The prince and a knot of fierce swordsmen were halfway up the marble steps leading to the library, surrounded by Ptolemy's troops and fighting for their lives. Bystanders gathered in clumps on the far side of the street, gesturing and shouting. Roxanne's heart rose in her throat as she caught a glimpse of a small blond head in the midst of the conflict.

"There!" Yuri cried. "I see Val!"

Kayan's barbarians were giving as good as they got.

Two Greek soldiers lay sprawled on the steps, and an Egyptian archer crawled away from the melee on his hands and knees. Roxanne estimated that the Bactrians were outnumbered at least three to one, but they gave no hint of realizing that the odds were overwhelming.

"Let me off!" Yuri cried. "They need my help!"

"You stay put or I'll knock you senseless." She must do something to help them. She knew the situation was desperate. But was it hopeless? If Kayan's band was doomed, then reason dictated that she flee with his little son as fast as she could.

"They'll kill my father!" the boy pleaded. "Let me down. I can fight!"

Reason be damned, she thought. Since when had reason guided her life? With a shout, she lashed the team toward the struggle, yanking the horses' heads back just in time to avoid running down the wounded Egyptian archer. "Get his bow and quiver," she ordered Yuri.

She was afraid to slacken tension on the leathers. The spirited black horses had caught the scent of blood in the air. Frightened, they pranced in the traces, tossing their heads and laying their ears flat against their heads.

"I can shoot!" Yuri said. "Let me—"

"Get the bow and give it to me before I toss you out like I did the driver."

Yuri did as he was told.

She grabbed the bow in one hand and passed the reins to the child. "Can you drive a chariot?"

"Watch me!"

"Keep the team moving," she shouted. "We don't want to make too easy a target."

The boy slapped the reins over the horses' backs. The blacks lunged ahead, running parallel to the steps. Roxanne fought to keep her balance on the swaying floorboards as she notched a feathered shaft and let it fly. The arrow missed the guardsman she was aiming for and struck a second in the buttocks. Yuri cheered.

Roxanne got off another shot before she was out of range of hitting anything in the moving vehicle. "Circle around!"

She decided that the boy's driving could use some technical refinements, but the chariot didn't turn over as they doubled back. Yuri's shouts goaded the team as he guided horses and chariot dangerously close to the confrontation on the stairs.

Roxanne saw Val dart from the cluster of defenders, carrying a Greek sword too unwieldy for him. He dodged an Egyptian marine and hacked at the legs of a soldier trading sword thrusts with a grizzled warrior Roxanne recognized as a veteran called Tiz. She looked for Kayan and spotted him—sword in one hand, curving Bactrian knife in the other—carving a circle of slashing death around him.

In that instant, Kayan looked over his left shoulder and saw Val. Kayan drove his sword through one Greek guard, twisted, and delivered a mighty sideways kick that tumbled his other opponent head over heels down the steps. With fierce determination, he fought his way past three Egyptians to reach Val.

"Slow down!" Roxanne commanded. Yuri wrapped both lines around his wrists and leaned backward, throwing all his weight against the horses' bits to hold them. This time, when she released her arrow, it pierced a Greek infantryman's cuirass and buried itself in his shoulder. The man fell to his knees, clutching the reed shaft.

One of the guards saw her, shouted the alarm, and charged down the steps, spear drawn back to throw at the closest horse. Roxanne held her shot, waiting until her aim was dead on. She released the arrow just as he began his cast. The arrow flew true. The arrowhead plunged into his throat, and his bronze-tipped spear clattered harmlessly down the steps.

Kayan had shoved Val behind him and was engaged in hand-to-hand combat with two of Ptolemy's city guards. Kayan wore no helmet or armor, but despite his size, Roxanne was shocked at the speed of his movements. He slashed and parried with the grace of a hunting cheetah, his untamed black mane of hair flying like a banner around him. Yet there was nothing wild about the precision of his swordplay as he kept his two enemy attackers at bay while defending his son and a wounded comrade.

"Steady!" Roxanne shouted to Yuri. She reached into the quiver for another arrow as he brought the team around. She found only one shaft remaining and left it. "Take the bow," she instructed the boy. "Give me the reins!"

Another two soldiers ran toward the struggle, but three of Ptolemy's original force had backed off. One man threw up his arms to spook her horses, but they were already in a state of panic and paid his shouts no heed. Roxanne widened her loop, driving the team across the square and guiding them to a spot near Alexander's shrine, where a groom waited, holding the bridles of two mounts.

"Can you ride?" she demanded of Yuri.

He shrieked with laughter.

"Take one of those!" she said. When she hauled the team up near the animals, the groom started backing away, pulling the horses after him.

Roxanne notched her remaining arrow and aimed it at the Egyptian's chest. "Do you want to die for your master?"

Yuri was off the back of the chariot and racing toward the sorrel. The groom dropped the reins on the cobblestones, waved at the animals to chase them off, and fled shrieking. Yuri grabbed the sorrel's trailing bridle leathers and reached for the gray's head, but the second horse shied away.

Roxanne watched, helpless. The horse was fifteen

hands, and Yuri was small and wearing a woman's skirts. She was afraid he would get tangled in the folds of linen and be unable to get up on the animal's back. And she feared that if he did manage to mount, the horse would be too much for him.

Yuri seized the sorrel's mane and climbed the gelding's leg as easily as a squirrel scampering up a tree. Once on the horse, he drove both heels in the animal's sides and went after the gray. When the two horses were side by side, the boy leaped from the sorrel onto the gray mare. The gray reared. The black wig slid off to be crushed under the mare's hooves, but Yuri stuck to her back like a burr.

Still holding the sorrel's reins in one hand, he wiggled far enough up on the gray's neck to get hold of her bridle. In two minutes, he was back at Roxanne's side, riding the gray horse, leading the sorrel, and grinning.

"I'll try to get your brother," she yelled as she finished tying the basket to the front of the chariot with a silk scarf. "Stay away from the fighting!"

Hoping the child would obey, she turned the team back toward the library stairs. More men were down, and the struggle had spread out. Some of the Greeks had backed off as if waiting for reinforcements. The onlookers had scattered: some had run into the public buildings and the tomb; others had retreated to the adjoining streets.

Yuri galloped past the chariot, and still leading the sorrel, he thundered across the square, whipping the horse and shrieking a war cry. When he reached the foot of the steps, he drove the horses up at a run, scattering guardsmen. "Val!" he yelled. "Val!"

Kayan broke away from the guard he was battling, seized one of his wounded men around the waist, and heaved him up onto the sorrel as easily as if he were a child. Val raced down the steps and vaulted up over the horse's rump to land behind the Bactrian warrior.

Kayan leaped onto the gray's back behind Yuri, and twisted around to cut down a charging Greek spearman. As the man fell, Kayan lifted Yuri and plopped him behind him on the mare. Yuri locked his arms around his father's waist. More Greeks backed away out of reach of Kayan's deadly sword blade.

An Egyptian guard darted forward in an attempt to tear Yuri off the horse, but another Bactrian spitted the man with a fallen Greek spear. The remaining barbarians regrouped and retreated down the stairs, flanked by the horses.

Roxanne was waiting at the bottom. "Here!" she shouted. "To me!"

Tiz leaped onto the chariot with a bleeding comrade over his shoulder. "Give me those reins!"

"Can you manage two?" Kayan shouted to Tiz. "Get rid of that basket!"

"No!" Roxanne cried. "I need it."

"Hand him over," Tiz roared. "If I can't get them out of here, there's no use in your trying."

Kayan dismounted long enough to move the injured warrior from the back of the sorrel to the chariot and to order Yuri up behind his brother Val. Roxanne was beginning to shake all over. It had all happened so fast that she hadn't had time to think. Now . . . now it seemed impossible for them to get away. From the left, a small group of Ptolemy's Greek guard formed ranks under an officer's command and trotted toward them.

Kayan seized her wrist. "You're coming with me."

"I—" she began. His eyes were fierce with battle madness.

"Quiet!" He tossed her up on the mare and mounted behind her. Tiz was already racing out of the plaza with the two boys in hot pursuit. Kayan slapped the gray's rump with the flat of his sword. He shoved her down on the horse's withers as a flight of arrows hissed over their heads, and then they were out of the plaza and fleeing for their lives down the avenue.

* * *

Coughing, Ptolemy surveyed the smoking ruins of Roxanne's apartments. Small fires still smoldered in two sections of the palace, but the damage had been contained, due to the immediate response of the well-disciplined soldiers. A captain had sent word to the king at the first sign of the emergency, and Ptolemy had ridden back from the execution site at Alexander's tomb to the palace and taken charge.

Hundreds of guards and servants had carried buckets of water from the artificial lake to throw on the flames, while others had blocked off corridors, removed furnishings, and torn away draperies and wall hangings that would give fuel to the fire. Much of the palace was stone, and the main areas were free-standing, joined only by covered passageways. The damage had been limited to less than ten percent of the palace.

"Where is she?" Ptolemy demanded of the chief eunuch. "Where is Lady Mayet? Was she injured? Has her body been carried to another spot?"

The eunuch fell to his knees in the warm ashes. The vizier and the officials who made up the king's party took several steps back, as if to distance themselves from the man's fate.

"No, Your Highness," the chief eunuch said. "None have seen her."

"Have you questioned her women?"

"Yes, yes," the man stammered. "But none . . . in the confusion of the fire . . . panicked . . . stupid girls . . ."

Ptolemy's grim expression turned hot with anger. "Find her or—"

"Your Majesty!" Two Greek guardsmen hurried toward the group around the king.

Ptolemy stopped and turned on them. "What is it? Have you word of the Lady Mayet?"

The taller of the two guards, a stocky Macedonian, nodded. "We saw her. She called for a chariot just before the fire broke out."

In twenty minutes, Ptolemy had the story, not just of Roxanne's ploy to leave the palace against his wishes, but of her later commandeering of the chariot and fleeing his guard. News of the struggle in the square came soon after.

"I want Kayan and the Lady Mayet captured alive," he ordered his commanders. "They must not get out of the city. Her weight in gold to the man who delivers her to me unharmed. Death to any who damages even her smallest finger. I want Kayan alive and fit to stand trial. The others are of no use to me. Find them or I'll strip you of your honors and find better men to fill your posts."

The alarm was late in spreading to the walls of Alexandria. No one tried to hinder their flight except for two city guards, but Tiz quickly discouraged them by lashing the chariot horses into a run and guiding the frenzied animals straight at the soldiers. The Egyptians leaped out of the way and flung curses after the chariot.

When they reached the shore of Mareotis, darkness was settling over the countryside. Kayan abandoned the chariot by dismantling it and heaving the wheels and parts into the lake. They had seized another small horse after the encounter with the guards. Yuri mounted the pony, while Val shared his mount with Bahman, who had lost a lot of blood from a wound in his shoulder but could still ride. The remaining man, Homji, was too badly injured to hold his balance on a horse. Tiz tied him across the sorrel's back, using strips of clothing ripped from Yuri's tunic.

Kayan still hadn't exchanged a single word with Roxanne, except for ordering her on his horse. Now he asked her if she wished to carry her precious basket or abandon it.

"I'll carry it," she replied. His manner was still cold, but there was no time to ask why. They could not be more than a hair's breadth from Ptolemy's justice, and the safety of their mountain kingdom lay half a world away.

Yuri took the chance to scrub off the remaining makeup and to rip off the women's clothing. He kept only enough linen to wrap around his waist in a loincloth, a garment dirty enough to pass as that of a farmer's son.

"Why are you doing that?" Val teased. "You make a good girl."

Yuri answered with an epithet fit only for a soldier's mess.

"How old is he?" Roxanne asked.

Kayan glanced at her with suspicion. "Seven. He's not yours."

"Your son?"

"Yes."

"Oh, you have a wife, then." She had the oddest sinking sensation in the pit of her stomach, as though she'd suddenly swallowed a rock. "I didn't know."

"It's been eight years since you've seen me," he replied, still with frosty disdain in his voice. "A lot has changed."

"I'm . . . I'm happy for you," she said.

"His mother's dead."

"Oh, I'm sorry." She drew a deep breath. "Val?" she asked hopefully. "Is he mine?"

"No, he's not. Both boys are my adopted sons. Both orphans."

"Brothers?"

"Brothers now."

"Where's my son? Is he alive? What have you done with him?"

"He's alive and well hidden. You'll have to trust me." Kayan motioned to the horses. "We don't have time for idle talk. Let's ride."

She touched his arm. "Maybe it would be safer for you if I didn't come. Ptolemy's pride will be wounded. He won't let me go. I may be putting the boys' lives in danger by—"

Kayan gestured to the sorrel, the animal's outline barely visible in the deepening night. Here and there, faint stars winked in the purple-black sky. "If you wanted to remain at Ptolemy's side, you should have thought of that before you killed his guards. All our heads are forfeit if we're caught." He cupped his hands to help her mount.

She swung up onto the gelding's back. "Is my father alive?"

"Yes, he is." He turned to the others. "Let's move. We need to reach the Nile if we're to have any chance of escaping the king's men."

"Kayan, what's wrong?" she asked quietly as he began leading the horse along the shoreline of the lake. "What have I done to anger you?"

"Zar and Izad both died at the Temple of Isis. Good men."

"I'm sorry. I didn't know them, but I'm sure they were." This was not the same Kayan who'd come to her at the Palace of the Blue Lotus, who'd proclaimed his love for her. What had happened to change that? The sick feeling in her stomach became nausea. "Are you blaming me for their deaths?"

"Did you lead Ptolemy's soldiers to the temple?"

The accusation made her speechless. "No," she protested. "I wouldn't—"

"Someone followed you to the temple last night, or there was an informer."

"It wasn't me. Even if I had chosen Ptolemy over you, why would I risk the children?"

"The children of a barbarian?"

"You told me I was as much a barbarian as you. I tell you, Kayan, I'm innocent."

"Only time will tell," he said.

"If I betrayed you, why would I fight with you at the library?"

"Guilt? A change of heart? What man knows a woman's mind?" he said brusquely. "Women are as deceptive as serpents."

"I didn't betray you," she protested. "No one followed me."

"Only time will tell."

Chapter 15

Two hours before dawn, as the fleeing group crossed a farm field, a band of Egyptians sprang up out of the darkness and surrounded them. Kayan and Tiz drew their swords and prepared to fight to the death, but a man jerked Yuri off his pony and pressed a knife to his throat.

"Drop your weapons and dismount. Get on your knees or the boy dies!"

"Don't hurt him," Kayan called in accented Egyptian.

"Two of our people are badly injured," Roxanne said. "They are tied on the horses." She caught a glimpse of Val's frightened face in the moonlight. Neither child made a sound.

"Tiz," Kayan said. The Bactrian's sword thudded against the earth.

"I'm dropping my bow," Roxanne said. She'd brought it, hoping to find arrows to fill the quiver.

The Egyptians moved out of the shadows, ten—no, more of them. The man who had threatened Yuri spoke to Roxanne.

"You are the Lady Mayet?"

"I am," she said. "But you don't want these people. They are—"

"I am called Debi," the Egyptian said. "You must come with us. You will not be harmed if you go quietly." By his voice and what she could see of his face, the man seemed to be middle-aged, but he moved and spoke with the authority of a military officer.

"Don't hurt the child," she said. "We'll do as you say." She slid off the horse and walked slowly to Yuri and took his hand. The boy's small hand gripped hers, but he made no sound.

"Don't try to escape," Debi said. "If you do, we will kill all of you."

"Where are you taking us?" Kayan demanded.

"Silence!" Debi ordered. His men tied Kayan's, Val's, and Tiz's hands behind their backs. "I will not bind you, lady, but do not be stupid."

"You have my word," she promised. "I won't do anything stupid."

"Make sure of it," Kayan warned in Parsi.

Debi struck Kayan on the shoulder. "I warned you not to speak."

"Please," Roxanne said in a low tone that was almost a whisper. "Give me leave to tend our wounded. They've lost much blood."

"We have a healer. He will see to them."

"Thank you." She wasn't certain how much Egyptian Kayan understood, so she translated for him.

Again, Debi repeated his command not to speak. The Egyptians led them across two more fields and down a lane to a walled compound.

When they reached a wooden gate wide enough to drive a four-horse team through, the leader called to someone inside. Two armed servants opened the door just long enough for the group to pass through the entranceway and then closed and locked it behind them. The twelve-foot mud-brick walls surrounded barns, sheds, storage buildings, servants' quarters, and a spacious farmhouse. Torches lighted the compound.

Roxanne could smell poultry and livestock. "This is a nobleman's farmstead," she said to Kayan. Dogs barked. Curious faces peered out to stare wide-eyed at the prisoners.

Their captors stopped before a windowless stone building. Debi produced a key, smashed a wax seal, and unlocked the door, which had been securely bolted. A man carrying a torch lifted it to illuminate the interior of what was obviously a granary. "Inside," the Egyptian said to Kayan. He motioned to Roxanne, who held Yuri to her side. "The boy too."

"I stay with them," she said, stooping and wrapping her arms around Yuri.

"No," Debi said. "The men and boys remain here. You are to come with me."

Two burly Egyptians dragged Tiz to the doorway and shoved him inside the granary. He cursed, staggered, and regained his balance.

Looking inside, Roxanne could see that the floor and walls were constructed of rough blocks of stone, set so tightly together that a knife blade could not pass between them. Two sleek cats stretched atop a waist-high pile of threshed barley. Rows of sealed clay jars, shoulder-high and wide enough to hold a grown man, filled the remainder of the structure.

One of the cats, a huge white male, arched his back and hissed at the Bactrian. Tiz hissed back. The cat fled through the open doorway into the yard.

Kayan strained at his bonds. "We remain together," he said. He lunged at the Egyptian captain, but two men grabbed his arms. Kayan threw them off and kept coming.

"Kayan, no!" Roxanne cried. Choking back tears, she felt each blow as if it were striking her flesh. Arms bound and outnumbered, Kayan had no chance to prevail over his captives. And what would she do if they killed him? There would be no chance of ever reaching her homeland or of laying eyes on her son.

Men threw themselves on top of him. A club flashed in the torchlight. Kayan groaned and fell to his knees. Val struggled against the man holding him.

Tiz dove headfirst through the doorway and butted one of the men attacking Kayan. In the midst of the confusion, Yuri twisted out of Roxanne's grip, dropped to the ground, and wiggled under the guards' legs to his father. "Leave him alone, you baboon turds!" he shouted, planting himself in front of Kayan and knotting his fists to defend him.

"Stop!" Debi shouted. He waved away his men, grabbed Yuri, and tossed him at Roxanne.

"No more," she warned the boy. "You will only put your father in greater danger." She wrapped her arms around him and pinned him against her.

Kayan raised his head, and Roxanne's heart lurched as she saw blood dripping from his temple, cheekbone, and mouth.

"The lady will be in no danger," the Egyptian said. "I give you my word."

"It's all right," Roxanne said to Kayan. "I'll go with him. Take care of Val and Yuri."

Once the four were locked inside the granary, the Egyptian relaxed. "Have no fear," he said to Roxanne. "My mistress is kind. I will call my wife Sheftu to tend you until morning. No one here will harm you."

"The injured," she said. "They've lost a lot of blood. If you would let me care for them . . ." Bahman had not even groaned when they'd carried him away. Homji was awake, but his face was pale and haggard. If their wounds weren't properly cared for, both would die in agony.

"They will be looked after," Debi said. "The healer is a good one. He served the Conqueror. If the men can be saved, they will be." He escorted her to the main house, where as promised he turned her over to his wife.

"Give me the children, at least," Roxanne begged. She

could imagine them shivering. Debi had ordered that Yuri's hands be bound as well, so that he couldn't untie the others. The boys were exhausted from traveling all night. They could easily take a fever.

Debi shook his head and smiled. "They are small scorpions. I fear their sting may be more than a man of my age should risk."

"The night is cold," Roxanne said. "If you will not allow the boys to stay with me, give them blankets against the chill."

"That I can do. But I warn you," he said, not unkindly. "Do not try to escape or to do harm to my mistress or any in this house. You will only bring disaster to all those accompanying you."

"It is me Ptolemy wants, not them," she said. Every instinct told her to flee this room, to do something—anything to rescue Kayan and the children. But reason told her that she must wait for the right moment to act.

Debi shook his head. "I have my orders, lady."

He left, leaving her with his shy young wife. The woman, Sheftu, also Egyptian, showed her to a bath and ordered a servant to bring food and drink.

"I don't understand," Roxanne said. "Why am I treated with the courtesy of a guest while my kinsmen and his followers are treated like common criminals?" She did not fear for her own life. Ptolemy wouldn't kill her; she was certain of that. But he had a merciless streak. She had no doubt that he would execute Kayan and both of his sons if she couldn't find a way to stop him.

Sheftu shook her head. "Make yourself comfortable. Bathe. Eat. Fresh clothing will be provided."

"I can't eat while the children remain hungry," Roxanne said. All she could think of was the four of them locked in that dark granary, waiting to learn their fate. "For mercy's sake, can't you see that they have water, at least?"

Instinct bade her to inspect the room she'd been welcomed into. It was plain but comfortable with a narrow bed, two stools, a high-backed chair with a leather seat, a table, and a sunken bath. The linens were spotless, the white walls painted in the Egyptian fashion with scenes of the Nile marsh. Woven reed mats covered the floor, and in a basket in one corner a white cat nursed three kittens.

"I will ask my husband to send food to the children," Sheftu agreed. "My mistress would not wish them to suffer until she has passed judgment."

"But who is your mistress?"

The woman shook her head. "I can answer no more of your questions. You must be patient. All I can tell you is that my mistress is a good woman and a loyal subject of the great lion of Egypt, His Majesty the King, as are all under this roof."

Dawn embraced the land of Kemet, washing over the rich green-brown waters of the Nile, glinting off the weapons of Ptolemy's soldiers, and warming the faces of the slaves already at work in the fields.

"My mistress will see you now," Sheftu said as she entered the room. "She has just completed her morning prayers and asks that you join her for breakfast."

Roxanne followed her down a passageway and into a room much like the one where she'd spent the remainder of the night. The wall paintings here were obviously the work of a skilled artist and told the legend of Isis's search for her murdered husband. The chamber floor was covered with brightly colored tile in a rainbow pattern, warm beneath her feet. A woven cage, suspended from the ceiling, held two birds.

On a stool by the window sat a Greek noblewoman with gray hair. She smiled at Roxanne and continued stroking the gray cat curled in her lap. "Lady Mayet." She rose and indicated a chair. "Welcome to my home."

"Thank you. I'm afraid I don't . . ." A stab of panic

knifed through Roxanne. Hadn't she regained all her memory? She would have sworn she'd never laid eyes on this woman before.

"Forgive me; I am Lady Alyssa, widow to Boreas and mother of Argo." She waited, as if those names should mean something.

"Oh, Argo's mother," Roxanne said. "Hesper is your daughter-in-law." She felt as though her heart had plummeted to the pit of her stomach. "Hesper speaks well of you." But what had Hesper said? Roxanne scrambled to recall the few times that her friend had mentioned her husband's noble mother. Argo was fiercely loyal to Ptolemy. Did that mean that his mother felt the same? Had they avoided the marshy wetland to fall even deeper into danger at Lady Alyssa's hands?

"I have never had the honor of meeting you," Lady Alyssa said. She pushed the cat off her lap and gestured to a slave. The girl brought a basin of water, soap, and clean linen for her mistress to dry her hands. The older woman washed and patted each finger carefully. "I fear I suffer from the affliction of the aged," she said. "My joints are not what they once were."

Roxanne noticed the wool spindle in a basket at the woman's feet and remembered that few Greek noblewomen bothered to learn to read or became involved with politics, concentrating instead on domestic matters. She doubted that this was true of Lady Alyssa because papyrus, ink, and a writing instrument lay on the table, along with a half-written list or letter. The woman's eyes were sharp, missing nothing, and the lines around her mouth made her appear kind rather than dour.

The question was, could she trust Lady Alyssa? Not knowing what else to do, she spoke frankly. "I am not the Lady Mayet."

"No, I didn't suppose you were." She put a finger to her lips as the slave girl returned with fresh water for Roxanne to wash. "I hope you don't dislike cats," she continued. "I'm afraid that I have quite a few of them."

"I am fond of all animals," Roxanne answered.

"So few of those newly come from the Greek states like them," Lady Alyssa said. "I think they're frightened of them, but they are both loving and useful. I can't think how much of our flour and grain would be lost to rodents if it weren't for my cats. One even killed a poisonous snake during the flooding of the Nile last summer. It had crept into the kitchen and terrified the cook."

More servants appeared with dates, melon, hot bread, and slices of lamb. "Please help yourself," Lady Alyssa said. "If you want anything else, I can have my servants prepare—"

"No, this is wonderful," Roxanne offered. "But my cousin and his sons . . . his men . . ."

"No one goes hungry under my roof," Lady Alyssa admonished softly. "Although that lion of a man has terrified my security troops. They feared to open the door without archers to protect them. Debi ordered the youngest child untied so that he might help the others eat. And my cook has cut the head off a duck to make a soup for the injured men."

"Could I see them? Bandage their wounds?"

"My healer has already done so. I believe he washed the injuries with vinegar and strong wine. One man, the older, was awake and able to drink a mug of beer."

"Thank you again." The servants had left them alone. "I must be honest with you," Roxanne said. "We endanger your household by being within these walls. King Ptolemy must be searching for me."

"I know that well enough. My son sent a messenger by boat just after sunset last night, warning me that Bactrian bandits had committed murder and fled the city with the Lady Mayet." She chuckled. "You appear to be well for a woman so badly treated."

"I told you that I am not Mayet. The king lies. I am Roxanne of Bactria and Sogdiana. Prince Kayan is my cousin. He has risked his life and that of his sons to find me and take me home."

"You claim to be the Princess Roxanne, wife to the Conqueror?"

"I do." She took a deep breath. "I know this sounds too strange to be the truth, but—"

"Tell me all. I am an old woman and seldom have anything to pique my interest, other than my son and his family."

"But where shall I begin?"

Lady Alyssa smiled. "I will not force you to relate the tale of your journey to India with the great Alexander. Start, instead, with what I know, that you and your son, Alexander IV, were held prisoner in a cave in Macedon for many years."

"Yes, seven years." She told her first lie. "Alexander's son died in that cave. He was always a sickly child, and . . ." The words spilled out, and the lady listened as Roxanne related all that had happened, her near-death and awakening here in Egypt without memory of who she was. She told everything, other than the exact relationship she and Ptolemy had shared and the details of the struggle at Alexander's tomb.

"So you see," Roxanne concluded. "If Ptolemy finds us . . ."

"Your lives are forfeit." Lady Alyssa took a sip of her wine and nibbled at the bread. "I must think on this matter," she said. "What to do with you?" She shook her head. "My heart goes out to you, but I must think of my son and grandson, and of Hesper, who has been a daughter to me as much as any of the poor, cold infants that came from my body."

"I understand," Roxanne said. "As I must think of my kinsman and his two children. The boys did not ask to come to Egypt, but they will suffer as much as Prince Kayan."

"You must give me time. This is too serious to decide on

a whim. There are many factors to consider, not the least of which is that, being old, I enjoy my comforts and have no wish to end my life as a slave toiling in the barley fields." She stood. "Meanwhile, I ask you to give me your word on whatever god you worship that you will do no harm to me or to mine within these walls. You must promise to make no attempt to free your men or to escape, yourself."

"If I can't?"

"Then you will be imprisoned as well." She shrugged. "I could not in good conscience lock you in the granary with them, but my steward assures me that we have other locations just as secure."

"May I see to my cousin's welfare?"

"If you give your word."

Roxanne nodded. She put her hands between Lady Alyssa's and swore the oath. "In the name of the holy light," she murmured, "I do so promise."

Roxanne went first to where Homji and Bahman were being treated. She examined their wounds and felt their heads for fever. Both were too warm, but it was to be expected. They were strong, and if evil humors did not develop and neither was taken with lockjaw—a mysterious and always fatal condition that often followed puncture wounds—she felt that they would recover fully. Whether they recovered only to be executed remained to be seen.

Following the customs of her people, she washed her hands three times in a strong vinegar solution and offered a prayer to the Lord of Light to dispel any power of darkness or jinni before she asked a servant to lead her to Kayan and the boys.

When the door to the granary was opened, Roxanne found that both Tiz and Kayan wore slave collars chained to the overhead rafters. Each man's hands were manacled together, but their legs were free, and there was enough slack in the chain to permit them to lie down. The boys had no collars, but each wore heavy leg manacles. Val sat with his head in Kayan's lap, while Yuri lay on his belly attempting to coax the cat to come to him. A single oil lamp hung near the door. The light it produced was feeble, but it was enough to keep the prisoners from total darkness.

Relief made Roxanne's knees weak. Kayan's right eye was swollen almost closed, and a gash ran through the brow above it. His lower lip was cracked, and several places on his head were encrusted with dried blood. Purple bruises covered his right arm, and his knuckles were skinned, but the one brown eye that met her gaze was clear and undimmed by fever.

"Are the boys well?" she asked.

Her heartbeat was strangely rapid. She cared desperately for the children, but for her cousin she felt more. They had been close since she was smaller than Yuri. Astrologers had once predicted that the stars decreed they should wed. He had been her friend—more than a friend, but never a brother. Once, she had fancied that she loved him as a woman loves a man, but now she was only confused. She had given herself body and soul to Alexander, and the feelings she felt for Kayan had changed.

Or had they?

She pushed away the sudden awkwardness she felt in his presence and went to him. "Is Val ill?" she asked.

Kayan nodded. "When we fought Ptolemy's soldiers in the square, a spear point nicked his hip. It is not a mortal wound, but he has lost blood."

"Val, why didn't you tell me?" she demanded. She put the back of her palm to the boy's forehead. "You're fevered." She glanced up into Kayan's face and read the concern in his expression.

The boy opened his eyes. Immediately she saw the yellow cast there, proof that what she feared most was true.

"Have Ptolemy's soldiers come yet?" Kayan asked.

She shook her head. "May I look?" she asked Val.

He winced as she pushed down his clothing enough to see the angry flesh that puckered around a four-inch cut. Val bit his lip as she gently fingered the injury.

"Has he taken water?" she asked.

"Little," Kayan replied. "He says he isn't thirsty."

"Worse. This needs to be treated immediately." She touched the child's cheek. "Be brave a little longer," she said. "I'll not leave you here."

"I stay with Kayan," he said.

"If you would be a warrior like your father, you must learn the wisdom of picking your battles," she said. "I will make them let me bring you into the house so that I can wash this and apply a healing poultice. You'll have to trust me."

"No," Val replied stubbornly. "I stay with my father and brother."

Roxanne looked at Kayan. "Speak to him," she urged. "Make him see that he must leave you long enough for me to tend his wound. Otherwise . . ."

"Do as the princess bids you, Val," Kayan said.

Tears welled in the child's eyes.

Roxanne leaned close and whispered. "A soldier must learn to follow orders."

"Keep him close," Kayan warned. "If harm comes to him, it will fall on your head."

"I will do what I can," she promised. "But you must pray for him, Cousin."

The dark eyes grew hard. "I have seen too much evil to believe in the power of God. If He exists, I fear my prayers would only anger Him."

Chapter 16

Lady Alyssa came to the granary, took one look at Val, and gave the order for Debi to release them all. "Take the boy to the Hermes room, at once. How could you leave him here in this condition? What kind of woman do you think I am to so mistreat a child?"

"Mistress, you can't mean for me to—"

"All of them." Lady Alyssa glanced at Roxanne and switched from Egyptian to Greek. "I assume you have some influence over your kinsman?" She turned to Kayan. "You'll not murder us all in our beds, will you?"

"No, lady, I can assure you that we won't," Kayan said in the same language. "But why—"

"We'll talk later. This child—"

"His name is Val," Kayan said.

"Young Val needs medical attention and a bath." Lady Alyssa glared at two of her servants. "You and you, what are you waiting for? Carry—"

"He is my son. I'll carry him."

"As you please." The woman clapped her hands. "Debi! Where are the keys?" She stooped and called to the cat that

Yuri had been attempting to catch. "There you are, Jarha." The tom leaped into her arms and rubbed his narrow head against her cheek.

Debi unlocked the collar that held Kayan. Once Val was free of his bonds, Kayan lifted the boy in his arms. He looked at Tiz and then glanced at Roxanne.

She saw at once that Kayan needed her to ensure that Tiz's needs were met. Turning to Lady Alyssa, she smiled and said, "My cousin's lieutenant needs aid as well. May I take him to the others?"

The Greek matron regarded the sinewy Bactrian warily. "Are you certain he's housebroken?"

Roxanne chuckled. One-eyed, lean, and battle-scarred, Tiz's roguish appearance was more than enough to make any gentle lady nervous. "I give you my word that your home will be safe. Tiz is many things, but not a thief."

"Indeed I am not," Tiz said, grinning wolfishly and offering his most courtly salute.

Roxanne didn't add that the line between thief and freedom fighter was a thin one at best. Even battered, sleep-deprived, and hungry, she guessed that Tiz with a sword in his callused hand could have easily bested any three of Lady Alyssa's young mercenaries.

She hadn't known Tiz well before yesterday, but she knew what kind of men Bactria and Sogdiana produced. Such heroes had marched with her father and held off the might of Alexander's Macedonians. In two years, the Conqueror had swept across mighty Persia, defeating the greatest army the world had ever known. But it had taken Alexander another two hard-fought years to defeat Oxyartes and his mountain-bred warriors.

It said much of her cousin Kayan that a stalwart such as Tiz would pledge him his loyalty. Kayan was noble born, but he had won the right to lead such men in hand-to-hand combat in a hundred nameless battles. Such respect and unflinching allegiance were offered only to a commander fiercer and more courageous than those who followed him.

"It's not my valuables I'm worried about so much as the morals of my maidservants," Lady Alyssa said. "Your man has the look of a rogue."

"That he is," Kayan assured her, "but an honorable rogue."

"Show him where his two comrades are," Lady Alyssa said to Roxanne. "Tell my servants that he is to receive the best care. And please ask my healer to come at once to tend to the boy." Her eyes narrowed. "But if Tiz causes any trouble, it will go hard with all of you." She motioned to a dark-skinned youth. "Take them to the Hermes room."

"Yes, mistress." He pushed an errant lock of dusty yellow hair out of his eyes.

"And you, boy," Lady Alyssa said to Yuri. "You look as though you could do with a bath and something to eat."

Yuri looked at his father.

"Thank you, lady," Kayan said. "That would be most welcome." With Val in his arms, he followed the servant toward the manor house.

"You seem to be fond of cats, young man," Lady Alyssa said brusquely. "Would you like to see our new litter of kittens?"

Yuri nodded solemnly. "I would," he replied with a final glance at his father and brother. "I have a cat at home, but it's bigger than these, and my grandfather won't let me keep it in my room anymore."

"Oh?" Lady Alyssa answered.

"No, and it's most unfair," Yuri complained. "Kerbadji wouldn't have eaten the cook's goat if it hadn't wandered into the yard and bleated so loudly that it gave him a headache."

"Your cat ate a goat?" The lady chuckled. "It must be a large cat indeed."

"Yes," Yuri agreed as they entered the house. "Grandfather thinks Kerbadji will be very big—even for a snow leopard."

Roxanne led Tiz across the farmyard, through a flock of scratching and strutting chickens, and past an attractive black-haired woman milking a goat. Despite his injuries, Tiz swiveled his head to wink at her. The servant blushed and giggled and turned her face away.

"Remember what Lady Alyssa said," Roxanne warned. "We're her guests, and I expect you to behave in a manner I would approve of."

"I'll be on my best behavior."

She grimaced. "Why does that fail to reassure me?" She folded her arms and planted herself in front of him. "I mean what I say, Tiz. Do nothing that will cause the lady to turn us over to Ptolemy's troops."

Tiz's shrugged. "And what makes you so certain she won't anyway?"

"Call it woman's intuition. I don't know why she'd endanger herself and her family for us, but I have the feeling that we can trust her."

"Trust her?" Kayan said a quarter hour later when Roxanne joined him at Val's bedside. "Lady Alyssa told me that she is the mother of one of the king's officers. We're safe here only as long as it takes for Ptolemy's soldiers to get here."

Roxanne shook her head. "I don't think so." She looked down at Val and felt his forehead again. "His fever isn't dropping. If anything, he's hotter than he was before."

"You think I don't realize that?" He'd undressed Val and used water and soap to bathe him. The healer had dressed the wound on the boy's side with malachite and anointed it with honey.

"You should try to get him to drink," Roxanne said as she stroked Val's damp hair.

"He choked on what I tried to give him."

She summoned a slave and requested clean water and a sponge. When a maid brought it, Roxanne sponged Val's cheeks and forehead in an attempt to cool his fever. An overhead fan of woven reed, powered by another slave outside in the corridor, kept the high-ceilinged room from turning into a bake oven as the Egyptian sun moved higher in the sky.

"We're trapped here," Kayan said. "Val's in no condition to be moved. Neither are Homji or Bahman." His conscience plagued him over his decision to bring the boys. It was clear now that they would have been in far less danger in Oxyartes's care. It was bad enough to lose Zar, Izad, Jandel, and Ram. If either of his sons came to harm, he'd never be able to forgive himself.

Roxanne eyed him skeptically. "I've seen you looking better, too."

He frowned. "A few bruises, a scratch or two. Nothing that would keep me from fighting our way out of here if—"

"A few scratches that need stitching. And an eye you can barely see out of. You're in sore need of a bath, too. There's a bathing pool in my room. I think you should make use of it."

He scowled at her. "And leave Val alone?" He felt helpless. He could cut out an arrow, dress a battle wound, or rough-set a broken bone, but when it came to a child's illness, he was useless. He could do nothing more than stand here and watch as his son grew sicker.

"I can stay here with Val," Roxanne said. "My chamber is only across the passageway. What good will you do your son—what good will you do any of us if your injuries—"

"What need to preen myself for execution?" Normally he prided himself in keeping clean, even while on campaign. He didn't need her to tell him that he was dirty or that his eye was swollen shut. By Ahriman's bowels! Could she not see that the chances were growing slimmer by the hour that any of them would survive Ptolemy's wrath?

She laid a restraining hand on his upper arm.

Her touch sent a jolt of heat through him. He brushed her away, angry that he could not control his emotions when he was near her. Furious with himself that even now while his son lay critically ill he couldn't keep from devouring her with his eyes and inhaling her scent. . . . from thinking what it would be like to take her to his bed.

He swallowed, attempting to dissolve the thickness in his throat. Damn her for her feminine wiles. He'd known her since she was a child, ridden and fished with her, eaten from the same bowl, and camped side by side on snow-capped mountains where wolves and Scythians prowled. He'd watched her be given in marriage to a foreign conqueror and had trailed her across Persia and India. He'd pledged to her his sword and his undying love. And she had returned his devotion by giving herself to Alexander's brother at the first opportunity.

"What's wrong with you?" she asked.

He clenched his jaw and spoke harshly to cover his pain. "Val lies gravely ill, and my men who died at Isis's temple and in the square in front of the Conqueror's tomb were as close to me as brothers. I brought them to Egypt. Their deaths and the fate of my son are on my head."

"But you blame me, as well."

He shrugged. "Someone betrayed us at the Temple of Isis."

"Someone? Must it be someone? Couldn't your men have been followed? Couldn't you have been?" She sniffed. "Why must a man always attempt to place fault? Ptolemy was suspicious of you. He probably had his spies watching you from the moment you set foot in Alexandria."

The sarcasm in her voice fueled his ire. "You think I'm too clumsy to move through city streets without being followed?"

"You have no qualms in judging me stupid enough not to keep from being trailed."

"You've changed." He shook his head impatiently. "You're not the woman I knew."

"I've changed? And you think you haven't? It's been eight years. You've grown your hair long, and it's turned as dark as a Scythian's. And you're . . . bigger. You've got new scars. And you're foul-tempered. You never were before. Where is the carefree cousin who trusted me to lower him down a cliff face to steal a fledgling from a hawk's nest? Or the rascal who helped me drag a wild lion cub into my father's throne room?"

"As you say, eight years is a long time." She was standing far too close, and her Egyptian tunic left nothing to his imagination. He could see the curve of her breasts and the deep pink of her nipples through the sheer linen. The pleated skirt was so transparent that she might have been wearing nothing. He tried to avert his eyes, but it was impossible not to seek out the shadow of auburn curls at the apex of her thighs.

"You were never this bitter," she said. "Not even when I was forced to marry Alexander."

This wasn't the way it was supposed to be. All those years of pining for her—of wishing she were in his arms. How could he have forgotten that she could block his best assault with words? That she could spur his fury quicker than any other person on the face of the earth?

Just once, why couldn't Roxanne be like other women? Soft and clinging, sweet. The room was suddenly too small and confining. He wanted to leap on the back of a horse and ride until sweat poured from his skin and his muscles ached. But he couldn't. He had to stay here—tantalizingly close to her without being able to take what he wanted most.

"You were my sanctuary," she continued, paring away at him with a blade sharper than obsidian. "I knew that no matter what happened, I could depend on you . . . on your love."

An ugly sound rose from his throat. "First Alexander, then Ptolemy. Maybe I got tired of waiting for you to—"

Her temper flared. She drew back her hand to smack him, but he caught her wrist. "Let me go!"

He held her.

Gold flames flashed in the depths of her nutmeg-brown eyes. For a long moment, their gazes clashed, and then she wavered. "I'm sorry," she murmured. "I shouldn't have—"

"No, you shouldn't."

Tears blurred her vision and she dashed them away. "You don't understand. I didn't know who I was. I remembered nothing. Not Alexander, not my child."

"And not me?" He lowered his arm, still careful not to hurt her, moving her hand behind her and drawing her closer.

"I died. Somehow I died and came back to life."

He grunted. "Did you come to believe the Conqueror's madness? That you're immortal as he was? You're lively for a dead woman. You walk and breathe and—"

"Stop it," she cried. "You can't understand what it was like. Ptolemy was my only friend. He—"

"You lost none of your beauty in those eight years of imprisonment," Kayan said, forcing her even closer. "If anything, you've become more radiant, more desirable." Her lips were full and moist. He could almost taste them.

"You mock me."

"Do I, Roxanne? How is that possible? You, the Little Star, the most beautiful woman in all of Persia, who could grasp a king by the stones and bend him to your bidding?"

"Ptolemy would have made me his queen," she said. "I chose to come with you instead. I chose to return to my people—to my son."

"Queen of Egypt. It must have been tempting. Especially since your Macedonian never crowned you."

"I was tempted," she admitted. "For a little while. But then I realized that I could never respect Ptolemy after he lied to me, convinced me that I was someone else."

"Ptolemy was more than a friend." Even as Kayan spoke the words, he knew that Roxanne hadn't failed him. *He'd* failed *her*. All those years, he should have found a way to go to Macedonia and release her from Olympias's prison. If he had, Ptolemy would never have taken what should have been his alone. "Did he force you—or did you go to him willingly?"

"So this is what you're angry about? That I shared my bed with him?"

"You were always passionate. I could hardly expect you to wait for me." He lowered his head, released her wrist, and kissed her.

For the space of a heartbeat, her mouth trembled beneath his and he tasted her soft sweetness. Then she took a step back and hit him, not with the flat of her hand but with her fist. Her knuckles slammed against his jaw, catching his tongue between his teeth and knocking his head back so hard he saw stars. He tasted blood.

"You're no different from Ptolemy! You think I'm someone to be used at your will." She faced him boldly, chin up, shoulders stiff, and eyes flashing defiance. "I'm a free woman, Kayan. My husband is dead and in his grave. By our laws and custom, who I share my favors with is no one's affair but my own."

He took a step back. "I'm sorry," he said. "I was wrong to accuse you." He'd been wrong. She hadn't changed. This was exactly the Roxanne he remembered—a princess royal—strong enough to stand up to the Conqueror, a woman who would die before backing down. He swore softly and turned away as pain knifed through his gut.

He'd lost her twice, and now, after he'd believed her dead, he'd been given another chance. But instead of embracing that gift, he was allowing his own jealousy to divide them again. "I want you," he whispered hoarsely, "more than I want to live. But not by force. I want you to come to me, to love me as I've loved you for half my life."

"Have you heard a word I said?" she asked him. "I didn't remember anything or anyone when I woke up in Alexandria. I didn't even know my own name."

"And now that you do know? What now? Do you feel anything for me?"

She covered her face with her hands. "Things are happening too fast. I need time to make peace with myself . . . with my memories of Alexander. How can I trust my judgment? I remember what you and I had. How I begged my father to let us marry. I remember how much you've always meant to me. But I had to learn to deny that love to save your life. I had to think of you as a brother, Kayan."

"I was never your brother," he retorted hotly.

"No, you weren't." She drew in a deep, shuddering breath. "We need each other more than ever. If we don't trust each other, depend on each other, we have no chance of getting out of Egypt alive. I have no chance of ever seeing my son again—Alexander's son."

"No," he agreed. "We don't." He opened his arms. "Truce?"

She went into them and laid her head against his chest. He held her lightly, savoring the feeling of her in his arms, wanting more but fearing her reaction.

"I've missed you," she said. "More than anyone. All those years in that underground prison, without sunshine, without seeing the sky, I survived because I knew that somewhere you were seeing clouds and rain and stars. Do you remember how we used to lie awake half the night staring at the sky? You made up tales about the constellations for me. Do you remember?"

He nodded, too full of emotion to speak.

"I could depend on you to keep your promise. I knew that you would keep my son safe and make of him a prince that his father would be proud of."

"That *you* would be proud of," he answered. "He is."

"He's there, waiting for me, at home, my little Alexander? You swear it?"

He was tempted to tell her the truth, but he couldn't. If she failed him, if she weakened and betrayed them to Ptolemy, everything they'd done all these years would be for nothing. "He and your father are close," he said. "Soraya adores him. She spoils all my sons, but I think he holds her heart."

"Soraya is well, then?"

"A little plumper, but well. She makes your father happy."

"It was a good day when they wed." She turned in his arms and touched his jaw.

He winced. "You still pack a punch for a girl."

"You deserved it—and worse. I've spent too long being manhandled. First Alexander, then Ptolemy. I'll not have it from the men I love any longer."

He tried to speak lightly, but the catch in his voice betrayed him. "So you admit that you love me?"

"Perhaps, a little," she said. "But it does not mean that I feel for you as I did for Alexander. Or that I want to marry you."

"Have I asked you?"

She shook her head and gave him a tremulous smile. "Not lately, but I haven't wanted you to. I meant it when I said I need time. Time to sort out my feelings. Can you do that? Can you give me time?"

"What choice do I have?"

"It would be wrong if I became your wife and couldn't give you what you deserve. A wife who will cling to you and love you more than anyone in the world. I don't know if I feel that way. I don't know if I've stopped loving Alexander. I'm confused, Kayan. In time, perhaps I can figure out what I want. If we can be friends again—"

He caught her hand in his. This time he made no attempt to hold her, only squeezed her hand and let her go. "So long as you don't expect me to call you sister."

She chuckled. "This is Egypt. Brothers and sisters here are said to be more than kin—at least those that claim the throne."

He scowled. "And they call *us* barbarians."

Roxanne dipped the sponge in water and wiped Val's face again. "He's strong," she said. "He'll fight this off."

"He has to," Kayan said. How had he forgotten his son so easily? "I was a fool to bring the boys with me. But I knew the journey was long. Both boys lost their mothers when they were small. I'm all they have. And our homeland is no longer the secure place it was for a child."

"Surely my father—"

"You must realize what dangers the Twin Kingdoms face," he said. "Cassander's troops have outposts on our borders. The Greek soldiers make regular forays into our territory. Within, at least three powerful warlords strive to unseat your father and seize power. We must deal with traitors as well as attacks from the Scythians and other steppe tribes."

"When did this happen? Bactria and Sogdiana were secure when—"

"When the Conqueror lived," he said. "But after his death, every handful of earth that he seized became a prize to be claimed by the strongest man. Under your father's banner, we drove the Greeks back valley by valley. But if we weaken, they will sweep over our lands again. The cities will fall, the rich farm fields will be graveyards once more, and another generation of children will feel the yoke of slavery."

"So that's why you couldn't come for me," she said. "I waited and hoped." She shook her head. "I knew it was impossible, but still I—"

"I wanted to come. It would have been easier to come and die at the hands of the Greeks than to feel I'd abandoned you. But your father convinced me that it would be a useless sacrifice—that I'd accomplish nothing but my own death and yours. Was I wrong not to come?"

"No," she admitted. "Not wrong."

"I've paid for that decision, night after night. I've called myself a coward a hundred times."

"You are no coward," she said. "You are the bravest man I've ever known."

"Braver than your Macedonian Conqueror?"

She shook her head. "It wasn't the same for Alexander. He believed he was immortal, and I'm not convinced he wasn't right. For all I know, he may have truly been the son of his Greek god Apollo. No, Alexander wasn't brave. Death held no reality for him. He may not even have been sane." She shrugged. "Your bravery is real, Kayan, the courage of a king, the courage to do what must be done for your people."

"So you tell me that I am the better man but your heart belongs to him?"

She sighed. "I'm telling you I don't know what I feel. I'm trying to give you honesty, something I never gave Alexander."

His gut clenched. "I find your truth poor compensation."

"Is he better?" Yuri called.

Kayan turned to see the child in the doorway and felt relief that he'd interrupted what was quickly becoming a quagmire of words with Roxanne.

"Why is Val sleeping?" Yuri demanded. "I had eggs and figs and bread. I saved him some honeyed figs." He held out his hand to reveal two pieces of plump fruit. "The lady showed me her kittens, too."

Kayan couldn't help smiling. Bathed and wearing a fresh linen kilt, Yuri looked three shades lighter. "No one would take you for a nomad bandit now," he said.

"I hope you were on your best behavior," Roxanne said.

"He was." Lady Alyssa entered the room. "How is Val?"

"Not good," Roxanne said.

"My healer is skilled, but he is no miracle worker. For that we must wait on the pleasure of the gods." Her gaze met Roxanne's. "I think perhaps we should have that talk now." She waved to a slave who carried Roxanne's basket and set it down on the table. "I believe this is yours," Lady Alyssa said.

"Yes, it is."

Kayan looked from one woman to the other. He'd supposed that the basket contained Roxanne's personal belongings, and he'd been annoyed with her when she refused to leave it behind as they fled. Now he wondered if he'd been hasty.

"Everything is there," the lady said. "Doubtless you'll need every item if you are to return to your far-off home." She paused, and when Roxanne made no reply, she continued. "Would you care to walk with me?"

"Whatever you have to say, you can say it in front of my kinsman. I have no secrets from him or from his sons."

"Very well." Lady Alyssa dismissed the two serving girls who'd followed her into the room. "As I told you before, I needed to think of the best course to follow. I am a loyal subject of King Ptolemy, as are my son and daughter-in-law."

Kayan nodded. "I understand."

"My late husband Boreas was a commander of infantry under the great king, Alexander III. Did you know him, by chance?"

Kayan shook his head. "No, lady, I didn't."

"Nor I," Roxanne said.

"Boreas loved him, not as some men love other men, but as his rightful liege. I don't believe he was ever the same after the king died." She walked to Roxanne and took her hands. "My husband was present on the day that a boy was brought to be judged for stealing a sword. The boy's name was Jason. Do you remember that day, Princess?"

Roxanne nodded. "I do."

"The king would have ordered Jason's hand to be severed, but you interfered."

"Yes," Roxanne said. "Jason wasn't a thief. He was a child who wanted to be a soldier. He thought that if he learned to use a sword, he could join Alexander's army."

"Boreas said that you fell on your knees and begged the king for mercy for Jason and for his young sister. You asked that King Alexander make Jason a royal page and that a family be found to foster Jason's young sister. They were orphans, and without his hand, Jason would not have survived."

"And neither would the little girl," Roxanne said.

"The king was furious, but you won. Jason went into service, and the girl Hesper was placed in the household of one of Alexander's Companions."

Roxanne smiled. "Yes, a good man by the name of Julian."

"My daughter-in-law Hesper was that homeless child. Her brother was the boy you saved. Hesper owes you not only her brother's life but her own, and through her, my grandchildren's lives."

"Tragically, Jason died later," Roxanne said.

"Yes, but he died honorably, not as a thief. And Hesper lived to grow up and marry my son. She acknowledges the debt she owes you."

"She owes me nothing," Roxanne replied. "What I did, I did because—"

"Because it was right," Lady Alyssa finished. "As it is right that I give you and your kinsman shelter in my home. Whatever wrong you have done King Ptolemy is not mine to judge. For the sake of Hesper, I will do all that I can to help you."

"The cost, lady," Kayan warned, "could be very high."

"Ah," she said. "But what price can be put on honor?" She smiled. "I am old-fashioned. My son would say that I am too soft-hearted. But this I know: My people are loyal to me, not to Pharaoh. Remain here until the boy is better. When he can safely travel, I will help you to reach the Nile."

"Thank you," Kayan said.

"If I do this, you must be certain that you wish to take the risk, Princess Roxanne," Lady Alyssa said. "If you return to King Ptolemy, he may spare your life. In time, you may even return to his favor. Are you sure you wish to remain here with these barbarians?"

Roxanne reached for Kayan's hand. This time, she clasped his fingers in hers and gripped them tightly. "Yes," she said. "Whatever comes, we will face it together."

"Then it's settled," the lady replied, as simply as if she'd decided the menu for the afternoon meal. "Consider yourselves under my protection. And may Hera keep you."

"There is no way that I can return your kindness," Kayan said.

"Yes, there is," Lady Alyssa replied. "You can avail yourself of a bath. If you're going to be a member of my household, I insist that you maintain a decent standard of cleanliness."

"That means you have to wash," Yuri said.

"I know what it means," his father said.

"I agree," Roxanne said. "Lady Alyssa, if you will do us another favor and sit by Val for a short time, I will show Prince Kayan to the bathing pool and personally see that he follows your command to the letter."

Chapter 17

An hour later, Kayan, clad only in a loincloth, waded into the bathing pool in Roxanne's chamber. Egyptian slave girls, arms laden with sponges, linen towels, perfumed oils, and a crock of lime-scented cleaning cream, stared and giggled. An elderly blind man with milk-white eyes and hair played a kithara, and a youth from the kitchen waited with a tray of roasted camel meat, fruit, cheese, and rounds of flat bread baked with sesame seeds and honey. Another lad carried an elaborate Greek wine cup sculpted in the form of a horse's head.

Kayan frowned. "Am I to bathe or take part in a performance?"

Roxanne cleared her throat to keep from laughing at him and waved all the servants except the musician from the room. "Leave the wine and food," she commanded.

Shedding her long pleated tunic and sandals, she pinned up her hair. Wearing nothing but her linen under-shift, earrings, and a necklace of golden cowry shells, she joined Kayan in the pool.

"I don't need your help," he said. "I've been washing myself since I was weaned."

"You fuss like an old woman," she chided him gently.

Kayan's mouth tightened.

"In my father's house I would do as much for any nobleman, especially one who was wounded and in need of medical care."

"You can hardly call these scratches wounds."

Scooping a little of the cream from the container, Roxanne brushed aside Kayan's hair and began to scrub his shoulders and back. He was bronzed by the sun and wind and scarred by old battle injuries, but beneath the skin he was all hard muscle and bone. She told herself that she would remain detached, treating him as she'd treat any other man who needed her healing touch. Still, she couldn't stop the flutter of excitement that made her just a little breathless as she stroked him.

Kayan groaned with pleasure. "You may have your uses after all," he admitted. He ducked his head under the water, and took some of the cream to shampoo his thick, long hair.

"Let me," she said. Kayan had always had beautiful, thick hair, but it had darkened to the black of a raven's wing in the years since she'd seen him. His features, which appeared as if they'd been carved in Sogdian granite, and his high cheekbones—a gift from some Asian ancestor—gave him the look of legend. Time had been good to Kayan. He was even more handsome now than he had been as a youth. She felt a mystery about him; as if she didn't know him as she'd always felt she had. That hint of danger intrigued her.

She wondered if attending Kayan was a wise decision. But it was too late to call back the body slaves. To do so now would be to admit weakness, and she had never been one to retreat from a challenge.

"To what do I owe this courtesy, Princess?"

Kayan's mocking formality sliced through her musings, and for an instant he was her girlhood companion again.

She responded as she would have when they were barely more than children. She scooped up a double handful of water and splashed it full in his face.

"Yeh!" He sputtered. "Thank you, my lady. That tastes like harness soap."

"You deserved it. Here, this will wash away the taste." She picked up the heavy, two-handled wine cup from the side of the pool and offered it to him.

He took a sip and then drank.

"It's watered," she assured him. "I remembered that you prefer it that way."

He looked at her over the rim of the cup. "A general lives longer sober."

"And a prince?"

Kayan lowered the wine cup, and a shadow appeared in his dark, liquid eyes. "It was Oxyartes's idea to adopt me and give me the title of prince to protect your son. I never meant to steal young Alexander's throne."

"But you haven't—have you? He's still to be king?"

"Of course he is."

"And he's well? Healthy? Normal?"

"He's all you could ask for in a son. But I warn you. He doesn't know you're alive. I thought it safer. Having a mother will be new for him. Don't expect him to fall into your arms and cover your face with kisses. You'll have to trust me that whatever I've done, I've done for the two of you, not for my own gain."

"You can't know how much I've wanted to hold him—to hear his voice." She smiled at him. "I take no offense where none was meant. I would easier believe that my father would turn traitor than you. Whatever else I've doubted, it was never your loyalty."

Emotion made her voice thick, and she covered her feelings with brisk movements. She accepted the cup from his hands and replaced it on the tray. Taking more of the lime-scented cream, she motioned for him to bend forward. He

was taller than she was, taller than either Ptolemy or
Alexander. She had to stand on tiptoe to work the shampoo
into lather and gently massage away the dried blood on his
scalp without doing further injury.

"Now rinse," she said. Heated water flowed through a
stone dolphin's mouth at one end of the pool and out a
drain on the far end. The efficient system was one that she
would like to install at home . . . if she ever reached home.

Kayan ducked his head under the water several times, and
she concentrated her efforts on his shoulders and upper
arms, tenderly rubbing and kneading the bruised flesh.
When she was eleven, her father's Indian concubine had
taught her a method of deep massage to relax the muscles
and speed recovery from injuries. She had always been fascinated by the art of healing. If she hadn't been born heir to the
Twin Kingdoms, she would have liked to study medicine.

A Persian magus had once told her that physicians in
Chin inserted tiny silver needles into the human body to
increase the flow of beneficial powers, but she had neither
the needles nor the training to attempt such a practice. As
the Lady Mayet, she might have been able to consult with
Egyptian physicians, but having no memory of her former
interests, she'd missed the opportunity.

"Ouch," Kayan protested. "If you want to kill me, use a
knife and do it quickly."

"Don't be a baby," she said. "You've so much dirt on
you, it's a wonder we were able to outrun Ptolemy's soldiers." She slid her hands up to soap his neck and broad
chest, careful not to injure the angry gashes that criss-
crossed his muscular arms. Carefully she washed each
forearm from elbow to wrist with the warm water, taking
care as she cleaned the blood from his skinned knuckles.

Kayan had little body hair, only a light sprinkling that
started on his chest below his nipples and continued down
over his hard, ridged stomach to disappear beneath the top
folds of his loincloth.

Kayan's hard thighs were those of a horseman; his well-formed and muscular legs were long, his feet high-arched, neither small nor overlarge. A deep laceration ran from knee to hip on his left side, and the other hip was bruised and swollen. She used the sponge in a slow, circular motion to wash away blood and dirt.

"You need stitches here." She touched his left thigh. "And over your brow."

"I'm certain you'll take pleasure in the sewing. Would you like to use a javelin or a *xyston* for a needle?"

"The long spear might be awkward, don't you think? A javelin should do nicely." She shook her head in exasperation. "Why would I wish to cause you pain? The gashes won't heal properly if they're not sewn."

"You think you're not causing me pain now?" His gaze lingered on her wet bodice.

Roxanne felt her cheeks grow warm. What was wrong with her that she could share Ptolemy's bed so eagerly, and now—after so short a time—lust after her cousin's body? Was she a trollop at heart?

Not your cousin, her inner voice chided. *No more than a distant relation and the man you were meant to marry.*

She closed her eyes and tried to clear her mind of such thoughts. "Do you ever think on Lilya?" she asked.

"Not often. You picked her as my wife, not me."

Long ago, Alexander had ordered Roxanne to choose a bride for Kayan, so that he might captain her personal guard without arousing gossip. She'd chosen the Lady Lilya, a Sogdian noblewoman lovely of face and form, but empty-headed, vain, and selfish. "I should have been wiser," she admitted.

"You knew exactly what you were doing," he said. "You knew that I could never love Lilya, and you wanted it that way."

"Many marriages of the nobility are political ones."

"Lilya was stupid and unfaithful."

"I'm sorry," Roxanne said.

"Don't be." He shook his head. "I never gave her a chance. I didn't want children by her. We bedded when it was convenient, but ours was a political union. I never wanted another woman but you, Roxanne. Not then, not now. If there was fault, blame me, not Lilya. She never pretended to be other than what she was—a greedy child in a woman's body."

"Perhaps I was the greedy child," Roxanne said, "to give you a wife that I knew you couldn't love."

"She's as dead as he is."

"Alexander."

He nodded. "Let him go. How long would he have mourned you if you'd died first? He married you to win the loyalty of our cavalry. He would have wed another princess in a month's time."

"Perhaps. I hated him in the beginning, but I think I loved him . . . in the end. Ormazd knows I didn't want to. We were at each other's throats most of the time. But there was something about him that—"

"He's dead and you're alive. You have a right to live . . . to love again."

"But how can I be sure of myself?" she cried. "I thought I hated Alexander, and I came to love him. I trusted Ptolemy, and he wanted me because I'd been his brother's wife. I never loved Ptolemy, but I liked him. I liked what we did in bed."

"Damn you, Roxanne! You always did go for the throat."

She drew in a shuddering breath and blinked back tears. "Honesty, Kayan. I can give you that if nothing more."

"It's not enough," he said.

Before she realized what was happening, he crushed her against him and kissed her. It was not the tender and hesitant kiss he'd given her an hour before, but a scorching caress that made her blood run hot.

Unwillingly she closed her eyes and parted her lips, allowing him to deepen the kiss, letting caution drop away, as his hands moved over the small of her back and clasped her buttocks, pressing her tighter against the burgeoning proof of his arousal.

She had expected his kiss to be like those she'd remembered from so long ago when they were young and thought they were in love. This was more, so much more that it frightened her and lured her to savor the sensation of his tongue against hers . . . to inhale his scent . . . to revel in his sheer, uncontrollable, male savagery.

She told herself that as long as she didn't actively kiss him back, she was resisting his advances, but she knew it was a lie. She, who had not hesitated to strike out at a king, trembled like a virgin in this man's arms and let herself wonder what it would be like to give herself completely to him.

His fingers brushed the neckline of her tunic and cupped her breast. Groaning, he lowered his head, pushed away the wet linen with his seeking mouth, and drew her nipple into his mouth. Sweet sensations swept through her, washing away all resistance. Her knees buckled, and she clasped his shoulders to keep from falling.

He laved her nipple with his tongue, causing the nub to harden and grow sensitive while he stroked her skin with tantalizing intimacy. Her head fell back, and the weight of the water loosened her hair. Kayan nuzzled her other breast, suckling and teasing until ripples of joy spilled to the apex of her thighs and she grew wet with desire.

He caught her hand and pressed it to his swollen phallus. Touching him excited her, and she lifted her face for his kiss. As their lips met, she gave as good as she got, kissing him with equal fervor, skimming her fingertips over his strong neck and shoulders, arching her hips against his.

It was Kayan who broke the embrace. Gently but firmly he pushed her away and exhaled softly. He smiled down at her with a teasing light in his eyes. "You've grown up," he said.

Stunned, unable to respond, she turned and dove under the water, coming up at the far end of the pool, about the length of two spear shafts from where he waited. "I don't know what to say," she admitted. "I shouldn't have—"

"No lies between us, Roxanne."

She tried to protest . . . to explain . . . but the words wouldn't come.

"A first," he said. "You, speechless? We should build a monument on this spot to mark the event." His smile became the crooked grin that she remembered so well. "I was nineteen when you wed your Conqueror," he said. "And you were what? Sixteen?"

"A lifetime ago." If she'd been confused before, now she was lost. What was solid? Kayan was the same and yet a stranger.

And she—who had known the physical love of two men—felt as though what was happening here was beyond belief or imagination. How could Kayan's touch make her feel like this? As though she'd been made of wood and not flesh and blood until this moment? It was as if she'd been a ghost wandering in the shadows and suddenly stepped into a meadow of sunlight.

She gazed at him through tear-filled eyes. "Were you really nineteen?"

"A green boy." He picked up the wine cup, drained it, and reached for a piece of meat.

She pulled the tunic up over her breasts, knowing full well that the clinging fabric was nearly transparent. "Now I'm an old woman who's given birth to a child."

"It's only made you more beautiful," Kayan said huskily. "I've aged, Roxanne, but those years you spent in prison . . . Time has passed you by."

She felt the blood heat her throat and face. "You've learned how to charm a woman with sweet lies since last we met."

"I never claimed to be a eunuch."

"No, you didn't. But neither am I a virgin, Kayan. If

we . . ." She wrung the water from her hair and tried to secure it off her shoulders with the remaining hairpins. "I
can't promise you anything."

"Promise me only that you will consider my offer."

"What offer? I've heard none." She hid her nervousness
as she climbed the steps and wrapped herself in a linen
towel.

"Marry me, Roxanne. Be my wife, my lover, my friend."

"Don't. It's too soon. I can't think. You . . ." She spread
her hands helplessly. "You were right to stop. If we'd . . . if
I had let you . . ."

He grinned again. "It felt good. Admit it."

"I'm not denying that. But maybe it isn't you. Maybe it's
me. Maybe I'm insatiable. Perhaps I'd react the same way
to a Scythian bandit or a camel driver. I find I like the physical act of sex. I like it very much, but that's hardly a reason to marry."

"I want you to give me children . . . daughters, I think.
Yes, daughters, three or four, all red-haired and snub-
nosed. And all as stubborn and endearing as their mother."

"What man doesn't want sons?"

"I have sons. No one could ask for two better ones." He
heaved himself up onto the rim of the pool. "And I must
get back to them. Val may need me."

"You're right," she said. "Go and see how he is, and then
come back so that I can stitch you up."

"You haven't forgotten that, have you?"

She chuckled. "No. I haven't."

He turned his back and stripped off the wet loincloth. She
tried to tell herself that the sight of his tight buttocks, slim
waist, and wide shoulders were not what made her pulse
quicken and her throat tighten, but she knew it wasn't true.
Kayan was every inch a hero, and she feared that whatever
else passed between them, it would not be long before she
knew him in a very elemental way. And if she let him possess
her body, how could she deny him her hand in marriage?

He deserved more than an unwilling wife. What if she could never give him what he should have?

"Wait," she said. "Give me a moment to dry off and put something on. I'll come with you."

"To see Val, or to make certain your next victim doesn't escape?"

"Maybe both," she admitted.

He fumbled with the short Egyptian kilt the servants had laid out. "How does this cursed thing—" he began.

"Let me." She knelt in front of him, tying the pleated linen so that it fell in a loop to his knees. "You'll never make an Egyptian," she said. "You're too big. There, that should do it."

"In all the ways that count," he replied. With a playful pat to her buttocks, he strode barefoot to the doorway. There, he stopped and glanced back. "Let him go," he said.

"It's not the way you think." Alexander didn't hold her anymore, did he?

"Let me love you."

"I wonder if I'm meant to be any man's wife?"

He shrugged. "Take what time you need, but know this. I'll not stand aside and relinquish you to any other man again. Least of all Ptolemy."

Val's fever rose. Lady Alyssa summoned her healer and bade him employ all his skills to treat the child. Roxanne questioned the man and searched through his supplies for familiar medicines. She bathed Val with cool water, not just his face but his entire body.

Kayan paced and swore and threatened the healer's life.

Yuri grew quiet and solemn. "He's not going to die, is he, Kayan?" he asked. "I don't want him to die."

"He's not going to die," Kayan said. "We won't let him."

Val had drifted from a half-sleep into a deep torpor, from which Roxanne was unable to awaken him. Still, she would not slacken her efforts. She used a goose quill to drip a mixture of wine and honey into the boy's mouth, drop by drop.

Still the fever raged.

Roxanne opened the wound on Val's side, examining the inflamed tissue and smelling for putrefaction. "This should not be," she said to Kayan. "The gash isn't deep, and it bled."

"An evil spirit has entered the child," the healer insisted. "We should summon a priest, offer sacrifices to—"

"We can't call a priest," Lady Alyssa said. "It would be too dangerous."

"Then the boy will die," the healer pronounced. "I am sorry, mistress. I have done all that I—"

"Go, then," Roxanne said. "But leave me your medical kit."

Kayan held Val in his arms. It seemed to him as though his son weighed as little as a bag of feathers. How could fever burn away his life before their eyes? "Do something," he said to Roxanne.

"We will fight fire with fire," she said.

"Ah," Lady Alyssa said. "I believe I've heard that Persians are fire worshipers."

"No," Roxanne said. "We are neither Persian nor fire worshipers. We follow the way of Zend-Avesta. We believe that Ormazd is the spirit of good and Ahriman of evil. The two battle, but in the end, good will triumph."

"So you have two gods?" the lady asked.

"No, there is but one Creator," Kayan said. "Fire is a symbol of our faith." He looked down at his son and wondered what right he had to speak of the Creator at all. "Of the faith of our people," he corrected. He was unwilling to admit his own doubts where Yuri could hear. And if he was wrong, if God existed and cared for the puny affairs of men, would He take out His anger on Val?

"I need a brazier," Roxanne said.

Kayan swallowed. "Is he strong enough to bear the pain?"

"He will have to be," she answered. "This much I know.

If the wound isn't purified, it will worsen, and we will lose him."

"Better it were me."

"Or me," she said, "but we don't have that option."

"My sword?"

Roxanne shook her head. "Too big. I will use my dagger."

Servants brought a clay brazier and set it on the floor. Roxanne washed the knife in vinegar and again in strong wine before placing the blade in the coals.

"What are you doing?" Lady Alyssa asked.

"She will use the power of the fire to combat the evil in my son's wound," Kayan explained. He cradled the boy against his chest and kissed his hot forehead before laying him on the bed. "I'll hold his shoulders and hands. We need Tiz to hold his feet."

The Greek noblewoman sent a boy for the Bactrian. "Are you certain of what you do?" she asked Roxanne.

"No," she murmured. "But I know nothing else."

Yuri crept wide-eyed to Val's side. "She's going to burn him, isn't she?"

Kayan nodded. "Watch and remember. It is a thing we do during war when bleeding is great or a limb has been lost."

"Will it hurt him?" Yuri asked.

He could not lie. "Yes."

Yuri rested small fists on his hips and glared at Roxanne. "If he dies, I will kill you," he threatened.

"Yuri!" Kayan admonished. "You should not—"

"Let him say what's in his heart," Roxanne said. She crouched and took Yuri's small hands in hers. "It isn't always easy to do what's right," she said. "I must have the courage to try to save him. Can you lend me some of yours?"

Yuri's eyes grew thoughtful, and he nodded. "If it will help Val."

"All right," she said. "You will stand by my side, and we will do this together. And if he doesn't survive, you may make up your mind then if you want to kill me."

"I will," Yuri said.

Tiz joined them, and Kayan instructed him to hold his son's lower body still. The Bactrian archer said nothing but took his place at Val's feet.

When the bronze blade of the knife glowed red, Roxanne glanced at Kayan and nodded. "May Ormazd guide my hands," she said.

Kayan steeled himself for what must come.

Val screamed.

Chapter 18

That night was bad. Twice Roxanne feared she had lost the child. Kayan alternately paced the floor, bathed Val's hot body, and sat talking for long periods, holding Yuri on his knee and clasping Val's small hand in his.

"Remember when you were little, Val, and I used to carry you out into the snow on my shoulders? And what about the time we made a snow leopard, and you hid behind it and snarled when I brought Yuri out to see it? Remember when you tried to shoot your first mountain goat—the one with the broken horn? It leaped off the ledge and scrambled away down that sheer precipice. You'd promised your grandmother goat for dinner, and she made us all eat gruel and flat bread . . ."

Roxanne listened, hearing tales of Val's childhood and Yuri's, of home, and of her beloved father and her stepmother Soraya, but never heard a word of the child she wanted to know most about. No matter how closely she listened to Kayan's voice, she heard nothing of little Alexander. So that her fear for Val became tangled in the suspicion that Kayan had lied to her to get her to go home with him. What would she do if he had lied—if her little Alexander was dead and Kayan was shielding her from the truth?

She could not sleep while Val lay suspended between life and death, and in the hours that her mind and body grew weary, she became more frightened. She wanted to ask Yuri about his brother Alexander, but she couldn't. How could she demand of a child what Kayan wouldn't offer? And what if Yuri told her the truth, and the truth was too awful to bear?

Again, she wondered if Val could be hers . . . or Yuri. Could Kayan have given the child another name to protect his life? But if one of these little ones was her child, why wouldn't Kayan tell them? Did he mean to hide who she was?

Val seemed too old to be the infant she had given birth to in Babylon. She studied his face, taking in the high forehead, the Greek nose, the beautiful lips that could have been Alexander's. She saw no real resemblance, but the Macedonian had been almost three times Val's age when she'd first laid eyes on him. He'd been a man grown, a man who knew the face of war, a man who'd burned a hundred cities and put their inhabitants to the sword. How could such deeds not have made a mark? And how could she know what Alexander had looked like as a boy?

Yuri's features she examined as well—the intelligent gray eyes, the curling blond hair, the dimpled cheeks. The boys looked enough alike to be blood brothers, but Kayan had insisted they weren't. Yuri could be no more than six, perhaps seven, but surely not eight. She could love this child with his stout heart and mischievous personality, but she could not see Alexander in him. Or could she?

Had Kayan lied to her about the fathers of these children? No man could be more loving toward a son who'd sprung from his own loins. He had a gentle manner with them, allowing them such freedoms that even she had not dared with Oxyartes. They obviously adored him, yet she could see respect in their eyes when they looked at him.

Could a man be such a wonderful father and still harbor deceit and betrayal in his soul?

"Tell me he will live," Kayan rasped, late on the evening of the second day after she had purified Val's wound with fire.

Roxanne started. Had she fallen asleep? She opened her eyes wide and her heartbeat quickened. Had the black horse and veiled rider come to steal the child while they slept? Quickly she leaned over Val to feel his breath on her cheek.

Yes, he lived. If anything, his breathing was easier. But his skin still felt hot and dry to her touch, and he had not opened his eyes in many hours.

"What? What did you say?" she asked, her gaze meeting Kayan's. His eyes were bottomless pools of anguish. But he had not slept. "I didn't hear . . . I must have dozed off."

"Will he live?" Kayan asked. Yuri slept soundly in his father's embrace, head back, arms outflung, cheeks ruddy with health.

What of my *son?* she wanted to cry. *What of the babe I entrusted to you? Why can't you speak of him? Or have you lied to me? Val could be mine. He could live and die without ever calling me mother.*

She wanted to speak, but the words would not come from her lips. Instead, she swallowed, and touched Kayan's face with her fingertips, trailing her hand over his rough unshaven cheek. "I pray . . ." she began.

The boy will live. A familiar voice echoed in her head. Tears welled in her eyes, and she began to tremble. *He will make a warrior I would be proud of.*

She sucked in a breath as she recognized her dead husband's voice. "He will make a warrior," she repeated, only half conscious of what she said.

Hair prickled on the nape of Roxanne's neck as the oil lamp beside Val's bed flickered in the cold gust of wind that blew through the room——flared up and went out.

"Alexander?" Roxanne called.

"By Ormazd's breath!" Kayan exclaimed as he leaped to his feet. "What was that?"

The air was still, the only sounds those of Yuri's sleepy sighs. Roxanne clamped her teeth together to keep them from chattering from the sudden chill.

"Take Yuri," Kayan said. He pushed the child into her arms. "Wait here."

Roxanne cradled Yuri against her breast and grasped Val's hand. It was still warm, still soft, still the hand of a living child. "May your holy light protect us," she prayed.

Was she mad? Had she lost her wits that she would hear Alexander's words in her head? And where had the wind come from? Was that real or supernatural?

Light glowed in the doorway. Kayan returned to the bed and used the flame from the lamp he'd fetched to light the one beside the bed. "The house is quiet," he said. "Whatever caused that breeze . . ." He looked down at Val. "He's not—"

"The same," she said. "No change." She shook her head. "We've been too long without sleep. It was a wind off the desert, no more, perhaps a sandstorm brewing."

"Maybe," Kayan agreed. "Here, let me take him." He reached for Yuri.

"No, let me hold him awhile," she answered. "Your arms must be weary." The fear returned, more insistent, forcing her to speak, to ask the question she dreaded to ask. "Did you lie to me, Kayan? What of my little Alexander? Why haven't the boys said anything about him? Why haven't you? He's dead, isn't he?"

"Dead?" Kayan looked at her as if she'd grown a pair of ox horns and sprouted a tail. "Dead? Whatever gave you that idea?"

"He's alive, then? You swear it?"

"Of course he's alive." The deep timbre of his voice burred with emotion. "I wouldn't have lied about that, Roxanne, not to you."

"But Yuri and Val never mention him. They never say—"

"They don't know him by that name. It wasn't safe. It still isn't safe. So long as the world thinks he's in a Macedonian grave, your son has the chance to grow to manhood without the shadow of the Conqueror's name. Without bringing the wrath of his enemies down on him. He's still a child. Would you want to put that burden on his shoulders?"

"No, no, of course not. But you never . . . you've told me nothing about him. I've . . ." She bit her lip and with a sob let her darkest fears burst out. "I was afraid. Afraid you'd lied. That he was either dead or afflicted of mind or body."

For an instant Kayan looked away, and her heart sank. But then he spoke quietly and firmly. "On my mother's soul, Roxanne, your son lives. Trust me," he said. "Trust me to care for him as I've cared for him since you gave him to me so long ago. He's well, and as strong and courageous as his mother."

"I'll see him? You swear it? You'll give him back to me?"

"If we live to reach home, I'll put him in your arms and tell him who you are," Kayan said. "I give you my word."

"How old is Val?" she demanded.

"Nine, going on ten."

"In what season was he born?"

"In winter."

"You swear to me that his mother is dead?"

"Yes."

"And Yuri?" she insisted. "When is his birthday? How old is he?"

Kayan shrugged. "It was a terrible time after the Conqueror died, naught but war and famine. Yuri's mother would have remembered, I suppose, but she was taken from him when he was young. Who would bother to record the birth of one more half-Greek baby? Most orphans never live past weaning. I'm no expert on children. Women tell me that he appears near to seven."

"He does to me, too." Regretfully, she realized, dimple-cheeked Yuri wasn't hers either. She sighed. "Thank you," she murmured. "Thank you."

On the morning of the third day, Val's fever broke. When the boy sat up and drank two cups of hot broth, Yuri did a handstand and Kayan was so relieved that he rushed from the room with eyes glistening with moisture. Roxanne, who was unashamed of her own tears of joy, would not allow the healer near Val again. She treated his burn with honey and gave the boy only liquids for the next twenty-four hours. By then, Val was arguing with his brother and complaining that she was trying to starve him.

Lady Alyssa came to see Val's recovery for herself, then invited Roxanne to join her in her private sitting room. "You saved him," Lady Alyssa said when the women were alone. "I was afraid that the child was beyond help."

Roxanne shook her head. "It wasn't me. It was his own will to live and youthful resilience."

"And perhaps the help of your fire god?" Lady Alyssa, elegantly but plainly garbed as always, picked up her spindle and began to wind a handful of raw wool into yarn. "Silly of me, isn't it?" she said. "Wool is of little use in Egypt, but my mother and her mother before her always had a spindle to hand. At my age, it's difficult to change one's ways."

One of her many cats batted and pounced on a ball of yarn that it had retrieved from the basket beside the lady's chair. The cozy room with its cheerful wall murals smelled of cinnamon and cloves.

"Perhaps the Creator was merciful," Roxanne agreed. "Or perhaps he sent you to assist us. If you hadn't risked everything to protect us, Val would be dead by now."

"I fear he would have been."

It was clear to Roxanne that the Greek noblewoman was nervous, eager to be rid of her dangerous guests. "Please," Roxanne urged. "Speak frankly."

Lady Alyssa gave a half-smile. "Patrols have crossed my

estate repeatedly in the last few days. All the countryside is up in arms in search of you. It isn't safe for you to remain here much longer." She hesitated, and then went on in a rush. "Hesper has written to ask me to return to the city. She needs me, and it will seem strange to my son if I don't come at once."

"You must do so."

"Yes, but . . ." Lady Alyssa pursed her lips. "Debi is dependable and absolutely loyal. But if my son should arrive, or if soldiers—"

"I understand," Roxanne said. "I believe that Val can travel. If you will give us until tonight, we—"

"You cannot travel by darkness. The roads are closely watched. Any who are about in the night are suspect. You would be arrested or worse. You could be murdered, and your bodies left to rot in the sun or torn to pieces by vultures."

"We must run that risk."

"No. There would be questions about where you had been for these last days, questions that could not be answered." She shook her head. "No, you must go in daylight. Your only chance to reach the Nile is to blend in with the honest citizens, to be taken for harmless inhabitants going about everyday tasks."

"There is much wisdom in what you say," Roxanne replied. "But how can we—"

"I have given this much thought. The estate regularly sends produce by river to Memphis. Your wounded may be hidden among the vegetables in carts, but not all of you. You must darken your hair and skin with cosmetics, and I fear that you must disguise yourself as a peasant woman."

"I have no qualms about that."

"When you reach the river, you'll go aboard one of my ships. I'll instruct the captain to put you ashore on the other side as soon as he feels it is safe. You will use the same ruse until you reach the fringes of the desert. After that"—she spread her hands—"you're on your own."

"It is more than enough. Words can't express our thanks. You—"

"Don't thank me yet. King Ptolemy holds Egypt in his fist, and his control extends far beyond the borders of this land. Your chances of reaching your homeland are impossibly small."

"I know," Roxanne said. "But I have faced such odds before. I've learned never to surrender hope. Deliverance can come in the final moments, and from the most unlikely quarters."

Lady Alyssa chuckled. "Oh, to be young and optimistic again. Hera be with you, child. And with those you love."

"And with you."

"I'll need her help if I'm to be rid of you without ending in one of Ptolemy's dungeons." She became serious again. "You told me that you hid the youngest boy by dressing him as a girl. Disguise could work again. The soldiers are looking for two Bactrian princes with fair hair and skin. No one would notice peasant children accompanying their mother."

"But what of Prince Kayan? No one would take him for a farmer or a slave."

"Ah, your brawny kinsman. He gave me the most concern," she admitted. "I agree that he is too fierce-looking to pass for anything but a warrior. For him, I have come up with a special solution. It's up to you to convince him that it will work."

At high noon, in the square in front of his main palace, Ptolemy confronted his troops from his chariot. Four hundred infantry soldiers and five score cavalrymen in full battle array were drawn up at attention behind their officers. Forty chariots waited, horses stamping impatiently, drivers and Egyptian archers standing with features rigid, their eyes riveted on their king.

"A handful of bandits?" Ptolemy exclaimed. "You tell

me that you are outwitted and outfought by this barbarian goat herder and his sorry-assed followers?" The king did not use a speaking horn, but so silent were the troops that his voice carried to the farthest ranks.

"Find them! Find the Lady Mayet and these Bactrians or you'll find yourself guarding lizard shit in the Sinai Desert! Do I make myself clear?"

"Yes, Your Majesty," General Nisus said. "Quite clear."

"Bring me their heads!" Ptolemy roared. "Their weight in gold for the severed heads of Kayan and his spawn! But the lady must not be harmed. If one nail on her hand is broken, I'll have the guilty man and his entire family skinned alive! By Ares's balls, I'll have every man he's ever tossed dice with skinned alive! Do I make myself understood? Do I?"

Hundreds of shouts assured the king that he had. Ptolemy nodded, seized the reins from his driver, and slapped them over the backs of his team. "I'll find her if I have to do it myself," he swore.

You may have to, answered the voice from within Ptolemy's head.

"What did you say?" the king screamed at his charioteer.

"Nothing, Your Highness." The man clung to the side of the speeding conveyance as Ptolemy whipped the horses faster. Behind them, chariots fell into position, two at a time. They sped through the streets of Alexandria with cavalry and infantry at their backs.

You heard me, Brother. She's outfoxed you, hasn't she?

"Shut up! Shut up!" Ptolemy cried.

You had to be greedy, didn't you? Alexander said. *But you're no match for her or that wily cousin of hers.*

"I'll not lose her this time," Ptolemy swore.

Again he heard his brother's laughter.

"Leave me alone!" the king cried.

She'll slip like smoke through your fingers if you're not careful, Alexander said.

Cold sweat ran down Ptolemy's back. The thunder of the horses' hooves, the clamor of the chariot wheels, and the cheering populace deafened him. He told himself that it was impossible to hear anything else—least of all the taunts of a brother dead eight years.

"You'll see, damn you!" the king swore. "You'll see! I'll get a son from her belly! A son to wear the double crown of Egypt!"

True to her word, Lady Alyssa had instructed her captain to carry their company across the broad Nile. The man had asked no questions, but had deposited them at an isolated landing only a few miles from where they had boarded the squat cargo vessel.

To ensure his silence, Roxanne had rewarded him with a gold chain from her store. The treasures she'd brought from Ptolemy's palace no longer filled a flimsy basket. Lady Alyssa had provided two sturdy but worn leather pouches and the leather straps to secure them. She had also given Roxanne a fine Greek sword and scabbard that she told her had once belonged to a brother. "Care for the weapon well," she had instructed. "And draw no more innocent blood than you must, lest you make of me a murderess."

The noblewoman had gifted Kayan's party with three goats, two carts and donkeys to pull them, as well as a covered litter, now jammed into the back of one of the high-wheeled vehicles. Bahman, hair cut short in an Egyptian style and wearing nothing but a filthy loincloth and a sling for his injured shoulder, drove the first cart, Tiz, the second.

Val, much to his dismay—clad in horsehair wig and a girl's tunic—was wedged into a corner of the trailing cart beside a crate of quacking ducks and several baskets of onions which concealed the recovering Homji. Yuri, naked and unencumbered, ran barefoot behind the last cart herding the goats.

"I must have been out of my mind to let you talk me into this," Kayan said from within the curtained litter.

"Be glad you don't have to walk in this heat." Roxanne snickered and balanced the basket of figs on her head, thanking her father's Indian concubine, Neerja, for that skill as well as many others. "Or that you didn't have to wear a woman's wig and tunic."

He swore a foul oath.

She laughed.

"I'm folded into this litter like a bean in a shell," he grumbled.

"Be glad you're not folded into a wet grave minus your head," she said.

His crude answer made her chuckle again.

Lady Alyssa had informed them that Ptolemy had put a price on their heads—all but the Lady Mayet's. The king wanted her back, unhurt. What he intended for her if he caught her, Roxanne wasn't certain. But she knew that she'd never allow herself to be captured alive. Seven years of imprisonment was long enough. One way or another, she would be free.

Yuri giggled, threw a stone at a clump of dirt, chased a frog, and ran to point out a circling falcon to Tiz.

"Save your energy," Roxanne advised the boy. "We have a long walk in front of us."

The muscles in her own legs were beginning to ache. It had been a long time since she'd walked any distance, and she was older than she'd been when she'd followed Alexander to India and back. Then, she'd ridden, on horseback, on a camel, and in a howdah on top of an elephant. It seemed another lifetime, and perhaps it was. So much had happened since her husband's death. She wondered if the trials she'd faced had made her stronger, or more vulnerable.

At least when she'd been Alexander's prize of war, she'd known her own heart. Her course had been set, and she'd known what she wanted of life. All her will and energy had been focused on escaping her husband's control, freeing the Twin Kingdoms from Greek tyranny, and putting her child on the throne of Bactria and Sogdiana.

Now . . . she straightened her shoulders and strode on. Her son waited for her in her mountain home. Her father . . . her people. Once she was there, she could think about Kayan. Until then, she could not allow herself the luxury of falling in love again.

They had traveled only a short way and already the fertile fields were giving way to pasture land. The green belt, which extended on either side of the life-giving Nile, did not run so deep on the far bank. Ahead lay trackless desert and beyond that the Red Sea. Soon they must turn north. Roxanne hoped that Kayan's sense of direction wouldn't forsake him.

The remaining Bactrian force waited with camels at a lonely oasis a week's travel from the shore of the Mediterranean. It was Kayan's plan to join his men and press hard for Gaza and then, Tyre. There they would follow the Conqueror's route along the Tigris River into Persia and from there to Bactria, Sogdiana, and home. All that stood in their way were hostile populaces, three Greek armies, bandits, deserts, rivers, mountains, and Ptolemy's legions.

Chapter 19

Roxanne, Kayan, and the others kept moving steadily north through the heat of the Egyptian sun. They passed fewer farms now, and the green irrigated fields were behind them. Even the flocks of geese and the occasional ibis flying overhead had given way to falcons and vultures. This was marginal grazing land where shepherds herded goats and sheep to feed on thorny shrubs, and the scorpion, speckled snake, and monitor lizard ruled supreme.

Only now and then did the group catch sight of other humans, none of whom showed any interest in the small caravan. At dusk, Kayan came out of hiding and dismantled the despised carrying chair with a few swipes of his sword. Yuri had long since become worn out, and he and two of the goats had been tucked into the back of one of the carts. Tiz had tied the animals' legs so that they would lie still and lend the child heat from their bodies. The remaining nanny, her bag heavy with milk, trailed close behind. At Kayan's insistence, Roxanne had reluctantly joined Yuri and the goats, and the little boy had fallen asleep with his head on her shoulder.

Kayan walked, and Tiz and Bahman kept urging the tired donkeys on as the stars winked into sight, one by one. The group had long since left the road and traveled now across flat, barren ground, sliced at intervals by deep gullies formed by rare desert rainstorms. Hour after hour they traveled until sometime after midnight when Kayan called a halt to rest the exhausted animals.

When the conveyance jolted to a stop, Roxanne jerked awake to find her right arm full of pins and needles. Yuri slept soundly as she eased him down between the goats, covered him with a blanket, and slid off the back of the cart.

Kayan was there to catch her. He had picked a sandy wadi to make camp, where the high banks would give some relief from the wind. "We're too close to outlying farms to chance a fire," he said. "We'll have to tough out the night."

"It's all right," she replied. "We have blankets. I can put Val in beside Yuri. I'll loose the animals long enough to give them water and grain, and milk the goats."

Kayan raised a brow quizzically. "Certain you remember how to do that, Your Royal Highness?"

She made a face at him. "Better than you. But it has been a while." She decided to let Yuri continue to sleep. He could eat later if he woke. She'd make certain to save milk for him.

Val was awake and moving stiffly. She knew that the boy was still in pain, but he made no complaint—not even when she changed the dressing on his side. He drank some milk and ate a few dates before willingly climbing in the cart beside his brother. Together, Roxanne and Tiz cared for Homji and Bahman while Kayan scanned the skyline for Ptolemy's soldiers.

The air was cold even in the sandy hollow, and a chill breeze whistled down the narrow wadi from the eastern desert. Roxanne shivered as she completed her tasks and carefully doled out the precious water to men and beasts. She ate little. Lady Alyssa had loaded the carts with provisions, but there was no telling when they could procure food or find a well with good water.

Long ago, Roxanne had crossed the Gedrosia desert with Alexander's army. The barren landscape of blowing sand and bare rock had cost the lives of sixty thousand men, women, and children, and had taught her lessons about survival that years could never erase. Kayan had accompanied them on that terrible march, but they had never spoken of it since the day they'd walked out of the nightmare. Some experiences were too deep for words.

"I can take the first watch," Tiz offered. The one-eyed warrior had three wounds, none likely to be fatal unless they turned bad, and seemed well on the path to full recovery.

"You go to sleep," Kayan commanded. "I'll wake you when I'm tired."

Tiz grumbled, but rolled in a blanket near the tethered donkeys. The other two men turned one cart on its side and curled up in its shelter. Roxanne tied the nanny to a dwarfed juniper where she could graze on succulents, then gathered dried grass for the goats in the cart. The ducks, heads tucked under their wings, were sleeping in their odorous crate.

"Baah," Tiz said. "We ought to wring the necks of these birds and have them for breakfast. They smell worse than Seth's arse."

"Leave my ducks alone," Roxanne warned. "You'll appreciate them a lot more when your belly's as empty as a drum and we can roast them over a fire." She was beginning to appreciate Kayan's grizzled lieutenant. He was smart, tireless, and absolutely fearless. She had seen him fight, and liked his protective manner with the boys.

"Promises, promises, it's all I get."

She smiled at Tiz, realizing that his complaints were mostly in jest. "You'll have the first drumstick," she said.

"I've eaten raw rabbits but never ducks," Kayan put in. "I have to agree with her. They'll taste a lot better cooked."

"Trouble with you is, you're getting soft since Oxyartes named you a prince," Tiz said. "You never used to put on such airs."

Bahman added a remark too low for Roxanne to understand, and Tiz laughed. Then the men fell silent, and minutes later, Tiz began to snore.

"My army," Kayan said. "The pride of the Bactrian cavalry."

"They are all brave men."

"The best."

She made no protest when he slipped an arm around her.

"You're cold," he said. "Take one of those blankets for yourself."

"I'll share with the boys. I've no wish to make a bed on the ground with the scorpions and snakes." She rubbed her arms and rested her head against his chest. "A thousand stars tonight."

"But not like home."

"No. Almost, but not quite." She closed her eyes. "High in the mountains, the stars are so close you can reach up and touch them." For a moment, memories of the long years in prison clutched at her, and she pushed them to the back of her mind. How many times had she stared at the rock walls of that cavern and prayed for the sight of the sky? "But beautiful, just the same," she said. "Do you suppose that my son is looking at those same stars now?"

Kayan chuckled. "I hope not. I hope he's sound asleep."

"I've missed so much of his life, his first steps . . . his first word. I don't even know what he likes to eat."

"Everything."

"Can he ride a horse?" She moved in front of him so that his back blocked the wind. She'd almost forgotten how solid he was. He carried not an ounce of fat. Kayan was all sinew and muscle.

"He rides like a Scythian." He nuzzled her hair.

"Shoot a bow?"

"I taught him."

"Hmm," she teased, looking up into his face. The moon made the night almost as bright as day, but Kayan's face was shadowed. "Then I suppose we'll need to work on that."

"Some appreciation I get for spending the best years of my life as a wet nurse." He rested his big hands on her waist, and her heart skipped a beat.

Steady, steady, she told herself. *You're no raw girl to be bewitched by a man's honeyed words in the moonlight.* "I knew you were up to it. You did see that he learned to read, didn't you?"

He tugged a lock of her hair free from the pins and wrapped it around his fingers. "Your father has seen that the boys have the best tutors. He reads Parsi and Persian and Greek. His Chinese characters are abominable, but he's learning to speak the language from one of Soraya's ladies."

"Mathematics?"

"Yes." He caught her wrist and turned it gently to place a warm kiss on the underside. "They tell me he has a knack for it."

"My hands are dirty," she said breathlessly.

"Mine aren't?" He pulled her closer.

"Tactics and medicine?"

"He's eight, Roxanne." He nibbled her wrist and trailed his teeth along her thumb, drawing the tip between his lips and suckling gently. "Can't you let him be a boy for a few years?"

She swallowed, her mouth suddenly dry. "He'll be a king. He'll need—"

He brought her palm to his bristly cheek and rubbed it against his face. "He'll need parents, a mother and a father."

She shivered, swallowed again. "He has them," she murmured. "Doesn't he?"

Kayan released her hand and took hold of her shoulders, bringing her nearer to kiss her throat and the hollow behind her ear. "He doesn't have a baby sister," he said. "Or two?"

She hadn't meant to kiss him back. She'd only wanted to

talk, here in the Egyptian night, to be with him and recall sweet memories. But when she tried to withdraw, her muscles wouldn't obey. She slipped her arms around his neck and parted her lips as their mouths met.

The magic shot through her with the intensity of a lightning bolt. Sweet shafts of sensation shook her to the core, melting her bones to water, thrilling and terrifying her at the same instant.

How was this possible? she wondered. How could their mouths fit so perfectly? How could their bodies mold together as if they were two halves of a whole?

There was no awkwardness . . . no hesitation . . . just the feeling that she had waited for this forever.

As their kiss deepened, he thrust into her mouth so that their tongues touched and she tasted and smelled him. His scent filled her head, clean and wild as the mountains of her birth, and she moaned softly, not caring that someone might hear. For seconds . . . minutes . . . intense longing gripped her, and she forgot everything but the need to be loved and protected by this man.

He kissed her eyelids and brows with teasing, featherlight caresses. He nibbled at her lower lip and whispered Sogdian endearments into her ear. His big hands moved over her, erasing the touch of other men, claiming her as his own.

And she let him . . . urged him . . . wanted more.

"Kayan . . ."

With a groan, he pushed her away. "Go to bed, Roxanne," he said hoarsely. "Now. With the boys."

"But I . . ." She stared at him in bewilderment. "What's wrong? What have I done?"

"It's more what you haven't done. Don't ask." He stepped back. "I want you," he said. "Ormazd strike me dead if I don't want you more than . . ."

"Then why?" She began to shiver in the cold moonlight. Somewhere in the distance a hyena yipped, an eerie sound that raised goose flesh along her arms. Another wailed in answer, and the nanny goat bleated in fear.

"That's why," Kayan said.

"Hyenas? They won't come—"

"Hyenas. Jackals. Bandits. Ptolemy's men." He made a sound of impatience. "There's no time for this tonight. No time for us. If I'm thinking of you instead of watching the night for them—"

"You're right," she said. "I didn't think. I—"

"Go to sleep," he said. "You're tired. Drink and eat something. And sleep. You walked a long way today."

"You need sleep as well." She rubbed her bare arms again. "I can stand watch. I've done it before."

"Not tonight, Roxanne."

"I'm no weakling."

"Damn you, woman. Can you never just accept an order? I need you strong. For the boys. Rest while you can."

"And you? Aren't you human? Don't you need sleep as well?"

The hyena howled again, closer this time. "They're real animals, aren't they?" she asked him. "Not Egyptian soldiers?"

Kayan shrugged. "They sound real enough. Likely our goats will seem easy prey."

"I've got a sword and my bow. I can fight; you know I can fight."

"I know it, but I hope you won't have to. Bring the nanny back to the cart. She'll likely bleat all night out there, anyway. A fire would have kept them away."

"And shown anyone hunting us where we were."

"So I thought," he answered.

"I'm not afraid."

"I am. Afraid I won't be able to protect you and my sons. Afraid that now that I have you, I won't be able to keep you safe."

"It's impossible, isn't it? What we're trying to do? Escape Ptolemy's wrath?"

He made a sound that might have been denial or assent. "Sorry you came with us?"

"Wouldn't have missed it." She tried to keep her voice light. "The Palace of the Blue Lotus and Alexandria were tame until you arrived. Poison wine. An occasional assassin in the night."

"I'm not joking. Are you sorry?"

"Yes."

"It's not too late to go back. He'd have you back. I know I would."

"I'm not sorry that I'm here with you, you idiot," she said. "I'm sorry you put yourself in danger to come for me."

"You'd rather have stayed with him?"

"You know that's not true."

One of the donkeys brayed and yanked at the tie rope. "They smell the hyenas. I'll bring them between the carts," she said.

"Wake Tiz."

Rivulets of fear chilled her spine. Hyenas were enormous beasts with jaws powerful enough to crush bone as easily as a bronze scythe cuts through ripe stalks of wheat. The creatures were fearless, and they would devour a child with the same cold savagery as they would a donkey or a goat.

"Now bring the donkeys, or let them loose and hope the hyenas will chase them and leave us alone."

"We need them," she answered. "Val and Homji aren't strong enough to walk yet." She was already forcing herself into the darkness between Kayan and the frightened animals.

When she reached the donkeys, they were braying, laying their ears back, and stomping the ground in fright. Her fingers were stiff and awkward as she untied the first lead and snubbed the rope around the animal's nose and between its teeth to make a crude bridle. Then she dragged the bucking creature back to where the terrified nanny was trying to scramble up into the cart.

Tiz was already awake and shaking Bahman. Homji grunted and pulled himself to his feet, reaching for his bow. Roxanne knotted the tie rope tightly to the back of the cart and went back for the second donkey.

A chattering yip sounded off to the left—not a laugh but the wailing scream of a madwoman. The donkey bolted, dragging Roxanne down the wadi.

"Let it go!" Kayan yelled.

The rope burned through her hands. She cursed and fell flat as the kicking donkey galloped away into the darkness. Kayan reached her side and pulled her upright with one hand. In his other, he grasped his sword.

"Are you hurt?" he asked.

"Stupid animal," she muttered. "Stupid, stupid—"

Her words died in her throat as a snarl came from the direction of the runaway. The donkey brayed. There was a screeching yip and a squeal. Hoofbeats thudded. Roxanne screamed as a shape loomed out of the night.

Kayan yanked her out of the way as the donkey, hotly pursued by two hyenas, sped past them. A flying hoof caught one of the predators in the head, flinging it backwards. Roxanne was driven to her knees as the second hyena twisted in mid leap to attack her and Kayan. His sword flashed. She caught a whiff of rotten meat and death before the sickly sweet smell of blood flooded her senses.

A heavy weight slammed into the earth only inches from her knee. Kayan grabbed her arm and pulled her to her feet. "Back to the others!" he shouted, dragging her after him. "Quick before they return!"

The squalling donkey fled past the carts and up onto the flat land. The second animal brayed and yanked hard on the tie, but the rope held. Kayan shoved Roxanne up into the cart amid the struggling goats and the frightened boys. Yuri whipped out his knife.

Roxanne scrambled for her bow and arrows, putting her hand on the quiver as the first shadowy shape moved along the ridge. Eyes glowed in the darkness, and Tiz sent an arrow flying at the moving target.

Yuri stood over a small basket, sturdy legs planted, knife held underhand in a fighter's stance. "I'll protect you," he cried.

More yips broke from the wadi. "Wait, wait," Kayan said. "Don't fire until you can see them clearly."

The ducks squawked wildly, beating their wings against the bars of the cage. "Loose them!" Roxanne shouted to Val.

The ducks spilled out of the box. Two flew up, and a third dove into a corner of the cart. Another fluttered to the ground, took wing, and vanished overhead.

A hyena leaped from the overhang. Roxanne got off a quick shot, and the beast fell to the ground, and then clawed up over the edge of the cart. Tiz drove a sword down the animal's gaping throat. Val slashed at the snarling creature with a curved saber, but the fight had gone out of it; it was mortally wounded.

Blood pulsed in Roxanne's ears. For an instant she heard nothing else but the donkey's braying and the nanny goat's strangled breathing. The animal had tried to climb under the cart, and had fallen and twisted her tie rope.

Then Tiz laughed. "Guess you should rethink that fire, eh, General?"

"That was a little too close, wasn't it?" Kayan answered. "Is anyone hurt?"

Roxanne leaped down. In the moonlight, she could see a dark stain across his chest. "You're bleeding," she said. "Did—"

"The beast's blood, not mine," he said.

"Look at the size of that monster," Bahman said, kicking the dead hyena with the toe of his boot. "He could have swallowed you whole, Yuri."

"I would have got him if Tiz didn't," the boy boasted.

Somewhere in the darkness the stray donkey brayed. His comrade bawled back.

"Give me horses instead of these flea-bitten asses," Tiz grumbled. "If this one doesn't stop making that racket, I'll finish him off." He grabbed the remaining duck and stuck it back in the cage. "I may have to eat the damned donkey, now that she let my ducks loose."

"Roxanne shot one of the hyenas," Val said. "With her bow. I saw it."

"Are you the Amazon princess in the stories?" Yuri asked her. "I thought your bow was supposed to be golden."

"I'm no Amazon," Roxanne said. She put her arms around Kayan and hugged him. "You're certain you weren't bitten? Their teeth carry disease. If it—"

"Didn't get that close," he said.

"You're pretty enough to be her," Yuri said. "Are you a real princess?"

She looked up into Kayan's face. "I'm not certain. Am I?"

"As real as those hyenas," he replied. "And prettier."

Roxanne leaned against him, taking comfort in his strength. "Are there more of them out there?"

"No doubt there are, two-legged or four." He indicated the cart. "Back up there with you. Get some sleep if you can. As soon as it's light enough to see, we'll try to catch the other donkey. If we can't, we'll put what's absolutely necessary in one cart and leave the other."

"So long as you don't throw out my leather bags."

"What's in them that you hold so dear? We've more need of water and supplies than a woman's sandals and extra tunics."

"What I carry is of more use than clothing."

"I'll make that decision when the time comes."

"You?"

"Aye. Me. You'll obey my orders when I give them, the same as Tiz or Homji."

"Are you certain of that?"

He nodded. "As certain as I am that we've not seen the last of Ptolemy's soldiers or that we have miles to cover tomorrow."

"As you say," she answered softly. "For now, I yield to your command. But I make no promises about tomorrow."

Chapter 20

On the second day after the attack by the hyenas, Kayan was forced to abandon the carts and the goats when the hard-packed earth turned to rock and shifting sand. He put Val on one donkey and strapped most of the remaining water-skins to the second, which had returned of its own accord. Homji and Bahman declared themselves fit to walk. Kayan and Tiz carried the provisions, and all the members of the party—including Roxanne and the boys—retained their own weapons.

"I'll take those," Kayan said when Roxanne lifted her heavy leather pouches out of the cart.

"Are you certain you want to burden yourself with tunics, cosmetics, and sandals?" she asked.

"Is there anything in here you don't need?"

"Look for yourself," she said. "Unless you'd prefer to examine the contents privately?"

Kayan regarded her with an expression of suspicion, but a hint of amusement twinkled in his dark eyes. The desert sun hadn't burned his cheeks as it had Yuri's and Val's; rather, the hard days of travel had simply honed his bronze skin to a burnish. He'd removed his Egyptian tunic and twisted it into a turban and allowed his long hair to fall loosely down his back. With his bare chest, short kilt, and boots, she thought he looked more like an Indian hill bandit than a Sogdian prince.

"I trust these men with my sons' lives," he answered. "There's no need for secrets between us."

"Suit yourself." Roxanne unstrapped a pouch and poured the contents onto the wooden bed of the cart. Gold necklaces and bracelets, jeweled earrings and amulets, precious stones and coronets fell in heaps and rolled across the rough-cut boards.

Tiz swore and reached for a ruby ring. "A lady after my own heart. No wonder your packs were so heavy. If you wore this on your finger, you couldn't lift your hand." He polished the gem on his tunic and held it up to the light. "Sparkles, don't it?"

Behind him, Bahman exhaled softly, and Homji grinned. "A king's ransom," Homji said.

"Just what I was thinking." Tiz tossed the ring to Roxanne. She caught it and dropped it on top of a pair of gold and jade earrings.

Kayan stared at the fortune and then glanced up, obviously waiting for an explanation. She shrugged. "You left Alexandria in a hurry. I thought you might need traveling funds."

"A crown." Yuri lifted a silver circlet set with raw emeralds the size of peas. "I guess you *are* a princess."

"Where did you get these?" Kayan asked.

"Ptolemy."

"You stole them?"

She shook her head. "Gifts."

Kayan began to laugh, as did the other three men. He laughed until tears rolled down his cheeks. "And all this time . . ." he managed, between gasps, "all this time, you've tried to make me think you'd been vain enough to carry—"

"Sandals, I believe you said," she reminded him. "Tunics and baubles?"

"I like you," Tiz said. "Any woman who can rob Pharaoh—"

"Not just any woman," Kayan reminded him. "Queen of Bactria and Sogdiana."

"Not queen," she corrected, gathering up the treasure and putting it back into the pack. "Not so long as my father lives and holds the throne."

"Why isn't Grandfather a king?" Yuri took a belligerent stance, legs apart, fists resting on his hips, dimpled chin thrust forward. "If you are his daughter, he should be King Oxyartes, not Prince Oxyartes."

"His Majesty is a prince because Princess Roxanne's mother, Queen Pari, was born royal," Kayan explained. "Her father took the title of prince when he married the queen, but under our laws, he could never be king."

"My son will hold that honor," Roxanne said. "When my father dies, I will inherit the title and the throne until my son comes of age."

"So your husband can't be a king," Val said. "Just a prince."

"My dead husband was a king in his own right. Our son will sit the throne of the Twin Kingdoms after me. He will be doubly royal."

"Sounds complicated," Val pronounced. "I think I'd rather just be a general."

"Not me," Yuri said. "I'm going to be a warrior, like Tiz. Nobody makes him take a bath when he doesn't want one. And he never has to give orders he doesn't want to, or be polite to boring people."

Tiz roared with laughter.

"Do you have a baby?" Val asked Roxanne. He slid down off the donkey to retrieve a wide gold armlet, crafted into the shape of a gazelle with ruby eyes, that had rolled off the cart and into the loose sand.

"I did," she said. "I had two sons. One died, but the other would be just a little younger than you are. I haven't seen him in a long time."

"My mother died too," Val said.

"Mothers aren't supposed to leave their babies," Yuri put in. "Good mothers take care of them. They don't die, and they don't run away and leave their—"

Val scowled and shoved Yuri hard. "Mothers can't help it if they die."

"Dying is stupid. It's just like running away."

"Is not." Val pushed him again. Yuri lowered his head and rammed his brother hard enough to knock him over backwards onto the sand. Before Kayan could separate them, fists were flying. "Take that back!" Val yelled.

He was nearly a head higher and outweighed Yuri, but the smaller boy made up in ferocity what he lacked in size. Val landed a hard blow to Yuri's nose as Kayan yanked them apart.

"Enough!"

Two pairs of blue-gray eyes glared. Blood from Yuri's nose spilled down his lip, and Val's left eye began to swell. Roxanne's chest felt tight. Yuri's remark about mothers who left their children had hit home, but her heart went out to both of them. She didn't know which boy to pull into her arms first.

"Shame on you," Kayan said to Yuri, "to strike an injured brother. Aren't there enough soldiers trying to kill us without you doing the same?"

Yuri blinked and dashed the back of a dirty hand across his eyes. His cheeks reddened with shame beneath the smears of blood and grime. His lower lip trembled, and he looked away, pretending to gaze at a circling vulture.

"And you!" Kayan glared at Val. "You're almost a man. I'd counted you as one when we faced Ptolemy's troops in the square. But I was wrong. Only a child would taunt a younger brother until he lost his temper. What do you two have if not each other?"

"But . . . he said . . ." Val stared at the ground. "I was wrong. I shouldn't have pushed you," he said without looking at Yuri.

"I didn't mean *your* mother," Yuri managed grudgingly.

"Your father is right," Roxanne said quietly. "Save your anger for the enemy."

"And save your strength to walk out of here." Tiz knelt and chose a round stone, rubbed it clean, and put it in his mouth. "From here on we ration our water. I like to suck on a stone so I can fool myself into thinking that I'm not thirsty."

"Me too," Yuri said.

"I know that," Val chimed in.

The grizzled lieutenant addressed the boys as solemnly as if they were soldiers. "Ptolemy might be pharaoh now, but he's a Macedonian warrior first. He's as smart and as tough as they come. He'll not let our princess slip easily through his fingers. He'll come after us with all he's got."

Homji grinned. "Let him. We'll send his soldiers running home with their tails between their legs."

Bahman added something too low for anyone but Homji to hear, and the younger man chuckled.

Kayan leaned over and hugged Val, then beckoned to Yuri. The boy came forward hesitantly, and his father drew him into a quick embrace. "Tiz is right," Kayan said. "Ptolemy will come with his hounds—not the pretty palace guards, but his old hands, men who marched with the Conqueror. If we mean to outfox him, we've got to put Egypt behind us."

"May Ormazd's luck be with us," Bahman said.

"That little one is lucky." Homji indicated Yuri. "You saw him driving that chariot back in Alexandria. He has Alexander's own luck. I would have bet a month's wages that chariot would turn over, but it didn't."

"Skill," Roxanne said with a wink at Yuri.

"Skill, my hairy ballocks," Tiz said. "Begging your pardon, Highness. Yuri's lucky, because he can't drive any better than a mincing Mede. I never saw worse, except the general here when he was ten and learning to handle a two-horse team. Wiped out two chariots in one day. His father was so mad, he had to hide out for two weeks in the mountains before he dared come home." Tiz laughed and then added. "Maybe some of Prince Yuri's luck will rub off on the rest of us. Because without it, we're screwed."

Kayan didn't comment. Instead, he lifted Val and put him back on the donkey, shouldered both of Roxanne's packs, a food container, and another skin of water, and started walking north.

Yuri dove into the cart and snatched a reed basket with a leather strap and slung it over his shoulder.

"What's that?" Tiz demanded. "No need to carry what we don't need. You'll just wear yourself out and end up dumping it along the way."

"It's mine," Yuri said stubbornly. "It's mine, and I won't leave it behind."

"He's got a—" Val began.

Yuri threw his brother a look that was black enough to melt sand into glass. Val clamped his lips together and rolled his eyes. Yuri's chin stiffened and he straightened his shoulders and stalked off to catch up with his father.

Tiz looked quizzically at Val, but the boy avoided the warrior's gaze. Tiz blinked and glanced at Roxanne.

"Who knows?" She shrugged and started walking.

For the first hour, Roxanne noticed that Yuri kept to himself, but gradually he moved closer to Val. By the second hour, Val was carrying the small woven basket balanced on his lap, and no one would have guessed that the boys had come to blows.

A day and a half later, Kayan gave a pitifully small ration of water to each of the two donkeys and motioned for Roxanne to mount the riderless animal. She shook her head and glanced at Yuri, who was walking.

Val's face was drawn, but he straightened his shoulders and said, "I don't need to ride anymore. I can walk."

"I'm not riding either," Yuri chimed in. "I—"

Kayan caught him around the waist and put him on the donkey. "Don't talk, don't argue, just ride." Yuri's mouth tightened and his bloodshot eyes narrowed, but he did as he was told. Val passed the basket back to Yuri.

"What's in that?" Kayan asked. "What are the two of you up to?"

"It's mine." Yuri clutched the basket against his chest.

"Let me see," Kayan said.

Yuri shook his head. Kayan reached for the basket. "He's mine," Yuri said. "He's mine, and I'm keeping him."

"Give it to me!"

The boy's face paled. Val slid down off his donkey and hurried to his brother's side. "Don't take Khui away from him," Val protested. "He can have my water."

"Mine, too," Yuri said.

Kayan's expression hardened. "What have you got in there?"

The basket hissed.

"A snake?" Roxanne stepped back. "All this time, you two have been carrying a snake?"

Kayan's patience snapped. "Open the lid!"

Yuri stood his ground. "You'll have to kill me first."

Kayan raised his hand, but Roxanne stepped between them before he could strike. "Please," she said quietly. "Let me see him. Khui? Is that his name?"

"Stay out of this, Roxanne," Kayan said.

"Please, Yuri," Roxanne said. "I won't take him away from you. I promise."

"He is scared," Yuri said. He scowled at his father. "You scared Khui." Slowly, reluctantly, he untied the leather thong that held the lid in place. There was a flash of white, and an angry kitten streaked up the child's arm to cling, hissing and arching its back, on the boy's shoulder.

"A cat?" Kayan said. "You brought a cat?"

"I've seen soldiers steal a lot of things," Tiz said, "but never a cat."

"He's a lovely cat," Roxanne said. The short-haired kitten was as lean as a ferret, almost pure white with vivid blue eyes and faint gray markings on his paws, ears, and tail. "How old is he?"

"Five months old. And I didn't steal Khui. The lady gave him to me."

"We can't take a—"

Roxanne cut Kayan off. "It will be fine."

"I won't leave him," Yuri said. "If you leave him to die in the desert, you have to leave me too."

"I told him not to," Val said. "He wouldn't listen. He never listens."

"Stay out of this," Kayan said.

"He's mine," Yuri repeated. "He's my friend, and Sogdians stick by their friends. You said so."

"Let him bring his cat." Roxanne glanced pleadingly at Kayan.

"The damn thing will just die and break his heart."

"Please," she said. "For me."

Kayan shrugged. "Suit yourself, but you carry it, Yuri. You tend to it, and if it puts any of us in danger—if it causes any trouble, I'll wring its neck."

Yuri nodded. "He won't, will you, Khui?"

The cat hissed.

"Any more surprises?" Kayan asked. "Or are we going to stand here until we're hyena bait?"

"No," Roxanne assured him. "No more surprises."

Roxanne kept walking, telling herself that all she had to do was put one foot in front of the other, telling herself that they'd find water soon, telling herself that the two vultures circling overhead weren't a sign of bad luck.

Yuri kept the cat's basket held tightly in his arms. And

whenever they stopped for water, the boy tenderly dripped water from his lips into the kitten's mouth. Kayan pretended not to notice the cat, but Roxanne observed that he never drank until everyone else had taken a share. Kayan never did more than take a small sip to wet his tongue.

The ground was nearly all rock. Sharp shards cut through the men's boots and ripped Roxanne's sandals to shreds, so that she had to wrap them in strips of linen from her pack. Homji's feet were so bad that he left bloodstains wherever he stepped. Roxanne thought she had more sand in her mouth and nose than in her hair, and her tongue felt twice its normal size.

Once, when she stumbled, Kayan reached out and caught her. "Want me to carry your bow and quiver?" he asked. She shook her head.

"Take heart," he said. "We'll make it."

She tried to smile at him, but her upper lip cracked and she winced. "Do you believe that, or are you just trying to make me feel better?"

Kayan was dirtier than ever, and there were tight lines around his mouth, but otherwise he might have been out for a stroll in the palace garden. She marveled at his strength and stamina.

"It's the children I worry about," she said. "They need water."

"They come from good stock. They'll hold up until we reach the camp."

"What we really need is a jar of that Egyptian beer," Tiz said.

"Two jars, at least," Homji said to Bahman.

His companion laughed. "So long as you're ordering, I'll have three jars of beer, a side of roasted beef, and a roomful of dancing girls."

"What would you want with girls out here?" Yuri demanded. "I'd rather have a horse."

Val joined in with the men's laughter.

Yuri scowled. "I hate girls. All they do is squeal."

That remark brought a peal of raucous amusement from Tiz. "Wait until you're a little older," he said in a strangled croak. "You'll figure out what they're good for."

At mid-afternoon, Kayan ordered a halt in the shade of a rock. While the adults were catching their breath, Yuri climbed the boulder and spied a column of dust ahead of them. "There." He pointed. "Beyond that ridge. I see something."

"Soldiers?" Val asked.

"No. They're coming from the wrong direction," Tiz said.

"Unless Ptolemy sent messengers up and down the Nile, and they're trying to cut us off," Roxanne suggested.

Kayan caught sight of the figures and shook his head. "They'd have chariots or camels. These men are on foot, driving or leading animals. It's likely a caravan." He motioned Yuri down. "You and Val stay here and protect Roxanne while we go take a closer look.

"There are only four of you," Roxanne began. "I can—"

Kayan silenced her with a look. "You do as I say when I say it. Stay here with the boys. Don't show yourself, and don't make any noise, no matter what happens." He threw off the packs containing her jewels and belongings. "Keep these here with you."

"And if they kill you?"

"Hide until you're certain they're gone. Then keep walking in the same direction we've been going. We can't be more than two days from the oasis where the others are camped."

Roxanne, Yuri and his cat, and Val hid in the rocks until dark fell. They could see the flicker of a fire more than a mile away, but none of the men returned. As it grew colder, Roxanne drew the two boys under the remaining blanket and they huddled together, taking comfort from each other. The kitten purred. The moon came out, and hyenas began to howl to the west.

"I should have gone with them," Val whispered, breaking the silence. "If they had to fight, I should have helped."

Yuri nodded, cuddling his cat. "Me too."

"Shhh," Roxanne said. "You'd best put Khui back in his basket."

"He's cold."

"Take him under the blanket with you, but keep him in his basket so he doesn't run away."

"He won't.

"Well, then, he might go hunting and get lost. You don't want to lose him, do you?"

"No."

"Then do as I say. Put him back in his basket and try to sleep. Don't worry. Your father will be back." She strained her eyes to see in the blackness.

After a long time, she heard what sounded like a rattle of gravel. Stealthily she pushed aside the blanket, slipped an arrow from her quiver, and notched it to the string. Val stirred, and she held her breath, hoping that the boy wouldn't give away their presence.

An owl hooted.

Roxanne felt sweat trickle between her breasts.

The owl called again, this time louder.

"That's Kayan," Yuri piped up. He replied with a screech that might have been a dying mouse captured by the same owl.

They waited for a short while, and then abruptly Kayan's tall form materialized out of the night. Roxanne sighed with relief. "Kayan." She lowered her bow. Joy at his return spilled through her, followed instantly by a warm tingling. It was all she could do to keep from crying out with excitement.

Val sprang up and threw himself into his father's arms. "Did you kill them all?"

"Thought we might have to," Kayan replied, rubbing the boy's head affectionately. "Yuri?"

Yuri ran to him. Kayan hugged him and then carefully handed something to the child. "It's a water-skin. Careful. Don't waste any."

Roxanne moved out of the shadows. "We were worried." She tried to keep her tone normal, tried to hide the pleasure she felt at seeing him, alive and whole. Safe.

"They claimed to be traders, but they're more likely bandits. We traded the two donkeys for three water-skins and some dates and stale flatbread. It took so long because we had to accept the hospitality of their fire. Then we moved on. There were seven of them, heavily armed. We didn't want them to guess that you were hiding here."

"You didn't fight them?" Yuri demanded. "I would have killed them and taken—"

"Hush," Val said. "I'd like to see you fight seven bandits."

"I could too, couldn't I, Roxanne?"

"Any man who fights when he doesn't have to is a fool," Kayan said. "Now give her some of that water. Tiz and the others kept moving. We'll catch up with them in the morning."

"What if we don't find them?" Roxanne asked.

"Tiz will find us. He may be getting gray, but he's a wise old wolf. Trust him to take care of his hide."

"I'm glad you got rid of those donkeys," Yuri said. "I'm a prince. I need a real horse, not a jackass."

"Me too," Val agreed. "Warriors don't ride donkeys."

"Some warriors will ride anything rather than walk," Roxanne said. "Even elephants." She lifted the water-skin and let the warm, sour liquid trickle over her tongue. It tasted better than the finest Sogdian wine.

"Just a little at a time," Kayan warned. "Your belly won't hold much after being so dry." Roxanne took another drink and passed the skin back to Val. "Can you walk a few miles more tonight?" Kayan asked her. He touched her shoulder, and she shivered.

"Yes." She wanted to go into his arms. She wanted him

to hold her as he'd held his sons, but this wasn't the time. When she'd thought he might not come back, the image of going on without him was too awful to contemplate.

She loved him.

Whether this was merely the love she'd felt for him as a child, for what they'd had and lost so long ago, she couldn't tell. She loved him as a friend and a cousin. But more? She was too tired to know her own heart. Maybe she was clinging to him because she thought he could get her away from Egypt and home. Or perhaps she was the kind of woman who loved whatever man she was with . . . Only time would tell . . . if they had time.

Yuri's luck held. The bandits didn't find them that night. And at daybreak, as lavender and tangerine ribbons of iridescent light spilled over the edge of the world, Roxanne caught sight of a man on a spotted camel loping across an open stretch of gleaming sand.

Val shouted, "Tiz! It's Tiz!"

In the distance the figures of other mounted camels appeared, vanished, and then appeared again as they traversed the undulating surface of the desert. "Yours?" Roxanne asked hopefully.

Kayan grinned, caught her shoulders, and kissed her. "Tiz isn't riding as though his ass is on fire. I'd say he's found our reinforcements."

"Fine talk in front of your sons," she said, but she was laughing too. And her lips tingled from the touch of his.

Yuri and Val shouted and jumped up and down, waving. Tiz waved back.

"Ptolemy won't catch us now!" Yuri proclaimed gleefully.

"He won't, eh?" Roxanne felt as excited as the children. "And why is that?"

Kayan nuzzled her hair. "They're Bactrian-Dromedary crosses," he said. "Well suited for desert travel and fast."

She closed her eyes for an instant, savoring the moment.

"Nobody will catch us," Yuri cried. "Not even Pharaoh's chariots!" He pointed to the camels. "You'll get to ride on a camel, Khui. You'll like that better than a donkey."

In the harbor at Alexandria, Ptolemy climbed the ladder to board the flagship of his fleet, captained by his old friend, Hector of Pella. "How many days to Gaza?" he demanded as his sandal touched the deck.

"This ship or all of them?" Hector asked. He handed Ptolemy a cup of wine. "I hear you've been playing games in the desert."

"Soldiers, horses, chariots. Get them aboard the ships. I want to be in Gaza ahead of that Bactrian bastard." By Ares's teeth, his head was splitting. Intense pain throbbed in his temples, pain made worse by every sound and the scorching sunlight. All he wanted was shade and something to drink.

"Not a problem," the wizened admiral said. "What are the chances he's survived the desert? If you couldn't find them, maybe the vultures or the hyenas did."

"No," Ptolemy said. "They're alive. I know it. I can feel it in my bones."

Feel it in your bones, hell, Alexander said. *You didn't think it would be that easy, did you? She's smarter than you are, Brother. And if you're not careful, she'll make a laughingstock out of you.*

"Shut your mouth," Ptolemy said, downing the dregs of the wine. "I've heard enough out of you." He resisted the urge to look over his shoulder. If this kept up, word would get out that he was losing his mind.

The admiral swore a foul oath and grinned wolfishly. "Since when do you expect me to turn lick-spittle? Save your bad temper for your generals."

"Not you," Ptolemy said. "I didn't mean you. I was . . . I was thinking about something. Didn't get much sleep in the last week." Rattling around in a chariot, eating dust while the Egyptian sun stewed his brains wasn't his idea of a good time. Maybe he was getting old. Or maybe he was mad. He wondered if madmen realized when they lost their wits.

Maybe he was crazy, but he'd not be the first king to be mad—or the last.

Hector chuckled. "You must have gotten a start on me." He took the wine jar from a sailor and poured Ptolemy another cup. "And a good thing, for I've more trouble for you."

More? Alexander asked. *I'd think big brother has more than enough on his plate.*

Ptolemy ground his teeth until pain shot through a back molar. Alexander's words were as clear as Hector's, more so, because Alexander had taken voice lessons as a youth so that he could be heard by his troops. Ptolemy's pulse was racing, and his gut was in knots. He kept his eyes on Hector. Damned if the admiral's head and shoulders weren't haloed with shimmers of light.

All Ptolemy had to do was ignore Alexander's voice and give all his attention to Hector. He refused to give in. He wouldn't turn and look—not this time.

Deep down, he was certain that if he did, he'd see not just a shadow as he had in his bedchamber, but Alexander standing there, gloating. He'd be in battle attire, sword at his side, that damned lionskin cap on his head. It was the way Alexander haunted his dreams. It was bad enough that he couldn't sleep, but lately . . . lately, his brother had been showing up several times a week.

No, Ptolemy told himself as he swallowed a mouthful of unwatered wine. He was just suffering from the strain of his efforts to make Egypt the mightiest nation in the Western world, or he might have contracted some illness that would go away in time. Alexander wasn't here on Hector's ship. He couldn't be here. He was dead, lying in his crystal coffin. And these headaches were just headaches, nothing more.

Think so, do you? Alexander asked cheerfully. *You're the bastard, trying to steal my wife. I told you to take care of her. You broke your promise to me, a promise you made on my deathbed. Have you forgotten that, you lying shit? I told you to watch over them. Where's my son, Ptolemy? Where is he?*

"Dead," Ptolemy answered. "As dead as you are."

You're wrong there. He's not dead.

Hector frowned and took a step back. "Picked up a fever in the desert, did you?" He shook his head. "I've got a good physician. Not on this vessel. But I can have him here in an hour."

More trouble? Alexander said. *I can't wait to hear what this is.*

"What's wrong?" Ptolemy asked.

"Below decks," Hector answered. "The queen. She came aboard and . . ." He shrugged. "I didn't think you wanted—"

Which one? Alexander said. *The Egyptian queen or the Greek? You've got so many wives to keep track of. You didn't need mine.*

"Artakama?" Ptolemy asked. He felt as though someone were driving a spike through the back of his head. The pain made his stomach queasy.

Hector shook his head. "Queen Berenice. She came aboard about an hour ago, insisting that you take her with you to Greece to visit her father. I told her I didn't know where we were bound but—"

"Get her off this ship," Ptolemy ordered.

Hector raised his hands, palms out. "I thought that's what you'd say, but I wasn't about to lay hands on your wife without—"

"Get the bitch off before I throw her overboard!" Ptolemy shouted.

Alexander's laughter echoed in his head. *Learn to man-*

age your own women before you take on mine. Roxanne's already made off with half your treasury. Make one more mistake, and she'll have your stones in a velvet bag hanging from her palace gate.

Chapter 21

For Roxanne, the weeks that followed the rendezvous with Kayan's cavalrymen had passed almost as a dream until today. Mounted on a swift cream-colored camel, she had ridden with them through each night and into the morning, stopping only in the heat of midday before starting off again. Relentlessly Kayan had pressed on toward the city of Gaza, not sparing her, his sons, the men, or the beasts.

As she traveled with Kayan's troopers, it seemed to her as though the years fell away and she was reliving her carefree youth. As heir to Sogdiana and Bactria, she had been expected to be prepared to lead her nation in peace or war. In the Amazon tradition, her father had insisted that she learn to ride and shoot like a Scythian. She had been instructed in swordsmanship by masters of the art, as well as in mathematics, science, linguistics, and history. More prince than princess, she had hunted and fished and roamed the wild mountains and valleys, not as pampered royalty but as an equal of her father's soldiers. Now, during this journey, she shared this intimate camaraderie again.

In her mind, the troubling times receded in urgency. Alexander's invasion of her country, her forced marriage, the years in prison, even Ptolemy and Alexandria didn't seem as important as before. All that mattered now was each moment and the men and boys who endured the hardships of this desert with her.

As the days passed, Kayan's followers lost their awe of her and began to consider her one of them. She treated their ailments, shared their rough camp meals, and warmed to their laughter. She listened to boasting of battles won and maidens lost, joined in the rowdy songs, and came to know these brave young men as patriots, brothers, and friends.

It was Kayan's careful planning that saved them from certain disaster. He had traveled this path on his way to Egypt, and he'd commanded his soldiers to cache stores of life-giving water, food, and grain for the camels at intervals in the desert. The sun was merciless, the landscape oppressive with shifting sand, but Kayan had chosen well. He'd picked only the strongest animals and men, all with bold hearts and an instinct for survival.

Kayan had ridden across the borders of Bactria with seventy camels, forty-two soldiers, and two young boys. Of the men, seven had met their deaths, the majority lost in hand-to-hand combat in Alexandria. Fifty-two camels survived; those that weakened were slaughtered and the meat eaten or salted and dried.

Night after night, Roxanne rode under the brilliant star-studded sky with only her thoughts to keep her company. Each camel carried a single rider, while the remainder of the animals were loaded with water-skins, tents, and supplies.

Kayan had insisted that she, Val, and Yuri be strapped to their saddles because of the danger of falling off their mounts and becoming lost in the dark or during the sandstorms that swept down from the north. At first she had argued, but Kayan would not budge, stating that either she gave in gracefully or he would tie her hands and feet as well.

"You want to upset the discipline in my troops?" he'd asked. "Or are you trying to foment rebellion in my sons?"

"I can ride a camel as well as you," she'd insisted. "You taught me."

"You can," he'd agreed. "But you're a woman. I'll not lose you because you weakened and fell."

"I'll not weaken," she'd flung back.

Kayan had won, as he'd won far too many contests between them recently. Reluctantly, after the second week of desert travel, she admitted to herself that he was right. The swaying of the beast was hypnotic, and she found it impossible to stay awake for the fifteen or twenty hours they remained in the saddle.

The boys lost weight. Their fair skins were burned nearly as dark as nomads, and weariness showed in their eyes. Val suffered the most. The wound on his side had healed, but he needed rest and time to recover from his ordeal—time that they didn't have.

When they did stop, Val made an effort to watch over Roxanne, bringing her food and water, often falling asleep holding tightly to her hand or lying with his head in her lap. Not only did Val seem to have forgotten his earlier distrust, he wasn't afraid to show his affection. It was impossible not to open her heart to Val, who obviously cared for her and who talked so reverently about a dead mother whose face he could no longer remember.

If she married Kayan, she told herself, she could be a mother to Val. Not just to him, but to Yuri and to her own son too. But she still wasn't ready to give Kayan an answer. And with the possibility that she'd never be ready, was it unfair to Val to allow him to become so attached to her?

As for Yuri, he troubled her. The mischievous child

who'd charmed her in Alexandria had become withdrawn and silent in the last few weeks. He shadowed Kayan, and seemed to resent the attention Val paid to her. It was almost as though the desert sun had scorched away the boy and left a small but determined warrior, one old far beyond his years. The only sign of the child in him was his devotion to Khui, a sentiment the skinny kitten seemed to return.

She and Kayan had never been alone since the night the hyenas had attacked. While his concern for her welfare remained unfailing, there was no opportunity for him to press her for a decision about marrying him. They were free to be what they had been for so long, the best of friends.

Again she found herself remembering the scrapes they had gotten into and out of as children and the way she'd always depended on him. She could see how the years had matured him, but only for the better. This Kayan was a wiser man, a better leader, less headstrong, and tireless in the care of his two sons.

She would not allow herself to consider the other memories . . . the excitement she'd felt when Kayan held her . . . the taste of his mouth on hers and the thrill of his touch. She could not dwell on what might have been her own sensual response to the attentions of a virile man. Her father's hot blood ran in her veins. If she could love a man like Alexander, who had conquered and slain her own people, how could she ever trust her own judgment again?

No, if she married again, it would not be for political reasons or because her father asked it. She wouldn't marry to win a protector or to fulfill a childhood promise. And she wouldn't take a husband because he made her heart pound, her hands sweat, and her loins ache. If she ever did wed, it would be for nothing less than true and everlasting love.

She wondered for the thousandth time if her heart had died

inside that dark cavern, or if Alexander had carried it away as a prize of war. Maybe she lacked the ability to love a man with all her soul. Could it be that she was so willful and headstrong that she didn't know the meaning of selfless love?

If so, she would be better off choosing her lovers discreetly and never becoming another man's wife.

This day had ended, or begun, like so many on this desert ordeal. When the sun was directly overhead, Kayan had ordered the men to erect the tents so as to protect them from the heat. After Roxanne had fed, watered, and hobbled her camel, she joined Val, Yuri and his cat, and Kayan in one of the shelters.

"Ptolemy will never catch up with us," Val said as he passed her a handful of raisins.

She shook her head reluctantly. "King Ptolemy won't stop at the borders of Egypt." She groaned and flopped back on the rug, glad to strip off her head covering and close her eyes. Every inch of her body felt gritty, and she longed for a hot bath, clean sheets, and a soft bed.

"Ptolemy controls everything between Syria and Carthage," Kayan said, "and his fleet is the greatest in the world. He commands more ships than all the cities of Greece together."

"He'll think the vultures got us," Yuri said. Khui curled in his lap, purring, his blue eyes nearly closed.

Kayan shook his head. "We can't rely on that. We have to get to Gaza and on into Syria before striking through the heart of the Greek occupation to Persia. Even there, Ptolemy's fist may close on us."

"Or Cassander's," Roxanne said. The Greek general was ambitious. He'd murdered Alexander's mother and most of his rivals in his attempts to seize Alexander's crown. Cassander had tried to kill her in Macedonia. If they were caught, she could expect no mercy from Cassander's troops.

"I'm not afraid of any of them." Yuri had finished his

bread and dates and was busy sharpening his knife. The boy had wrapped his head and face so that only his eyes and a little of his forehead showed. He wore a belted man's shirt, trousers, and soft hide shoes, which Tiz had fashioned out of goatskin.

So young and so fierce, Roxanne thought. She couldn't help wondering what kind of man he would be if he lived to grow up. "I'm not afraid of Ptolemy," she said, "but I am afraid of what he can do to us. The important thing is to get home safely."

"Bactria and Sogdiana aren't safe," Val said. "They'll just come after us. They always do. The Scythians, the Greeks, the Persians. So now it will be Egyptians."

"The Twin Kingdoms defended their borders for over a thousand years," she said.

"Until the Conqueror came." Kayan's gaze met hers. "Now—"

"Don't talk about him. I hate him!" Yuri said. He sliced a bit of dried camel meat with his knife and fed the tidbit to Khui. "If I'd been a warrior, I would have beaten him. I'd have put a sword through his black heart."

"Don't waste your energy hating a dead man," Kayan said. "It's the living conquerors we have to worry about."

"You and Grandfather drove the Greeks out after Alexander died," Yuri said. "If we can fight Greeks, we can fight Egyptians." He paused and glared at Roxanne. "But we wouldn't have to if you hadn't gone after *her*."

"She's our queen," Val declared. "We had to rescue her."

Yuri's blue-gray eyes turned hard. "I would have left her there with Ptolemy."

Val leaped to his feet. "Liar!"

"Am not!" Yuri rose and launched himself at his brother. Khui squalled and dove into its basket.

"Coward!" Val shouted.

Kayan pried the two apart. "Enough," he said. "The

princess will be our queen and your mother if I have any- thing to say about it. Yuri, you owe her an apology."

"No!" He tried to twist out of his father's grasp. "I hate her. She married Alexander for his crown, and now she wants Ptolemy."

"Not another word!" Kayan said.

"She's a traitor!" Yuri flung back. "I don't want you to marry her. I don't want her to be my mother. I wish she was dead!"

The boy's bitter words shocked Roxanne. Hurt welled up in her chest, and she blinked back tears. "I don't hate you, Yuri. I care about you—"

"No, you don't!" he said. "You lie! You care about your- self. You don't want us."

"That's not true," she protested.

"Where's your son?" Yuri cried, kicking and struggling to get free. "Why didn't you keep him with—"

Kayan clamped a hand over Yuri's mouth. "Apologize!"

"I won't!" Kayan's fingers muffled Yuri's protests. "I won't."

"Please," Roxanne said. "Let him go. Let Yuri say what he feels about me."

Kayan released the child, and Yuri scrambled up and darted out of the tent. Kayan made a move to go after him, but Roxanne lifted her hand. "No," she said. "Let me. I'll bring him back."

The sun struck her with the force of a blow. She stood up and squinted, shading her eyes with her hand as she looked around the camp. None of the men were visible, and she assumed they were in the other tents. The camels, staked and hobbled, stood with their backs to the wind, shuffling their wide feet, grunting and groaning.

The land around them was treeless. Either Yuri had gone into one of the other tents or he was hiding among the camels. Roxanne went to the lines of animals, and found Tiz examining a brown camel's hind leg.

He glanced up at her. "Looking for the little one?"

She nodded.

Tiz pointed to the tents. "He'll be all right. I'll look after him."

Roxanne covered her eyes. "What's wrong with the camel?"

"Nothing a little salve and time won't fix. Got kicked by one of the others, I suppose." He fixed his single eye on her. "Boy's fighting mad, isn't he?"

She nodded again. The camel sheltered her from the worst of the wind-blown sand, but the sun was relentless. "He says he hates me."

Tiz shrugged. "Jealous. Thinks you're going to take his father away."

"I'd never come between them," she said. "I love him." She realized as she said it that she did love the boy. Whether she'd allowed herself to be captivated by Val and Yuri because she longed for her own child so much, or whether it had happened because of their natural charm, it didn't matter. She found that she cared deeply for both of Kayan's sons.

"You love the lad or love the general?"

"I've always loved Kayan."

"That's not what he wants, that *always loved*."

"It's hard, Tiz. I'm not a lovesick girl. I'm a widow who—"

"Right. Heard that before." Tiz grinned and spat sand, taking care to spit downwind so he wouldn't hit her. "You loved that Macedonian bastard, didn't you?"

"Yes, I think I did."

"Well, for all one can say about him, and I've spoken my share, he was a man to be reckoned with."

"Yes, he was, wasn't he?"

Tiz busied himself with anointing the camel's cut leg. "Married three times myself. First one was Mahin, Ahriman's own whelp. Meanest woman to ever draw breath, and the sneakiest. Got herself with child by my best friend. I would have had to divorce her, but she died when the Greeks overran her village."

"I'm sorry. And the babe?"

"Never drew breath. Soldiers killed Mahin when she was in her eighth month." He glanced back at her. "Truth is, I cried over her when I found out she was dead. Hated her, but hated to think of her dying that way." He patted the camel and stepped away. "I always heard that losing a woman was like falling off a horse. Best thing to do is get right back on. Otherwise, you get to thinking too much and get shy of what threw you. I married Lalagul second."

"Lalagul?"

"Fifteen, with a face like a new moon and the heart of a lion. She already had a baby with no father and she needed a provider. No reason why she should have taken to a one-eyed rascal like me, but she did. She gave me two sons a man could be proud of before fever took them all in one week."

"Tiz." Roxanne grasped his forearm.

"What I'm trying to say is that I made up my mind not to bother with marrying no other women. I'd love them and ride out when my captain gave the orders. But when we got to India, I found Vrinda, and she was sweeter than the other two put together. She was swelling with my child when she died of a cobra bite."

"How could you bear it?"

"You bear what you must in this life, Princess. But I'm telling you that if I find another woman that takes my fancy and she's willing, I'll marry again. I'll marry and we'll try to make more children to take the place of the ones I lost. My Vrinda's dead, and so are Lalagul and Mahin, but I'm alive. If I was happy with one wife, I might be happy with another. It wouldn't be the same, but I wouldn't expect it to be. And I'd rather make a mistake ten times over than to give up living because I might pick the wrong girl."

"Roxanne!"

She turned to see Kayan coming toward her. "Where's Yuri?"

"In my tent," Tiz answered. "I'll tend to him, General."

Roxanne rose and kissed the veteran on the cheek. "Thank you," she said. "For everything."

He grinned. "My pleasure, Princess. Just don't hurt the ones I care about most. I'm not bright, but I'm loyal."

She chuckled. "You're bright enough." She turned and walked to Kayan. "I'm sorry about Yuri," she said.

He motioned her back inside the tent. "Get some rest while you can. I'm going to have a talk with my son."

"Don't punish him because of me. He's angry enough."

Kayan grasped her arms. "Roxanne . . . I . . ."

She was facing toward Tiz's tent and saw a small hand push the flap aside. "Not now," she said, stepping away from Kayan.

For a second, the boy's gaze met hers. Then he crawled out, stood, and marched stoically to his father. "I need Khui," he said.

"You need your bottom striped," Kayan replied.

"No," she said. "Don't."

Yuri stopped and looked up at her. The wind howled around the tents, driving sand like needles against their skin, but the child ignored it. "I was wrong to insult you," he said stiffly. "I deserve to be whipped."

"When have I ever beaten you?" Kayan asked.

Yuri stood his ground. "I owe you allegiance," he said to Roxanne. "But I don't have to like you."

Kayan grabbed for him. "You little—"

Yuri ducked into the tent. Roxanne and Kayan followed him. Yuri had Khui's basket in his arms. "Don't whip me in front of her," he said.

"I don't understand," Roxanne said. A single tear spilled down her dirty cheek. "What have I done to you?" she asked the child. "I thought we were friends."

Anguish gleamed in the boy's eyes. "Why should you come back from the dead?" he demanded. "Why you and not my mother?"

"Yuri," Kayan said. "You don't—"

"Stop it!" Val cried, running into the tent. "She's dead, and she's not coming back. Just like *my* mother. But"—he grabbed Roxanne's hand—"you're here, aren't you?"

"Yes, Val, I am here," she said as she knelt and embraced him.

"Have her, then!" Yuri shouted. "Let her be your mother."

"Go on," Kayan said to Yuri. "Go with Tiz. We'll talk about this later when you've had time to think about how much you've hurt Roxanne. Maybe you'll feel different then."

Yuri carried Khui to the entrance of the tent, glanced back at Roxanne, and addressed his father. "I won't change my mind. Nothing you can say will make a difference. She'll never be my mother." He ducked out of the tent and let the flap drop closed behind him.

"Go with him, Val," Kayan said. "Make certain he does nothing foolish."

Val looked up at Roxanne.

"Go," she said softly. "Care for your little brother. He needs you."

"Remain with him until it's time to set off again," Kayan ordered.

"I will," the boy promised. With a shy smile for Roxanne, he followed Yuri outside.

"Will they be all right?" she asked.

"A hundred feet? From one tent to another? They've camped alone in the mountains for a week at a time." Kayan shook his head. "They're growing into men."

She swallowed. "They're too young to be men yet."

"Not in these times."

The tent was small. He had only to reach out and take her hand to pull her to him. "What's wrong?" she asked. "What have I done to turn Yuri against me? I wanted him to like me."

"He does." Kayan embraced her and lowered his head to kiss her mouth.

Desire surged through her body. One instant, they had been discussing Kayan's son, and the next, he was kissing her and she was kissing him back. Trembling, she pulled away. "This isn't the right time."

"Isn't it?" He kissed her again and pushed her down onto the rug, pinning her to the ground and tangling his fingers in her hair. "How long do you expect me to wait, Roxanne?"

All the years that had passed between them were nothing now that Roxanne was here alone with him in this tent. For weeks they had gone without sleep, exposed to sun and wind, yet she was more desirable to him than she had ever been. Being near her made him crazy. He couldn't deal sensibly with his sons. He couldn't worry about the lies he'd been forced to tell her or the repercussions when she found out the truth. All he could think of was claiming this woman that fate had denied him for so long.

"I love you," he murmured as he pressed feather-light kisses on her face and mouth. He wanted her—not just her body, but her general's mind, her laughter and wisdom. He needed her compassion and her faith, a faith in the Creator and the power of good over evil that had never failed.

Even now, as he grew hard, as his body ached to possess her, he knew that he could not take her by coercion. He believed Roxanne loved him as he loved her. But she was stubborn. If there was any hope of happiness for the two of them, it would come only if they were joined as one heart, one soul.

"Please," she begged. "I can't think. The children may come back."

Heat flashed under his skin. Reason warred with pas-

sion. He didn't care who might discover them. Tomorrow
might bring death, but they were together here and now. "I
want you," he rasped. "More than life, I want you."

He kissed her again, slipping his tongue between her lips,
delving deep into her, feeling the warmth and texture of her
body. "Roxanne." He groaned, fighting to maintain control.

"Not this way," she whispered.

"We've been betrothed since we were children. By our
laws, we are husband and wife."

She turned her face away and whispered. "Not until I
give my consent."

He released her and sat up. "I'll join my soldiers if you
don't want me here."

"No," she said. "Kayan. Don't go." Tears spilled from
her eyes, scalding him as no torture could ever do. "Can't
you see what it's like for me? Always, one man or another
has forced me to his will. Even my own father chose you to
be my husband. Now, for the first time, I have the freedom
to decide for myself. You must know that I love you, but—"

"It is a strange love, and one I find hard to bear." He
rose to his knees and moved away from her. "I'm not a boy
any longer," he said. "This isn't a board game of foot soldiers and elephants. You can't manipulate me as you did
Alexander."

Her eyes widened. "You've never used his name before."

"Maybe I should have." He reached for his sword belt
and strapped it around his waist. "Alexander came between us."

"Do you blame me for that?" She was sobbing, and he
wanted nothing more than to take her in his arms and kiss
away the hurt. But he knew that if he touched her, they
would end up making love. He would win this battle of
wills but lose the war.

His gaze locked with hers. "I've never blamed you," he
said. "He forced you to become his wife, but you main-
tained your honor. You never broke your marriage vows—

we never broke them. But Alexander is dead, Roxanne. Will you let him divide us forever? Does he have to take you to the grave with him?" He didn't wait for an answer, but turned his back on her and left.

As he walked away from the shelter, he could hear the sound of her weeping.

Chapter 22

That evening when Kayan assembled the men and camels to ride through the night, he motioned Yuri to him. "I want you to trade Friya for Chubin, the big spotted male. He's the strongest of our riding stock."

Yuri waited, his expression unreadable. He didn't ask why, as Val would have done. Nevertheless, it was clear to Kayan that his son expected a reason for this order to change mounts. Camels were stubborn beasts at best, with likes and dislikes. Friya, the animal that Yuri usually rode, was young and fast, and Yuri handled her with the same skill he exhibited as a horseman.

"This desert is hard on Princess Roxanne. I'm afraid her strength is failing," Kayan said, which certainly wasn't a blatant lie. "I want you to take her on Chubin with you."

Yuri's blue-gray eyes took on a steely hue. "Let her ride with Val. He likes her."

"I'm not asking," Kayan said. "It's an order."

"I hate her."

"That is your right. As your father and your commander, it's my right to insist you obey a direct command."

Yuri stiffened to his full height and snapped a military salute, right fist over his heart. "Yes, sir."

His face showed not the slightest expression, but his eyes flashed with a defiance that Kayan knew all too well. Of his sons, this one had always been the more difficult.

"The princess is heir to the Twin Kingdoms. You will guard her with your life."

Yuri didn't blink an eyelid. "Yes, sir."

"And you will be on your best behavior," Kayan added.

"As you wish, sir."

Roxanne was no happier than Yuri with Kayan's decision, but she had the good sense not to argue the point in front of the men. Within minutes, the tents were struck and the supplies loaded. Kayan watched as a grim-faced Yuri led the big brown and white camel to where Roxanne stood, tapped Chubin to make him kneel, and waited for her to climb onto the saddle.

"Remember what I said," Kayan told him.

Yuri grimaced.

Roxanne sighed and tried to look Kayan in the eyes, but he turned his back to talk to Tiz. She couldn't guess why Kayan wanted her to ride double with Yuri. She was perfectly capable of managing her own mount, and the boy obviously resisted the idea of being in such close contact with her for hours.

Yuri made a sound of impatience, and she hurried to climb onto the camel's back. Once she was seated securely in the saddle, Yuri hopped up behind her and gave the command for the animal to rise.

Chubin grunted and groaned in protest. "Up!" Yuri said. The surly beast moaned and rolled his large, doelike eyes. Yuri repeated the command and smacked the animal's rump with a switch. Chubin bawled, snapped at the nearest camel with yellowed teeth, and unfolded his long, powerful legs.

"This was not my idea," Roxanne murmured as the camel got to his feet. "But I'm glad we have a chance to talk."

Yuri didn't answer.

He guided Chubin into the forming column. Warriors called to him, and he smiled and returned their greetings. It was clear to her that the child was well liked among Kayan's troops, and that he idolized the soldiers.

She didn't know what to say to Yuri to ease his pain. She realized that she shouldn't take his rejection personally, that he grieved for his own mother and nothing could alter the fact that she wasn't coming back.

"Wait!" Val called. He reined his camel next to Yuri and held out the cat's carrying basket. "You forgot Khui."

"You take him," Yuri said. "He doesn't like her."

"Yes, he does," Val said. "You're being dumb."

Yuri flung back a phrase more suitable to a cavalryman's mess hall than the presence of Sogdian royalty. Val blushed and tied the basket to his saddle.

"Mind your tongue, boy," Tiz said, trotting past on a gray animal that Roxanne recognized as Zirak. "Any more of that talk and I'll wash out your mouth with saddle soap."

"You say that all the time," Yuri said. "I heard you call Bahman—"

"Yuri!" Kayan glared at him. "Bring Chubin up behind me. You know he and Zirak have a blood feud. We can't have them ripping pieces of hide out of each other all night."

"Sir." Yuri touched the camel's rump again with the switch, and Chubin jogged ahead to the place his father indicated.

"You handle him well," Roxanne said. "He's a big camel."

"And I'm not as big as Val," Yuri finished.

"I didn't say that," Roxanne replied.

"Bigger doesn't mean stronger."

"I didn't mean to insult you."

An hour passed, and then a second hour. Brilliant stars glittered against a velvet canopy of night sky, and the luminous moon glowed with a cold and eerie radiance that lit the desert nearly as bright as day. She might have been riding alone except for the small hands locked around her waist. Twice she tried to start a conversation. Each time, her venture was met with silence.

The wind wailed; camels grunted and coughed. Saddle leather creaked, and water sloshed in the water-skins. Another hour passed.

"Homji's a handsome man," Yuri said abruptly in a tone too cheerful to be genuine.

"Yes," Roxanne agreed, somewhat startled at the child's choice of subject after not speaking for so long. "He is quite handsome."

"He's brave."

"Yes."

"He would make a good husband for you."

"For me? Homji?" Roxanne tried to hide her amusement. She liked the young nobleman well enough, but he couldn't be many years out of his teens. She'd be surprised if he was past twenty-one.

"He likes you. He told me so."

"Oh."

"Homji doesn't have a wife. He wouldn't care that you're so much older than he is."

"Not that much older," she protested. "How old do you think I am?"

"Old. Twenty-five, at least."

She cleared her throat. "And you think he would make a good prince consort?"

"He likes fine clothes."

"And that makes a ruler?"

"They have to get dressed up a lot—for talking to other kings."

"Don't you like fine clothing?"

He considered. "Sometimes," he answered. "But I am too young for you. Besides, I hate you."

"Val—"

"He doesn't like girls. He's never going to get married."

Roxanne clamped a hand over her mouth to keep from giggling. "I didn't mean I wanted to marry Val. I meant that your brother doesn't hate me."

"No. He doesn't. Just me."

"Your father has asked me to be his wife," she reminded him when she could speak almost normally.

"He told me," Yuri said. "But you aren't the right woman for him."

"No?"

"You're a widow. Kayan should marry a virgin."

Roxanne nearly convulsed. "And what do you know about virgins, Prince Yuri?"

"I'm not a baby. I know stuff. Virgins are quiet and obedient and don't argue with men."

"I suppose you intend to marry an obedient woman yourself?"

"I suppose. Some day. After I hunt all the lions and defeat all the Scythians. I won't have time for a wife for years."

"Ah," she said. "I can see how that would be a problem. What with all those lions to track down."

"And Greeks. I have to chase them out of the Hindu Kush and Persia, back to where they came from."

"You're going to be a great warrior, then."

"You don't believe me, but you'll see."

"Just how old are you, Yuri?"

"I don't know, not exactly. My mother would know. If she was alive, she'd know. Mothers know that stuff."

"Yes, they do. I'm sorry about your mother. Do you remember her at all?"

"Sometimes I think I do. Sometimes, if I shut my eyes, I think I'm going to see her face. But I never do."

"It's hard to lose a mother. I lost mine when I was a baby."

"I don't want to talk about her."

"What shall we talk about?"

"Nothing. Virgins are quiet, too. They know when not to talk."

Yuri didn't speak to her again for the better part of an hour, and then offered, "So what do you think about Homji?"

"I think I'd rather marry Tiz."

Yuri made a sound of approval. "Tiz is a better fighter than Homji, but he won't marry you."

"No? Why not?"

"He likes fat women with big breasts."

"And mine aren't big enough?"

"No. Tiz likes women with really big ones. He says it gives him a good place to lay his head when he's had too much wine. Besides, if you are a princess, you can't marry a common soldier, even if Tiz is Kayan's second in command. It will have to be Homji."

"And he won't care that I'm not a virgin?"

"I'll ask him if you want me to," Yuri offered hopefully.

She laughed. "No, don't do that."

"What's wrong with Homji?"

"Nothing. He's a fine young man, but I'm betrothed to your father. We'd have to break the marriage contract before making any arrangements with someone else. Otherwise, Kayan's honor would be challenged. He'd have to fight Homji."

"Oh. He'd kill him. Kayan is the best."

"Is he?"

"Yes. Better than anybody."

"Then maybe I should marry him."

"No. You forgot, didn't you? I told you why you can't."

"Ah, yes, I'm not a virgin and my breasts aren't big enough."

"What are you telling my son?" Kayan demanded, reining in his camel beside Chubin.

"We were discussing my shortcomings as a possible bride."

"What?" Kayan said.

Roxanne chuckled. "It's a private discussion. Between Prince Yuri and me."

"You said for me to protect her," Yuri said. "I was just giving her some advice."

"Yuri thinks that Homji would make a good husband for me. If you'd be willing to release me from our betrothal."

"So you wouldn't have to kill him," Yuri added.

"I think you two have had enough discussion," Kayan said. He moved his animal close to Chubin and held out his hand. "Princess?"

"Thank you, Prince Kayan," she replied, throwing her knee over the saddle. She pushed off and Kayan caught her, lifting her and neatly depositing her in front of him.

"I'll take over this duty for the rest of the night," he said to Yuri. "Fall back and ride in front of your brother."

"Sir," Yuri replied. He pulled Chubin out of the line. "But I still think Homji would be a better husband for her than Tiz."

Roxanne stifled a giggle.

"When I want your opinion on choosing a wife, young man," Kayan said, "I'll ask for it. Tomorrow, she rides with Val."

Yuri reined in his animal, and Kayan and Roxanne moved up to take the lead position.

"What was all that about?" Kayan asked. "You told him that you wanted to marry Tiz?"

Roxanne chuckled and leaned her head back against him. The night was cold, and Kayan was warm. "If I told you," she said, "you wouldn't believe a word of it."

"Try me."

The following day, Roxanne did ride double with Val, and she found it a more pleasant experience than sharing a camel with prickly Yuri. It was impossible for her not to love both children, but Yuri's hostile attitude stung.

Val was warmer and seemed more receptive to the possibility that she might become their mother and Kayan's wife. She longed to make the same connection with Yuri but wasn't certain how to bridge the distance between them.

Stubbornly Yuri refused to return to the tent she shared with Kayan and Val during their rest periods, remaining instead with Tiz and the soldiers. The boy's attitude troubled Kayan, and he threatened to order Yuri to sleep with Roxanne and Val, but Roxanne begged him not to. Instinctively she felt that it would be better to earn the child's affection bit by bit rather than force him to be near her.

Much to her disappointment, there was no opportunity to be alone with Kayan again. He didn't suggest they ride together, and she was reluctant to question his decision. She found herself remembering Kayan's words about allowing Alexander to take her to the grave with him, and she couldn't help wondering if her indecision was ruining any chance they might have of a future together.

Kayan seemed distant and preoccupied, almost as though he was losing interest in her. The thought made her uncomfortable and more confused than ever. She found herself watching him, listening for his voice, and wondering if she had made a terrible mistake.

On the evening of the fifth day after Yuri had left Roxanne's shelter, Kayan ordered the two boys to ride together. Tiz led out Friya—the female camel that was Yuri's favorite—for Roxanne. Once she was mounted, the lieutenant took the lead, with Yuri and Val riding behind him. Kayan dropped back to last place in the column, the worst position of all, due to the dust kicked up by the other animals.

Roxanne reined in and waited until the column of soldiers passed before guiding Friya alongside Kayan's camel. "Do you mind if I ride with you?" she asked.

"No. I've been wanting to speak to you without Val hearing," he said.

"Me too."

Daylight was fading. The sun glowed crimson-orange on the western horizon, and the camels cast elongated shadows on the sand as they trudged tirelessly along. A flock of birds flew over, too high for Roxanne to identify them, but she was pleased to see them. It had been days since she'd seen any birds. "The animals seem eager tonight," she said. "Friya hardly protested at all when I mounted her. Usually she groans as pitifully as all the rest."

"The camels smell water," Kayan said, "and grass. There, ahead of us, that low ridge. Can you make it out?"

The dusk was coming so quickly she could barely see the rise. "Yes, I think so. Yes, I see it."

"Beyond that, an hour, maybe two, and we'll come to an oasis. There used to be a small settlement there, but there were only ruins when we passed before. The water isn't the best, but we can drink it, and there's grazing for the camels."

"I noticed lichens today where we camped, and a few sprigs of grass here and there. Are we really across the desert?"

"This one, yes, almost. The land is barren for another day or two, but then we'll pass the first village."

"Was that what you wanted to tell me? That we'd made it across the desert?"

"No."

She waited impatiently, wondering what he wanted to say, thinking how much he reminded her of Yuri.

"I want to say I was wrong—what I said the day we fought our way out of Alexandria. About not being able to trust you."

"So you've changed your mind?" she said. "You do trust me now?"

"I was wrong to blame you for the deaths at the temple. You're right. Ptolemy could have had my men followed as well as you. You risked your life for us in the square. I never thanked you."

She shook her head. "You don't need to thank me," she said. "We should be beyond that. As many times as you've saved my neck . . . what you did for me in Babylon . . ."

"You're right. It's hard, Roxanne. I didn't know. . . . There are things I should have told you."

An icy chill gripped her spine. "What things?" She put her hand over her mouth. Had he lied to her about her son? Was he dead? "My baby—" she began.

"He's fine, not a baby anymore. He's alive and well. I would have told you if he . . ." Kayan exhaled slowly. "I would have told you if he'd died."

"You scared me," she admitted. "I thought . . . I'm tired. The heat and this infernal wind has gotten to me. Maybe Yuri's right. Maybe I am old." Relief made her limp so that she leaned forward and rested her head on the high pommel of the saddle.

Kayan laughed. "Yuri can be a little pisser, can't he? But it's Val I wanted to talk to you about. I should have said something before this, but I wasn't sure that—"

"Kayan!" Val's scream echoed down the line.

The column wavered and came to a halt. Warriors shouted in alarm and scrambled for their weapons. Bellowing commands, Tiz swung his mount in a circle and loped toward them. "Chariots!" he yelled. "From the north!"

"Stay with the pack animals!" Kayan yelled at Roxanne. He kicked his camel forward to meet his sons. Roxanne urged Friya after him and fumbled for her bow.

"Chariots!" Yuri cried. "Egyptians!"

Roxanne peered through the gathering darkness and saw a group of small moving objects heading toward them. As she watched, one chariot pulled away.

"Tiz! How many chariots do you count?" Kayan shouted.

"Eight, maybe ten. One is turning back."

"There are more to the northeast," another man called.

"Tiz! Take a half-dozen men! Don't let that lone chariot get away."

The one-eyed lieutenant whooped with glee. In less time than it took to exchange the orders, Tiz was lashing his camel into a gallop with his platoon hot on his heels.

Kayan motioned to the boys. "Take Roxanne back to the pack animals and keep her there if you have to knock her senseless." He pointed to several soldiers. "You and you! Where's Homji!"

"Here, General!" the young man shouted.

"Take these men and six more. Guard the princess and my sons."

Roxanne's heart sank. Kayan wasn't going to run from danger. He meant to launch a full attack. She wanted desperately to ride with them, but she knew that her place was here protecting the children and the pack animals. Friya moved restlessly, but Roxanne held her from bolting as the bulk of the cavalry surged forward toward the oncoming chariots in a flying wedge, with Kayan at the center of the charge.

Chapter 23

As clouds shrouded the crescent moon rising on the horizon, the shouts and cries of dying men and animals drifted on the desert wind. Fear such as she had never experienced gripped Roxanne and chilled her to the bone. She had witnessed many battles, but not knowing what was happening to Kayan and his troops was torture far greater than being in the midst of the fighting.

"How many chariots did you see?" she asked Homji as she rested a hand on her sword.

"Twenty, maybe more."

"We shouldn't be here!" Yuri said. "We should be helping Kayan."

Val slid down off Chubin and began to saddle one of the riderless camels. "He needs us," the older boy insisted.

Homji remained firm. "You will obey orders. The general said for you to remain and guard the princess. You will do as you have been told."

"What if there are more chariots than we counted?" Roxanne shifted anxiously in the saddle. "They could be facing infantry or cavalry as well as chariots."

"If there are too many to fight, Prince Kayan will pull his men back," Homji said. "Until then, we wait."

Roxanne's mouth felt dry. Her heart raced. "You seven could make the difference," she argued. "I'll not have you risk the prince's life for me. Not when we're not even in danger."

"Think of it as my life you're protecting," Homji answered. "If I disobey the general's orders during battle, he'll use me for target practice."

Yuri backed Chubin away from Homji toward the pack animals. "Watch him," Roxanne said. "They'll both be in the fighting if you let them. We can't let—" She stopped in mid sentence as she heard the pounding of horses' hooves and what could only be the clatter of chariot wheels on rock. "There!" she shouted, gesturing toward the oncoming racket.

Instantly Kayan's warriors formed a defensive ring around her and the children. Roxanne notched an arrow to her bowstring and stared into the gloom, prepared to meet the attack. Val drew his sword and reined close on her right. Yuri took the left position.

The sounds of the approaching horses and vehicle intensified. Yuri nudged his mount into the circle between two Bactrian archers and readied his small bow.

Abruptly there was a crash and a thud. Wood splintered. A horse whinnied in pain. Out of the night rolled a single detached chariot wheel.

Homji shouted a command. Three warriors drew swords and urged their camels toward the collision, leaving the rest to hold their defensive positions around Roxanne.

A man groaned.

Silence.

"It's all right," Homji called.

The other men moved forward. Yuri slapped Chubin's neck. Roxanne and Val followed.

They didn't have far to go. Not twenty yards away, an Egyptian lay sprawled on the rocky earth with his head at an unnatural angle. The smashed chariot littered the ground. One horse, tangled in harness, a shaft trailing behind, struggled to rise. A Bactrian dismounted and approached the animal. A few yards away, the second horse stood on three legs, head down, favoring a right foreleg.

"Nothing broken," the soldier said as he examined the horse with the injured leg. "He won't go far on this sprain. What do you want me to do with him, Homji?"

Homji knelt over a fallen archer wearing Greek armor. "This one's gone to meet his maker." He glanced toward the horse. "Set him loose. He'll find his way to the oasis."

Roxanne tapped Friya's shoulder and commanded the camel to kneel. She slid off and went to the downed horse. Speaking in soothing tones, she untangled the harness and freed the bay gelding from the remains of the chariot. Looping a leather strap around the animal's neck, she tied the end to Friya's saddle and got back on the camel.

In the distance, Roxanne could hear more fighting. The sounds of struggle continued for about a half hour, then there was nothing.

"Someone's coming," a dark-haired Bactrian warrior said.

The soldiers drew their weapons again, then visibly relaxed as it became evident that what they heard were the muffled footfalls of camels.

Two mounted men loomed in the darkness. "It's over," one said. "We got them."

"Ptolemy's men?" one of his comrades asked.

"Can't say. A mixed unit of Egyptians and Greeks. Mostly Egyptian drivers."

"Foot soldiers?" Homji asked.

"No infantry. No cavalry. Just archers and spearmen."

Tiz arrived with three of his original group. "No one will be taking word back to the main force, Princess," he said. "It took us a while, but we caught up with that lone chariot the general sent us to stop." The lieutenant looked around. "He's not back yet?"

"Haven't seen him," the bearded man who'd freed the injured horse replied.

"We lose any?" Homji asked Tiz.

"Jivaji. Daradast. Adarfra," Tiz answered. "Stivant took an arrow through his shoulder. Pulad's beast stepped in a hole and threw him. Pulad's banged up, but not hurt bad."

Roxanne watched as other soldiers rode in. Where was Kayan? Her anxiety increased as more of the cavalry joined them. One man she recognized. "Bahman!" she called. "Was the prince with you?"

Men eased aside to allow Bahman to approach her. He was leading a riderless animal. Roxanne's heart skipped a beat as she saw something black staining the saddle.

"That's Delir," Yuri cried. "That's my father's camel."

Roxanne stiffened.

"That's blood," a trooper said.

"Quiet, you fool." Tiz reined his camel to block Roxanne's view.

She began to tremble. "You've got to send out riders to search for Kayan," Roxanne said, trying to hide her terror. "We don't have much time. More enemy—"

"You're right there, Highness," Tiz said. "We'll find him."

"Ease your heart," Homji said to Roxanne. "The prince is not so easy to kill."

Roxanne dismounted and walked to the uninjured chariot horse. Swiftly she fashioned a steppe bridle from a length of rope and vaulted up on the saddleless bay's back.

"What are you doing?" Tiz asked her. "You're not going anywhere."

"I'm going to help you find Kayan," she replied. "And I'll be far more efficient on horseback than on that camel."

"Princess . . ." Homji said. "You—"

Tiz shook his head. "Let her come. From the looks of her, it's the only way to prevent more bloodshed." He began to issue orders. "Prince Yuri, you and your brother stay with the princess. Keep close to the rest of us, and keep quiet. Voices carry. You find the general, give a jackal's call. And if we're attacked by a force too big to fight, you boys guide the lady to the Street of the Tanners in Gaza. There's an alehouse there called the Ram's Head. We'll meet there on the evening of the fourth day."

Roxanne dug her heels into the horse's sides. The animal pranced nervously, shook his head, and snorted. She spoke to him in Egyptian, and he broke into a trot. Yuri and Val guided their camels to follow her.

"Look smart," Tiz ordered as Roxanne rode into the darkness. "Let's find the general and be miles from here before sunrise."

Searching the battlefield for one live man among the dead was not a task Roxanne looked forward to. Darkness and rough terrain made the hunt more difficult. Time and time again, she dismounted to examine a body, only to find that it wasn't Kayan. Horses, still hitched to their empty chariots, wandered the field. Other animals were trapped by fallen teammates. Archers, drivers, and spearmen lay where they had fallen or crawled. She discovered two of the enemy soldiers alive, one Greek and one Egyptian. She offered water to both men and moved on without speaking to them.

"They tried to kill us," Val whispered. "Why give them water? Why not just cut their throats?"

"We're not Greeks," Yuri admonished.

His brother was unrepentant. "If you let them live, we'll just have to fight them again."

"The Master teaches us that compassion is never wrong," Roxanne said. "You're both right, but both wrong. Not all Greeks are heartless. Didn't the Lady Alyssa risk her life and those of her family for us? Those men that I gave water to will both die, but if I've eased their passing, it may be that the Creator will forgive me for some of the sins I've committed."

"Kayan doesn't believe in God," Yuri said. "He says that either the Creator has died or that He's too busy to notice what happens to us."

"He says God died when the Greeks captured Sogdiana Rock," Val said.

Roxanne closed the eyes of a dead Bactrian, a young man she thought she recognized, and offered a quick prayer for the safe journey of his soul. "Your father is wrong," she said to the boys. "The Creator of all things cannot die. We may not have our prayers answered in the way we want, but that doesn't mean He doesn't care or that He has forgotten us. His ways are sometimes a mystery."

She walked on, leading the horse. Fear made her clumsy and clutched at her throat so that it was hard to breathe, but she wouldn't give up. She refused to weep for Kayan, and she wouldn't allow herself to believe that he was lost. Surely he was too strong, too full of life, to die here in this nameless spot. *Please*, she murmured silently. *Let him be safe, not just for Val and Yuri. If there is a price to pay, let me pay it.*

A jackal howled.

"That's the signal," Val said. He whacked his camel on the rump. "Come on! They've found Kayan!"

Roxanne turned to mount the horse.

A cavalry horn wailed. Not Bactrian, but Greek. Close by.

"What are you waiting for?" Roxanne cried to Yuri. "Ride!" She bent and snatched up a stone and flung it hard at Chubin's rump. The camel bawled in pain and exploded into action, galloping away at a full run.

Roxanne flung herself onto the bay as the first of the Greek riders spilled into the valley. It was still too dark to see clearly, but she could tell by the sound of the horses' hooves that it was a full company. She glanced once in the direction the boys had gone and whipped her gelding the other way.

"Help me!" she screamed in Greek to attract the soldiers' attention. "Help me!"

The bay raced over the uneven ground, leaping over low bushes and broken chariot shafts. Roxanne shrieked again. Behind her, she heard some of the horsemen break away to chase her.

She leaned low over the little horse's neck and smacked his rump with the trailing end of the rope bridle. The bay lengthened out and ran as though Ares's hounds were after him. Roxanne sucked in a deep breath and screamed as loudly as she could.

Sweat rose on the bay's neck. Foam flew from his mouth. The way lay uphill now, over loose rock and deep sand. Roxanne glanced over her shoulder. Horsemen galloped behind her. She caught the gleam of helmets in the moonlight.

She gained the summit of the hill and urged her mount down the far side at breakneck speed. The horse stumbled and nearly pitched forward, regained his balance, and slid on his haunches. Roxanne clung like a burr to the close-cropped mane.

The ground gave way in front of them. The horse fell, got his feet under him, and landed, shaking but unhurt, on the floor of a dry riverbed. The far bank was too steep to climb. Roxanne reined the gelding's head left and set off down the wash at a canter.

She rounded a bend, came face to face with a column of Egyptian chariots driving three abreast, and yanked hard on the bay's head. The animal reared, sank his hind leg into a soft spot, and fell over backwards. Roxanne threw herself off the horse's back, and the ground came up and hit her.

She opened her eyes to the sound of clapping.

"Bravo, bravo," Ptolemy said. "Magnificent attempt."

Roxanne blinked. "Ptolemy? Is that you?"

He chuckled. "Were you expecting my brother?"

"No." She closed her eyes and held on to the earth until it stopped spinning. "What are you doing here?"

"I might ask you the same." He touched her cheek. "Are you hurt?"

"Other than my dignity?" She stifled a groan and sat up. It took a few minutes to regain her senses. She really was getting too old for this sort of thing.

"You've led me quite a chase."

"Good." Her head felt as though she'd been kicked by a camel, and her mouth tasted of dirt and blood. Somehow she'd bitten the side of her tongue.

"You must have as many lives as a cat," he said. "Captain Eurystheus said you'd broken your neck in the fall. You've been senseless for nearly an hour."

"Your soldiers . . . they were chasing me."

"Some of my cavalry. Yes. They did catch you, but not until you'd landed nearly in Captain Eurystheus's lap."

Ptolemy took her hand and pulled her to her feet. "How many of my soldiers did you kill tonight, you little hill savage?"

She started to shake her head, but the effort was too great. "None," she answered. The bay horse was on his feet and trotting back and forth nickering at the chariot horses, seemingly none the worse for wear. She was glad of that. He was a game little animal, even if he wasn't the fastest horse she'd ever ridden.

"You didn't shoot any? Run a sword through one or two?" Ptolemy asked caustically. "I'm almost disappointed, Roxanne. I know Alexander would be. I expected more."

"If you don't mind, could we wait until later to trade insults? If I don't sit down, I'm going to throw up."

He called to two aides. "Carry her to my chariot. Unless you'd prefer to be dragged behind it?"

"No," she answered. "I wouldn't." She spat into the sand. "At least you seem to have recovered."

"From what?" Ptolemy asked. "Oh, yes, you tried to burn me alive in my own palace, didn't you?"

"I did not," she protested. "The fire was a diversion, nothing more. If I'd wanted to set you alight, I'd have found a more certain way. But you should know me better. I've a tender heart."

He swore and then laughed heartily. "Ah, Roxanne, you will make a splendid Egyptian queen. You're as blood-thirsty as the best of them."

A Greek soldier took her by each arm and half carried, half led her to Ptolemy's chariot. There were not so many as she had first thought, no more than fifteen, each with a driver and an accompanying officer. Roxanne sank down on the floor, sitting with her feet on the ground, and leaned her head against the reed sidewall. "Have you anything to drink?" she asked.

The king snapped his fingers. "Bring wine for the princess."

Someone shoved a wine-skin at her, and she uncorked it and took a drink. "Thank you." She wiped her mouth with the back of a dirty hand.

"Was it worth it?" Ptolemy asked. "Weeks on the desert for a carnal taste of your barbarian kinsman?"

"It's not like that," she protested. "I haven't—"

Ptolemy uttered a sound of amusement. "Don't bother with excuses, my dear. Do you think I care, one way or another? My other two queens are hardly known for their virtue. But I hope you've gotten it out of your system, because you'll share no beds after this but mine, even if I have to chain you to it. I want no other man's son to inherit my throne."

"Why?" she demanded. "Why did you lie to me?"

"I saved your pretty little ass. You'd be nothing but bones in a grave if I hadn't had you drugged and carried to Alexandria."

"Why the pretense? Why did you tell me that I was Mayet?"

"The fault's yours. You made it all too easy," he answered. "I wasn't ready to announce to General Cassander and the powers that be that I was making Alexander's wife my queen."

"And now?"

He shrugged. "Since I've taken the trouble to assemble my troops, I'll take the opportunity to avenge my dear, departed stepmother, Queen Olympias."

Roxanne rubbed her aching temple. "Since when do you harbor affection for that monster?"

"Since it advances my cause. The world will hardly be the poorer for Cassander's death." He caught her chin and lifted it so that he could look into her eyes. "Don't tell me you're going to plead for mercy for Cassander."

"Why would I? He would have murdered me."

"Exactly." He pressed a mocking kiss to her forehead. "For once, we are agreed on something. I find it refreshing."

She took another drink of wine and passed him the skin. "Why did you come after me, Ptolemy? Don't you realize that I might have married you willingly if you'd been honest with me? I respected you. I considered you a real friend."

"Even after I deserted you and your son when Alexander died?"

She wished he would just leave her alone. All she could think of was Kayan and the boys. Had they escaped? Had Tiz and the others? Or had they all died in the darkness under a hail of Greek arrows and sword blades? She wasn't up to sparring with Ptolemy, but she couldn't back down. If she did, he might well kill her too. And as long as she drew breath, there was a chance that she would get home to her own son.

"I never blamed you for that," she said. "Perdiccas would have killed you if you'd stayed."

"He should have done it then."

"Because you killed him when he came to Egypt," she finished.

"Yes."

"I could forgive you anything for that deed."

"You amaze me, Roxanne. Most women would have called it cowardice for me to abandon you to your enemies and flee to Egypt."

"You're no coward."

"No, I'm not. But my brother would have said so."

"Alexander had little patience for human frailties," she said. "I always knew that your decision wasn't personal. I thought that you'd help me some day, if you could."

"And I did." He bent and kissed her lips.

She tried to turn her face away, but he held her and forced the kiss. "Don't," she said. "I said I *might* have married you if you'd been honest with me. I might have made exactly the same kind of logical decision you did when you claimed Egypt."

"But now your pride is injured. You're going to hold a grudge. After all I've given you." He scoffed. "You're beaten, Roxanne. You will admit defeat and accept what must be."

A messenger arrived on horseback.

"Stay where you are, and don't try to escape," Ptolemy said to her. He moved away to a spot at the rear of the chariots and summoned four men. They were too far away for Roxanne to hear what they were saying, but Ptolemy seemed impatient. They spoke for perhaps half an hour before the courier rode out again.

Ptolemy returned to where she waited. "No," he said. "We don't have them yet, but we will."

"Give me your word that you will spare the children," she begged. "You've no quarrel with them."

"You're in no-position to ask for favors. Do you have any idea what this expedition has cost me?"

"Forgive me if I can't sympathize with you."

"Everything has its price, Roxanne, even you." He touched her cheek, and she shrank back. "That was one of Alexander's failings," he said. "My brother never considered the cost of his actions, or of yours. I won't make that mistake."

Horses coming down the dry riverbed drew Ptolemy's attention, and he turned to watch a unit of his Greek cavalry riding pell-mell toward them.

When Ptolemy glanced toward the sound of the approaching horsemen, Roxanne leaped to her feet and seized his dagger from the sheath at his waist.

He advanced on her. "Drop that!" he said, "or I'll knock the—"

She stared past him at the Greeks still coming at a hard gallop toward the king's chariot. She tried to estimate how many there were—perhaps thirty, all in bronze helmets and armor. Greek cavalry was among the finest in the world, but something seemed odd about the way they sat their mounts. Almost as if . . .

A soldier from one of the chariots behind Ptolemy's shouted, but the horsemen didn't slow their pace. Ptolemy took a step back and glanced over his shoulder at the oncoming men and riders.

With an oath, Ptolemy lunged for Roxanne and grabbed hold of her left wrist. She slashed at him with the knife, nicking his right forearm and jerking away. He came after her, and she retreated up into the chariot.

A Bactrian arrow plunged into the chariot wall between Roxanne and Ptolemy. Not Greek, but Bactrian. Hope blossomed in her chest. In a final effort, she scrambled over the side and dashed toward the charging horses.

The lead rider reined hard to the left and leaned down. Roxanne looked up into Kayan's face and uttered a cry of joy.

"Are you coming?" he shouted.

She seized his arm, and he swung her up behind them. Soldiers swarmed the king and formed a wall of bronze around him. The horsemen barely slowed as they plunged through the spaces between the massed chariots.

"Hold on tight!" Kayan bellowed.

Ahead of them, a single chariot, halted at an angle, blocked their path. Roxanne clung to Kayan's waist as the horse soared up and over the chariot and panicked driver.

Then her Bactrian countrymen were past the last of the Greek chariots and plunging unopposed down the hard-packed riverbed to freedom.

Chapter 24

A drop of liquid fell on Roxanne's lips. Only half awake, she licked it away with the tip of her tongue. *Wine.* She sighed sleepily. A second drop struck her nose. She opened her eyes.

Alexander stood over her, a goblet in hand, his cap of gilded curls framed by a shaft of sunlight filtering through the foliage of a blossoming citron tree. "Am I dreaming?" she asked sleepily.

Alexander's blue-gray eyes sparkled with mischief. *Eleven days in Gaza, and all you've done is sleep—and eat.*

"You shouldn't be here. You're dead."

He chuckled. *Woman, you would argue with Apollo himself.*

"It cannot be. You died in Babylon."

When did I ever bind myself by the rules of mortal men?

She reached out to touch him. Her fingers passed through Alexander's flesh without disturbing his image. She felt not the slightest obstruction. "You are a dream."

You're wrong, Roxanne. I am as real as you and as alive as ever.

Her heart pounded. "How is it possible?"

In time you will learn the great mystery. For now, there is much for you to do. Where is the Amazon I married? Has Ptolemy completely destroyed your sense of adventure? Are you content to lie on your back while kingdoms fall?

She drew in a ragged breath. She was as light-headed as if she'd drunk the contents of an entire skin of Scythian spirits. Struggling for control, she bit the inside of her lip. She tasted the salty sweetness of her own blood, but Alexander remained as vivid as before. "If you're real, why can't I touch you?"

Always questions. Can you never accept what I tell you as fact?

"Never trust a Greek."

Your arguments are as illogical as always. How many times must I remind you that I'm Macedonian? He grinned boyishly. *You are a thorn in my flesh, Roxanne. Your barbarian deserves you.*

"Kayan?" She could not stop staring at Alexander. If this was a dream, it was more real than any she'd ever experienced. And if it wasn't . . .

He's waited long enough, hasn't he? Such devotion should be rewarded.

Her dead husband's face was younger than she remembered it in the last year of his life, the high brow and sculpted nose smooth and unblemished, the scars of war oddly absent. He wore a short cavalry tunic and cloak of gold with purple borders, and his bronze cuirass glittered brightly in the sun. Alexander's favorite sword hung ever-ready at his hip, and golden sandals were laced at his ankles.

This is Kayan's time. Ours? He shrugged. *Who knows what the fates may have in store for us in the future?* He leaned over and kissed her tenderly on the lips.

She closed her eyes and savored the taste of his mouth on hers. "You've been eating apricots," she said.

I like apricots.

"Is this good-bye?" she asked him.

He smiled. *Fly free, Little Star. Cherish my son and live every day of your life.*

"I mean to make him a warrior-king to drive out your Greeks."

I would expect no less of you . . . or of him.

"I was always faithful to you."

I know. I should have trusted you, above all of them. Especially Ptolemy. Be on your guard. He's a formidable opponent. If you let him, he'll destroy everything you love. And he was always lucky.

"So was I," she reminded him.

A horse whinnied.

Take care, Roxanne. Your mountains are a long way off, and your path is strewn with danger. Make one mistake, and my son will find an early grave.

"Wait, Alexander! I—"

He did not vanish so much as simply fade into the sunlight. His image grew hazy and indistinct. She blinked, and only his face remained. For what seemed forever, Alexander's magnetic gaze held hers. *Farewell, Roxanne.*

"Good-bye," she whispered.

You were the dearest thing I ever conquered.

She waited, but there was nothing more than the echo of horses' hooves growing ever fainter. She sank into white clouds of oblivion.

Roxanne supposed that time had passed, but she couldn't be certain. The scents of citrus and sandalwood drifted on the air. She opened her eyes and smiled as she realized where she was.

This was the home of Tahm the Merchant in Gaza.

Tahm's high-walled garden of lime, citron, and apricot trees was as close to paradise as she'd been for a long time. Lying here on soft cushions, listening to birdsong and the trickle of bubbling water from the fountain, seemed more fantasy than reality. She had the vague memory of a dream . . . a dream about Alexander. The details were hazy, but she had the distinct impression that he had kissed her.

She moistened her lips and tasted apricots. Odd, she thought. She hadn't remembered eating apricots. She stretched and yawned, feeling stronger and more rested than she had in many months. She had rested long enough. She and Kayan had been hiding here in Gaza for a week and a half.

The hours after Kayan and his men had rescued her from Ptolemy remained a blur in her mind. Kayan had divided his forces into small groups, the better to blend in with the local populace. Some wore the armor of slain Greeks and rode their horses as they had when they'd swooped down on Ptolemy and his officers. Others donned the drab garb of camel drivers and common farmers.

After much deliberation, Kayan had placed his sons in Tiz's care, explaining to her that Ptolemy's men would be scouring the countryside in search of a beautiful Sogdian princess traveling with two young princes. Thus the boys would be safer dressed in rags and accompanying Tiz, who might pass for a mercenary, bandit, or slave trader.

Kayan had sent Bahman, who spoke fluent Aramaic, to purchase two goats and clothing suitable for a shepherd and his wife. As a decent countrywoman, Roxanne could keep her face veiled and her hair covered. Ptolemy's soldiers were everywhere. But by leaving their mounts to Homji and leading the goats, she and Kayan had strolled leisurely through one of Gaza's gates and under the noses of the Egyptian charioteers without causing the slightest suspicion.

Gaza was a center of trade; the dusty streets were crowded with merchants, tradesmen, soldiers, slaves, and freemen. Silks from China, grain from Persia, gold from the steppes, furs from the far north, and spices from India arrived weekly by camel and donkey trains. In a city full of foreigners, individual Bactrians, especially those disguised as Greeks or Persians, Medes, or Indians, could easily be missed by Ptolemy's troops.

The king had not given up the search. Daily his chariots rolled through the city streets. His officers posted notice of rewards for Kayan's head and a prize of gold for Roxanne's safe return. Egyptians searched private homes, raided temples, taverns, and pleasure houses. So far, only one of Kayan's Bactrians had been discovered. The young archer had dispatched three of Ptolemy's men before an Egyptian killed him with an axe.

Roxanne was well aware that she and Kayan couldn't remain in hiding in the home of Tahm the Merchant much longer. But after the desert, the comfortable house was a godsend.

Tahm was an acquaintance of her father and a dealer in fine rugs and olive oil who had dwelt in Gaza for more than forty years. The merchant had taken a wealthy Syrian widow to wife, and after her childbearing years had passed, he'd married his wife's younger sister, also a widow with a wealth of olive groves, sheep, and land. A pillar of the city, Tahm was father and grandfather of well-to-do citizens. But he'd been born in Balkh of Sogdian parents, and in his heart he still owed allegiance to the House of Oxyartes.

When Kayan had asked for shelter, Tahm had given it willingly. Not only had he welcomed them into his house, but Tahm had taken his wives and family to one of his country homes and left Roxanne and Kayan with a staff of loyal servants.

"Lazybones." Kayan gazed down at her. "Do you mean to sleep the day away?" He brushed a tendril of hair away from her face with feather-light tenderness.

"I wasn't sleeping. At least I don't think I was."

The smell of the citrus blossoms was sweet, but not so sweet as the eddies of warmth that flowed through her when Kayan smiled. "I was worried about you," he said. "The desert is no place for a woman."

"That's not the first desert we've crossed together." She slid over, patted the pillow beside her, and made room for him to sit on the wide divan of heaped cushions.

"Lazy wench." He handed her a cup of sweetened lime juice mixed with water. "Drink it."

Their fingers touched, and she felt her face grow warm with pleasure. "Is that an order?"

"It is." Pinpoints of light glittered in his dark eyes. "You need to recover your strength before we leave the city."

"I'm fine," she said, before sipping the delicious drink. "Just sleepy." And strangely restless . . . uneasy with this man she had known and loved all her life.

"What have you got on your . . ." He touched her nose. "Sticky." Kayan licked the tip of his index finger. "Wine." He chuckled. "Have you been bathing in our host's wine? I prefer to drink it."

"No, it was . . ." She averted her gaze, unwilling to share her dream of Alexander. "Just sloppy, I suppose."

"No wonder you're so sleepy. But you've played the great lady long enough. We have plans to make."

"We or you?"

He fixed her with an unwavering gaze. "Who's the general here?"

"And who's the princess?" she countered.

"A prince tops a princess."

"Always?" She chuckled. "I can think of other interesting positions."

"Wanton," he teased. "This is hardly the time for your bawdy humor." His dark eyes sparkled with amusement. "I've brought you a gift from the marketplace." He took the empty cup from her hand and brushed his lips against the rim at the spot her lips had touched.

"Another goat? The last one had mange."

"It's lucky for you I'm not a shepherd. If I were, you'd be useless as a wife. You'd let my sheep and goats be eaten by wolves or fall into rivers and drown. I'd have to beat you every day."

"You could try," she said. He refilled her cup and offered it to her, but she shook her head. "Later."

"If I were a common soldier, you'd never do either. You'd take up with another man as soon as I rode over the first hill."

"Would I?"

Hard muscles rippled as he stretched beside her and propped himself on one elbow. "You are a poor example of a woman," he accused in a deep, resonant voice. "You can't cook, and even Tiz can sew a seam straighter. What exactly are you good for?"

She tilted her head. "I'm not bad at archery," she offered.

"Archers can be had at any crossroads. And I'd never have to buy them silks or jewelry."

"Hmmm." She pretended to consider. "I can train a horse."

"No." He shook his head. "I've no use for another horse handler. Every man in my cavalry unit considers himself a master trainer."

"Wolf catcher?"

"I can trap all the wolves I want myself."

"Elephant mahout?"

Kayan folded his massive arms over his bare chest. As hard as she tried, she couldn't look into those dark, liquid eyes and keep a straight face. She had to smile at him. How had she ever believed him less than beautiful? Kayan was all rugged male and untamed sexuality.

His hair was clean and shining, as black as pitch—except for the single lock of snow white that sprang from the crown of his head—and as straight as hers was curly. Kayan had braided two thin plaits on either side of his face and decorated them with red beads, letting the mass of his thick hair fall in a silken curtain midway down his back.

His nose and chin were roughly hewn, a mountain man's

features, proud and fierce. His lips were both firm and sensual. For an instant, she had the almost overwhelming urge to kiss the hairline scar at the corner of his mouth, the souvenir of a near-fatal swordfight with a Scythian when Kayan had barely entered his teens.

Apricot blossoms tumbled in the pit of her stomach . . . or perhaps it was the incipient flutter of desire. She gazed up at him through slanted lashes and felt joy spill through her body. I came too close to losing him, she thought. *How was it that I never knew what I held in my hand until he was nearly lost to me . . . forever?*

"Kayan," she whispered, just because she wanted to say his name.

He lifted her hand and pressed it palm to palm against his. "You are my strength," he said, lacing their fingers together with a lock of his own hair. "If you had died on that field, I would not have rested until both Ptolemy and Cassander were no more. And then I would have turned my face to the east and withered like a stalk of wheat in winter snow."

"You have children," she said. "You would have lived for them."

"My hands might grasp a sword or a bow, my eyes might see, but without you, I could not breathe. My heart would wither. Water from the clearest mountain stream would choke my throat like sand, and roasted ibex taste of naught but crumbling shale."

She swallowed, trying to dissolve the lump in her throat. There was no mistaking the emotion etched on the angled planes of his face. These were not idle words such as men might offer to women they wished to seduce. Kayan meant what he said to her.

"There would be no music in the world, Little Star," he continued huskily, "nor any laughter. You are more to me than my honor . . . more precious even than the lives of my sons."

She clasped his hand and brought it to her lips, kissing his scarred fingertips and inhaling the clean, virile scent that was his alone. How many times, she wondered, had she thought of him in the past years? Alexander's words surfaced from the darkest corner of her mind. *This is Kayan's time,* he had said. She felt the haze dissolve around her, and the clouds of doubt part to reveal the shining promise of the sun.

. . . As though she had awakened from a long sleep.

Tears blurred her vision. "Without you," she said, "my life would be empty and meaningless."

Kayan's dark eyes were luminous. His gaze held her spellbound. "You must go home and lead our people to freedom," he said. "Without you, we are lost."

Sudden giddiness seized her. "Without you, freedom is a word as hollow as Ptolemy's heart."

Kayan pressed his warm lips to her shoulder and nipped the skin lightly. Shivers of bright excitement cascaded from the crown of her head to her toes. She flattened her palms against his chest, feeling the coiled power of muscle and bone barely leashed beneath his bronze skin.

He groaned and whispered her name as he kissed a path of caresses to the hollow of her throat. "I would have you be my wife," he said. "I want to wake beside you every morning. And I want your face to be the last thing I see at the end of every day."

She moistened her lips with the tip of her tongue. "You would soon tire of my foul disposition."

"Never," he answered. "I want to make red-cheeked babies with you. I want to see you swell with life and know that part of me will be forever joined with part of you." He skimmed his callused palm down over her breast until he brushed her nipple. Instantly Roxanne felt her flesh tingle and become more sensitive. Her stomach contracted, filling her with a curious hot excitement. "Kayan," she murmured. "I've been such a fool."

"Haven't I?" He thumbed the hard bud of her nipple and kissed it through the azure silk bodice of her gown.

Hot, reckless excitement ignited a pulsing ache at the pit of her stomach. She could not keep her hands off of him. Fierce urgency made her bold. "I do love you," she murmured.

"Tell me that you'll have me to husband, Roxanne. Take pity on a man who has loved you forever."

"Can you forgive me for not seeing what was right in front of me?"

"There is nothing to forgive. There is no yesterday, only today and tomorrow." He cupped her breast tenderly. "I love you," he repeated. "I will always love you."

"Can it be that my father was right all along?" She gasped as his strong hands ignited flames beneath her skin. "That the magi were right when they said we were destined to be together?"

"Destined to save Sogdiana and Bactria from darkness." He kissed her mouth. "Mmmm. Apricot."

His kiss deepened, and she opened to it, losing herself in the scent and taste of him. She wrapped her arms around his neck and clung to him. "Kayan, Kayan," she whispered. "Is it possible to feel this way?"

Gossamer ribbons of need wafted through her as he pushed her back against the cushions and kissed her mouth, her throat, her breasts. She tangled her fingers in his thick hair as tears of happiness filled her eyes.

Kayan groaned and moved lower, kissing her bare midriff and down over her belly. She closed her eyes and tossed her head from side to side as he stroked the curve of her hipbone and laved her navel with his warm tongue. She arched her hips as his tongue flicked against her bare skin, sending exquisite sensations rippling to the apex of her thighs.

"Let me pleasure you," he begged. His hands were on her legs, sliding the silk material higher.

She drew in a shuddering gasp as his fingers brushed the damp folds of her womanhood.

"Sweet," he whispered. "So sweet."

His breath was warm.

"Kayan . . ."

His teasing kisses gave way to a gentle probing. Her heart thundered in her chest when she felt his hot tongue plunge deep, filling her with an urgent drive for fulfillment. Kayan chuckled and clasped her buttocks in his powerful hands, lifting her hips to give him free access to nuzzle and plunder her throbbing, wet core.

She felt his teeth on her flesh, his searing lips . . . his hard, thrusting tongue. Involuntarily she tightened her sheath around him. Fevered desire drove her wild. "I can't . . ." she whispered hoarsely. "I must . . . Please! I want you in me—all of you."

He laughed and raised his beautiful eyes, heavy-lidded with passion, to meet her gaze. "Not yet," he said. "Not yet." He lowered his head and continued the bittersweet torture until her cries became screams of ecstasy.

Chapter 25

Still washed by sweet waves of iridescent pleasure, Roxanne lay in the circle of Kayan's strong embrace while he kissed her face and hair and throat. She sighed, still too caught up in the intensity of her climax to speak.

"Do I pass muster?" he asked.

She sighed and smiled at him. How could she explain how much at peace she felt? That everything she'd ever done had led to this moment?

"Is that a yes?"

"You know it is." She brushed his stubbled cheek with her fingertips, and bright shards of utter bliss pinwheeled through her. She wanted to laugh—to sing. She was jubilant—as lighthearted as a sunbeam. Not from the physical gratification Kayan had given her, but from the realization of his unselfish and eternal love, a love that she'd been too blind or foolish to see until now. "But . . . it's not fair," she murmured. "You pleasured me, but I didn't do the same for you."

"I've waited a long time for this. I can wait a little longer." His eyes glittered with desire. "You are what I want most . . . you in my arms. I've dreamed of this so many times, it's hard to believe that you're real."

She kissed him and gently nibbled his lower lip. "I'm real enough," she murmured. "And so are you." She caressed his hard-muscled shoulder and brushed her fingertips over his deep chest, lingering on his nipple. It hardened under her teasing touch, and he groaned.

"Careful," he warned. "You'll light a fire that may not be so easy to control."

"Perhaps I know best how to deal with such a condition."

She chuckled and pressed a kiss on the tight nub of flesh. He rolled onto his back, pulling her on top of him. His long, sinewy legs were entwined with hers, and she shifted her hips so that the length of his engorged shaft lay against her inner thigh. The feeling was wonderful, but she wanted more. The thought of having him inside her brought a rush of excitement, and she molded her body to his.

This is right, she thought. *This is what was meant to be.*

Kayan's muscles tensed. Again he groaned. "Roxanne, Roxanne," he whispered. "You'll be the death of me."

"Tell me what you want," she whispered.

"I want you to love me as I love you. As I've always loved you."

"I do," she answered. And it was true. This was no brotherly love she felt, nor friendship, although that remained as solid and unyielding as the earth. This was more . . . a mating of souls that she had never felt before with any man.

Kayan kissed her mouth hungrily and ran his hard, lean fingers down her back to caress her buttocks and press her even closer to him. How sweet his body felt to her, but it was not enough. Sighing, she wiggled free of his embrace and slid down until her fingers could grasp his swollen phallus.

"Mmmm, very nice," he said.

"And this?" She brushed his taut erection with her fingertips.

Kayan inhaled sharply.

She flicked the tip of her tongue along its length. He moaned. "Or this?" she said, laving the tip of his shaft.

"Yes," he rasped.

"Turnabout is only fair," she murmured, before giving full attention to his need.

She took him to the brink and then withdrew, moving higher so that she could sit astride him. He kissed her breasts, licking and nipping at her nipples, suckling until heat flared within her and she writhed with urgency as great as his. His hands closed on her waist and he lifted her so that she could feel him nudging her most intimate folds. "Now," she said. "Now."

"I want you . . . not just for a morning or a night. I want you for always."

"Prove it," she dared.

She opened to take him in, but he held her and kissed her until beads of perspiration rose on her skin and she felt she must quench the hunger coursing through her or die. "Please," she whispered. "Love me."

"Will you marry me?"

"Kayan? This isn't the time to—" She caught her breath as he rolled over, pulling her with him until she was on her back and he was over her.

"It's exactly the time. Swear!" His eyes were glittering jewels of promise as he lowered his head and nuzzled her breast. "Swear to me that you will be mine."

Her excitement became a throbbing, incandescent heat. She could feel how slick and wet she was. She wanted him as she'd never wanted another man. "Yes . . . yes."

"You will marry me?"

"Kayan!"

He laughed and plunged deep within her, thrusting hard, sliding back and sheathing himself to the hilt. She cried out with delight as she adjusted to his size and length and wrapped her legs tightly around him. He began to move, slowly at first and then faster. She met him willingly, crying out in ecstasy as they discovered the ancient rhythm of giving and receiving, letting the tides of passion carry them beyond the bounds of human limitations. And when the highest wave crested and broke, they drifted together in a sea of joy and contentment.

"You promised," he reminded her when the sun reached the highest point overhead and she still had not stirred from his arms. "You are bound to marry me by your own will."

She looked up at him through thick lashes. "And you to me," she said.

"See what you've been missing all this time?"

She struck him playfully on the shoulder. "Beast. Now is the time for honeyed words, not boasting."

"I'm good."

She laughed. "You are."

"Better than Pharaoh?"

"Kayan!"

"Am I?"

"And if I say *yes,* you'll be impossible to live with."

"So that's a maybe?" he teased.

She laughed. "No, not a maybe. Let us say that there are more ways to win a woman than by offering her the crown of Egypt."

"I knew it. I knew I was better than any Greek."

"My experience with Greek men is limited. I've only bedded two."

"But I'm better."

She rolled onto her back and threw a pillow at him.

"Forget the Twin Kingdoms. We'll stay in Gaza. I'll learn to sell olive oil, and we'll never leave this garden."

"How much oil will you sell from my bed?"

He moaned. "Not yet a wife and already a nag. Merchants must come here if they wish to buy my oil. I'll not let you out of my sight. If I did, you'd be off to Crete or India or the Misty Isles."

She caught his hand and brought it to her lips, nibbling his fingers until he freed himself by kissing her. That led to laughter and tickling, which ended with Kayan on his back and Roxanne astride . . . which led to the inevitable.

Twice more they made love before hunger and thirst made him summon the servants for food and drink. Later, they bathed in the fountain and shared wine and bread hot from the bake oven, cheese, and dates.

Kayan led her that night to the flat roof of the house, where they could lie on their backs on heaped cushions and see the stars strewn in the sky like handfuls of glittering pearls. They made love and talked of small things and large: last spring's foals, her years in Greek captivity, their family and friends, and the dangers facing Bactria and Sogdiana from their many enemies. Kayan told Roxanne of his design for a new saddle and his plans to raise a great army to drive the Greeks back from the borders of their homeland once and for all.

They spoke of Tiz and the brave band of men who'd come with Kayan from the Twin Kingdoms to rescue her, and of Yuri and Val. But most of all, Kayan told her stories about her son's early childhood.

"He would drink nothing but camel's milk until we found him a wet nurse. But he's strong. He had his cranky nights when he was cutting teeth, but he's never been sick."

"Never?" she exclaimed.

"No. And he's the only baby I've ever heard of who didn't crawl. He went from pulling himself up on the nearest dog to toddling. By the time he was a year old, he was the terror of the palace."

"If you only knew how many nights I cried for him."

"No more tears."

"What's he like? Is he happy? Is he good at sums? Can he read?"

"Sometimes he's quick to anger, but he never holds a grudge. By three, he was riding his own pony. He's smart and agile, and he has a merry heart."

"I can't wait to hold him."

"You will, soon." He cradled her against him long after she fell asleep only a few hours before dawn. Even then, he did not sleep. His happiness was tempered by the knowledge that once she discovered that he'd deceived her, she might never forgive him. These hours might be all they would have together, and he had to make the most of them. And if there was a price to pay, he would pay it. Later.

Roxanne woke with the first light and they watched the sunrise together. "We can't stay here any longer, can we?" she asked him.

He leaned over and kissed her. "No," he said when they broke apart to catch their breath. "We can't. It's too dangerous."

A shiver of apprehension passed down her spine, and she remembered the words Kayan had said in jest the night before. *You'll be the death of me.* She'd lost so many who were dear to her. If he was taken from her . . .

She clung to him. "Promise me you'll be careful," she said. "Promise that nothing will happen to you."

He shook his head and pulled her close. "I can't do that," he murmured into her hair. "None of us can see the dark rider of death until he comes for us."

"Kayan . . ." Her throat constricted so that she couldn't speak.

"I know that we have been bound forever," he said, taking her hand in his. "But I would have your pledge in marriage, and I would give you mine."

She nodded. "Yes. Gladly."

"I hoped you'd say that." He slid a braided circlet of hair

on her finger. "With this ring made of my body, I, Kayan of Sogdiana, freely take you, Roxanne, as my true and only soul wife. By my sword and by my honor, I swear to have no other love all the days of my life."

She turned to look into his eyes, and the love shining there warmed her more than the sun's radiance. "I, Roxanne, princess, heir to Bactria and Sogdiana, take you, Kayan, to be my chosen husband and consort."

"In light and darkness," Kayan said.

"In peace and war."

"By mountain peak and water's flow."

"By grass and rock, by wood and bronze."

Still facing him, Roxanne pressed her palms to his and together they recited the ancient blessing that a holy man should have recited over them at their wedding.

"Not two, but one," Kayan said.

"Forever and always."

He sealed their vows with a kiss and held her for a long time. "Tomorrow," he said, "we have to meet Tiz and the boys and rejoin the other men."

"Ptolemy won't give up."

"No, I don't think he will," Kayan agreed. "But neither can he leave Alexandria for too long. Cassander would love to snatch that prize away. And I hear that there is war with Carthage. If we can keep a jump away from Ptolemy's army, he may be forced to return to Egypt."

"We can hope."

"Yes, but . . ." He hesitated. "There's something I should have told you, but I didn't know how."

"You've got another wife?" she said lightly.

"No. It's about Ptolemy."

"You know something about him that I don't?"

He nodded. "Yes. Years ago he fathered an illegitimate child by a Persian noblewoman."

"Yes, I'd heard something about that. The woman died, didn't she?"

"The child was a boy. Ptolemy named him Paris."

Puzzled, she stared at him. "You know what happened to the boy?"

"I do."

She waited.

"I named him Val."

"Val? Our Val?" She swayed and would have fallen if he hadn't caught her. "Why did you hide this from me? How is it possible?"

"Val's mother was a cousin of Homji's father. I learned of the lady's death and told your father. He sent me to inquire about Paris's fate. So many children were orphaned by war. If he'd not had a Greek father, some of the mother's family would have taken him in. As it was, he'd been left in the care of a nurse, who planned to sell him to a slave trader as soon as he was weaned. I bought him for a pair of pearl earrings."

"A king's son," she said. "Sold with as little regard as a sheep." Tears blurred her vision. "You're certain it was the same child?"

"Have you looked at him? Your father claims that he is the image of Ptolemy."

"And you kept him as your own?"

"I already had a son. It wasn't so hard to take another."

She wiped away the tears. "Or another, when you adopted little Yuri?"

"Yes. It got easier. Besides, Ptolemy was your friend and Alexander's brother. For the sake of kinship, I thought it was what you would have wanted."

"Yes," she agreed. "I would have. But . . . why didn't you say something in Alexandria? It never occurred to you to tell me, or to tell his father?"

Kayan's eyes narrowed. "I am his father . . . the only one he's ever known."

"You don't mean to give him up."

"What's mine, I keep." He exhaled slowly. "I was afraid

to tell you, at first. Afraid you would betray the boy's birth to Ptolemy."

"And later?"

"I was waiting for the right time."

"Val doesn't know?"

"No, and he never will, if I can help it. He's a prince of the Twin Kingdoms. Isn't that enough?"

"Some would say it's more than enough," she answered.

"Would you say it? Can you be a mother to him?"

"I love both Val and Yuri. I'd be honored to be their mother."

"Good, that's settled." He kissed the crown of her head. "I thought you would be angry with me for not telling you sooner."

"No, it's better that I didn't know," she said. "Better that I came to love him first. Ptolemy doesn't deserve him."

They left the rooftop and Roxanne retreated to her chamber to bathe and dress for the morning meal. She waved away the maid who came to assist her, and plaited her hair into a thick braid that hung down her back. Once they'd arrived in Gaza, she'd dyed it dark. If Ptolemy saw her, she'd never be able to fool him, but there was no sense in helping them capture her. Now she stared into a polished bronze mirror at the face of a married woman. So much had happened to her since she'd fled Alexandria that it was difficult to keep from being overwhelmed.

She tried to picture Val as last she'd seen him. Did he resemble Ptolemy? And if so, how had she failed to see it? Ptolemy's soldiers had come close to murdering them all. What would he have done if he'd realized that he'd endangered his own son by his actions? And what would he—a king without an heir—do to get Val back if he knew the truth?

Kayan had ordered the servants to bring breakfast to the

garden. Once Roxanne and Kayan were alone, he took her hands, drew her into his arms, and kissed her. She hugged him tightly, and when they parted, she glanced down at her wedding ring. "You braided this from your own hair, didn't you?"

"Yes." He lifted her hand and kissed the ring. "It's not the first ring I ever made for you. Do you remember when we camped by that waterfall, years ago?"

"I remember. I was fourteen, and you made me a ring of horsehair."

"And what did you do with it?"

"I hid it in a stone wall beside the great stables at the west palace. It may be there still."

"We'll go and see."

"Promise?"

"Yes, that's a promise." He chuckled. And I promised you something else. Have you forgotten that I said I brought you a gift from the marketplace?"

"If I did forget, I had good reason," she teased. "It's not every day a woman becomes the wife of a prince."

"Keep laughing." He clapped, and a maid came from the house with a bundle. "Wait," he said.

Roxanne didn't open the package until they were alone. "What is it?" she asked as she looked at the emerald-green pieces of silk. "You can't expect me to wear this?"

"I do." He broke into a grin. "Do you remember the time that you danced for Alexander and his guests?"

"I do, but . . . I don't understand."

"By now, Ptolemy's soldiers will have alerted all the authorities between here and Persia. The country is too unsafe to travel through in small groups, but a Bactrian cavalry unit would attract too much attention. We'll disguise ourselves as a group of performers seeking the protection of a merchant's caravan. Several of my men are musicians, and Tiz can juggle six wine cups at a time."

"A dancing girl? You want me to dance for strangers?"

"Have you a better idea? Sometimes the best place to hide is in full view." He grinned at her. "Be a good sport, Roxanne. I'd wear the costume myself, but I think you'll attract more of a crowd."

Chapter 26

The following day, Kayan and Roxanne slipped out of a back gate of the merchant's house, wearing the clothing they had worn to enter Gaza. They met Tiz, Yuri, and Val at the Ram's Head on the Street of the Tanners. It was all Roxanne could do not to hug the boys with relief, but Kayan had insisted that it was safer to pretend they didn't know each other.

Kayan ordered a large bowl of beer and deliberately spilled it on his tunic. Roxanne was veiled, and her hair covered in a dirty length of rough homespun. Both were barefoot. Val, disguised as a servant, led a donkey ridden by Tiz. The animal was so small that the cavalryman's bowed legs dragged on the ground. Tiz had covered his eye patch and his good eye with a length of filthy cloth that made him appear blind. Yuri, veiled and dressed in a girl's skirt, joined Roxanne and Kayan, so that they appeared to be a family returning to their country home after a visit to the city.

The tax for entering or leaving the city was a single copper coin or the equivalent in material goods. Armed city guards claimed a toll from every traveler, but for the last two weeks there had been an additional detachment of Ptolemy's Egyptian marines at each gate, inspecting each passerby and questioning any who appeared suspicious. As Roxanne, Kayan, and their "daughter" approached, a lone man carrying carpenter's tools was snatched out of the line by two marines and roughed up. An Egyptian shouted questions at him, but the detainee didn't answer. A second soldier shoved him to the ground, bellowing in Greek. The man made no reply, simply pointed at his mouth.

Roxanne's heart sank as she recognized Bahman. She knew he didn't dare speak or his accent would give them away. She genuinely liked Bahman and feared for his life, and he was a favorite of Yuri. She squeezed Yuri's hand, not wanting to say anything that would attract attention, but hoping that the boy wouldn't panic and expose them.

She need not have worried. Instead of crying out or becoming alarmed, Yuri plopped down on the hard-packed street and began to pick at an invisible splinter on the bottom of a dirty foot. Kayan leaned on a staff, muttered about the inconvenience to honest farmers, and assumed a bored expression.

A chariot drawn by a single horse drew up by the gate, and a Greek officer got out of the vehicle and strode over to see what was causing the delay. Bahman got to his feet and, still not uttering a sound, pointed at his mouth again.

"This fellow's a mute, you turds!" the officer said. "He's a carpenter, not a savage. Let him go."

"Next!" a city guard shouted. "Move along, here! We haven't got all day!"

Roxanne held her breath as she stepped forward with her group. Kayan paid the fee with a single scrawny pigeon. A potter passed through the guard station behind Kayan, Roxanne, and Yuri, and after the potter came the blind man and his servant.

Tiz held up the line, supposedly searching for his copper, in an effort to allow Kayan and Roxanne to get as far from the city gate and the Egyptian marines as possible. The ruse consisted of a great deal of creative obscenity, kicking Val, crying aloud to the Almighty, a choking spell, and finally finding the missing coin in a fold of his grimy turban.

Kayan and Bahman were laughing about the close call when Tiz and Val joined them in a lime grove several miles from the city gates. "I didn't dare say anything," Bahman explained.

"Where'd you get the tools?" Yuri asked, ripping off the hated girl's clothing.

"In the marketplace. If they didn't let me through, I was planning on throwing myself on the ground and faking a seizure," Bahman said.

Val and Yuri conferred excitedly, and Roxanne heard Val teasing his brother about the skirt. "Next time, you have to be the girl," Yuri protested. "Doesn't he, Kayan?"

"All right, enough of this. We've a ways to travel before we meet Homji and the others with the camels," Kayan said. "And we have to do some rehearsals if we want to convince the locals that we're really entertainers."

"I don't know," Tiz put in. "Yuri don't need much practice. He's a born actor. Maybe we need to think about adding a tragedy to the show."

"You," Bahman said, "are tragedy enough, poor old blind man." He grinned. "When I laid eyes on Tiz, I was afraid he'd pick the pockets of the marines before we could get out of there."

"He did," Val said. "I saw him."

"You didn't," Roxanne said.

Laughing, Tiz tossed her a small leather bag. "Not too much in there, but more than enough to buy a few rounds of drinks at the next tavern."

*   *   *

By the time Kayan's company reached Samaria, Roxanne had practiced enough to feel comfortable entertaining strangers. When she was hardly more than a child, her father's Indian concubine had instructed her in dance. Although she hadn't danced in nearly ten years, the rhythms and movements quickly came back to her. Disguised by the new color of her hair and a veil that concealed her face, except for her eyes, she was able to put aside her modesty and give a convincing performance in village squares and caravan campsites.

The ruse worked. Ptolemy's soldiers had set up roadblocks and stood at the entrance of every town and oasis, but never considered that the princess and her rescuers might be right in front of their eyes. As Kayan had promised, some of his soldiers were excellent musicians, and one had a beautiful voice and a command of languages that enabled him to sing poignant ballads in Greek and Egyptian, as well as Aramaic and several Persian dialects.

Tiz sold an herb from the East that would miraculously restore a man's youth when taken for four weeks. He also juggled, threw knives, and told lewd jokes that kept the audience in stitches. Even Yuri and Val did acrobatics with Homji and another cavalryman, a young man named Emet from Samarkand. Kayan's job was to protect Roxanne, billed as the beautiful Taamina of Babylon, from overeager fans, and to play the part of owner and manager of the troupe.

Ptolemy and his army remained a constant threat. He'd put both cavalry and charioteers into the field and commanded the local authorities to be on the lookout for the Bactrians. He'd also doubled the reward for Roxanne's capture. On the outskirts of the ancient city of Samaria, Kayan's troop avoided a face-to-face confrontation with Ptolemy by less than an hour.

In Tyre, following a particularly profitable performance, a captain of Egyptian marines approached Kayan with a

now-familiar offer. The Egyptian, who'd been drinking
heavily, offered Kayan four silver tetradrachmas stamped
with the image of Athena for one night with the seductive
Taamina. When Kayan refused, the captain raised his bid
to five tetradrachmas. A burly slave dealer from Sardis interrupted the negotiations by tossing a heavy bag of silver
Alexanders at Kayan's feet.

"I'll buy Taamina from you," the Greek said.

Kayan glanced at Tiz, who ushered Roxanne out of
sight, much to the disappointment of the raucous throng,
now clapping and stamping for an encore of her dance. De-
laying the inevitable, Kayan made a show of counting
the silver. Heated words flew between the Egyptians and
the Greeks. When the Egyptian officer drew his sword, the
slave dealer's hired mercenaries and marines leaped into
the quarrel. Kayan hurled the silver Alexanders into the air.
When coins rained over the crowd, the melee became a
brawl. Kayan and his group fled the square as city guards
rushed in with spears and clubs to quell the riot.

Again, Roxanne believed that it was the camels that
saved them. A ruby ring from her hoard bribed the guards
to open the city gate in the middle of the night and allow
them to escape into the countryside. Kayan's cavalry troop
was well disposed to abandon all pretense of being entertainers and ride east as hard as humanly possible to Da-
mascus. There, they turned north and then east again to
cross the Euphrates River near Thapsacus.

The chief dangers now were the Greek armies and warlords that held parts of Persia. During Alexander's rule, the
Royal Road had been safe for travelers. Now, bandits, de-
serters, and rogue units of Greeks and Persians roamed the
lawless land at will. Weeks became months as Kayan led
his band from Babylon to Susa—where they traded their
mounts for Bactrian racing camels—and on into the rugged
Zagros Mountains.

The journey and the skirmishes along the way had taken

their toll on men and beasts. Twenty-three cavalrymen, Tiz, Bahman, Homji, Kayan, and the two boys were all that remained of the original party.

"Hardly enough of us to fight a major battle," Kayan said as he and Tiz lingered by the campfire.

Tiz had hired two guides to take them through the passes. The tribesmen were probably in the employ of a local robber baron, but Tiz ordered a couple of men to keep watch over them. He'd pay no fees until they reached the agreed-upon village. There, Tiz would acquire new guides and pay off the old ones. It wasn't the best solution, but it seemed the only practical one.

"Tired?" Kayan asked.

Tiz laughed. "Who isn't? But I'm not ready to turn in yet. Go to your lady. I'll sit up awhile."

Kayan and Roxanne had declared themselves husband and wife, but there was little chance for rest, let alone privacy. Gaza and the hours they'd spent together seemed to Kayan like a dream of paradise. Now he joined Roxanne and Val in the tent. Both were sleeping, but she stirred and opened her eyes when he touched her hand.

"Is something wrong?" she asked.

Kayan shook his head. The light from the fire shone on the front of the shelter, but the interior remained in shadows. "There's a pool beside the waterfall. I thought you might like the opportunity to wash while most of the men are sleeping."

"I would," she agreed. "Should I wake Val?" She picked up two blankets and rolled them into a bundle.

Kayan shook his head. "He's a boy. Dirt is his friend. Let him sleep."

"Yuri?"

Kayan didn't answer. Since they'd announced that they had given and received wedding vows, Val had been delighted with the idea of having Roxanne for his new mother. Kayan's younger son, as usual, was proving difficult. Yuri no longer avoided Roxanne, and he treated her with guarded respect, but he always remained at Tiz's side.

"It's time I learned what it means to be a warrior," Yuri had declared. "The place for a warrior to sleep is with the men."

The breach that had opened between his son and the woman he loved seemed impossible to close, and it troubled Kayan's sleep. He blamed himself for not taking Yuri's stubborn nature into account. Each day, Kayan pondered what to do to bring an end to the separation, but while they were running for their lives, fighting mile by mile to reach the relative safety of Bactria, he was afraid to make things worse by addressing the problem directly.

Roxanne rose, still fully dressed in a man's trousers and tunic, and followed him outside. He took her hand and led her through the camp and up the steep trail to a hollow where a shallow pool lapped at the bottom of a thirty-foot cascade. The way had been too difficult for the camels, and the troop had spent several hours carrying water to the animals.

"It's even more beautiful by moonlight," Roxanne said, gripping his hand tightly.

Heat suffused his skin. Being constantly near Roxanne and unable to make love to her was agonizing. It took no more than a touch of her hand, a glance, to melt his heart. Now, as he looked at her, his exhaustion fell away, and he felt his heartbeat quicken and his groin grow taut with need.

Roxanne glanced around. "Is it safe here?"

He nodded. "As safe as anywhere. For the moment." He'd posted guards on the mountainside around the camp, and the pool and waterfall lay within the perimeter of his lines. The campsite nestled against a face of sheer granite several hundred feet away; the camels and horses grazed on lichens and tufts of grass on a terrace below the tents.

The air was cool and the water fed from snow-capped peaks, but Roxanne didn't hesitate. She stripped off her clothes and waded in. "Ah," she said. "Cold enough to shrivel even your ardor."

He followed her into the water and swore. "There goes any hope of future children."

Roxanne laughed and ducked her head under. The water was chest deep on her, and the bottom of the pool was rock and sand, making the footing extremely treacherous.

"Be careful," he warned.

She reached down in the water and grabbed a handful of sand to scrub herself clean. "What I wouldn't give for soap," she said. She waded out and wrapped herself in one of the blankets. He followed in another minute.

"When we're home, I'll find you soap," he said.

She pulled him into her blanket and kissed him. "Do you know how much I love you?" she asked.

His heart hammered in his chest. What had he done to win such a woman? Here, with her hair dripping wet, without jewels or silks or furs, she was so beautiful that he felt he would weep for joy. When he spoke, his words came out in a husky rasp. "How much do you love me?"

She laughed and kissed him again. He held her tight against him, and for a long time they didn't speak. He simply held her and thought how incredibly lucky he was. When she began to shiver, he peeled away the damp blanket and enfolded her in the dry one. She sat on a rock and watched him dress. "I'm afraid," she admitted softly. "Since we passed through Babylon, I've been having dreams about something bad happening."

He gathered his hair into a club and fastened it with a leather tie. "Sometimes dreams are only dreams."

"Kayan . . . I dreamed that Alexander would die in Babylon, and he did."

He sat on the rock beside her and put his arm around her. "Soon we'll be home, all of us." He kissed the crown of her head.

"That's what I'm afraid of," she admitted. "I keep seeing an arrow in flight."

"I won't let anything happen to you, Roxanne. I swear I'll protect you." He kissed her mouth, and she tasted as sweet as wild honey. "Just believe in me a little longer," he said. The talk of dreams and death made him uneasy. He didn't fear dying, but he was afraid of failing her, of failing his sons.

"No, it's not me I'm afraid for," she said. "I should have died in that prison, and I've been granted so much that I thought I'd never have. I've known your love, and that of Val and Yuri. I'd reconciled myself to never seeing my son in this world, and now I have hope. It's not my life that I fear to lose. It's you, or the boys. I couldn't bear to part with any of you. So many people that I loved are dead. I need you, Kayan. I need you more than I've ever needed anyone. Don't leave me."

"Shhh." He placed his finger over her lips. "I'm here. I'm fine. Just be brave a little longer. The green valleys of home are waiting. Your father is waiting for me to bring you back to him."

"And my son? Young Alexander? Is he waiting too?"

"He's waiting."

Her teeth began to chatter with the cold, and he was overcome by the need to keep her safe.

"Ptolemy's out there. I can feel him," she said. "He'll never stop until he finds us, not if he has to follow us to Sogdiana Rock."

"If he crosses into Bactria, he'll never see Egypt again. That much I promise you."

"But I want you to promise me that we'll grow old together, that we'll make beautiful babies and live to see them grow up."

"You know that's impossible," he said. "I can't give you that assurance. Life is as fleeting as a snowflake."

She trembled in his arms. "Then love me," she said.

"Make love to me here. Let's seize whatever happiness we can."

"That's one thing I can give you," he answered. He began to cover her face and throat with hot kisses. "Roxanne," he whispered. "Roxanne, I—"

A stone rolled.

Kayan turned and reached for his sword.

"Wait," Roxanne said. "It's Yuri."

Kayan swore softly. "What is it?"

The child stood motionless, eyes wide with distress. "Kayan," he stammered. "I wanted to . . ." He took a step back. "I didn't think . . ."

"You didn't think," Kayan said. "Go back to the tents. Your mother and I—"

"She isn't my mother!" He half turned to run.

"Yuri, come here," Roxanne said. "Please. Don't go away." She wrapped the blanket around herself, covering her nakedness, and beckoned to the boy.

He looked at her warily.

"It's all right," she said. "Please, Yuri. Come here."

The small jaw firmed. His shoulders straightened. Slowly, as if he were going to his own execution, he walked to her. "What?"

"You wanted your father, didn't you?"

Yuri stared at the ground.

"Didn't you?"

"No," he mumbled. "Wanted you." The moonlight reflecting off his face showed two rivulets of tears running down his cheeks.

Roxanne touched his face. "Don't," she said. "Whatever is wrong, we can make it right."

"You can't," he said. "She's dead, and she's not coming back. Ever."

Kayan came toward him, but Roxanne glanced up and shook her head, warning him not to interfere. "Your mother," she said.

Yuri nodded.

"Did she love you, Yuri? Did your mother love you?"

"I don't know," he said. "Maybe."

"I think she did," Roxanne said in a voice so tender that it made a lump rise in Kayan's throat. "I think she would have given anything, even her own immortal soul, for you."

"Why do you think that?" the boy asked.

"Because I would, if you were mine."

He raised his head and gazed into her eyes. "Really?"

"Really." She opened her arms, and he flung himself into them. "I want to be your mother," she said. "Yours and Val's, but if I can't, I'll settle for being your friend."

Kayan went to them, knelt, and hugged them both. "Your timing is a little off," he said to his son, "but your aim is true."

Yuri wiggled free and rubbed his eyes with the backs of his fists. "I lied," he said. "I don't hate you."

"I never thought you did," Roxanne said. She offered her hand to him. "Maybe we could be friends first, and if that works out, maybe I could fill in for your mother."

Yuri took her hand hesitantly.

"Friends?" she asked.

The boy nodded. "If you don't tell Val I cried."

"It will be our secret," Roxanne promised.

Kayan put his hands on his son's shoulders. "It's late. You should be sleeping."

"I couldn't," he said. "I was thirsty. And I wanted to talk to her, to tell her that . . ." He broke off shyly. "You know."

"And who told you that Princess Roxanne was here at the waterfall?" Kayan asked.

"Tiz."

"I thought so. Remind me to thank him for that." He looked at Roxanne, and she chuckled.

"I think we all could use some sleep," she said. "But since you're going on watch, I'd feel better if someone was with me in the tent." She glanced at Yuri.

"Val's there," he said.

"He is," Roxanne agreed, "but he's already asleep. Would you mind bringing your blanket into my shelter. Just for tonight?"

"I could do that," Yuri agreed. "Just for tonight."

They were halfway back to the tents when a flaming arrow streaked across the sky. "Look!" Roxanne said, pointing.

"A warning!" Yuri said.

The distant wail of a Greek battle horn echoed through the hollow, and the three headed back toward camp at a dead run.

Chapter 27

Ptolemy listened to the young captain's report. "You're certain it's the Bactrians?" he asked when the man had finished. "There's no chance you're mistaken?" It was still several hours before sunup, and weariness showed in the soldier's face.

"The whore from the village we just passed through told one of my men. He said there was only one woman traveling with the caravan. One woman and two children, both boys."

"How many men?" Ptolemy asked.

"Perhaps two dozen. She wasn't certain. They had good camels, and the men were all fit. They carried weapons. She said they were from the Twin Kingdoms. She heard them talking among themselves."

"And the woman the whore saw? Did she say what color her hair was?"

"No, King Ptolemy. She said she didn't get a good look at the woman, and she said that her face and hair were covered."

"It's got to be them." Ptolemy nodded. "Be certain that

the trollop is rewarded. We may need information from the villagers in the future. Return to your command."

The king turned away and returned to the torch-lit tent where he'd been drinking all night with General Ixion, a soldier he'd fought beside during Alexander's Persian conquest. Ixion was an ally of Cassander, or had been. The troops he commanded were a tough mixture of Persians and Macedonians, all familiar with mountain campaigning.

General Ixion looked up as Ptolemy entered the shelter. "It's them."

"I thought so." Ixion poured a bowl of wine and handed it to him. Then the man lifted his own cup. "To a successful conclusion," he said.

"And to our continued cooperation." Ptolemy settled onto a stool and leaned his back against an upright support. By Ares's staff, he was tired. This riding all day and half the night and drinking for hours afterward was for younger men. He'd never expected the barbarian to lead him a chase across half of Persia. He'd nearly had them when they crossed the Euphrates, and again outside the walls of Babylon.

Damned if the wench didn't have Alexander's luck! Ptolemy had killed countless men and horses to reach these mountains. He could have built another palace for what it had cost him. If he didn't catch them here . . . But he would. There was no way they could escape this time.

And the expedition had been good for him. He hadn't been troubled by Alexander's specter since he'd shaken the dust of Gaza from his sandals. He'd lost nearly a stone in weight and was hard and lean, more physically fit than he'd been in years.

"What's the news of Carthage?" Ixion asked. "We're so isolated here, we might as well be on the dark side of the moon." He downed his wine and spat the dregs on the ground. "I've a wife in Stagira, a son I haven't seen in seven years. Cassander promises to send someone to replace me, so that I can assume a more important position closer to civilization. But so far, his promises are as empty as his treasury." Ixion leaned forward. "My men haven't been paid in six months."

"Once we've disposed of Prince Kayan and his hounds, I think we can remedy that," Ptolemy said. He reached for a slice of lamb and chewed deliberately.

"You'd pay my men for past service to Cassander?" Disbelief showed in Ixion's expression.

"You were loyal to Alexander and, after his death, to Perdiccas."

"Who died in Egypt," Ixion supplied, "at your hand. You know I was Perdiccas's man, and you hold me no ill will?"

"While Alexander lived, Perdiccas and I fought on the same side. It wasn't until he tried to take what was mine that I killed him. You're a soldier, not a sailor. But you should still understand that a wise man trims his sails according to the wind."

"And the wind blows now from the Nile." Ixion's grim face relaxed and he grinned, revealing one blackened bottom tooth. "Cassander warned Perdiccas that you'd be no easy mark."

"Who could blame you for supporting the strongest candidate?" Ptolemy said. "But that's no longer Cassander."

"You look beyond the borders of Egypt?"

"When I make Alexander's widow my wife, she brings Bactria and Sogdiana as her dowry. Once, the Twin Kingdoms were rich beyond measure. Bactria is the crossroads of the world, where spices, furs, silk, gold, horses, and women are traded. Name what men desire most, and I'll show you how Princess Roxanne's country profits from those luxuries. The wealth of the East passes through there. I mean to make the Twin Kingdoms mine, and then I mean to claim my brother's throne—the throne I should have had when he died."

"It's true, then, what men say?" Ixion asked. "You are the Conqueror's brother?"

"I am the son of Alexander's father, King Philip II by the Lady Arsinoe. I am Alexander's elder by eighteen months."

"Illegitimate."

"Since when has that been an obstacle for kings? Alexander himself claimed that his mother cuckolded Philip with the god Apollo. Perhaps he was more bastard than I."

Ixion chuckled and scratched his three-days' beard. "What would you have of me, Highness?"

"Supplement my forces. Help me to destroy the Bactrians, and then join us as we drive on to seize the throne of the Twin Kingdoms. Above all, the princess must not be harmed."

"Arrows don't always discriminate between the guilty and the innocent. What if your bride-to-be is accidentally killed in the fighting?"

Ptolemy uttered a sound of amusement. "Impossible. So long as any red-haired woman draws breath in Bactria, the Princess Roxanne will wear the crown of Egypt and I will claim Bactria and Sogdiana as my rightful due."

When Roxanne, Yuri, and Kayan reached the tents, men were astir. A scout waited by the fire, breathing hard. Tiz was already calling for the animals to be brought up from the lower terrace and arms readied.

"Prince Kayan," the scout said. "The Greeks—"

"I heard the horn. How far are they?" He exchanged a few words with the man, and then glanced at Roxanne and his son. "It's Ptolemy. He's joined with a Greek company under a commander named Ixion. Wake Val. Make yourselves ready to travel. Dress warmly. There are still the high passes to traverse."

Within minutes, the troops had struck the camp. Kayan ordered six camels to be heavily laden. One carried a tent; the other five carried supplies and blankets. "I don't understand," Roxanne said. "Why are these animals packed differently from the rest? What's happening?"

Kayan drew her aside. "What was always meant to be." He gestured to Tiz, who took the rope of the lead camel. "Homji! Bahman!" Kayan called. "It's time."

A chill passed through Roxanne. "What are you doing?" she demanded.

Kayan's features hardened. "Tiz, Bahman, and Homji will lead you and the boys on ahead, while we hold our pursuers here."

"You think I'd leave you?" she cried. "I'm your wife. I've been trained to fight. My place is beside you."

"Your place is on the throne of the Twin Kingdoms," he answered. Muscles tightened in his throat and jaw. "Take the children home. Do what you must do."

"Without you?"

"I'll follow."

"Follow? By Ahriman's foul breath! You mean to play the hero and die here."

Val and Yuri appeared at Roxanne's side. Yuri carried his bow and quiver; Val clutched a man's sword. "We're ready to fight," Yuri said. "Tell us what to do."

Kayan laid his hand on Val's shoulder. "You have a decision to make, son. You know the name of your birth mother, but I never told you who your father was."

The boy's eyes widened in bewilderment. "I thought you didn't know," he said. "What difference does it make? I belong to you."

"Yes, you do, but you were sired by another."

"Another who didn't think enough of my mother to marry her. A stinking Greek. May he burn in Hades."

"Four hundred of General Ixion's men march on our camp. I don't know how many Ptolemy has, but he's here. The truth is that none of us may live to see Bactria. But you have a choice, Val. Despite your years, you've played the part of a warrior, and you deserve the respect I'd give a man. You have another name. When you were born, your father acknowledged you and named you after his own grandfather. He called you Paris."

"I don't understand," Val said.

"You carry the blood of Alexander," Kayan said. "You're the natural child of his brother, Ptolemy, King of Egypt."

"No!" Val said. "That's a lie! I'm not his son. I'm yours."

Kayan embraced him. "You'll always be mine. But Ptolemy will accept you. He has no son and heir. You could wear the crown of Egypt after him. It would be selfish of me to rob you of that chance."

Tears ran down the child's wind-burned face. "No," he protested. "No. I'm not. He's evil. I'm not his son."

Roxanne touched Val's cheek. "He's not evil. He is a brave man and a great king. No matter what is between us, I know he would be good to you. You would come to be proud of him."

"I would not!"

"Think, Val," she said. "Among our people, you're a prince, but you'll never inherit the crown. It's a big decision, and we should have told you before, but—"

"Kayan is my father." He sobbed. "Not Ptolemy. And I fight beside him and Yuri."

"You're certain?" Kayan knelt to look into his son's eyes. "You don't want time to think about this?"

"No. You said I was a man," he said. "You said I could choose. I choose you."

Kayan rose, closed his eyes for an instant, and swallowed. "Ormazd grant that I haven't wronged you, Val. If I did, remember that I did it because I couldn't bear to part with you."

"I don't care if Ptolemy's your father," Yuri said. "You're still my brother, even if you are part Egyptian."

"Not Egyptian," Roxanne said gently. "The blood of King Philip runs in his veins. Ptolemy may hold Egypt, but he is pure Macedonian, as was his brother, Alexander."

Val wiped away the tears and threw back his shoulders. He was growing again, Roxanne thought. He was more than a head taller than Yuri, and if she looked hard, she was certain she could see a resemblance to Alexander in Val's mouth and nose. His hair was darker than his uncle's, despite being bleached by the sun, but his eyes were similar in color.

"Can you take orders like a man?" Kayan asked.

"Yes, sir." Val slammed his clenched fist against his chest in a military salute. "Give me my orders, Father."

"Very well. You and your brother are to escort the princess home to Bactria."

"And leave you?" Val demanded.

"I'm not going," Yuri said, clutching his cat.

"To disobey a commander during wartime is high treason," Kayan said sternly. "You will guard my wife with your lives."

"No," Roxanne said, putting her arm around Yuri's shoulders. "We all stay together. If I'm the crown princess, my word overrules yours. We live or we die, but we don't desert each other."

"Tiz! Put my wife on that camel. By force if you have to. You are to take her and my sons to safety in the Bactrian mountains." He seized Roxanne and kissed her hard before releasing her and stepping back. "Go for me," he said. "For us."

She shook her head. "You can't ask this of me. I won't run and leave you—"

"You will!" he thundered. "You will. If not for us, for Yuri—for Alexander's son."

She stared at him as her arms and legs went numb, as her feet welded to the earth. She'd heard wrong. She must have heard wrong. Kayan couldn't have said what she thought he'd said.

Kayan hugged Yuri and pulled Val into his arms. "The two of you are first cousins," he said. "And brothers of the heart."

"Yuri?" Roxanne said. Her voice sounded as though it came from far away. Black spots danced in her head, and she felt faint. "You lied to me when I asked you if he was my son?"

"I did what I had to. To protect him."

"From me?"

"What are you saying?" Yuri asked. "She—"

"You are the lawfully born son of Princess Roxanne and King Alexander," Kayan said. "And after your mother, the heir to the Conqueror and to the throne of Sogdiana and Bactria."

Wind whipped Roxanne's hair and stung her face as she followed Tiz and the guide up a narrow track so steep that they had to lead the camels single file where only mountain goats and golden eagles dared traverse. Often the footing was crumbling rock and the stone face so close that the camels' loads brushed the wall. If they strayed even an arm's length, they risked falling off a sheer precipice thousands of feet to the valley floor. Val and Yuri came behind Roxanne, with Bahman and Homji guarding the rear.

Roxanne's fury at Kayan's deception had flared and quickly drained away. Since she'd forced him to swear an oath to protect Alexander's son with his life, she could hardly blame Kayan for doing whatever he thought necessary. Hadn't she been the one who'd substituted a foundling for a prince? Hadn't she deliberately risked little 'Zander to save Yuri?

For eight long years she'd lived for her son. Now that she'd found him alive and well, all she could think of was that Kayan would die fighting against overwhelming odds . . . that her last words to the man she loved had been bitter ones.

As for Yuri, her precious son had not spoken to her, had not even looked at her since they'd left the camp. Whatever he thought remained inside him, making her wonder if she and Kayan had destroyed any chance of her ever having a normal relationship with either Yuri or Val.

In an hour's time, Roxanne guessed they'd traveled no more than half a mile from the campsite when one of Kayan's troopers came running after them. They couldn't stop, but had to continue on for several hundred yards before there was a spot wide enough to halt the camels and for Tiz to retrace his steps to meet his comrade.

"What is it?" Roxanne called.

Tiz didn't speak until he was beside her. "Kayan's received a message from King Ptolemy. The general wants you to read it and give him your reply."

Her heart hammered against her chest. Kayan was still alive. He'd been alive when he'd sent the runner. Perhaps there was still a chance . . .

But when she unwrapped the scroll, her hopes fell.

"What does it say, lady?" Tiz asked.

"Ptolemy has made a generous offer. If we surrender to his mercy and I agree to become his wife, he will pardon Kayan and the children."

Tiz offered a cheerful obscenity. "Sure he will. Right after he makes me his chief concubine. Likely he'll make Homji and Bahman guardians of his harem."

Homji laughed. "At least King Ptolemy's kept his sense of humor."

Bahman's suggestion concerning the king was both ribald and physically impossible. "Begging your pardon, Majesty," he said as an afterthought to Roxanne. "You don't believe him, do you?"

"He's a liar," Val said.

Yuri's gray eyes gleamed with a grim expression that Roxanne had seen so often in Alexander, she wondered that she'd not recognized it before.

"If Ptolemy's brother had offered these terms," she said, "he would have kept his word. Whatever else Alexander was, he was a man of honor."

"And Ptolemy isn't?" Val said.

"I don't know," Roxanne replied honestly. "All I do know is that your grandfather was King Philip of Macedonia, and he wouldn't have kept his word to Zeus himself if there was profit in it for him."

"I guess that means we're going ahead up this swiving trail," Tiz said.

"No, it means *you're* going ahead," Roxanne said. "I'm going back to Kayan."

Tiz stepped in front of her to block her path. "I don't think so."

"Val and Yuri are what matter most," she said. "If Ptolemy's willing to bargain, we can stall, gain time."

"You're going to trust him, aren't you?" Val asked.

"I don't know what I'm going to do. But this doesn't feel right. If I go, I'll regret it forever. There may be a way to save Kayan—to save all of us. If Ptolemy's bargaining, he's not sure we're in the palm of his hand."

"I can't let you go," Tiz said. "The general ordered me to—"

"He gave that order, yes," she agreed. "But that was before Ptolemy sent the messenger. Everything's changed now."

"I can force you to go on."

"For how long?" she demanded. "Would you strike me? Struggle with me on this ledge, or another just as dangerous? I'm your princess, not your prisoner."

"The general said—"

"Prince Kayan is my husband. If I can save him, I will. And if you don't let me try, you might as well put an arrow through him yourself. You know what he means to do. He has less than twenty men. Against how many? A thousand? Two thousand? Even the Spartans couldn't have held out against those odds."

"You're just a woman."

"You know better than that, Tiz. You know that whatever I am on the outside, I have a warrior's heart. Don't underestimate me. Alexander did, to his own regret."

For the space of a long minute, Kayan's lieutenant considered her words, and then he grinned and saluted her with his fist over his heart. "Give them fire and brimstone, Highness," he said. "And Ormazd protect us all from the general's wrath if anything happens to you."

She glanced back at Val and Yuri. "Remember that I love you both," she said. "Never forget it."

"Don't go," Val said. "Don't."

As she turned and retreated back down the mountain track, she listened, hoping to hear Yuri's voice. But she heard nothing but the crunch of scree under her boots and the high-pitched shriek of a diving gyrfalcon.

Chapter 28

"What are you doing here?" Kayan demanded when Roxanne appeared with his runner. "Have you decided to accept Ptolemy's terms? Will you return to him?" He stood immobile, unable even to draw a breath. He'd failed her, and no matter what the outcome, nothing would be as he wanted it. Either he would lose her to Egypt and Ptolemy's bed, or he would die here and never know the joy of her love again.

She came to him, but she didn't fling herself into his arms or kiss him. Instead, she brushed his cheek with warm fingertips. "You wear the mark of the griffin," she said too softly for any of his soldiers to hear. She drew her hand away and looked down at the stain of blue paint on her skin. "The oath of the hero."

He looked into her eyes, and the overwhelming grief he saw there was nearly his undoing. He sucked the thin mountain air into his lungs and said, "I have sworn to hold this pass, as have my men. So that the royal house of Bactria and Sogdiana will survive."

"You will lay down your lives for me."

"And for Alexander, your son . . . our son."

She glanced at his cavalrymen, seeing that they too had chosen the way of honor. Each man had freely taken his vow to stand beside Kayan and fight until their last drop of blood was shed.

Roxanne's eyes glistened with moisture, but she did not weep. "If I accept Ptolemy's offer, he may let you go," she said.

"You know better than that." He ached to hold her one last time. Shards of white-hot pain splintered in his chest. He wanted her to live at any cost, but he would not sacrifice his sons on the altar of Ptolemy's ambition.

"Should we have given him Val?" she asked. "Were we thinking about what *we* wanted, rather than what was best for him?"

"It's not too late, if you believe that would be best. But you risk the chance that Ptolemy may pretend to accept the boy and then slay him out of doubt. He'd not be the first man to rid himself of an unwanted bastard."

"My father once said that you were the bravest warrior he'd ever known but you didn't have the wisdom to be a king. He was wrong, Kayan," Roxanne said. "I've known the love of two kings, and you are the greatest of them all. How many men would take the child of their most hated enemy and love him as their own? How many would lay down their lives for sons sired by others?"

He shrugged. "We all meet the veiled horseman. For some, there is a chance to choose the time and hour. If I die today, I'll know why, and I need not hang my head in shame when I face my Creator."

"I love you, Kayan," she said. "More than I have ever loved another—more than I love my own son. And I would give my immortal soul to see you live to make men out of Val and Yuri."

He gripped her shoulder. "You're going to Ptolemy."

"It's a chance," she said. "A chance for you and the boys; a chance for the new life I carry under my heart."

A giant fist twisted his gut and crushed his chest. "You carry my child?" he asked her.

The tears burst forth. "You have Ptolemy's son, and I fear he will have yours." Her lower lip quivered. "Kiss me, my love, one last time."

He kissed her, hard and quick, inhaling the scent of her hair and skin, feeling the heat of her in his blood and bones, savoring what might be his last taste of paradise.

"Kayan, I—" she began.

He drew away, knowing that to hold her like this would be his undoing. He did not release her, instead lifting her into his arms and pinning her against her body. "Pulad!" he shouted. "Stivant! Bind the princess. Let no harm come to her. If she escapes, I'll use your entrails for bowstrings."

"No!" Roxanne cried, struggling wildly. "Let me go. What are you doing? I have to—"

He clamped a hand over her mouth. "Quiet, lest you tell our enemies more than you mean to. I've a plan that requires you to observe without interfering—a task at which you've had little experience."

"Kayan," she mumbled.

He pressed his palm tighter. "Shhh! Trust me, woman." He handed her over to his men. "Tie her hands, throw a cloak over her shoulders, and let down her hair so that Ptolemy will recognize her even from a distance. "We need her to look free, without having the ability to do anything noble and stupid."

Roxanne's nutmeg-brown eyes flashed fire.

"Accept it," he said, meeting her gaze with his own determined one. "And listen and watch to see if Prince Oxyartes was right all along."

Roxanne frantically worked the ties on her wrists as she walked to the ridge overlooking the terrace where Tiz had tethered the camels and horses to graze the night before. Below, in the trees and along the rocky slope, massed the legions of Ptolemy and Ixion, Egyptians and Greeks beyond number. Above, dark clouds threatened, and thunder rumbled in the distance. Gusts of wind whirled leaves and bits of bark and grass into the air before howling away down the valley.

Ptolemy and several of his officers stood within bow range, but carrying shields, on an outcropping of solid rock that jutted out from the mountainside below the grassy area. The opening greetings had already been shouted, and Ptolemy's numerous titles and honors proclaimed by his spokesman, General Ixion, who had to yell because of the gathering storm. Ptolemy repeated his offer to spare Kayan and his sons if the barbarian leader would free his captive, the Princess Roxanne, to her betrothed, King Ptolemy.

"What of my men?" Kayan shouted back. "Are they to be held responsible for following my command?"

Ixion conferred with Ptolemy before declaring, "Pharaoh, in his mercy, will pardon the criminals from execution."

"Which means they will be enslaved, probably in Ptolemy's copper mines," Roxanne said quietly.

"Smile," Kayan murmured. "Look queenly and bored."

"What say you?" demanded Ixion.

"That's your cue," Kayan said to Roxanne.

"If King Ptolemy wishes my hand in marriage, why doesn't he speak for himself?" she cried. "Why must he hide behind you, Ixion?" She had to shield her eyes from the flying debris.

"Heed your tongue, woman!" the Greek general bellowed. "King Ptolemy—"

"She's right," Ptolemy said, stepping forth and shoving Ixion aside. "I will speak for myself. I would have you to wife, Princess Roxanne. You bring me Sogdiana and Bactria, and I will give you the crown of Egypt."

"You must let Prince Kayan's followers go unharmed," she replied. "He and his sons must be allowed to return to their own country without hindrance."

Ptolemy's face darkened and veins stood out on his forehead. "You expect me to forgive those who have murdered innocents, who have robbed the temples and destroyed my palace?"

"I do!" She waited, not speaking again until the onlookers grew impatient. The wind increased as peals of thunder boomed down the valley and echoed off the mountainside. The rolling clouds blocked out the sun, hiding the snow-covered peaks and turning day to ominous twilight.

"Very well," Ptolemy shouted. "As a wedding gift to my queen."

"One more thing!" Roxanne called out. "There is an ancient custom in my country! If two compete for the same bride, they must submit to a rite of combat!"

"If you want her, fight for her!" Naked sword in hand, fierce face painted for war, Kayan leaped down onto the flattened area of torn earth and grass.

Kayan had stripped away his tunic so that he faced Ptolemy with bare chest and arms. Wide bands of Scythian gold encircled his biceps. His long hair, braided with nuggets of raw gold, thin strips of silk cord, and hawk feathers, whipped around his face. Around his throat he'd clasped a silver-mesh torque bearing the golden image of a griffin.

An uproar arose from Ptolemy's troops. Shouts echoed and reechoed off the ridges. "No! No!" Bronze rang as the Greeks and Egyptians struck swords against shields.

"Kill the barbarians!" they howled above the wind.

But Kayan's men were equally vocal. "Coward! He will not fight! Crawl back to Egypt, coward!"

"I accept the challenge!" Ptolemy cried. Despite the protests of his men and officers, he settled a helmet on his head and strode out onto the terrace to meet Kayan. Fat raindrops splattered on his polished armor as he drew his Greek short sword.

Roxanne's heart clenched. Kayan was a mighty warrior and ten years Ptolemy's junior, but Ptolemy had been trained from boyhood by the finest swordsmen. The Greek was no mean opponent. She knew all too well that the outcome of such a contest could swing on a single misstep or weakness of a blade.

Save him, she prayed silently. *Please, Ormazd, in your mercy, let Kayan live.* Overhead, the gyrfalcon dove from the black maelstrom and screamed again. It came to Roxanne that this was no real hawk but an omen. Whether it was an omen for good or evil, she could not tell.

For what seemed forever, the two men circled, mentally taking the measure of each other. Bronze swords clashed. A parry. A thrust. Ptolemy slashed low in an attempt to slice through Kayan's knee. He leaped out of the way and delivered a powerful blow that would have taken Ptolemy's head off if the Greek hadn't blocked it with his round shield.

Lightning flashed, followed by a crack of thunder. Roxanne heard a sharp intake of breath in the silence following the roll of thunder and glanced down to see Yuri standing beside her. "Untie me," she said.

Pulad shook his head. "No, Prince Kayan said—"

"Stand off!" Val cried, drawing his sword and putting himself before Pulad.

Yuri's knife flashed, and he shoved aside Roxanne's cloak and sawed through the leather ties. "Touch my mother at your peril," he threatened Pulad.

Another bolt of lightning struck. Horses whinnied. A soldier cursed.

The swords rang again. Ptolemy went down on one knee. Kayan stepped back to allow him to get to his feet.

"Don't!" Roxanne called. "He'll show you no mercy!"

Ptolemy leaped up. Kayan swung his sword, and the

king blocked it with his own weapon. Bronze grated against bronze. The men sprang apart and rushed at each other fiercely.

"Why are you here?" Roxanne demanded of her son.

"You need me."

She laid a hand on his shoulder, and needles of rain slanted across her cheek. Yuri took a solid stance, legs slightly apart, body angled toward the enemy force, knife ready. "You cause a lot of trouble," he said.

The wind gusts tore at her cloak and tangled Yuri's hair.

"But you came back," she said.

She fixed her gaze on the two combatants as they slashed and thrust. The rain came harder, turning the terrace to mud and making it difficult to see. Ptolemy's blade flashed, drawing a thin line of crimson across Kayan's bare chest. Roxanne felt the pain of his wound as sharply as if it had been her own flesh that had been scored. She clenched her teeth to keep from crying out.

"Would you expect less of me?" Yuri shouted between crashes of thunder. "Would my father?"

"Our country needs you," she said. "Without you—"

Suddenly, almost too swiftly to see, Kayan lunged, blocking Ptolemy's sword thrust and continuing on to slam his shoulder into the Greek's chest. Ptolemy went down with Kayan's boot on his chest. Kayan raised his sword to deliver the death blow.

"No!" Val shouted. "Don't!" He threw himself off the ridge and tumbled to slide down toward Ptolemy. At the same instant, Ixion seized a spear from an Egyptian charioteer and hurled it at Kayan.

Roxanne screamed as Val scrambled into the spear's path. Kayan tried to block the missile with his own body, but the iron spear head buried itself in the child's thigh.

Lightning struck the far side of the valley, blasting the mountainside and sending boulders the size of warships skyward.

Arrows from both camps hissed through the air. Greeks and Egyptians surged forward, the battle cries issuing from their throats drowned by a roll of thunder. Kayan's Bactrians leaped forward to defend him.

"Tiz!" Roxanne shouted. "Take Yuri!"

She needn't have given the order. Even as the words came out of her mouth, Tiz snatched the boy off his feet. Dodging arrows, the doughty warrior ran through the downpour back toward the mountain trail with Yuri flung over his shoulder like a sack of grain.

Roxanne flung herself over the edge of the slippery bank, climbing over a fallen Bactrian to reach Kayan and Val. Kayan, his sword cutting an arc of death around him, had his wounded son in his arms and was backing toward the rise. Blood flowed from Val's leg and pooled on the muddy earth.

Ptolemy was on his feet, advancing on Kayan. Flanking him were Ixion and two more officers, all with drawn blades. Around them, men were struggling and dying.

"Stop!" Roxanne screamed as she darted in front of Kayan. She was no more than a spear's length from Ptolemy, but sheets of rain made it hard to see him. "Hear me, Ptolemy! Would you murder your own son? This is Paris! Your son Paris!"

Ptolemy lifted his hand and shouted a command. Ixion bellowed the order to halt. The storm of arrows thinned and ceased as a final shaft plunged between Roxanne's deerskin boots.

"If you're lying to me—" Ptolemy seized her arm.

"It is the truth," she insisted. "Look at his face. He is your son by the Persian woman. If you don't do something, he'll bleed to death before your eyes!"

Ptolemy motioned his soldiers back. Another peal of thunder shook the ground. "Let me have a look at the whelp," he said.

Val's eyes were open, his teeth gritted against the pain.

Roxanne turned her back on the king and ripped a length of material from her soaking tunic. "Put him down," she shouted at Kayan. "If you don't let me stop the bleeding, neither of you will have him!"

Kayan nodded and lowered Val to the ground. Still gripping his sword, he knelt in the mud beside the child and leaned over him, trying to shield him from the storm. "Be brave a little longer," he said to the boy.

Ptolemy stared at Val. "He has the look of Alexander," he said finally. "Is it possible?" He glared at Kayan. "How dare you keep my son from me?"

"How dare you abandon him?" Kayan flung back.

Roxanne tightened the cloth around Val's leg.

Val winced. "It hurts."

"Yes, it does. But you'll be all right." She knotted the tourniquet and glanced up into Kayan's face. The rain had streaked his war paint to thin lines.

"Am I going to die, Mother?" Val began to shake.

"No," she answered. "No, you won't die. I won't let you."

"Good." He sighed and went limp, his taut face suddenly pale.

"Curse you for a fool!" Roxanne cried to Ptolemy. "Send for a physician!"

The king's physician arrived—a Hebrew, Roxanne noted by his beard, side-locks, and garb, a man with gentle hands who seemed to pay no more heed to the pouring rain and thunder than the bared swords around him. "We cannot do this here," the man said after examining Val. "We must get him warm. I need a tent, a fire, my instruments."

"Will he live?" Roxanne pleaded.

"With the Almighty's grace, lady."

She kissed the boy's damp forehead and whispered a silent prayer. "Remember that I love you, Val. Never forget it."

"Take him," Ptolemy commanded the physician. "What are you waiting for?"

Roxanne sliced a lock of blond hair from Val's head with her knife and looked up at Ptolemy. "He's been raised as a prince of Bactria. Swear to me on your immortal soul that you will treat him as a son."

"Why shouldn't I?" Ptolemy answered. "He's the only son I have."

Roxanne moved back to let the Hebrew gather Val into his arms. "Don't lose him," she said.

"I will care for him as though he were my own," the physician replied as he carried him away.

She drew in a deep breath and moved back to stand in front of Kayan, who had risen to his feet. "Let him go," she whispered. "It is his only chance."

Ptolemy folded his arms. "Have you had enough drama, my dear? You're not parting with the boy. You're coming with him. With me."

"Only if you let Kayan go," she said, shivering with cold.

"No!" Kayan thundered. "Never!"

"As you wish," Ptolemy said, drawing his sword again. "Take the woman, and kill them all."

A bolt of lightning struck the terrace. The dazzling flash and ensuing clap of earth-shattering thunder knocked Roxanne to her knees and deafened her. Greeks, Egyptians, and Bactrians toppled to the earth as if smitten by a giant's hand.

The air sizzled with the smell of brimstone. Tingling sensations radiated through Roxanne's limbs and pricked her scalp. Black starbursts blazed behind her clenched eyelids. Then Kayan flung himself over her.

How dare you, Brother? Alexander demanded.

The force of the lightning strike drove Ptolemy belly down in the muck. He felt the warmth of urine trickle down his inner thigh. His mouth gaped, and he spat dirt. He stared in disbelief at the burn on his right palm where his sword-hilt had scorched his flesh.

Have you lost your wits? the mocking voice demanded.

Ptolemy gasped. His eyes widened in fright.

Alexander, clad in full battle armor, stood between him and Roxanne. In his right fist he held an upraised sword. Fury gleamed in his gray eyes. *Be gone, Brother*, he commanded. *Take what belongs to you and leave my son alone!*

"Alexander . . ." Ptolemy stammered. "You . . ."

Be gone, I say! Alexander repeated. *You shall not have Roxanne. Let them go, or you will feel my wrath.*

"You can't—" Ptolemy began.

Know when to walk away, the taunting voice in his head commanded. *Go or lose all. By all that's holy, I'll cast you down into the depths of the earth and use your rotting eyes for dice!*

Ptolemy sank onto the churned grass and covered his head with his hands. "Let them go," he croaked. "Let them go in peace."

"What in the name of Ormazd?" Kayan said.

Men wept and cried out—some to their gods, others to their mothers.

Roxanne opened her eyes and blinked. For an instant, she thought she saw a golden-haired man in full battle armor standing over Ptolemy. The shimmering image was that of a man, yet not a man of mortal flesh and blood, his form almost too bright to look upon. It happened so fast that she couldn't be certain what she had seen, but she could have sworn that . . .

The apparition materialized again. And in the heartbeat before it faded, Alexander of Macedon grinned at her.

And winked.

"Farewell," Roxanne whispered.

Ixion rushed forward. Kayan leaped to his feet, jerked Roxanne up, and thrust her behind him. He raised his sword, prepared to do battle to his last breath.

"No!" Ptolemy bellowed. "I said, let them go!" He lifted

his head and clawed at his helmet. His features were waxen, his sandy brown hair suddenly frizzled and hoary.

Kayan swore softly.

Roxanne heard Tiz singing a death chant.

"Go, damn you!" Ptolemy shrieked.

Ixion blinked and lowered his spear. He stared dumbly at Ptolemy and then back at Kayan. "Go on," he said. "You heard the king."

Some Greeks and Egyptians were fleeing down the mountainside. Others sat in the mud and stared or turned to their companions with frightened eyes. One charioteer was on his feet, but turning slowly in a circle, clutching his eyes, and moaning.

"A lightning strike," Kayan said. "Lightning." He glanced at her and swallowed. "Are you all right?"

"Come," she said. "We have to go."

"I don't understand," he said.

"We have to go *now*," she insisted.

"Val," he said, taking a step forward.

Roxanne shook her head. "We have to leave him, Kayan. To save his life. Come; it's over."

"Get away!" Ptolemy bellowed, half sobbing. "Get out of my sight, you demon witch!"

Roxanne nodded, turned away, and began to climb the muddy slope.

"Why?" Kayan asked Roxanne three days later, when the survivors had put a mountain range between them and Ptolemy's host. "What happened there? Why did Ptolemy change his mind and let us go?"

"He has Val," she answered. "Maybe that was enough."

"The lightning bolt . . ."

Roxanne met his gaze and wondered if she'd really seen what she'd thought she'd seen on that terrace. Had Alexander returned from beyond to save them, or had she simply been suffering shock from the lightning strike? She smiled up at Kayan. "As you said, it was just lightning. Too close for my liking." She shrugged. "Maybe the Good God saved us. Or maybe the storm affected Ptolemy's wits. In any case, we're rid of him."

"For now," Kayan said.

"Forever, I hope."

She and Kayan and Yuri had walked on ahead of Tiz and the others. The way ahead was easier; the trail led down into a green valley watered by a swift-running river. Beyond another mountain range lay the familiar path to home. But the storms had passed, the sun shone brightly, and the air was sweet with the scent of wildflowers.

"I wouldn't have let Ptolemy have Val," Yuri said. "We could have taken care of him. Mother could have fixed his leg."

Roxanne handed Kayan her horse's reins, crouched down, and took her son's hands. "Val needed more than we could give him," she said. "Medicine, a warm bed, hot food. Ptolemy's physician will care for him until he's well."

"But the king won't let him come home," Yuri said.

"No," Kayan said. "He won't. We had to give him to Ptolemy to save his life. We didn't want to, but it was best for Val."

"I'm going to get him back," Yuri said. "I will."

"I hope you do," Roxanne said. She stood and rubbed the small of her back. "Actually, a soft bed wouldn't feel too bad, would it?"

Kayan grinned. "I gave you one in Gaza, but you weren't content to sleep in it. Kept me up all night, as I recall."

"*Kayan!* Is that any way to talk in front of our son?"

"I will get Val back," Yuri repeated stubbornly. He slipped his hand into Roxanne's and, leading his camel, walked alongside her, Khui on his shoulder.

"Did your mother tell you that you're going to be a big brother?" Kayan asked.

Roxanne grimaced. "It's too soon," she said. "What if something goes wrong?"

"Nothing will go wrong," Kayan said. "If you've carried her this long, she's tough."

"A baby?" Yuri said. "I guess that would be all right, if it doesn't make too much noise. Not that I'll hear it. Tiz is taking me to the mountain pastures to help bring down the mares for foaling. We're going to hunt wolves too. Val likes . . ." He trailed off. "I miss him," he said. "He's still my brother."

"He'll always be your brother," Kayan said. "Sometimes brothers take different roads, but nothing breaks the bond between them."

"If I have a new baby brother or sister, I won't like it more than Val," Yuri said. "Don't try to make me."

"Love is like sunlight," Roxanne said. "There's enough to go around for all of us. I think you'll find you can love the baby and still love Val."

"Prince Yuri!" Tiz called. "Come here and look at this track. See if you can tell me what kind of animal left it."

"Coming!" Yuri said. He turned and went to the troopers.

Kayan took Roxanne's hand. "We'll be home in time for the solstice," he said. "We have work ahead of us. Your father will crown you queen, and the ruler of the Twin Kingdoms has more to do than wear jewels and fine silks."

She smiled up at him. "I've never been afraid of work."

"They say that the solstice is the luckiest time for a wedding."

"You won't be ashamed to stand before the magi with a bride whose belly is swelling?" she teased.

"I'd be proud to lead you around the sacred fire, and swear to love and care for you and defend your honor forever. It's all I've ever wanted."

She laughed. "All you've ever wanted? What of your mighty army to drive out the Greeks? Your treaty with the Scythians and the other steppe tribes? Our hordes of future children? A kingdom so strong that none dare threaten her borders? I think you want more than my hand in marriage, Prince Kayan."

He stopped and took her other hand. "And what do you want, Little Star? What does your heart desire?"

Tears sparkled in her eyes as she put her arms around his neck and pulled his head down to kiss him. Their lips met, and she felt a tide of happiness fill her to overflowing. "I have more than I ever dreamed," she murmured. "I'm going home, and I have you and Yuri and our coming child."

"But grief for Val's loss."

"More joy than sadness," she answered, looking deep into his dark, luminous eyes. "Our son's not lost forever. Didn't Yuri promise to bring him home? With your love, and hope for tomorrow, what more could I ask?"

The Conqueror

Judith E. French

For two long years her father's tiny mountain kingdom had withstood the conqueror's sweeping forces, but now the barbarians storm the mile-high citadel and the women cower in fear. All but the one called *Little Star*. Famed as the most beautiful woman in all Persia, Roxanne has the courage of a fierce warrior and the training of a prince of her people. When she learns that slavery is not to be her lot, but a brilliant political alliance, she vows to await her bridegroom with her snarling leopard at her side and silken seduction at her fingertips. For she is no plaything, but more than a match for any man, even . . . Alexander the Great.

CARNAL GIFT

PAMELA CLARE

Her body and her virginity are to be offered up to a stranger in exchange for her brother's life. Possessing nothing but her innocence and her fierce Irish pride, Brighid has no choice but to comply.

But the handsome man she faces in the darkened bedchamber is not at all the monster she expected. His tender touch calms her fears while he swears he will protect her by merely pretending to claim her. And as the long hours of the night pass by, as her senses ignite at the heat of their naked flesh, Brighid makes a startling discovery: Sometimes the line between hate and love can be dangerously thin.

THE SPARE
CAROLYN JEWEL

Captain Sebastian Alexander is The Spare, but as the younger son he inherits more than a title after his brother's murder. He acquires a family estate with dark secrets that threaten his life. He takes on a quest to avenge his brother. But most troublesome of all, he finds a red-haired beauty who is either a guileless witness or a ruthless seductress.

Olivia Willow is missing three days from her life. She'd been a guest at Pennhyll the night of the murder, but now she can recall nothing. The new earl is determined to help her remember. He charms, he beguiles—he matches wits with her. And soon, instead of trading barbs they share kisses, and instead of seeking out the past, they are fighting for a future.

HANNAH HOWELL

His Bonnie Bride

When Storm Eldon is kidnapped by her family's ancestral
enemies, she knows there are rules to be honored by both
sides. If her stepmother agrees to the ransom demanded,
Storm will not be harmed by Tavis MacLagan, the handsome Highland warrior who holds her captive. But as days
of waiting turn into weeks, it begins to be clear that in this
contest of wills, no one is fighting fair. Tavis's hands-off
policy has changed into an all-out siege of the senses, and
Storm realizes she is less interested in guarding her virtue
than becoming . . . *His Bonnie Bride.*

The Temptation
CLAUDIA DAIN

In England of 1156, a gently bred lady is taught to obey, first her father, next her bridegroom. But ever since Eve it has been in every woman to defy any lord. And Elsbeth of Sunnandune is determined to trade the submission of the marriage bed for the serenity of the convent. Yet never did she suppose the difficulty of her task, for the husband given her is a golden knight of godly beauty and grace. His every word and look is a seduction, his every caress cause for capitulation. In this war of wills, she discovers, blood, honor, even the thrill of victory, can take on new meaning, and no matter how much time a wife spends on her knees in prayer, every path can lead into temptation.

- -

TO BURN
CLAUDIA DAIN

He has sworn to battle the empire wherever he finds it, and an isolated Roman villa in Britannia seems the perfect target for his revenge. He and his fierce Saxon warriors will sweep through it like an inferno, destroying all in their path. From the moment he sees her, he knows she embodies all that Rome stands for: pride, arrogance, civilization . . . beauty. She is a woman like no other, fighting with undaunted spirit even as he makes her his slave. She calls him barbarian, calls him oaf, calls him her enemy. Yet when he takes her in his hard-muscled arms, her body trembles with excitement. But will the fire flaring between them conquer him or her? Is the passion that burns in their souls born of hatred, or of love?

CLAUDIA DAIN
THE MARRIAGE BED

It starts with a kiss, an explosion of longing that cannot be contained. He is a young knight bent on winning his spurs; she is a maiden promised to another man; theirs is a love that can never be. But a year's passing and a strange destiny brings them together again. Now his is a monk desperately fleeing temptation, and she is the lady of Dornei, a woman grown, yearning to fulfill the forbidden fantasies of girlhood. They are a couple with nothing in common but a wedding night neither will ever forget. Eager virgin and unwilling bridegroom, yielding softness and driving strength, somehow they must become one soul, one purpose, one body within the marriage bed.

___4933-3 $5.99 US/$6.99 CAN

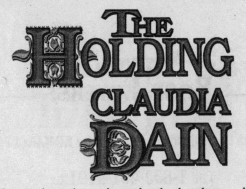

THE HOLDING

CLAUDIA DAIN

It is done. She is his wife. Wife of a knight so silent and stealthy, they call him "The Fog." Everything Lady Cathryn of Greneforde owns—castle, lands and people—is now safe in his hands. But there is one barrier yet to be breached. . . . There is a secret at Greneforde Castle, a secret embodied in its seemingly obedient mistress and silent servants. Betrayal, William fears, awaits him on his wedding night. But he has vowed to take possession of the holding his king has granted him. To do so he must know his wife completely, take her in the most elemental and intimate holding of all.

___4858-2 $5.50 US/$6.50 CAN